YANNI'S STORY

THE SPENCER COHEN SERIES

N.R. WALKER

COPYRIGHT

Cover Artist: Sara York
Editor: Labyrinth Bound Edits
Yanni's Story © 2017 N.R. Walker
Spencer Cohen Series © 2017 N.R. Walker
Publisher: BlueHeart Press

Warning

Intended for an 18+ audience only. This book contains material that
maybe offensive to some and is intended for a mature, adult audience. It
contains graphic language, explicit sexual content, and adult situations.

Trigger Warnings:

Descriptions of violence, suicide, and sexual assault.
Reader discretion advised.

Trademarks:

All trademarks are the property of their respective owners.

BLURB

When Yanni Tomaras is kicked out of his family home, his parents' final words are religious insults and an order to never return. Homeless and desperate, he's lured in by Lance—charming on the outside, an evil predator underneath—who abuses Yanni until he finds the courage to leave.

Yanni should feel free. But by the time Spencer Cohen finds him, he's resigned to being handed back to Lance and once again being caged by fear.

Starting school and a part-time job, Yanni begins to reclaim his life. But a love for silent films leads him to Peter Hannikov, a man with a kind heart but who's twice his age. An unlikely friendship between them blooms into so much more. Neither man knows what he wants, at first. Finding out exactly what he needs is Yanni's story.

"I'd spent years as a bird, caged with my wings clipped, tormented and beaten.

I thought I'd escaped when I'd left my abuser, but in hindsight, I could see that I was still caged, this time by fear and self-doubt.

Spencer and Andrew, and Andrew's parents, opened the door to the cage that confined me.

But it was Peter who taught me how to fly."

DEDICATION

Because every Yanni deserves a Peter

The Spencer Cohen *Series*

YANNI'S STORY

ACT ONE

LEARNING TO WALK

PROLOGUE

SPENCER COHEN SAVED MY LIFE.

I didn't know it at the time. Actually, when Spencer first found me and introduced himself, I thought my worst nightmares had found me again. I'd fought hard for my freedom, and I'd foolishly thought I was free. But instead, Spencer found me living a half-life—a scared-as-hell half-life. I'd spent years as a bird, first with my family and then with Lance, caged with my wings clipped, ridiculed, tormented, and beaten.

I thought I'd escaped when I'd left Lance, but in hindsight, I could see I was still caged, this time by fear and self-doubt.

Spencer and Andrew, and Andrew's parents, opened the door to the cage that confined me.

But it was Peter who taught me how to fly.

CHAPTER ONE

I COULDN'T REALLY REMEMBER much about that afternoon. A guy I'd never seen before, with an Australian accent, and a beard and tattoos, told me his name was Spencer. He said he was given my description—tall and thin, black curly hair, green eyes, olive skin—he knew my name and said *Lance* had sent him.

Lance. A name that made my blood run cold—a name I didn't like to even think of, let alone speak—and everything was a blur after that. I remember getting into a car with Spencer, the bearded guy, knowing whatever he planned to do to me couldn't have been worse than what I'd already been through.

He had a warm hand, a gentle hand, and worried eyes. I wasn't even aware he was holding my hand in the back of that car until I realized I was squeezing something to death, and looked down to see his fingers threaded with mine. He looked at me like he was scared I would break.

But I was already broken. And with that realization, that all-too-real, "I'll never be free of *him*" realization, came the tears I was helpless to stop. I hadn't allowed myself to cry in a long time. 'It was a sign of weakness. Only girls cry', Lance had said. Is that what I was? A little girl? He had taunted me, ridiculed me. He'd done the most unspeakable things to me, things that still haunted my dreams. It was part of the reason I didn't sleep. I was too scared to close my eyes…

But this kind man never let go of my hand. His name was Spencer Cohen, and he kept apologizing for scaring me. Spencer explained that he helped couples reconcile, a kind of matchmaker who helped put relationships into perspective. That was why Lance had contacted him. Lance wanted me back, but Spencer didn't know Lance had abused me. He knew now though, and he was so very sorry. Spencer was taking me somewhere safe, where *he* couldn't find me.

It didn't matter. None of it did.

Even if he did take me back to *him*, I wouldn't fight it. Because I understood now. I'd never been free of him. I could see now, the darkness that followed me was the memory of *him*, and even though I'd made my escape, I was never free.

I was so utterly exhausted. A tiredness that words couldn't explain. My mind was enervated, slow, and disengaged, and I couldn't focus no matter how I tried. Everything whirled out of my grasp.

When we stopped and Spencer got me out of the car, I half expected Lance to be there. But he wasn't. I found myself at Spencer's place, on a couch with a blanket, and I sank into my mind. It was the only safe haven I had, where I was safe, truly safe, from those who hurt me.

I didn't know how long I sat there. I had no recollection of time passing. Then we were on the move again and things got surreal, and I wondered if I'd lost grip on my sanity. Because Spencer took me to a huge house, a secure house, supposedly, and who should open the door but the one and only Helen Landon.

I sat on the sofa in a daze. I could barely ask her if any of this was even real when Mr Allan Landon walked in. *The* Allan Landon and Helen Landon, the powerhouse couple of theater in LA, sat staring at me with kindness and sympathy in their eyes.

"It's so cliché," I said, feeling foolish for doing so. "But he really was charming in the beginning. I didn't even realize he'd isolated me. By the end of the first six months, I was living with him, I had no friends, no one but him." I didn't know whether to laugh or cry. "I really was so naïve."

Mrs Landon put her hand on my arm. "No, you weren't," she said. Her voice was kind but determined. "The fault is his, not yours."

I had to blink back tears. "Then in the last six months, he started to get possessive and mad if I was late." I swallowed down the taste of bile that threatened to come up. "The first time he hit me, he'd been stressed at work, and he was so sorry. And I believed him." I scrubbed at my tears. "I'm sorry."

"Don't apologize," Mr Landon said gently. "You're allowed to cry. You've lost a lot. You need to grieve for that."

Grieve? I hadn't grieved for anything. I'd barely survived it.

I continued with my story, unwrapping my past, my guilt, and my pain for them all to witness. "I got through my first year at the Actors Academy and knew I had to come out to my parents. I couldn't put it off. But they…" I shook my head and let out a shaky breath. "They kicked me out at the beginning of my second year. I spent a while living rough, then I met *him*. He paid for me to go back to college, something I could never do on my own. I lived in his expensive apartment. And at first, it was exciting that I could do these things because I had no money, no family.

"It took him less than twelve months to completely own me." My voice shook, but I needed to get this out. "The last time he hit me, it was my birthday. The only thing he gave me was a black eye and a split lip. I swore it was the last time. I left with nothing. I had nothing. Everything I thought I had was his. It was always his. I quit my job. I left school. I left my cell phone he'd given me on the kitchen table and never went back. I stayed at a homeless shelter with my backpack and one change of clothes." I glanced at the bag at my feet. It was everything I owned. "I never thought I was a materialistic person until I had nothing."

Spencer frowned. "But those few things mean a lot. They're your worldly possessions, and they're everything."

I nodded at him, and I knew all eyes were on me. "Then you found me," I said, still looking at Spencer. I thought I'd escaped…

"I had no idea," he said again. "Well, I knew something was off with him, but I didn't realize, and I'm so sorry to drag you back through this." Spencer explained for everyone, "Yanni's ex-boyfriend contacted me to find him. It's not what I usually do, but he lied so convincingly."

God. I almost laughed. "He's a piece of work."

"But you went back to college?" Mrs Landon asked me.

I nodded sadly. "He took everything, but I couldn't let him take that from me. Acting is what I do. It's the only good thing in my life. I left the Actors Academy and started at Pol's Acting School." I looked down at my hands, trying to speak with a conviction I just didn't feel. "It's not as revered or exclusive, but I'm doing it on my own, and that's more than he gave me."

Mrs Landon's eyes were glassy, and she raised her chin before rubbing my arm. "Yanni, that's the sign of a true actor. One who fails to give up on his craft when he has nothing. That is a sure sign of strength and drive, and believe me, to make it in this industry, you need both in spades."

"I can't go back to Pol's," I said softly. It was starting to dawn on me that everything I'd gone through in the last few weeks was all for naught. "If he knows I went there…"

"I never told him," Spencer said adamantly. "I told him nothing. Actually, when I had a feeling he wasn't what he seemed, I told him you had a job in a bookstore in the city. We went to see if he turned up there looking for you."

I almost didn't want to know. "Did he?"

Spencer and Andrew both nodded. "Yeah."

I fought back more tears. "He won't ever stop."

"Did you tell the police?" Andrew asked.

"Yes. I filed a restraining order, but it doesn't mean anything."

Spencer nodded like something made sense. "That's why he asked me and not the police or a detective agency to find you."

I put my coffee back on the tray and sagged back into the sofa, and for a while, no one spoke. Mr Landon eventually broke the silence. "Yanni, when did you eat last?"

God, I couldn't even remember. I tried to think… I didn't even know what day it was. Mr Landon stood. "I'll go see what I can find," he said as he walked toward the kitchen.

My God, this was all too bizarre. I shook my head in

disbelief, scrubbing at my face and letting out a crazy-sounding laugh. "This is so surreal. I can't believe I'm here sitting beside you, and *the* Allan Landon just offered to get me food. I don't know what I did to deserve this, or is there a *Punk'd* camera hidden somewhere?"

Andrew snorted. "No cameras. They're just my parents. Spencer said you needed help, so I helped."

Mrs Landon put her hand on my arm. "Yanni, I want to tell you something. I have been where you are. It was a long time ago, before I met Allan. Actually, it was Allan who helped me leave my first husband."

All I could do was stare at her.

She smiled at me. It was a warm, motherly look that made my chest ache for my own mother. Another loss I couldn't bear to think about right now. "I've known the fear and hopelessness you feel. That exhaustion you feel in your bones, I've felt that. You will get through it if you let us help you."

I started to cry again. She understood me, what I'd been through. She just described everything better than I could.

Mrs Landon kept on talking. "I'm the Managing Director at Acacia Foundation. It's a center for men and women who are going through the same thing. We help people understand their legal rights and help them with police proceedings. We help them get back on their feet, find them somewhere to live, and employment placement."

Mr Landon came back into the room then, carrying another tray. Food; I could smell it from across the room. "It's just leftovers," he declared, putting the tray in front of me. There was Mexican beef, rice, and vegetables with flat breads, and I ignored the pity on their faces as I ate it. Lance had always been so particular about what I was allowed to eat, and for the last month, I'd been at the shelter with no money, no food. I was lucky to see half a meal a day. And God, I'd never tasted food so good. I ate far too much and my stomach threatened to explode. When I was more than done, I sagged back into the seat and closed my eyes. Relief, guilt, and shame washed over me.

Then I realized I hadn't waited for permission... Oh God. "I'm sorry," I said quickly, panicked.

"What for? Come on," Mr Landon said, standing up, waiting for me to do the same. "You can sleep in the guest room, and we'll deal with tomorrow after breakfast."

Not wanting to see the pity on their faces and not wanting to risk angering anyone, I picked up my backpack and followed Mr Landon obediently out of the room. I followed him down the hall, keeping my head down and seeing no more than his shoes and legs in front of me. He stopped at a door, opened it, flipped on a light, and stood aside. "This guest room has its own bathroom. Use whatever you need. Sleep well, and we'll see you for breakfast. Any requests? Helen will probably insist I eat yogurt and fruit, but I make a mean bacon and eggs."

I stepped into the room and held my bag in front of me. This was so strange. Today had gone from survival mode, to nightmare, to the Twilight Zone. I mean, I stood in the fanciest house I'd ever seen, I'd been fed a hot meal, and had a bed that wasn't a dirty cot. Had my own private bathroom, and he'd just offered me breakfast. And *he*, who was offering, was Allan fucking Landon. "Uh, I don't expect anything... You've already done so much."

He gave me a smile that tried for bright, but there was a sadness underneath. "Okay. If you need anything, Helen and I are upstairs. Just call out. Nothing is a problem. Goodnight, Yanni."

He pulled the door closed, and the quiet click of the

latch made me jump. I walked slowly to the bed and took in the room. It was huge; the bed was queen-sized and looked as soft as clouds with the white duvet and pillows. The curtains were white, matching the bed, and the walls were a pebble brown. There were fancy plates as wall decorations down one wall, and it was very clear that the Landons had impeccable taste or an interior designer who charged like a wounded bull.

I looked down at the carpet, only to find my dirty shoes instead. I quickly took them off, careful not to mark the plush floor coverings any more than I already had. Then I noticed how filthy my socks were, so I pulled them off too, only to reveal my dirty feet.

Oh God.

I was going to ruin their carpet. I ran to the first door, only to realize it was a walk-in closet, so I pushed on the second door to reveal the private bathroom. I turned the water on and stripped down as fast as I could, and not even caring about water temperature, I scrubbed my body with soap. My face, arms, torso, neck; I even washed my hair with soap, scrubbing harshly at my scalp. I scrubbed down my legs, but the dirt on my feet was too ingrained. I sat on the shower floor and scrubbed them raw, but I couldn't get them clean.

I would never be clean.

I didn't even know I was crying until my lungs burned for oxygen. I sucked back a breath and sobbed. Holding onto my knees, I let the water wash over me. I cried—for everything that hurt, for everything I'd lost. I cried for what had been taken away from me: my dignity, my pride, my self-worth.

I cried for the person I used to be. Because he was gone. My innocence, my youth, was ripped away from me, and I felt old. I was twenty-one, yet I felt I'd lived a hundred years.

I was so, so tired. I was battle-worn. I'd fought with everything I had, and I lost.

All I could do was cry. I cried until my tears ran dry, until I remembered where I was.

Eventually I stood up and shut the water off. I dried off and buried my face in the towel. It was soft and warm; two of the simplest things so easily taken for granted, until you're on the street with nothing. I'd missed towels. *The stupid things you think of at times like this.*

Then I realized I had no clean clothes.

I couldn't very well sleep in their nice clean bed in unwashed clothes. I certainly wouldn't sleep naked. I doubted I ever would again… I picked up the clothes I'd taken off and inspected them. I hadn't realized what state they were in. I thought I'd been doing okay…

With the towel wrapped around my waist, I went back out into the room to my backpack, with hopes of finding my spare clothes cleaner than my others, when I noticed a neatly folded pile of clothes on the end of the bed.

Mr or Mrs Landon must have put them there when I was in the shower.

I wondered if they'd heard me crying.

The clothes they'd left me were a pair of track pants, a T-shirt, and a long-sleeve sweatshirt. They had clearly been someone's once, loved and worn, no longer wanted. The significance wasn't lost on me.

I dressed quickly, relishing the comfort of clean and warm fabric against my skin. I climbed into the bed with my backpack and sank down in the mattress. I pulled the blankets up to my ears, too exhausted to think about how very surreal this was.

My tears had dried up, though my heart still ached. Like every night for the last month, I'd slept with my backpack under the blankets with me. I closed my eyes and tried not to panic. I told myself over and over I was safe here.

I'm safe here. I'm safe here. I'm safe here...

I slept with the light on.

CHAPTER TWO

IT TOOK me a minute to figure out where I was when I woke up. I was comfortable, and that sent a jolt of fear through me, as though the last month had been a dream—like I hadn't left Lance, and I'd woken up in his apartment. I shot upright, my stomach in knots. Then I remembered where I was.

The huge bedroom, lavish furnishings, the quiet... No, this definitely wasn't *his* place. *His* apartment was cold and debilitating. But I could feel the difference in this house. There was a peacefulness here, a home of warmth and laughter.

I was in the spare bedroom of *the* Allan and Helen Landon's house. I tried to not let that freak me out. It was surreal. Actually, I needed a better word than surreal.

Snippets of yesterday ran through my head. Spencer, my world coming down around me, then Andrew bringing me here. Mr Landon gave me food. I got to shower, wash my hair, and brush my teeth. I slept without fear of being robbed, bashed, or worse. The homeless shelters were better than sleeping on the streets, but they were far from perfect.

I didn't even know how long I'd slept. I had no way of knowing what the time was. I had no watch, no phone. In the shelters, I slept with one eye open and made myself scarce before anyone took too much notice. I kept track of the time, usually by clocks in stores, and it seemed unlikely and something I never even considered, but I had a pretty good idea of what the time was by where the sun was.

There was bright daylight peeking from behind the curtain, and I knew the Landons were probably waiting for me to make an appearance. I used the bathroom, washing my face and brushing my teeth again. I had no choice but to venture out wearing the clothes they'd graciously left out for me.

I felt every bit the charity case I was. Trying to ignore the shame I felt, I didn't want anyone to think of me as ungrateful. So I folded my clothes and shoved them along with my shoes into my backpack, and with a deep breath, I opened the door. The hall was empty, but I could hear signs of life coming from the kitchen.

It was sad how adept I'd become at listening to what part of the apartment *he* was in and how to go about not disturbing him. I padded down the hall and was soon following my nose.

Someone was cooking something that smelled divine.

And whistling, and chattering, and humming.

It was the sound of happiness, and I almost didn't want to disturb them. I could have stood on the other side of the door and listened all day, but an ingrained compulsion to face my fate pushed me forward.

Mr Landon was at the stovetop, whistling to a pan of frying bacon, while Mrs Landon sat at the counter top reading a newspaper. There were coffee cups, plates, a loaf of bread placed haphazardly. Casual, carefree, and completely relaxed. Nothing needed to be immaculate or aligned just so.

It was strange the things I noticed now. I wondered if there would ever be a time when I didn't notice such things. If there would ever be a time I wouldn't be so jumpy.

"Ah, good morning!" Mr Landon said, noticing me first. I flinched even though I was expecting him to speak. Mr Landon pretended he didn't notice.

Mrs Landon looked up, and she glanced at my backpack, how I was holding it like a shield, but still she smiled warmly. "Yanni. Did you sleep okay?"

"Yes, thank you," I managed. "And thank you for the clothes. I didn't realize how dirty mine were."

"We can wash them today," Mrs Landon said.

"Breakfast first," Mr Landon said, scraping a pan full of bacon onto a plate of waiting scrambled eggs. "Yanni, do you want coffee? Juice? Water?"

"Um…"

Mrs Landon was quickly on her feet. "You sit down at the table, love. I'll bring it all over."

"I don't want to be a bother," I said, clutching my backpack.

Mrs Landon's eyes fell to my bag, and when she met my gaze, her face softened. *She understands. She's been where I've been.* "You're no bother at all, Yanni."

I sat at the table and shoved my bag onto my lap and tried to make myself as inconspicuous as possible. Mr and Mrs Landon moved around the kitchen, bringing plates to the table, followed by cups of coffee and juice, and trays of bacon, eggs, and toast. My mouth watered, but I didn't dare touch it.

When Mrs Landon put the cutlery down, I instinctively

straightened it so it aligned with the plate and the edge of the table perfectly.

It was ingrained in me now. A force of habit.

When I noticed Mr Landon watching me, I slid my hands from the table and sat on them instead. He gave me an awkward smile and started to dish himself up some breakfast, and Mrs Landon did the same. Yet I didn't move. I would wait my turn.

"Are you hungry?" Mr Landon asked. He took a mouthful of eggs and waited for me to answer.

I opened my mouth to speak but wasn't sure what to say. I nodded instead.

Mrs Landon's smile was sad; her voice was quiet and reassuring. "You can eat, Yanni."

"Thank you," I whispered, both grateful and ashamed.

I ignored the silent conversation between Mr and Mrs Landon and ate my breakfast. The scrambled eggs were possibly the best I'd ever eaten, the bacon was delicious, the juice fresh, the coffee expensive.

When I couldn't have fit another bite in, I realized Mr and Mrs Landon were long finished and waiting for me. I silently set my knife and fork at twelve and six the way *he* had always insisted on and put my hands in my lap. "Thank you."

"Was it good?" Mr Landon asked.

"Very." I smiled at his cheerfulness. He was an attractive man, an older version of his son, Andrew. There was a gentleness to him, a kindness, which I found reassuring. Mrs Landon was the same, though she had the grace and confidence of a queen, and it was easy to see why. Because Mr Landon treated her like one. "You've both been very kind."

Mrs Landon drained her coffee. "Yanni, would you

mind sitting with me in the living room? I thought we could chat. Is that okay with you?"

Talking about what I'd been through was the very last thing I felt like doing. The thought alone made my breakfast sit like an uneasy lump in my stomach. I swallowed hard. "Yes. Of course." Then I looked at the table and stood up. My backpack fell to the floor, but I ignored it and stacked the empty cups. "I'll clean away the breakfast dishes and be right with you."

She gently put her hand on mine, stopping me. "Sweet boy, you don't have to do that."

I quickly took my hand back and stood up straight. "Sorry."

"No need to apologize," Mr Landon said. He finished stacking the plates. "I'll take care of these."

I wanted to object, say that it was certainly not his job to clean up after me, but I didn't want to speak out of turn.

Mrs Landon stood up and gave me a soft smile. "Would it make you feel better if I said you can help clean up after lunch?"

I half-nodded, half-shrugged. "Yes."

She laughed quietly and gestured toward the door at the end of the kitchen. "Come with me, Yanni."

I collected my backpack and followed obediently, giving a final glance at Mr Landon, who was already loading the dishwasher with plates. I sat beside Mrs Landon on the same sofa we'd sat on last night and held my backpack on my lap.

"So I was thinking today we could talk about what you want and what steps you'd like to take," Mrs Landon said.

I didn't understand. "What I want?" I shook my head. "I don't want anything. I don't expect anything. You've already been more generous than I can ever repay."

She smiled patiently. "You don't need to repay

anything. I was referring to which steps you'd like to take in getting yourself a place to stay, maybe a part-time job so you can continue your studies. Your future, Yanni. What do you want for your future?"

"Oh." It was a lot to get my head around. "I've just been concentrating on getting through each day. I haven't really thought much about my future."

Mrs Landon let out a breath and sat back in her seat. "That's the hardest part, isn't it? When you're in a relationship you can't get out of, like you were, like I was, you don't just lose your freedom and self-esteem. You lose sense of who you are, your identity. Your dreams, your direction. They take everything away."

I nodded, but I refused to cry. *She understands. She's been where I've been.* "Everything."

She patted my knee. "But this is you taking it back, Yanni. You're taking back control. This is your life. You make the decisions from here on out, and I know that's scary right now, and it's overwhelming. But that's why I'm here to help. It's what my Acacia Foundation does. We help you get on your feet."

"It is scary."

"It's frightening as hell," Mrs Landon said. Then she raised her chin. "But you know what? You are strong enough and brave enough to get through this. I'm not just saying this, Yanni. I'm not reading a spiel from a pamphlet." She took my hand and squeezed. "You were strong and brave enough to leave him. *You* did that. And I can tell you why. Because you said 'no more.' You said you wanted better because you deserve better. You deserve to not be afraid. To not live in fear."

I blinked back tears. "I didn't want to be that person anymore."

Mrs Landon was teary too. "Because you deserve better."

It took everything I had, but with a deep breath, I nodded.

She breathed in deeply through her nose and lifted her chin. There was defiance there, a strength. Her eyes told a story, a depth, a history, a fire that burned from a place only a few people knew existed.

"Now," she continued. Her tone was different, like the second act had begun. "What did you want to do about Lance?"

I recoiled at his name. Words failed me. "N-n-nothing."

She squeezed my hand. "You said you'd taken out a restraining order. Him engaging Spencer to find you violated that order."

"A piece of paper was never going to stop him."

"If you want to report him, I can drive you to the police station."

I shook my head. "I don't know…"

"You don't have to, Yanni. I would never pressure you."

"But you think I should."

She took another deep breath. "I do."

"What good will it do? It won't stop him."

"Maybe not. But it paints a picture for the police. If you report him, they have his name on record. If he does it again to someone else, they'll know he has a track record."

My gaze shot to hers. *Does it to someone else?*

She nodded and patted my hand. "Just think about it. You don't need to make any decisions about that right now."

Speaking of decisions. "I'll need to call Pol's and ask if I can defer or withdraw…"

Mrs Landon frowned.

"I can't go back there," I said. "If Spencer found me there, then surely he could too."

"Spencer did say he never told him."

"I know."

"But it's too close?"

I nodded. *She understood.*

"Then I think we can find you a new school. Through the Foundation, we can find placement housing, but we don't need to rush that. My point is, once we do find a place for you to live, then we can find a school that's close."

Right. My future.

"I know it's daunting, but it's exciting too, yes? A new beginning? New life?"

I was still stuck on overwhelmed. "Sure."

Mrs Landon gave me a pained look. "Yanni, the Foundation also provides resources like therapy and counseling. It's not compulsory, but I would recommend it. You've been through hell, and I think you could benefit from some professional perspective and advice. We can take care of all the physical things, but we shouldn't forget the mental and psychological."

I could barely nod, swamped with information and emotion. It was all moving in the right direction, but it was too fast, too soon.

"Okay, that's enough of the heavy for now," Mrs Landon said. "How about we get your clothes in the washer. I actually have some clothes put aside for Goodwill. The other week, I cleared out our wardrobes of all the clothes we hadn't worn in a while. I'm sure we can find you something to wear in the meantime." Then she brightened considerably. "Oh, and we have a collection of classic film and theater DVDs to rival the BBC's library. It wouldn't be a Friday night in the Landon household without a feature presentation."

I found myself smiling, despite the conflict in my head. It also implied I had somewhere to sleep for the night. "That sounds great."

She stood up. "Come on. Let's go sort these clothes out."

I followed her to the laundry room, where she showed me how to use the washing machine, then she showed me the DVD collection, while she went in search for the bag of clothes for me to look through. She wasn't joking about their film collection rivaling the BBC's. There were rows of classics in both film and theater, ranging from Orson Welles and Charlie Chaplin to Errol Flynn and Humphrey Bogart. The theater greats were there as well. So much so, that if the British Theatre ever lost their archives, they could use the Landons'. I adored Shakespeare, but my heart was with the silent movies.

My breath literally caught in my throat when I realized they had Carl Theodor Dreyer's 1928 film *The Passion of Joan of Arc*. I pulled it out, running my fingers along the cover. It was a masterpiece.

"Ah, when you said you liked the classics, you weren't joking." Mr Landon's voice made me jump. He flinched but was quick to smile. "You have impeccable taste."

"Oh, yes," I said, turning the DVD over to look at the back, waiting for my heartbeat to stop hammering. "It's genius cinematography."

"So ahead of its time."

"It really was."

Mr Landon shook his head with a smile. "You know, as much as we tried to get our kids into the classics, their tastes never quite did gel with ours. I think Andrew's idea of a classic is *Blade Runner*."

I chuckled. "Semantics, I guess."

He grinned at me. "True. Helen wanted me to tell you the clothes she mentioned earlier are in the front living room."

"Thank you."

He turned to leave but stopped. "And bring the DVD. It'll be our Friday night cinematic spectacular!" He waved his hand dramatically, as though the words were up in lights, before disappearing down the hall, whistling a tune. I couldn't help but like him. He gave off positive energy, and I remembered reading that other actors he worked with loved having him around for that very reason also.

Though it was a little different for me. I felt safe around him. I felt safe in this house. And that said a lot for me.

I grabbed the DVD of Laurence Olivier's *Hamlet*, as well, and ventured back out to the front living room. Mrs Landon was there, pulling folded clothes from a large bag and refolding them, organizing them into a pile on the sofa.

I showed her my selection of films, and she beamed. "Oh, you do have impeccable taste."

I smiled. "Mr Landon said the same thing."

"Only someone who appreciates the art of acting would pick those two."

Her words warmed through my chest with something that felt like pride. I allowed myself a moment to bask in that feeling. Then I noticed the folded shirts and pants. "Oh, that's a lot of clothes."

She waved her hand. "Well, I buy clothes for Allan, trying to instill some sense of fashion, but it's no use. He's a lost cause."

"I heard that," Mr Landon called from somewhere down the hall.

Mrs Landon laughed. "It's true." She held up a yellow

knitted sweater. "Like this. Paid a small fortune for it, but he won't wear it. Now I don't buy him anything."

"I have more clothes than the men's department at Bloomingdale's," came a reply from down the hall.

Mrs Landon rolled her eyes, and I smiled at her. "It's a lovely color," I said, nodding to the sweater.

She handed it to me. "It's yours. All of these are for the taking. Whatever you don't want will go to the Foundation or to Goodwill. Someone who'll appreciate them might as well have them." Then she pulled out a pink and purple handful of silk. "Oh, this was mine. There's nothing wrong with it, it just went out of fashion. I really need to stick to buying classic pieces and not get caught up with trends..." She was chattering away and put the silk item off to the side. I couldn't stop staring at it. It was vibrant and looked incredibly soft. Mrs Landon noticed me staring at it, so she picked it up and offered it to me. "You can have it if you want?"

"Oh, I..." I shook my head. "I'm not into wearing women's clothes. Not really. And not that there's anything wrong with that, it's just..."

She kept her hand out, still offering the fabric, and gave a daring smile. "Just touch it. It's glorious."

I took it and it was like water in my hands. Smooth, cool, luxurious. She was watching me, and there was no point in trying to hide it. My smile gave me away. "It feels incredible."

"Doesn't it just?" she said casually, like we weren't discussing me enjoying the feel of women's clothes against my skin. "It's supposed to be a jacket, like a wrap. You could wear it as a robe if you wanted to."

I held it up and could see the length of the jacket itself would come down to my thighs. The long sleeves were bell shaped, and it was gloriously bright pinks and purples. I could never see myself wearing it out in public, but to wear it in private…

It was foolish to think I'd ever be in a place where I could wear it. I'd never have my own room, let alone privacy, and that stark realization killed any hope that might have started to form. My good mood deflated. I folded it up and handed it back to Mrs Landon. "I don't really have anywhere I can wear that."

Mrs Landon took the jacket with a sad smile, though she recovered quickly by grabbing a pair of trousers. She flicked them out and held them up, inspecting them. "I think he wore these once." Then she stage-whispered with a wink, "Said they were too tight. They might fit you. What size are you? A thirty-two?"

"I'm not sure. I used to be a thirty-four, but my jeans were loose."

"Give your body time," she said, like it was just a matter of fact. "You haven't had the opportunity to eat properly for a while. Add in an incredible amount of stress and hardship, and your body's taken quite the hit." I wasn't sure what to say to that, and Mrs Landon seemed to understand. "Oh, what about this one?" She held up a plain white tee.

We went through the bag and I ended up with half a wardrobe of clothes. Some I wasn't sure would even fit properly, but any clothes were better than the none I had. We must have sat there for an hour, slowly going through the clothes, but with each garment, Mrs Landon chatted away, making me feel more comfortable—more human—than I'd felt in a long time.

She explained what the Acacia Foundation does on a daily basis, how busy she is, how she loves it. She told me some success stories of people she'd helped, how their stories were similar to mine, and how they've made new lives for themselves.

I helped her with lunch and she had me chop peppers, mushrooms, and cucumber for the salad while she told me stories of what a disastrous cook Andrew turned out to be. We talked about our favorite foods and recipes, and it was dreamlike and decidedly normal.

And so very wonderful.

I'd forgotten what normal felt like.

After lunch, I was all too happy to help clean up. It was the least I could do given their generosity, but it also felt good to be productive. As I wiped the sink down when I was done, Mrs Landon stood beside me. "It hasn't been this clean since it was installed."

I chuckled, but a rush of pride bloomed in my chest. "Thank you."

She tilted her head, her brow furrowed. "Everything okay? You were frowning at the sink just now."

Oh. *Was I okay?* I wasn't sure if I'd ever be okay again, but the truth was, even though I'd only been in their house for less than twenty-four hours, I felt more comfortable than I could remember being. Not comfortable in a pleasant-living way, but more comfortable with myself, and even though I was hesitant to use the word confident, I was pretty sure I knew what I should do.

"I think I should tell the police," I said. "About what he did."

Mrs Landon's smile was slow spreading, and her eyes filled with warmth. "I can take you."

I realized I was wringing the dishcloth, so I quickly folded it neatly and put it down, then wiped my hands on the tea towel, fidgeting and unable to keep still.

"It's okay to be nervous and scared," she whispered

softly. I shoved my hands in my pockets. "I'll be with you the whole time."

"It's the right thing to do, isn't it?" I asked.

She put her hand on my arm. "He should be stopped."

I nodded but felt so unsure. He *should* be stopped, yes. But I just wasn't sure I was strong enough to do it.

CHAPTER THREE

IT WAS irrational to be scared of the police. I'd done nothing wrong, yet I felt like a criminal. From the way they looked at me, their barely concealed judgment felt like an unwanted touch. Like it was *his* hands on me, uninvited. It made my skin crawl.

I could see in their eyes what they were thinking. I had no fixed address, no family. I was gay. I wasn't masculine. I wasn't strong enough to stop him.

Men weren't the abused. They were the abusers. In their eyes, that made me the weaker one, the battered wife. No doubt, I'd probably be the punch line of a few jokes when they had a coffee break. When the truth was, domestic violence, violence of any kind, wasn't fucking funny.

When we'd finally been allocated an office with two uniformed police officers, Mrs Landon did most of the talking. She spoke with a no-nonsense confidence and seemed to know the jargon, the right words that ensured action. Mr Landon sat on my other side and put a reassuring arm around my shoulders. I felt like a child, certainly not the twenty-one-year-old I was.

I nodded at all the right times, and I answered yes or no. I gave my account of what had happened the day before, and I signed the statement to make it official. I knew they'd be calling Spencer for his side of the story, and I felt bad about that. I didn't mean to involve anyone else. I didn't even want to involve me.

An older policeman asked if he could speak to the Landons in private, leaving me with the female officer. She had dark curly hair pulled back in a ponytail, dark brown eyes, and a dimpled chin. She'd already introduced herself, but her demeanour was different now. "My name's Detective Serena Hernandez. But you can call me Serena." She smiled at me and spoke in even tones. "You did the right thing, Yanni. It was a pretty brave thing for you to do."

I nodded.

She pointed her chin to the door Mr and Mrs Landon walked out of. "They seem like real nice people."

"They are. They didn't have to help me, but they did." I shrugged and looked down at the yellow sweater I was wearing. "They gave me these clothes. And food."

Serena's face softened.

I don't know why, but I felt compelled to defend myself. I couldn't look at her, though, so I spoke to my hands in my lap. "I'm not a weak person. Well, I didn't use to be. I didn't think it would ever happen to me."

"It's not your fault," Serena said. I looked at her then. "You just trusted the wrong guy."

I nodded. "Then I couldn't leave. I had nothing, and he…"

"Made you feel worthless," she finished for me.

I went back to looking at my hands, and she reached over and slid her hand over mine. "You did the right thing.

It wasn't easy, but you did it. You have more courage than he will ever have. Don't ever forget that."

I looked up at her again, and I could see in her eyes, *she understood. She's been where I've been.* "Thank you. I'm just trying to get through one day at a time."

"That's all you can do. One foot in front of the other, one breath at a time. And you will get through this." Serena gave me a hopeful smile. "Come on, let's go find Mr and Mrs Landon."

She held the door for me, and we went down a corridor where Mr and Mrs Landon were talking with the officer they'd left the interview room with. Unfortunately, we walked in on the end of the conversation. Mr Landon was talking, "… starving hungry but too scared to eat without permission——" The three of them stopped and looked at me. Mr Landon looked sorry and upset, and I hated that I was the cause.

I don't know why I said what I did. There was a strange detachedness to admit this stuff out loud. "Only sometimes. I was only not allowed to eat sometimes. I think he preferred me to not know what to expect. It was scarier that way. But I'd have to wait to be told to eat. Or sometimes he'd put my plate on the floor like I was a dog."

The policeman recoiled with a frown. I'd wondered if he didn't believe me up until now. He seemed sorry to have doubted me. Serena put her hand on my arm, her eyes filled with a familiar sadness. And with that, our meeting was done.

Mrs Landon had tears in her eyes, and Mr Landon was quick to put his arm around me. "I think we need takeout, ice cream, and popcorn," he said, as brightly as he could. "We can't have Friday night movie night without takeout, ice cream, *and* popcorn."

We made our way out of the building, and Mr Landon

never dropped his arm from my shoulder. "What's your favorite ice cream?" he asked as we crossed the lot to the car.

"Um, chocolate?"

"Mine too!" He unlocked the car. "Helen, where's the closest Ben and Jerry's?"

So that's what we did. They bought ridiculous amounts of Chinese food, tubs of ice cream, and bags of popcorn. We laid all the food out on the kitchen counter, and truthfully, it was enough to feed ten people. But Mr Landon handed me a plate and looked me right in the eye. "You don't ever need permission to eat. Not in this house, not anywhere. For as long as you're here, anytime, day or night, there's fruit or bread, milk, coffee, whatever. If you want anything, you help yourself. Okay?"

I nodded. "Thank you."

"Well," Mrs Landon said thoughtfully, waving a fork. "About not needing permission from anyone... unless you have dinner with the Queen of England, I'd probably hold back until someone gives the nod."

Mr Landon smiled and bowed his head. "Oh, but of course."

"Or Judi Dench," Mrs Landon added.

I fought a smile. "I thought that was who you meant when you said the Queen of England."

They both burst out laughing, and Mrs Landon gave me a half, side-on hug. "Oh, you are a man after my own heart."

We ate our dinner and took our ice cream in front of the TV for our movie night. *Joan of Arc* was just as I'd remembered, and the ice cream was divine, but my favorite part was sitting in a family home doing something that families did. They weren't my family—I hadn't had a family for a long time—but for one night I could pretend. I had no clue how long I'd be staying with them, so I just allowed myself to imagine.

When the movie was done and my stomach full, Mr Landon suggested the second film, but I could hardly keep my eyes open. I'd spent the last year barely sleeping at all —first with *him*, then at the homeless shelter—but it was barely eight o'clock and I was nodding off. Mrs Landon took our empty plates. "Can I get you anything else, Yanni?" she asked on her way to the kitchen.

"No, thank you. I think I need to go to bed," I admitted. "I don't know why I'm so tired."

Mr Landon waited until we were alone. "You'll be tired, and you'll need to sleep," he said quietly. "I remember when we finally got Helen away from her ex, she slept like she hadn't slept in months. So if you feel yourself getting tired, don't fight it. It's perfectly normal."

I swallowed hard. I didn't think I'd ever be used to discussing such things so casually. "I feel like I could sleep for a week. I guess a full belly and feeling safe here helps. So thank you."

His smile was a mix of proud and sad. "You're more than welcome."

"Good night," I said, standing up. "Please tell Mrs Landon I said good night and thank you."

"Will do. Sleep well."

By the time I'd changed and brushed my teeth, I was so exhausted I almost fell into bed. Yes, I felt safe here, but I still slept with my backpack under the covers with me, and I slept with the light on.

Small steps.

———

THE NEXT FEW days were a blur of sleep and meetings

at the Acacia Foundation. Mrs Landon wanted me to go with her so I could see what my options were. With her holding my hand, I called Pol's and requested a temporary leave on my studies until I decided what I wanted to do. Mrs Landon didn't want me to quit school or acting but didn't want me to deal with ultimatums or deadlines right now, and to be honest, after I'd made the call, I felt relieved.

"You need to look after your health. Physical and mental," she said. She showed me a list of housing options, though she wasn't sure any were suitable for me. All the readily available placements were basically like halfway houses for people from the LGBTQI community getting back on their feet. People who the Acacia Foundation were helping get their lives back on track after being kicked out of their homes or abused, beaten.

People exactly like me.

"I'm not playing favorites," Mrs Landon said, looking over the housing options. "But, and this is only if you want, how about you stay with us for a little while longer? It can't be permanent, but we have the room, and you're such a joy to have around."

"Oh."

"Maybe it'll only be a few weeks, but there's a place I have in mind for you. It's close to our performing arts school and there's a ton of cafés and restaurants where you could get some part-time work. It would suit you so much better than these." She nodded to the list. "All of our houses are situated close to colleges and shopping outlets because the majority of our clients are young adults. But the one I'm thinking of would be perfect for you."

I wasn't sure what to say.

"Have you heard of LA's School of Performing Arts?"

"Yes, of course. It's an incredible school. But I can't

afford fees like that. I could barely afford Pol's with the money I made at the café. I only did a few shifts a week, and staying at the shelter, my wages went on tuition and food."

She gave me a sympathetic smile. "It's not often I'll use my name or credibility to pull strings, but have you forgotten who I am?"

I chuckled at her attempt at fake indignation. "Certainly not."

"And if my name isn't enough, I'll just sleep with the boss."

I'm sure my eyes almost bugged out of my head, and she burst out laughing. "Los Angeles School of Performing Arts is Allan's pride and joy. He's run that school for fifteen years."

"Oh." I put my hand to my heart, still not over the shock of her sleep-with comment. "Thank goodness."

She laughed again, delighted by my reaction. "Yanni, my dear. You are the sweetest child."

Good lord. LASPA was a small, leading school, which produced some award-winning stage actors. I would never have imagined in my wildest dreams… I couldn't get my mind around it, and one question begged to be asked.

"Why are you doing this?" I asked. "Not to sound ungrateful, because I'm *so very* thankful for everything you and Mr Landon have done for me, I truly am. But why me? It can't be just because Andrew and Spencer dropped me off on your doorstep. You could have taken me to one of the placement homes the next day and wished me luck, and even that would have been enough, but this…"

Mrs Landon stared at me for a moment, the papers on her desk in front of her long forgotten. "Because you remind me of me. You *are* me. Thirty years ago I was in your shoes, a broken soul who just dreamed of being on stage. But where you have no one, I had Allan, and he saved my life. Literally, if it weren't for him, I wouldn't be here today. So I pay what I can forward, and if that means I need to be someone else's Allan, then that's what I'll be."

"So it's kind of like some universal general ledger," I surmised.

"Exactly! And in a few years' time, when you're a successful actor and settled down with some gorgeous man, *you* can pay the universe forward."

I laughed at that. "Neither of those things seems likely at this point."

"You can have both or neither. Whichever you want. It's your choice."

I thought about that for a moment, and even the idea of having the freedom to choose sent a thrill through me.

"Speaking of choices," Mrs Landon continued, "have you thought any more about therapy or counseling?"

That surge of excitement at taking back some control made me smile. As daunting as it was, I knew it would be good for me. "Yeah, I have. I'd like to try it, if that's okay."

By the time we left her office, I had an appointment the following day with a therapist, and we had plans for a home-cooked dinner, and apparently Mr Landon wanted me to do a script read-through with him of his latest stage adaption. And they wanted me to stay with them for another week or two. In just a few short days, with the Landons' help, of course, I'd taken huge steps in a positive direction.

And for the first time in a long time, something began to bloom in my chest. I didn't want to get ahead of myself, but it felt a lot like hope.

CHAPTER FOUR

MY THERAPIST WAS a woman by the name of Patrice Clare, who could have been a professional impersonator for Whoopi Goldberg. She looked like her, spoke like her, smiled like her. She had an open warmth about her, and I felt comfortable being alone in a room with her from the second we met.

I wasn't too comfortable with strangers, especially those who were scrutinizing me, but something about her put me at ease. She had a great professional relationship with Mrs Landon, and I trusted her judgment in character, which helped.

She asked me a lot of questions about my life, my family, my childhood, and I'd mentally prepared myself for those. But then she asked me what I hoped to get out of our meetings together. "I don't know," I replied.

"Well, let's set some goals. What do you want in a week, a year, three years, ten?"

"Mrs Landon asked me something similar. And like I told her, I haven't actually allowed myself to look to the future in so long, I've kind of forgotten who I am. But I've been thinking about it since she asked. I want what Mrs Landon has. Not the money or the house." I shrugged. "I want to live like her: be happy and healthy, to have someone to love me, who knows what I've been through without judging me. But for me to recognize my past without fear or shame."

"That's a wonderful long-term goal, and one I have no doubt you can achieve. What about short term? What's the next step for you?"

"Well, Mrs Landon's trying to get me into housing. One that's close to a new acting school. I'm excited about that. A new start, ya know? I'm truly grateful for the Landons, I really am, but I want my independence. I want to stand on my own two feet. Well, I want to try."

She smiled at me. "It's perfectly natural to want to reclaim your life. I'm sure the Landons know how appreciative you are."

"I hope so. I mean, I've told them, but it doesn't seem like enough."

Patrice leaned forward and whispered with a motherly smile. "Yanni, they know."

I didn't know why, but that made me feel better. The very last thing I wanted to be was another disappointment to the people who had been the kindest to me.

"The hardest part about what you've been through," Patrice said, "is the isolation. You finally have your freedom and are regaining your independence, but it feels deficient because you've lost all connections with your old life."

I nodded. "Exactly. I've lost my family and my friends. I mean, my family was lost to me before… him… but my friends, that hurts, ya know?"

"Could you contact them?"

"My family?" I shook my head. "No. I spent my entire

childhood afraid of who I was because they were so anti-gay. And when I actually came out… well, they made it pretty clear I wasn't welcome."

She blinked and I knew we'd be coming back to that topic at some point. "What about your friends?"

I took a deep breath. "Maybe."

"But you feel like you'd need to explain and apologize."

"Yeah. And I'm not above doing that, but…"

"But it's an emotional hurdle you're not ready for."

I nodded. "I didn't know them for very long. I didn't really know them at all, to be honest."

"You'll make new friends."

"Eventually, maybe."

"Why do you say that?"

I shrugged. "I dunno. It just feels so out of reach right now."

"Like you're at the foot of the mountain you need to climb," she elaborated.

I smiled at her. "You get this, don't you?"

"I've helped a lot of people who've been through what you've been through."

"I think I can tell."

She chuckled quietly. "Our time is up for this session, but it was an absolute pleasure to meet you."

"You too."

"Yanni, I want you to think about something for me. If the opportunity comes up for you to be social, though only if you're feeling up for it, get out of the house and talk to people. It will help you feel connected again. Only in small doses. Half an hour this week, a little longer next week. How does that sound?"

"Okay, I guess. I'm not sure if Mr or Mrs Landon want to babysit me, though."

"It doesn't have to be a babysitting mission. Even just a quick trip to the store."

"I went shopping with them the other day. We got ice cream."

"Excellent. Try again this week sometime. Nothing you're uncomfortable with, of course. And if you're not ready this week, then that's okay too."

I let out a deep breath, gave her a nod, and promised to see her next week. Which I was strangely eager to do.

And a week later, she welcomed me warmly. "How's your week been? You've had a haircut?"

"Pretty good," I admitted. "Great, actually. And yes, Mr Landon took me to a barber." My black curly hair was still a little long on top, but at least the sides were neater. "It was nice."

"You're still living with the Landons?"

"Yeah. They're very kind. Some days I have to remind myself it's only temporary. They seem to like having me there."

Patrice smiled warmly. "I've known the Landons, professionally, for twenty years. If you're still there, it's because they want you there." Then she quickly added, "Not to say that when you do leave, it's because they want you to leave."

I laughed. "No, I know exactly what you mean. Mrs Landon's hoping I can get a place in that house near their acting school."

"How's that looking?"

"She thinks in a few weeks," I said. I couldn't stop the smile that stole across my lips.

Patrice smiled right back at me. "That *is* good news." Then she got back to business. "So, you had a few more social interactions this week?"

"Yes." I ran my hand through my newly cut hair. "The

barber. Andrew and Sarah both came to the house. Mr and Mrs Landons' kids."

"Yes, I know them."

"They came and stayed a while. They're very funny. And I went to the store again with Mrs Landon. We bought some personal things for me."

"Such as?"

I shrugged. "Underwear. That kind of thing."

"It must be nice accumulating some belongings again."

More than I could say. "Yes. I'm keeping tabs on how much they're spending on me. I want to pay it back one day. I don't know how, but I will."

Patrice's smile had an edge of pride. "That sounds like a goal."

"It is."

She studied me for a moment. "How are you feeling, Yanni?"

"I feel good. Better than I have in a year. I'm eating and sleeping better than I can remember, and that helps my frame of mind. I understand that. But I feel… I don't know, positive, for my future. And that's a real good feeling."

She went on to set me little homework tests for the week to follow, which included some pen and paper notes, but more mental than anything. She gave me a notebook, like an exercise book I had in school, and wanted me to write down notes, thoughts, reflections, and emotions. Keeping a journal was a great way to keep on track, but she wanted me to keep being forward-thinking in my social outings.

I thought about her words a lot, and when Andrew stopped by on Friday, I was kind of excited to see him. He was wearing gray trousers and a pink and gray argyle sweater. He was very handsome, and when he smiled, he looked just like his father.

"You look great!" Andrew said as soon as he saw me.

I was sure being showered and dressed in clean clothes would have been any kind of improvement to when he first saw me. But still, I'd seen him since then. "You saw me just a few days ago," I said. "Not sure I've changed that much."

"Yanni, you look like a million dollars, even compared to the other day."

"Your parents keep me well dressed," I said, looking down at myself. If he recognized his father's clothes on me, he never let on. "And well fed."

"Dad?"

I snorted. "Yes. He likes to see me eat."

Andrew grinned. "Sounds about right. But yes, you look like life with my parents agrees with you."

"They're so lovely. I really need to thank you and Spencer."

"No thanks necessary. Spencer said to say hi, by the way."

"Oh, please tell him hello for me. And that I'm grateful for what he did."

"I will." Andrew smiled warmly. "Are Mom and Dad here?"

"No, they're both at work."

He clapped his hands together and grinned. "So you can tell me the truth. Are they driving you insane?"

"No! Absolutely not."

"Not making you do screenplay readings and ad-libbing in the living room?"

"Well, once or twice—"

"I knew it!"

"But I love it!" I said with a laugh. "Truly, I do!"

He put his head back and groaned. "Another actor, I forgot!"

Now I laughed. "Your dad told me you and your sister never caught the acting bug."

"No, never!"

It was nice to talk with someone closer to my age. As much as I loved spending time with Andrew's parents, Patrice's words came back to me about making new friends. Actually, it wasn't even that he was my age or that his parents weren't, but just someone *new* to talk to.

And talk, we did. He told me about his work, which was interesting to say the very least. He drew animation boards for Universal, so for a digital artist, it didn't really get much cooler than that.

We sat at the kitchen island while I plated up some left-over pasta and told Andrew all about my week so far and his mother's hopes of finding me a place in a house so maybe I could go back to school.

"That's awesome!" he said with a mouthful of food. He pointed his fork to his bowl of *pastitsio*. "And this is really good."

"It's a family recipe," I explained. "I cooked it for your parents."

He chewed and swallowed thoughtfully. "Your family…?"

"Don't make for pleasant conversations." I frowned at my meal. "I shouldn't have brought them up, sorry."

"It's perfectly fine. You don't have to talk about them if you don't want."

"Thanks. My therapist asked a bunch of questions, stuff I hadn't thought of in a long time, so I guess it's been on my mind. I don't normally like to talk about it. I thought they were the worst thing to happen to me until I met… him."

"Well, he won't be bothering you anymore," Andrew said. "Spencer and Emilio paid him a little visit at his work the day after he found you. Gave him a taste of his own medicine."

My stomach twisted, threatening to expel my dinner. "They hit him?"

"No!" Andrew said quickly. "No, not like that. Just told him they knew what he'd done and threatened him. Apparently that was all it took. He almost crapped himself."

I wasn't sure how I felt about that. "Was he angry? Does he know where I am?"

Andrew stood up and came around my side and put his hand on my arm. "No. Yanni, you're safe here. He knows nothing. And from what Spencer told me, he won't be looking for you. He wouldn't be game to try."

My mouth was dry and I had trouble swallowing. "He won't ever stop looking for me. He told me that."

Andrew moved his hand to my back and rubbed reassuringly. "He's finished. He's done. Mom told me you went back to the police. Out of all the things he is, a monster, an asshole, a snake, the one thing he is the most is a coward. He wouldn't survive five minutes in jail, and he knows it. Yanni, he's out of your life for good."

I tried to take comfort in his words, but I wasn't sure I'd ever believe it. If not now, I knew I'd have to face him again at some point. And that was something I couldn't even think about right now.

"You know what?" Andrew said. "How about we get out of here for a while? We can just drive downtown, grab some beers if you want?"

"I uh, I don't drink.

"Soda? God knows Mom and Dad don't have sodas in the house. What kind of soda have you been craving?"

I almost smiled. I hadn't had soda in so long. "Root beer."

Andrew grabbed up his keys. "Excellent, let's go."

We drove down to the Boulevard, a place I hadn't seen in what felt like forever. When I was a kid, I dreamed of coming here. When my relationship with my parents came to an abrupt end, this was the first place I went. It was where I was going to make it big and make it on my own.

Until life, and *him* made sure that didn't happen.

Though as Andrew drove, it was hard not to smile at the lights and the strictly LA feel. Maybe it was why Andrew chose it. To let me see the lights, the people, how life hadn't actually stopped around me.

We pulled up at a store but Andrew had to double-park. He took out twenty dollars and handed it to me. "You all right to go in on your own?"

"Sure." I wanted to prove I could do this. A simple thing like going into a store by myself. It was all very normal; no one paid any attention while I found what I wanted, and the cashier even smiled. God, it was such an everyday thing to do, yet something that felt so unreal. It was ridiculous how excited I was. I collected my six-pack of root beer, and when I got back in Andrew's car, he was on his phone. He held it to his chest and looked at me. "Spencer is at a diner just down the road. He asked if we wanted to join him, but only if you want to."

I thought about what Patrice had said, about being more social in situations where I felt safe. But then Andrew added, "He's having coffee with a friend. So you know there will be somebody else there. I've never met this guy, but Spencer trusts him."

I wasn't sure if I wanted to meet strangers, but I wanted to see Spencer to thank him. And if he trusted this man, then I would too. "Um, okay."

When Andrew said it was just down the road, he wasn't kidding. Literally two blocks later we pulled up to a small diner and went inside. Spencer stood to greet me, and I didn't know what came over me, but I was so pleased to see him that I hugged him. He was the man who saved me. I hadn't known it at the time, but I knew it now.

I think I surprised him more than I surprised myself, but we settled into our seats, and it was then I noticed the man across from me. He was possibly early forties, with short blond-gray hair, blue eyes, and a kind face. He was also wearing a tuxedo, so he looked every penny of a million dollars. A quick round of introductions later, I discovered his name was Peter, and he had a smile that made me feel safe.

Spencer spoke first. "Yanni? How's life with the Landons going?"

"Oh, it couldn't be better," I said. "They're just the nicest people ever."

"But they're driving him crazy," Andrew added.

I laughed and shook my head vehemently. "No, no. They've been very generous. I really do owe you everything, Spencer. If it weren't for you…"

Peter exchanged a questioning glance at Spencer, so I quickly explained. "My ex hired Spencer to track me down and… befriend me. He… wasn't a nice man, and Spencer took me in. He saved me."

Spencer looked modestly embarrassed. "Well, I don't know about that. I couldn't leave you where you were, that was for certain. It was Andrew's parents who took you in." Peter was staring at him, so Spencer added, "I kinda just did what was right."

"You're one of the good ones, Spencer," Peter said. Then, with a heavy sigh, he gave me and Andrew a sad smile. "My ex is exactly that. My ex. It was confirmed tonight that he has no interest in returning to me."

"I'm sorry to hear that," Andrew said. I nodded sympathetically.

Peter simply shrugged it off. "Well, if he can move on so easily, it should be easy for me to do the same, right?"

"If only it was," I answered quietly.

Peter smiled at that. "So very true. Anyway, Spencer here very graciously offered to keep me company, for which I'm grateful."

Our conversation was interrupted by a waitress delivering our dessert. Coffee and pie was such an everyday thing, and I tried not to let on that it was special to me. I remembered Mr Landon telling me that I didn't need to wait for permission to eat, and I didn't want Spencer or Peter to think that I was weird or damaged, so as they began to eat their pie, I picked up my fork and did the same. Spencer and Andrew were playfully bickering over their shared plate, so any hesitation on my part, or any uneasiness, thankfully went unnoticed.

I wasn't sure what to say or how to contribute to the conversation. I used to be outgoing, used to be the loud one, the one whose laughter would make everyone smile. But I hadn't been that Yanni in a long time. Thankfully Andrew prompted a conversation about silent movies, of all things, and I knew that small piece of information must've come from his parents, but most surprisingly, Peter looked up at me and said, "Oh, I love silent movies!"

"Me too! I thought I was the only one! Most of the people I went to acting school with were all about Tarantino or Scorsese. And I do appreciate them, but silent movies are my favorite."

Peter sipped his coffee but was quick to nod. "I agree! The characterization, the portrayal of emotion and sentiment without saying a word is a talent lost in today's cinema."

I stared at him. "I said the same thing to Andrew's dad just the other day. We were watching *Joan of Arc*, talking about the craft of method acting and cinematography."

Peter swallowed his mouthful of pie and smiled. "Oh, I haven't seen that in years. But my favorite is Charlie Chaplin. I guess he's everyone's favorite. The most famous, most likely."

I was almost giddy, getting to talk about my passion outside of acting class or away from the Landons. I was having adult conversation, being social without judgment, and that felt pretty amazing. I couldn't wait to tell Patrice. But soon enough, our cups were empty and our plates cleared away, and I was hit with a pang of sadness when Peter announced he should be going.

"Thank you for this evening."

Spencer was quick to reply. "No worries at all."

And as they both began to slide out of the booth, Peter said it was nice to meet me and something came over me. I didn't know what it was. Bravery? Foolishness? But the words were out before I could stop them.

"If you want to catch a movie," I said, "there's a cinema in West Hollywood that plays silent films."

"Oh," Peter said, clearly surprised. He swallowed hard and spoke kindly. "I'm truly flattered, but I'm not looking for that right now. I think I need to give my old heart some breathing room."

I felt the blood drain from my face when I realized he thought I'd just asked him out on a date. "I didn't mean…" I shook my head and turned to Andrew for help. "I didn't mean… Oh God."

Andrew gently put his hand on my arm before I could

have a complete meltdown, but he looked to Peter when he spoke. "I don't think Yanni meant it like a date."

I shook my head again and swallowed down the pie that was now a roiling lump in my stomach. I could feel the cold spread of panic starting to seep from my chest. "No, I'm so not ready for that. Like really, *really* not ready for that. But my therapist said I should try and make new friends. You like silent films and I love them, and I just thought, well, I don't even know what I thought."

I didn't know whether he took pity or if he was worried I was some fragile little kid. "Yanni," he said warmly. "I'd love to see a film with you. Spencer and Andrew can come along if they'd like"—he looked to Spencer and nodded before turning back to me—"if you'd prefer. Because having *friends* sounds perfect to me right now. Well, friends, popcorn, and Charlie Chaplin."

Oh, thank God. I nodded. "Okay."

"Spencer can give you my phone number and email," Peter added.

"I can," Spencer said, giving me a bit of a grin. Peter put his jacket on and said goodbye and left.

Spencer let out a long sigh. "Man, I wanted him to be one of my success stories."

"He's a nice guy," Andrew offered.

"He is. Decent and honest. Which is rare these days."

"Except for me." Andrew sniffed indignantly. "I was honest and decent, right?"

Spencer laughed. "Honest, yes. Decently indecent. In the best of ways."

Andrew threw his scrunched up napkin at Spencer's face. "Just because you're looking all hot in your tux with your bow tie off and buttons open doesn't mean you can say those things."

I tuned their playful banter out until I heard my name. "Yanni? You okay?"

"Oh, sure. Well, not really. Do you think I should have done that? Asked Peter if he wanted to be friends? I mean, who even does that outside of kindergarten? But he seems like a nice guy? Doesn't he? I know my ability to see people for what they are isn't great, but we like the same movies, don't we? No one else I know loves silent films."

God, I felt so foolish. I felt like a kid. Peter was probably twice my age and certainly didn't want to be babysitting a kid with more issues than *Cosmopolitan*.

As always, Spencer was quick with a sympathetic response. "I think you and Peter would be good friends. I've only known Peter a week, but we've talked a lot. I've asked him a bunch of personal questions, and he was honest with me every time. I've been to his house, I've been in his car, and I felt one hundred percent comfortable with him at all times."

It was like he knew exactly what to say. "Good."

"And you didn't ask him if he wanted to be friends," he added. "You asked him if he wanted to hang out sometime. And that's what new friends do. You did good."

My anxiety reduced to a simmer, and I reminded myself that even small steps were still steps forward.

Then Andrew said, "We better get going. It's getting late."

As we made our way back to Andrew's car, Spencer asked if it was okay if he tagged along, and I realized that Spencer was entitled to be there, and *I* was the one tagging along. "If you two wanna go, I can…" I looked off down the street. I wasn't sure what I'd do exactly. I had no money, no phone. I couldn't call a cab. Hell, I couldn't even catch a bus.

Andrew sighed and looked at us both over the roof of his car. "Would you two just get in?"

I climbed into the backseat, leaving Spencer to get in the passenger seat. "He's always bossy like that," Spencer said to me as Andrew got into the car. "Don't let his geeky sweater vests fool you. He was on the cover of *Bossy Geeks* and everything."

Andrew started the car and stared at Spencer. "I hate you."

Spencer took his hand and kissed his knuckles. "No, you don't."

It was so obvious they were very much in love. They bantered and teased, but it was all so very lovely to watch. I ignored the ache in my chest, the longing. "You two can stop being so cute now."

"Well, Spencer can," Andrew deadpanned. "I, unfortunately, am cute all the time."

Spencer laughed. "It's true. He is."

They dropped me back at Andrew's parents' house and said a quick hello to Mrs Landon while I put the root beer in the fridge. After they'd gone, Mrs Landon met me in the kitchen. "How was your night?" she asked, like she wanted me to dish on all the gossip.

"It was fun. Andrew and I only intended to go to the store, but Spencer was literally just a block away. He invited us to join him. We had coffee and pie."

"Sounds lovely."

"Spencer is a great guy, and it's pretty obvious that he's in love with Andrew. You know that look?"

Mrs Landon tilted her head and smiled. "I think so."

Of course she knew. Mr Landon looked at her like that all day long.

Then I blurted out, "I asked someone if he wanted to go to the silent movie theater sometime, and he thought I was asking him on a date. It was so awkward, and I was horrified because that's not what I meant at all. I'm trying to be sociable, like Patrice suggested, and this guy is a nice guy. His name's Peter and Spencer trusts him, and he likes silent movies as much as I do." I let my head fall into my hands. "I almost died of embarrassment. Thankfully Andrew saved the situation."

Mrs Landon gently rubbed my shoulder. "What did he say?"

I looked up to find her smiling. "Who? Peter or Andrew?"

"Peter."

"He said, yes. Just friends, though," I stressed again. "Apparently he just broke up with his boyfriend. Well, his boyfriend dumped him, so we probably make for good company right now."

Her smile was wide and warm and she gave me a bit of a hug and bid me goodnight. I went to my room, showered, and changed into pajamas. I picked up my backpack and climbed into bed, then stopped.

Did I need to sleep with my backpack under the covers anymore? Certainly no one in the Landons' home was going to steal it. I let it fall gently beside the bed and snuggled down in the warmth and softness.

My mind whirled back over the evening, and I smiled at the ceiling. I was taking back control of my life. I had a friendly non-date outing to see a silent film. Not only was Peter gorgeous and smart, but we seemed to hit it off. As friends. And even though I still slept with the light on, I closed my eyes, and I was sure it was the first time in years that I fell asleep with a smile on my face and hope in my heart.

CHAPTER FIVE

WHEN PETER HAD to contact Spencer, who then had to have Andrew pass on a message to his mother to get in touch with me, Mr Landon went on a mission. "Aha!" he cried, victoriously holding up a white phone charger as he came out of his office. "I knew I had one!"

He handed me the cord that went along with the phone he'd handed me earlier. It was an old model iPhone, still newer than what most people had. "I got a free, new upgrade, and this has been in the drawer in my office since then."

I turned the phone over in my hand. "Thank you. I'm not sure what to say."

Mr Landon pretended not to notice how thankful I was. "It was literally just lying around. You may as well have it."

I was grateful, and I was very humbled by his generosity, but he was forgetting one thing. "I don't have any money to pay to use it. Like, I can't afford a bill or credit."

"It's funny you mention that." Mr Landon was trying

not to smile. "Something came up at the school today. A job, if you want it."

"What?" I shook my head. "No, I can't accept that. You've already given me too much. Done too much. Everything, you've given me everything."

He put his hand up as if calming a wild animal. "It's nothing too flashy, and it's only temporary. Probably four weeks, at the most. Christopher will want his job back; he was quite adamant about that." Mr Landon smiled fondly. "Christopher has worked at the school for eight years. He takes his janitorial supervisor role very seriously. But he twisted his knee, and his doctor insisted he take some time off work."

"Janitorial?"

"Yeah, I said it wasn't too flashy a job. Is that okay?"

I wasn't sure what to say. He must have taken my hesitation for uncertainty. "I just thought it would keep you busy, give you something to do during the day before you start classes."

"Oh no! Of course it would be okay. I just wasn't expecting it. I'd love to do it! Cleaning toilets and sweeping floors is not beneath me." The more I thought about it, the more I looked forward to it. I held up one finger and tried not to smile. "On one condition. You don't pay me. You've already given me enough—clothes, food, this phone."

Mr Landon smiled like I amused him. In a good way, though, not a patronizing way, like he found my principles admirably cute. Yes, I was grateful for everything they'd done for me, but I didn't want to be a charity case.

"Then how will you pay for your phone?"

"Oh." I felt a little deflated. "I hadn't thought of that."

"How about you get paid base wages? You can pay for your phone, and I insist that you buy me pizza at least once a week. Just don't tell Helen." He rolled his eyes. "She keeps telling me I have to eat healthier for my age."

"Deal." I laughed. "When do I start?"

Mr Landon grinned at me. "Tomorrow morning, seven o'clock."

ARRIVING at LA's School of Performing Arts—or LASPA, as it was known—with Mr Landon was something out of a dream. The school itself was small, and while most of the acting world called it *elite*, the Landons would call it *intimate*. They were so humble, and that trait in LA was disgustingly rare. And incredibly wonderful.

Mr Landon was a presence in any room. A bubble of energy, larger than life, and people smiled just because he was there. He could be living off the glory of his stage career, charging ludicrous amounts of money to give lectures, appearances, and advice to this whole town of wannabes, but instead, he gave his time to budding actors, spending hours with them honing their craft, helping them achieve their dreams.

He put his hand on the auditorium doors, looked at me, and smiled. "You excited?"

I nodded, practically bouncing on my toes. Walking into any stage theater, even an acting school—*especially* an acting school—made my heart want to burst.

Mr Landon chuckled and put his hand to his chest. "That feeling? I still get it. Each and every time."

"Really? It never goes away?"

Now he laughed. "Yanni. If it ever goes away, it's time to give it away. Walking into an auditorium or an amphitheater or a community hall with a stage will always give me a rush."

"It's breathtaking," I said quietly. "Like the moment an artist puts a brush to a blank canvas."

Mr Landon paused, and something in his eyes softened. "Oh, my boy, you get it, don't you."

It wasn't a question, but I nodded anyway. "Acting is all I want to do."

He took a breath and seemed to bask in my response for a moment. "Come on, we better get in there. Christopher doesn't stand for tardiness." He grinned, then he pushed on the doors, and we walked into the seating area of the auditorium.

"Mr Landon, you're late," a man said. He had to lean on his crutches so he could tap his watch. "Seven oh-five. You're supposed to be here at seven."

Mr Landon checked his watch as we walked down the aisle toward the man near the stage. "Oh, I'm sorry, Christopher. I didn't realize the time."

"Is this the guy who will do my job?" Christopher asked, looking me up and down.

"Yes," he answered. "Christopher, this is Yanni."

Christopher, as I just discovered, was a man with Down's Syndrome. He was kinda short, maybe in his thirties, with neatly brushed brown hair and a firm, warm handshake.

"Hello, Christopher," I said with a smile. "Mr Landon told me I'll be doing your job until your leg is better."

Christopher looked down at the crutches. "The doctor said four weeks."

"It was very nice of you to come in today to help me learn the ropes," I said. I wanted him to know I wasn't trying to steal his job. I just wanted to help.

Christopher finally smiled at me. "That's okay. You ready? We're already late, and I have a schedule to get it all done before the classes start."

I clapped my hands together. "I am very ready."

Mr Landon put a gentle hand on my arm. "You all good here?"

He wasn't asking if I was capable of the work, he was asking if I felt comfortable being left with a guy I just met. I gave him a smile. "I am all good."

"Okay, this way," Christopher said, starting to walk to the side of the stage. He was slow with the crutches, but I didn't mind. I stayed beside him at his pace and listened as he gave me detailed instructions on what my duties were.

I swept, mopped, cleaned mirrors, organized, emptied trash, and changed the paper towels and toilet paper in the bathrooms. I vacuumed, wiped doors down of hand marks, and unstuck some gum from carpet. All under the watchful eye of my supervisor, Christopher. He seemed pleased with my work.

"Class starts soon," he said, looking at his watch. I got the feeling that time and routine were important to him. "I normally take my break now." He turned and walked to the staff room, where everyone who saw him greeted him with a fond, "Hello, Christopher," to which he replied with their full name in return. Some asked how his knee was doing, some wished him a speedy recovery, and mostly people ignored me, and that was fine by me.

I would soon be a student here. I didn't need the small teaching staff to all know I was a special case, living with, and the latest charity case of, the Landons.

Christopher had a lunchbox in the staff room, where he neatly set out his food and proceeded to eat it. He asked if I liked the work, if I liked Mr Landon. He admitted Mr Landon told him I was starting classes soon, and he asked what kind of acting I liked most. But soon after, Mr Landon appeared with a woman who had come to drive Christopher home, and he promptly told Mr Landon I did a good job and would be all right to work on my own for the four weeks only, until such time he would be fit for duty.

Mr Landon took it all in stride and shook Christopher's hand, thanking him for being such a good mentor.

After they'd gone, I followed Mr Landon to his office, where he offered me a seat. "So, how was it?" he asked. "Not too horrible?"

I couldn't help but smile. "You know what? I actually enjoyed it. It feels good to be productive, and Christopher is a nice guy."

"He is," he agreed. "Loves his job."

"Yes, he does. But it was nice to chat with him. He asks a lot of questions," I said with a bit of a laugh. "But he doesn't judge. Just nods and keeps going."

Mr Landon chuckled warmly. "Perfect. Now, I know it's early, but how about we celebrate your first day with a sim card for your phone and a slice of pizza."

AFTER A QUICK STOP by the phone shop for a new sim card and ten bucks credit, courtesy of Mr Landon, he pulled up at a pizzeria I could never afford. "Uh, if we're taking a rain check on this weeks' 'wages in exchange for pizza' deal we have going, then maybe we should choose somewhere more in line with a janitor's wages."

Mr Landon grinned. "Well, you can pay next week. This one's on me. Plus, they have the best Italian wood-fired pizza on the entire West Coast, and Helen doesn't let me eat here because 'heart health is important, Allan,'" he said, mimicking her voice perfectly. It was said good-naturedly, and I knew he meant no harm. "But this is man time. We're being pizza-eating men!" When he got out of the car, he quickly added, "I'll eat bran for breakfast tomorrow and do an extra mile on the treadmill tonight."

And it was real good pizza. Worth every ridiculously overpriced penny. But I could see why he craved it. When we were done eating and I'd set up my new phone, Mr Landon took out his cell and sent off a quick text message. It beeped not a moment later with a reply, and he turned it around so the screen faced me.

"That's the guy's number about the silent movie. You had to text him, right?"

"Oh. Peter, yes." My face flamed. "Yeah, but I don't have to right now."

"No time like the present." He studied me for a moment. "Are you embarrassed?"

I sipped my soda but figured I owed the Landons nothing but the truth. "Well, yeah. I felt like a kid in kindergarten asking if he wanted to be my friend."

"I'm sure it wasn't that bad. He said yes, right?"

"Well, at first he thought I was asking him out on a date. That was horrifying. But yes, in the end, and I'm certain out of pity, he agreed."

"Pity?"

"Well, yeah. You know. Considering I'd just asked him if he wanted to be my friend."

Mr Landon chuckled. "Send the text. If he doesn't want to go, I'm sure he'll say so. Go on, just type his number in so you have it anyway."

I did that, even though it made me nervous. I had no other contacts, just Peter, a guy I'd met only once and briefly, at that. I couldn't remember his last name, so I added him as Peter-Charlie-Chaplin and turned the phone off without texting him.

Right then, Mr Landon's phone rang and Helen's name flashed on screen. His whole face lit up, then he answered, "Hello gorgeous." He laughed at whatever she replied with. "Yes, I got the number, thanks. I'm having lunch with Yanni. He's just about to text that guy about the silent movie, and we needed his cell number." He waved his hand at me and my phone. *Text him*, he mouthed, then spoke to Helen. "Where are we having lunch? Well, we're absolutely not at Alberto's Wood-Fired Pizzeria, that's where we're most definitely not." He grinned without shame and laughed at her response. While they chatted, I summoned the courage to actually text Peter. With conviction I didn't feel, but with Mr Landon's and Patrice's words in my head, I typed out a text.

Hi, this is Yanni. I met you with Spencer and Andrew the other night and mentioned maybe catching a movie at the silent film theater. Let me know if you'd still like to.

I read it and re-read it, trying not to dwell on how lame I sounded. Then, in case he needed an out, I added, *If not, that's okay.*

My thumb hovered over the Send button, but I couldn't bring myself to press it. But the waiter appeared at our table and startled the hell outta me when he spoke, and I must have bumped the screen.

I could literally feel the blood drain from my face when the phone pinged in my hand. *Message sent.*

"Yanni? Everything okay?" Mr Landon asked. He had that talking-to-a-frightened-animal tone again. He handed over his credit card without taking his eyes off me, and the waiter was gone.

I put my hand to my heart, feeling the staccato under my palm. "Oh, um, I didn't mean to send it, but he scared me and it sent. He's gonna think I'm a loser."

"No, he won't," Mr Landon said kindly. "And if he does, then he's not worth your time, okay?"

I nodded, though it was wooden at best. My lunch

rolled in my stomach. Because now I had that dreaded emotion hanging over me, wondering if Peter would reply or not, and if he did, what would he say?

Hope.

It was a dangerous thing.

When the waiter returned, Mr Landon signed the check and tried to smile for me. "You ready to go?"

I was suddenly very tired. "Yeah."

"Helen said we're having salad for dinner," he grumbled on the way out. "But it was worth it. That pizza is the best this side of Italy. I don't care if I have to eat salad all week, it was worth every calorie."

I smiled, despite my downturn in mood. "It was good."

Mr Landon put his hand on my shoulder. "You can admit it. It was the best. Though if we need to come back next week to make sure, I won't mind."

I chuckled, feeling a bit better. "You'll get me into trouble with Mrs Landon."

Now he laughed and snorted. "Never. She loves you! And believe me, she knows damn well whose idea it always is to come here."

We climbed into his car, and my nerves about texting Peter were forgotten. Maybe Mr Landon didn't realize what he'd said. Maybe he said it on purpose. I didn't know. But he said Mrs Landon loved me, and the warmth that bloomed in my chest made me smile the whole way home.

MY SMILE and my good mood lasted all afternoon. Mrs Landon came home, pretended to chastise Mr Landon, but her smile gave her away. She wasn't joking about the salad, though, and the three of us stood in the kitchen, washing and chopping vegetables, getting dinner ready, laughing and telling stories, like a… family.

It made something squeeze in my chest that felt a lot like longing and heartbreak.

I missed my family. Despite everything I'd been through in the last twelve months, or because of it, I wasn't sure, I missed my family. The way my mother would laugh when she told stories from her youth as she cooked dinner. The way my father would smile, even though he'd heard each story a hundred times before. I missed my sisters. I even missed the way they would hog the bathroom every morning. Even if they'd been staunchly religious and homophobic, there were times I missed them.

But that was before. Before they knew what I was. Before everything I knew, and everyone I loved, was taken away from me.

Standing in the Landons' kitchen, slicing avocados and telling Mrs Landon about my work with Christopher, I was torn between relishing in this safe haven with them, a feeling of warmth and acceptance, and a hollow, empty feeling that would accompany memories of my family.

Rejection, in any form, was never easy. But when it came from those who were supposed to love you unconditionally, it left a wound I doubted would ever heal.

"Yanni, you okay?" Mrs Landon's expression was soft and sad. "We lost you there for a minute."

"Yeah, I'm okay. I was just thinking…"

She put a gentle hand on my shoulder. "Did you want to talk about it?"

I shook my head. God, I could barely stand thinking about it. "No."

She seemed to understand and thankfully didn't push. She took the plate of avocado and put it on the table.

"Come on, let's have dinner and we can talk about our plans for tomorrow."

Mr Landon talked about auditions and getting classes ready, and Mrs Landon talked about the Acacia Foundation, board meetings, and funding. We talked about the planned productions for the next semester, and by the time dinner was done, I'd almost forgotten the dull ache in my heart caused by thinking of my family.

The loss of my family was like a dripping faucet. Constant background noise that never went away. Sometimes it was drowned out by other noises, but it was always there just drip, drip, dripping in the back of my mind.

I knew it was a subject choice that Patrice would want to autopsy with both hands, but I wasn't sure I was ready or brave enough to face it yet. She had years of work ahead of her just peeling back the layers of damage done to me by *him*, without even touching the surface of what my family, what my father, did to me.

A vibration and a buzzing coming from my pocket scared the life out of me. I almost jumped off the chair. The sound of my fork hitting my plate was louder than it should have been, and I knew my reaction startled Mr and Mrs Landon. I realized it was my phone in my pocket, and I put my hand to my heart and tried to laugh it off. "Oh my God. That scared me."

I'd forgotten all about the phone, and I'd certainly forgotten about my text message to Peter, but I fished the phone from my pocket and put it on the table. The name Peter-Charlie-Chaplin was on screen.

I had a text message.

"Oh, it's from Peter." Of course it would be from Peter. He was the only one who had my number.

"Well, what did he say?" Mr Landon eyed my phone, trying to read the screen. "Go on, open it."

Trying not to think about what I would do if he said no, I opened the message.

Hi Yanni.

I'm glad you messaged me. I'd love to catch a movie with you. There is a lunchtime matinee of City Lights *this Saturday, if you're interested. Let me know what you think.*

Peter.

Mr and Mrs Landon were both watching me read the message. I looked at them both and I knew my smile gave the answer away, but I said it anyway. "He said 'yes.'" I read the text aloud for them, and it was ridiculous how happy it made me.

Mr Landon did some weird hand gesture. "Quick, you need to reply!"

Mrs Landon shook her head. "No, not just yet. You don't want to sound too eager."

"Good point," Mr Landon said. He tilted his head, looking at Mrs Landon all confused. "What's an acceptable wait time? He doesn't want to sound too willing, but he also doesn't want to sound like he doesn't care."

She just laughed at him. "Yanni will do what feels right for him."

"Is Saturday okay, though?" I asked. It wasn't like I had a car or even the money to go to the cinema. God, why hadn't I thought of that before? "This is starting to feel like a bad idea."

Mr Landon frowned. "What? Why?"

Mrs Landon seemed to understand. "It's okay Yanni. One of us can drop you off and pick you up, and you will have been paid by then. You're working now, remember?"

My smile was back. "Thank you." *For this. For everything.* "I'll reply after I've cleaned up after dinner."

Which literally took all of ten minutes. That was a good wait time, and it let Mr and Mrs Landon know I wasn't about to bail on my responsibilities. When the dishwasher was loaded and I'd wiped down the sink and countertop and table, then started to wipe the sink again, Mr Landon stopped me. A gentle hand on my arm was all it took. "Yanni, reply to him. Friends don't keep friends waiting." He winked. "And don't be nervous."

"I really am nervous."

"I can tell. If you keep scrubbing the sink, you'll hurt yourself."

I laughed. It might have sounded a little crazy. "Okay. Sorry."

"So, how about we check out the cinema times so you can see if you're free." Mr Landon took out his phone and started scrolling. "He said matinee, right?"

"Uh, yeah. And why wouldn't I be free? It's not exactly like I have a social calendar."

"Yes, but he doesn't know that." Mr Landon didn't even look up from his phone. "Ah, here it is. It starts at twelve fifteen. Is that okay?"

I nodded. "Yes. It's not a date."

He looked at me then. "I know that." Then his eyes narrowed. "Does *he* know that? Do I need to meet him first and lay down some ground rules?"

I bit my lip so I wouldn't smile, but couldn't help it. "Ah, no, it's okay. He knows." I really liked that he was protective of me. "But thanks anyway."

I picked up my phone and hit Reply to his text.

Matinee sounds great. Meet you out front?

I took a deep breath and hit Send. "Done," I announced. "First step in making new friends has been made." I cringed at my own words. "I sound so lame."

"It's not your first step," Mr Landon said gently. "Your first step was letting us help you. You've agreed to see Patrice, said yes to a job. You're already miles ahead of where you think you are." He clapped his hand on my shoulder. "Give yourself some credit."

I didn't know what to say to that. And even before I could open my mouth, my phone buzzed in my hand. It was another message from Peter.

Do you need a ride? I could pick you up on my way.

Instinctively I took a mental step back. The Landons' home was my safe haven, and I liked the fact that nobody knew where I was staying. There was a comfort in that, a security blanket, almost. Anonymity was a form of defense. Even though Spencer said he trusted Peter, a part of me was always wary. Would probably always be wary after the hell I'd gone through, then doing my best to escape only to realize I still wasn't safe. But I was safe here, and the idea of letting a stranger into the Landons' safety net made my stomach sour.

I quickly thumbed back a response. *It's fine, thanks anyway. I can meet you on the steps out front. Is noon okay for you?*

His reply came back a few short moments later. *Sounds good. Will see you there.*

I let out a long breath, and Mr Landon gave me a reassuring smile. "Excellent. Right, then, I'm turning in early. Don't forget we're up with the sun tomorrow. We can't be late, or Christopher will never forgive me."

I smiled to myself as I reread Peter's message. Now I just had to get through the next five days without getting too excited. Or without texting back to cancel.

PATRICE GAVE ME HER WIDE, warm smile. "Come in, Yanni. Take a seat and tell me, is there anything you want to discuss this week?"

I sat in my allocated seat, wrung my hands together,

and took a deep breath. "I started work as a janitor at the LASPA. It's only temporary, probably just four weeks' worth, but I like it. It feels good to be productive. I made plans to see a movie with a new friend for this Saturday. I'm trying really hard not to talk myself out of it. I've been thinking about my parents a lot, and it hurts each and every time. They kicked me out when they found out I was gay. They told me I was 'a mistake in God's eyes. A stain on their faith,'" I quoted bitterly, using finger quotes in the air. "And I feel safe at the Landons' house, I really do. I know *he* can't get me there, but I still have to sleep with the light on."

Patrice blinked, then gave me half a smile that was a mix of pride and sadness. "Thank you for telling me. It really shows me that you're ready to move forward, and I promise we will get to each and every one of those things. But to begin with, how about we start with one at a time."

CHAPTER SIX

I SAT in the car trying to catch my breath. I'd almost canceled a dozen times, but like a masochistic test on myself, I was going through with it. It was Saturday, five minutes to noon, and Mrs Landon gave me a reassuring smile.

"You have our numbers. You can call at any time and we will come get you. You remember what we discussed?"

I nodded. If I felt unsafe or if I felt overwhelmed, I was to go to the coffee shop half a block down, call them, and wait for them to find me. It was a backup plan, Mrs Landon explained, so I knew I wasn't alone. I was to think of them as my wingmen, Mr Landon had joked.

It was so utterly ridiculous that such a simple thing like going to the movies was such an ordeal for me. But it wasn't *just* the movies, and it wasn't a reflection on Peter. It was putting myself in a vulnerable position when every cell in my body screamed "no" at me.

And I wasn't doing this because Patrice thought it was a good idea to broaden my social circles or because Mr and Mrs Landon agreed with her. I was doing this because I wanted to.

I needed to.

I had always been the life of the party. I needed social interaction, and I loved being surrounded by people. Well, I used to. Before *him*. And I wanted that part of me back again. I wanted to take back everything he had taken from me. And like Patrice had said, even the smallest steps forward were still steps forward.

I looked out the windshield and saw a familiar figure on the steps outside the cinema. "That's him," I breathed. "That's Peter."

He looked as handsome as I remembered, and even though the last time I saw him he was wearing a tuxedo, he still looked just as good in jeans and a light blue, button-down shirt.

Mrs Landon was surprised. I could tell even though she tried to hide it. She studied the man across the street. "He looks…"

I think she was going to say old or mature, so I prompted her otherwise. "Nice? Handsome? Friendly?"

She nodded quickly. "Yes, all of those things."

I grinned at her. "Were you expecting someone younger?"

She gave me an eye-crinkling smile, and I knew I was right. "Oh, hush. Now hurry along. You don't want to keep him waiting."

So with a deep, fortifying breath, I opened the car door. "Wish me luck."

She grinned. "Break a leg."

And with that, I got out of the car and jogged across to the cinema steps. Peter smiled when he saw me, and he looked different in the sunlight. Younger, happier. Though I was reminded, the night I had met him, he just had his heart broken. He had just found out, with Spencer's help, that his ex had really moved on. He'd had an air of sadness about him that night, the kind of melancholy that dulled the fire in his eyes. But the brightness in them now almost took me by surprise. "Yanni, nice to see you again." He looked me up and down. "You look great!"

I had no idea what to say to that. I just looked down at my outfit, which was made up of Mr Landon's hand-me-down navy pants and a shirt that was far too expensive and miles too big on me. I was pretty sure Peter knew I was wearing someone else's clothes, and I ignored my own embarrassment. "Thank you for agreeing to see the movie with me."

"Ah, my pleasure!" His blue eyes glittered with gold in the sunshine. "I love Charlie Chaplin. Though *City Lights* is not my favorite, it is one of his best."

We headed inside. "Which is your favorite?"

Peter held the door for me and put his hand on my lower back as I walked past him. "I know it's an unpopular opinion, but I liked *Modern Times*. I thought it was clever. His use of comedy to portray political references and social realism was forward thinking, especially in the 1930s."

"It's ironic that he was criticized for being outspoken in silent film."

"It's also ironic that the resistance is always led from the arts."

I smiled at him, and any worries I'd had simply flittered away. We paid for our tickets and Peter insisted on buying soda and popcorn and we took our seats. It had been so long since I'd been to this theater. And as I sat back in my seat next to Peter and we settled in to watch the film, I knew I was taking a tiny piece of my old life back. It was just a sliver, a simple moment, a poor attempt at independence and normalcy, but it was mine.

And when the movie was done, Peter and I stayed in our seats. He talked of the subtleties, the nuances in Chaplin's expressions, and his ability to portray emotions without saying a word. "It's an art form that is lost in today's cinema. Everything today is about CGI and special effects, surround sound, and it's digitalized and remastered to within an inch of its life."

"Agreed. That's what I love about theater. There is an openness, an honesty in live production. You can't just call cut; you can't do a dozen takes to achieve perfection. It has to be right the first time. The audience is right there; they see every look, every expression. There is no hiding."

"I love live theater. It's been too long since I've seen anything. I love musical theatre, too, but haven't been in years."

"We should totally go," I said without thinking. I was caught up in the excitement, the comfortableness. "I mean, we don't have to——"

"Ah, excuse me, guys." A theatre usher with the dustpan and brush waved from the doorway. "We need to clean up now."

I'd been so caught up in our conversation, I hadn't even realized they'd turned the lights on. "Oh, of course," Peter said, quickly standing up. "We should get going."

Peter led the way and held the door for me, again putting his hand on my lower back. It was strange, but I liked the way he did that. It didn't feel sleazy or like a show of ownership. Perhaps this was simply Peter's way of being a gentleman.

We made our way outside, and the sun was a little lower than I had expected. I took out my phone to check the time and realized we must've sat talking for forty-five minutes after the film ended.

"Everything okay?" Peter asked.

"Oh, sure. I just didn't realize the time."

"Do you have to be somewhere?"

"No, no. Nothing like that. I just need to text someone when I need to be picked up. They're probably worried."

"Did you want to grab a cup of coffee?" Peter looked down the busy street toward the coffee shop. "I've just really enjoyed chatting with you, and I'm not quite ready to go home just yet."

I smiled at his nervousness. I'm sure it matched my own. "I'd like that."

The coffee shop was busy, but we ordered and found a table for two. I was suddenly very nervous, and not in a good way. Seeing a movie was one thing; the conversation was limited. But going out for coffee was where the personal questions started. Questions I wasn't ready to answer just yet. Remembering Patrice's words, I took out my phone and recaptured some control of my situation. "I need to be picked up by three thirty," I told Peter. "Is that okay?"

He glanced at his watch. It was forty minutes away. "Perfect."

I'm sure he could see the relief on my face, in my smile. By setting time restraints and having Peter know someone was expecting me was a safety net for me. And instead of waiting for Peter's questions to fire at me, I aimed first.

"So, tell me about you." Then I realized, if he'd have asked me that, I would have died. So I lightened it with, "As a friend, that is, what do friends know about Peter?"

He smiled at my lame cover-up. "My name is Peter Hannikov, and I'm forty-three years old. I'm a third-generation Russian-American. My great-grandparents came here from St. Petersburg just before the Great Depression. Not exactly the land of opportunities they were seeking, but they survived. I'm a project manager in corporate finance, which is probably boring to some, yet strangely fulfilling for me." He smiled to himself. "I like my job, and I'm paid well to do it. I like 80s music, good food, good company, and silent films, as you know."

God, he was so put together. So confident, like nothing could faze him. And I was in a complete shambles. I sipped my coffee and had to consciously make myself swallow it. It felt like my throat had closed over because I knew it was now my turn.

Peter gave me a patient smile. "So what about you?"

And there it was.

"Well, my name is Yanni Tomaras. My parents are from Greece, but I was born here. I'm twenty-one years old and I love acting. I know that's so cliché, especially in this town. Every second person you meet is going to be the next big thing." I shrugged. "I don't care for fame and fortune, though I'm sure those things are nice. I just want to be on stage, even in a small production, but something I can put my heart into…"

No, I hadn't given him much personal information, but what I'd given him was deeply personal. His smile was slow-spreading and heartfelt.

I sipped my coffee again, almost spilling it because my hands were shaking. I put the cup back down carefully and sat on my hands. "I'm starting classes soon, at LASPA. I started at the Actor's Academy, but that didn't…" *Didn't what? End well? Because my parents kicked me out and stopped my tuition, then my asshole ex was paying for it because he controlled everything in my life and he took it all away from me.* "Anyway, I'm starting over and starting class next month hopefully."

Peter studied me for a moment. I knew he saw what I was.

Damaged goods.

Yet he never missed a beat. His smile was kind, as were his eyes. "Tell me, what's your favorite class?"

"Well, theory and technical elements are not my favorite. And voice, or singing, isn't exactly my favorite either, but I still enjoy them. I do enjoy the history element."

"Such as silent films."

"Exactly. But stage acting, that's what I love."

"I think I can tell."

"What do you mean?"

"Your smile just now. When you mentioned stage acting, it was written all over your face."

"Oh." I wasn't even embarrassed. "I guess I need to work on my acting skills. You know, not to give away all my secrets."

Peter laughed as he sipped his coffee. "To the contrary. Never hide your passion. It's a rare and beautiful thing."

His words embarrassed me. Not in a humiliating way, but in a humbling way. He didn't stop though. "There's a self-sufficiency and empowerment in acting that I'm envious of."

"You? Envious?"

He chuckled. "Yes. Why wouldn't I be?"

"I don't know. You're successful, you're intelligent, you're focused, you've done well for yourself, clearly. Why would you be envious of anything?"

"Because you can put yourself in front of an audience and, like you said, put your heart into a performance. That takes guts." He blew a breath out of puffed cheeks. "I get to do performance criteria meetings in front of twenty people and loathe every minute."

"Because that's you. That's Peter Hannikov. When I'm on stage, it's not Yanni up there under scrutiny. It's a character. And I don't know about empowerment. Self-sufficiency, yes, but empowerment…"

His eyes sparked with humor. "Definitely empowerment. Would you not call the likes of Laurence Olivier, Judi Dench, or Paul Scofield empowering?"

"Yes, of course." I could see now that I'd walked right into his point. "But not really what I do. Not yet, anyway."

Peter shrugged. "I don't know. I'm no expert. But I'd say anyone who studies and is driven to act, whether they walk out on Broadway or at a local community stage, is empowering. They push their voices to the back wall. With their hearts on their sleeves, they hold the audience captive with every word, every movement."

I found myself smiling at him. "Fair point."

Peter met my gaze and didn't look away. Eventually he smiled. "See? Envious."

My phone buzzed with the message. It was Mrs Landon. *Out front and ready when you are.* It was then I realized the time. "Shoot! I have to go."

Peter stood with me, and together we made our way back up the street to the front steps of the cinema. "I've really enjoyed this afternoon," Peter said. "I'm glad you asked me."

"Me too." I highly doubted he understood the significance, that this was such a huge step for me. Before, I was hesitant to meet him, and now I wished I'd told Mrs Landon a later time so we could talk some more. But her car was parked in the no-parking zone, waiting for me. "I was worried we would run out of things to talk about. But I somehow don't think that would be a problem between us."

"Me either." Peter's smile seemed brighter in the sunshine. "You know, they're running Charlie Chaplin films every Saturday for fifteen weeks," Peter said. "I think we've missed the first three, but if you aren't doing anything next Saturday…"

I stopped walking, almost to the car now, and it was then I saw a flash of vulnerability in Peter's eyes. And I realized, despite how confident I thought he was, he was putting himself out there too. "I'd really like that."

His smile was immediate. "Same time?"

"Sounds good." I turned and walked to Mrs Landon's car but stopped before I opened the door. "You know, you can text me, if you're bored or whatever."

He nodded and appeared like he was trying not to smile too widely. "Okay."

"See you next week, and thank you."

"Anytime."

I opened the car door and slid into the seat. I tried to hide my smile, but half a block later when Mrs Landon asked, "So, how was it?" my happiness and relief won out, and I laughed.

"It was really good. Better than good. The film was great, as I'm sure you know, but even better on the big screen. Then we had coffee, and I remembered what you said about setting my own boundaries, so I told him I was on a time limit. You know, in case it got awkward or if I needed to get out of there, and it was probably just as well too because I think if you hadn't texted me, we would've stayed chatting for hours."

Mrs Landon looked like she might very well burst. "What did you talk about?"

"Acting, mostly. He spoke of the complexities or the dual persona of an actor and how he found it empowering." I shook my head, knowing I sounded too excited, but I couldn't bring myself to care. "He's very smart. He's some corporate project manager who deals with numbers and figures all day long, but he's, I don't know… worldly."

"And you're seeing him again?"

"Yes, next Saturday. Same time, same place. They're screening Charlie Chaplin feature films every Saturday."

"That's so wonderful, Yanni. I'm proud of you."

Oh. Her words resounded in my chest. I didn't think I'd made anyone proud before. It took me a moment, and I had to clear my throat before I could speak. "Thank you. I couldn't have done it without you. I couldn't have done any of this without you."

"You're stronger than you know." She gave me a soft smile and leaned over and squeezed my hand. "Now, I can't decide between Korean barbecue or Italian pasta for dinner. Which do you feel like?"

"Korean barbecue. I've never had it before, and given today is a day of firsts…"

Mrs Landon did a little happy dance in her seat. "Perfect. Korean, it is."

THE DAYS that followed were peaceful. I helped Mrs Landon rearrange her bookshelves, and I helped Mr Landon in the yard. We ate good food, watched a documentary on the new generation of filmmaking, and talked and laughed a lot.

I tried every day to ignore the nagging feeling in the back of my mind that things were going too well. But I couldn't help but wonder when this dream life would come to an end.

I continued cleaning the school in the mornings, and on Wednesday afternoon I met with Patrice. I told her of my non-date with Peter, about how nervous I was beforehand, and how relieved I was it had gone well. I told her I was meeting him again this Saturday and how I hoped it would be a weekly thing. I explained how my janitorial role at the school was going well and how at ease I felt with the Landons.

I bit my lip and studied a cuticle on my thumb. "Can I ask something?"

"Of course you can." Patrice tilted her head in a patient but expectant way.

"I know it's early, and I know I have a long way to go. And things right now are wonderful. If anything, it's too good. I keep waiting for the ax to fall. Like my own brain won't let me be happy."

Patrice nodded as though she fully expected me to say that. "I think it's reasonable to be wary, Yanni. A false sense of security can be just as harmful in the long run. Walking around as though the ground might give way underneath you at any moment is frightening."

I nodded. "It does feel a bit like that."

"Staying with the Landons isn't permanent. Is that what's bothering you?"

As hard as it was to admit my fears out loud, I nodded. "Yes. They've been like a life preserver, keeping me afloat, and I'm not sure if and when I don't have them anymore that I won't keep from drowning." I frowned. "They're such nice people, and Mrs Landon told me she was proud of me. No one's said that to me before. God knows my parents never did. I've come to think of the Landons as my parents, even though I know they're not. I want to be independent, but I just don't want to lose that sense of family. Again."

"Why can't you have both?"

"Well, when I move out, I won't have any reason to see them again. And what if the new place doesn't work out? Where do I go then?"

"It's okay to be nervous about moving into a new

house, cautious even. There will be new people who've been through what you've been through. It will be a safe place. You'll make new friends, find new work, and start classes. Isn't that what you want?"

"Yes." That all sounded great, exciting even. I did want that, I really did. "But I want to stay with the Landons too."

"I don't think the Landons would ever make you do something you don't want to do," Patrice said. "Before you met with Peter, it was scary and it was unknown. You said you wanted to call and cancel because the fear of the unknown was almost too much. But you went, and it was wonderful. And moving into your own place and being independent will be just like that. Scary, yes. But wonderful. You will be safe there, and you can call the Landons at any time. You can still meet with them, have dinner and watch movies any night of the week."

"I guess."

"You won't lose them, Yanni. And if it doesn't work out, then we move on to Plan B. You'll always have options." Patrice studied her pen for a moment. "Now can I ask you something?"

I nodded warily.

"What was the last thing your father said to you before he threw you out?"

CHAPTER SEVEN

MR LANDON PICKED me up from my appointment with Patrice, and thankfully he could see I needed some time to decompress, and he gave it. He never said a word the entire drive home, but as we walked into the kitchen, he offered me a bottle of water and some advice. "Some sessions aren't easy. In fact, some are rough as hell. It feels like for each step forward you take two back. And that's all you can do, Yanni, just keep inching forward. Do you want to talk about it?"

I swallowed hard and let out a shaky breath. "I'd rather not, but thank you anyway. Patrice wanted me to talk about my father… And it drains me."

Mr Landon squeezed my shoulder gently. "Go lie down, rest for the afternoon. Read a book, watch a movie, have a nap. I'll come find you when it's time for dinner."

I gave him the best smile I could manage and went to my room. I flopped down on the bed, feeling the very literal weight of emotional dissonance on my chest. I wasn't sure why wounds had to be reopened in order to heal. I trusted Patrice, I trusted her methods, but making me name how I felt when my father disowned me hurt like tiny razor cuts all over my heart. The words she made me list still clung to my skin.

Failure. Shame. Regret. Pain.

She wrote each one down, and I knew we would be covering them in further sessions. It made me realize how far I had yet to go. If we would spend each session breaking down one word and the meaning behind it, the dam of emotions behind it, then I really did have years to go.

She seemed focused on what happened with my parents rather than what happened with *him*. We hadn't even begun to discuss what had happened with *him* yet.

I wanted to be better, and I wanted to be better now. I knew Patrice had her reasons, and she told me the path I was on would be a long one. I guess I had to break down before I could rebuild, and that did nothing to ease the ache in my chest.

I closed my eyes and dozed off to images of myself being picked apart at the seams.

THE BUZZ in my pocket woke me. I startled but was quick to realize it was still light outside, the room wasn't dark, and my heart rate slowed until I could swallow. I took out my phone and smiled

It was Peter. *You said I could text. Hope you don't mind?*

I thumbed out a reply. *Don't mind at all. It's a nice surprise.*

I really enjoyed last Saturday. They're showing The Kid. *Looking forward to it.*

I was still smiling at my phone. *Me too.* I considered adding that maybe I could stick around a little longer this time, for coffee and conversation, but thought I best check that it was okay with the Landons first. I hit Send and rolled off the bed and padded down the hall. The kitchen was empty, so I wandered to the front room only to find an upset Mrs Landon whispering something to Mr Landon.

I froze. My heart skidded to a stop, and it almost took a conscious thought to make it beat again. I tried to move backward, but my feet wouldn't budge. I was struck with fear and dread, and my insides curled like ice.

Mrs Landon looked up. "Oh, Yanni." Her frown deepened. "Please, come in and take a seat."

My mind raced with possibilities. Had Lance done something? Had he found me? Did he blame Spencer? Did he retaliate? Oh God, was someone hurt?

Resigned to hearing whatever bad news she had to say, I walked numbly to the sofa. I sat down like it was my execution chair, timid, yet reconciled with the fact my fate would always find me. *He* would always find me.

Mrs Landon tried to smile. She delicately shook her head and straightened her back. "I don't know why I'm upset. This should be good news."

I squeezed my fingertips and let out a breath. "What is it?"

"That position in the house we wanted for you has become available. The one near the school and the cafés? It's perfect for you, really…" She sniffed.

I blinked. It didn't make sense. Her reaction didn't make sense. "Pardon?"

"The house I wanted for you? Notice has been given on a room…" Her words trailed away and she tilted her head. "Yanni, are you okay?"

I almost laughed. "I thought he must have found me."

Horror washed over her face, and Mr Landon closed his eyes, his nostrils flaring. "No, no no no," Mrs Landon breathed the words. "Oh honey, no."

"You were upset…? I assumed the worst." I shrugged one shoulder, not sure what else to say.

Mrs Landon wiped her cheek and regrouped. When she spoke again, it was with poise and softness, and there was a dignified humor in her eyes. "I'm only upset because I'll miss you. You can ask Andrew and Sarah. When they both moved out, I cried for a week."

"It's true," Mr Landon added. "She did."

Mrs Landon raised her chin. "And for selfish reasons, I don't want you to go. You're a breath of fresh air, Yanni, and I have loved having you here."

"Oh." Relief and happiness soared in my chest, leaving a trail of tears in my eyes. "And I am so very grateful. I always knew I couldn't stay here forever. As much as I wanted to. I even talked about it with Patrice just this week. I knew it would come to an end."

"Nothing has to end," Mr Landon said. "It just changes. We'll still be a part of your life. You still have to buy me pizza once a week." He shot his wife a look. "Heart-healthy pizza, of course."

I smiled despite the ache in my chest. "When? I mean, how long do I have?"

Mrs Landon frowned. "Three weeks."

Relief surged through me, dousing the panic in my belly. "Oh, that's okay then," I said with a bit of a laugh. "I thought you were going to say tomorrow."

Mrs Landon's face was a picture. "Oh, my Lord, no! We'd never do that. The girl that was in the room gave twenty-one days' notice, as per her lease. I brought home a copy of the standard lease for you to have a look at, to make sure you're happy with it before you sign. I'm sorry if I scared you earlier." She frowned again, her eyes misting over. "I don't want you to think we're kicking you out because we're not. And I know that you need this, you need to do this on your own, but I'm going to miss having you here."

Mr Landon studied me for a moment. "Are you comfortable with the three weeks?"

Was I? Was three weeks enough time? Granted, it was better than a day or no notice at all. But I'd been with them now for four weeks, and I'd come so far. How far could I go in another three weeks? I still had issues, and who knew, maybe I always would. But the truth was, I did want to stand on my own two feet. As much as I'd love to stay with the Landons, what I wanted most in the world was to take back everything *he'd* taken from me.

Slowly I started to nod. "I think I am."

Mrs Landon started to cry and laugh at the same time, and she leaped off the sofa to come and give me a hug while I was still sitting down, which was kind of awkward and amazing at the same time. "I'm so proud of you."

Mr Landon looked on fondly. "We both are. You're a good kid, Yanni. And you deserve the good things that will come your way."

I was on the verge of tears, happy tears, my face burned with emotions, and my throat was tight. "Thank you, both, for everything. I owe you so much."

Mrs Landon fixed my hair, the way a mother does her child. "The only thing we want from you is for you to be happy."

A tear slipped down my cheek, and I laughed as I wiped it away. "Do Andrew and Sarah know how lucky they are to have parents like you?"

Mr Landon snorted and grinned right at me. "Probably. But we tell them all the time just in case they forget."

I laughed at that. "Oh, that reminds me," Mrs Landon said. "Sarah will be here for dinner on Friday night. She's bringing Amani and Saanvi. Just so you know"—she looked right at me—"it will be a loud night. Those girls are so much fun."

"Duly noted, thank you."

"It'll be good practice for you." Mr Landon winked. "Having a loud and busy house. I remember college housing—"

"Yes, well," Mrs Landon cut him off. "I'm sure Yanni doesn't need to hear stories from your college days."

I chuckled. "Uh, that reminds me as well. I was texting with Peter earlier. I didn't want to mention it to him before I run it past you, but maybe I could stay a little later after the film?"

Mrs Landon smiled warmly. "Of course you can."

"It wouldn't be too much later," I explained quickly. "It would be before it got dark."

Mr Landon stood, crossed his arms, and pursed his lips. "I'm thinking I should meet this Peter guy. Make sure he's good enough."

Mrs Landon laughed. "You might find you have things in common with him."

Mr Landon was confused. "What do you mean?"

She winked at me. "Like those college stories you were talking about before. Maybe you went to college at the same time."

I put my hands over my ears. "God no, don't say that!"

Mrs Landon laughed and leaned against her husband, patting his chest. "Peter is more our age than Yanni's."

"Oh," he said, nodding. Then his eyes went wide. "Ohhhh."

"It's not like that!" I cried, falling back into the sofa with my hands over my face. "We're not like that."

"There's nothing wrong with liking older men, sweet-ie," Mrs Landon said, giving her husband a nudge.

"I'm twelve months older than you," he griped. "And you remind me about it every year."

"Some things bear repeating," she smiled winningly. "And yes, there's something to be said about an older man. More charismatic, more confident."

Mr Landon grinned wickedly. "More experience."

I shot up off my seat. "Oh my God, this is so embarrassing. If you're done mortifying me, I'll just go to my room."

They both laughed and high-fived each other. Mr Landon was proud. "It's our parental right to embarrass the kids with sexual innuendoes."

Mrs Landon added, "What he means to say is, our job isn't complete until we've mortified all our children to the point where they want to run screaming."

I couldn't even be mad or embarrassed. She'd said *our children* like I was included in that. I walked over to her and kissed her cheek, then did the same to Mr Landon. "You're both ridiculously amazing. Crazy, but amazing." I headed to the hall. "I'll be in my room. I will let Peter know our *non-date*—thank you very much—can go a little later than last week. Then I'll come back out and help with dinner."

When I gave them a parting glance, they were both sitting back on the sofa, holding hands and smiling. Like proud parents. And after such a shitty day with horrible memories of my real parents, I now had a smile and a ridiculously full heart.

———

FRIDAY NIGHT with Sarah's friends around for dinner was a lot of fun. Amani and Saanvi brought a dish of food each, and I made souvlaki, and we feasted on Iranian, Indian, and Greek food. Yes, they were loud and they laughed a lot, but they included me. They asked me questions, genuinely interested in me as a person. They asked me about my job cleaning at the school, and they asked me about my pending non-date with Peter. They asked me about the classes I wanted to take, and they asked me about the house I would be moving into in a few weeks.

"I'm going to have a look at the house on Sunday," I explained. "I haven't seen it yet, but your mom swears I will love it."

Sarah gave me a beaming smile. "Then I'm sure it will be perfect."

"And hopefully I'll get to meet my new roommates," I said. And made a nervous face. "Fingers crossed no one's too scary."

Mrs Landon, who just happened to be walking past, put one arm around my shoulder and gave me a squeeze. "They'll love you." Then she straightened and put a finger in the air like she'd just remembered something. "Oh, that reminds me. Sarah, don't forget we have our annual soirée coming up. I do expect you and Andrew to both be here. You too, Yanni."

The look of panic on Sarah's face made me nervous. "What's an annual soirée?"

Sarah rolled her eyes. "Every year Mom and Dad invite a hundred of their actor friends to the house to talk about how fabulous they all are."

Mrs Landon pursed her lips and gave Sarah a mock glare before she turned to me to explain. "We have a party once a year to get together with old friends. We're all so busy, it's hard to catch up." She turned back to Sarah. "People look forward to it, and the invitations have already gone out, and I've told people you and Andrew will be here."

Sarah groaned. "He'll have Spencer this year. Who will

I talk to?" She shot me a hopeful glare. "Yanni, you can be my life preserver… I mean date."

"Oh, Sarah, it's not that bad." Mr Landon shoved a mouthful of papadum, curry, and mint yogurt into his mouth. He hummed, "Mm-mm. Saanvi, this is so good."

"Thanks," she said brightly. "Family recipe."

The thought of facing a hundred people, who would all ask me questions like "Where do you fit in here?" and "How do you know the Landons?" made my stomach churn. And if they were friends of the Landons, then there was a very good chance they would be famous stage or screen actors. My nerves shriveled up at the thought. I could meet three people at a time, like Sarah and her friends, but not a hundred. "I uh, I don't think crowds are a good idea right now."

Mrs Landon gave my shoulder a squeeze, and I pretended not to see the pointed look she gave Sarah. "That's fine, dear. I understand."

The conversation moved on, and the girls were soon laughing again at something they'd seen on social media. But there was a tug at my conscience, that Mrs Landon wanted her family here for her annual soirée, and yet I couldn't do it.

I was reminded that no matter how far I thought I'd come, it wasn't as far as I'd hoped, and instead of being leaps and bounds, it was still one small step at a time.

———

I MET Peter on the steps of the cinema, as we had the week before. He grinned when he saw me, and I tried to play down how happy seeing him made me. He looked more gorgeous today. His dark gray trousers matched the gray hair at his temples; his blue shirt matched his eyes. He was the epitome of understated confidence, like he needed no one else's approval for anything.

"Hi," I said as I approached him.

"Hello." He slid his hand to my elbow and greeted me with a soft kiss on the cheek. "Shall we go in?"

By the time we got our tickets and had taken our seats, my heart rate still hadn't returned to normal. A kiss on the cheek wasn't foreign to me—I came from a Greek family! —but something about Peter doing it made my heart flutter and my skin flush. It wasn't unwelcome; it was unexpected, and I liked it.

"You okay?" Peter eyed me as other patrons took their seats.

"Yeah." I tried to keep my grin to a moderate smile but failed. "I'm good."

Peter settled back in his seat and smirked. "How was your week?"

"Good. Busy. How was yours?"

Peter's eyes sparkled with humor and light. "Good. Busy."

I laughed and ignored the butterflies in my belly. Thankfully the movie started and was a welcome distraction. Until it wasn't.

Chaplin was outstanding; the direction, cinematography was all on point. But maybe watching a film about an orphan losing the only family he'd ever known wasn't the best idea.

When the lights came back on as the credits started to roll, Peter looked at me, and his smile died. "Yanni?"

"I'm okay," I said too quickly. I took a deep breath and stared at the screen. I didn't want to see the pity on Peter's face.

He reached over and took my hand. Warm, strong, and

gentle. He waited for everyone else to leave before he spoke. "It's okay not to be okay."

I looked at him then, and I must've looked like a scared rabbit, but he never faltered. There was no pity in his eyes, just concern. "The movie was just a little too close to home, that's all." I tried to smile. "And some days I'm fine, but then other days I'm… not okay."

He squeezed my hand and threaded our fingers together like he had no intention of going anywhere. "Being not okay is perfectly fine. It makes you human. We all have good and bad things happen to us, but how we deal with what we've been given is what matters. And I think you're doing pretty good. Now, I don't know much about anything that's happened to you. All Spencer told me the night I first met you in that diner was that you'd had a rough time, and he kind of told me to tread carefully. But here you are, despite the bad, trying to find the good in life, and that tells me you're a pretty remarkable guy."

I let out a shaky breath. "A rough time is one way to describe it. But thank you for understanding and for not running a mile just now."

He gave a smile but seemed to sense I wasn't done talking. "I *am* trying to find the good in life. And I'm trying to take back what *he* took from me. But it's not easy."

"He?"

I blinked a few times and forced the answer out. "My ex."

Peter squeezed my hand, rubbing his thumb across my knuckles. I got the feeling that the armrest between us annoyed him, and if he could have, he would've pulled me onto his lap. Or maybe I just wished he would.

He looked back at the screen and his brow furrowed for just a moment, and I knew he couldn't quite get the puzzle pieces to fit. So I filled him in. "The fact that I was disowned by my parents or orphaned like the kid in the movie was just the beginning."

Peter's knee bounced, and he frowned. "And it wasn't the worst, was it?"

I shook my head and whispered, "No."

He took a moment, then squared his shoulders. "Yet, despite all that, here you are trying to find the good."

I let out a bit of a laugh so I wouldn't cry. "I'm trying."

Just then, an usher walked in, surprised to see us, and kindly asked us to leave. This time when we walked through the doorway, Peter put his hand on my lower back and kept it there like he wanted to protect me. "Still up for coffee?"

I nodded. "Yeah."

He let his arm fall, and I missed his touch immediately. But we walked to the coffee shop, ordered, and found a table at the back. I wondered how this would go, considering I'd killed any chance of a light conversation. I didn't want it to be awkward. I didn't want to spill my entire life story either. Maybe I'd already said too much, or maybe he deserved a better explanation. Maybe this was all too complicated, too soon.

But Peter never seemed to miss a beat. "So, tell me about all the good things in your life right now."

I didn't know how he knew what to say, but having me focus on the positives without disregarding the negatives, or brushing them aside completely, was the perfect thing to do.

"I'm getting my own place. Well, it's a shared house. I'm moving in a few weeks, but I'm going over tomorrow to check it out and maybe meet my new roommates. Mrs Landon lined it up for me because it's close to the school and some coffee shops where I might be able to score some work. I thought I might hand in my résumé to a few next week, you know, to try and get in early. I'm going to need an income while I study."

And so, for the next three hours we talked, we drank coffee, we ordered cake, and we talked some more. I learned his two best friends were old college buddies and had been important people in his life ever since. Mike and Rob were both the same age as Peter, which I already knew to be forty-three. The three of them were successful in their corporate careers, both Mike and Rob were married to lovely women and both had kids, but Peter had remained single.

"You'd just broken up with your last boyfriend when we met at the diner," I said.

"Ah, yes. His name was Duncan. He was a student when we met; his career was just starting out. We wanted different things. I wanted quiet nights at home, dinner parties, movie nights. He wanted to sleep with random people at nightclubs." Peter smiled ruefully. "I can joke about it now."

I smirked and spun my empty cup slowly. "Now, I'm not one to judge people I've never met, and truthfully I'm the last one to talk about stupid decisions, but Duncan sounds like a fool."

Peter chuckled quietly. "The funny thing is, I don't blame him. I was his age once. I get it, I really do. But I could have done without the deception."

"I don't blame you. Honesty is not a difficult concept."

"No, it's not. My friends keep telling me I should date someone closer to my own age. And who knows? Maybe they're right."

"Maybe. Maybe not. You just need someone on the same page as you, not the same age as you. Then their age wouldn't matter, would it?" I was feeling so much more relaxed and comfortable with him now. I almost felt like my old self.

The blue of Peter's eyes seemed to intensify. "No, it wouldn't matter." He sipped his coffee to seemingly distract himself.

"Because I like older men, and I'm pretty sure my therapist thinks I have daddy issues."

Peter choked on his coffee and coughed with his hand to his mouth, making me burst out laughing.

"We're a perfect match. It's a shame neither of us is ready for anything more."

Peter composed himself, coughed a bit, and straightened his shirt. "Yes. It's a shame."

CHAPTER EIGHT

WHEN WE LEFT the coffee shop, Peter put his hand on my lower back as we walked through the doorway and kept it there for a few beats before we headed back toward where Mrs Landon would be waiting for me.

"I really enjoyed today," I told him. "I'm sorry if I freaked out a little bit earlier. Thank you for not freaking out on me."

"I've had a great time too." Peter's brow furrowed, as though he was trying to figure out how to tell me he thought it was best if we didn't meet again. Not that I could blame him. My life was a circus, and even as a friends-only arrangement, it was a lot to take on. And just when I thought he was about to let me down as gently as he could, he didn't. "I mentioned last week that it had been too long since I'd seen a stage production, and that got me thinking, which got me googling. Have you ever been to the Bootleg Theatre?"

I shook my head. It was an old 1930s warehouse that had been made into a theater. "No, but I've heard it's beautiful."

"The local amateur production of *West Side Story* is running for the next few weeks, but only on Tuesday and Wednesday nights. I'd like to catch it, if you want to come with me. It will be my treat."

"Really?" I was sure I was grinning like a madman. "I'd love that! Though I can pay for my own ticket."

Peter's smile was pure relief. "I know you can. But I'd like to pay for this. The show starts at seven o'clock, but we can text and work out the details. Is that okay with you?"

Was I okay with going out at night, alone with Peter? If the question was *did I trust him*, then the answer was *yes*. "That's very okay with me."

Then he stopped walking, faced me, and took my hand. "Yanni, I know we've both said that we're not ready to date yet."

Oh God. I was not ready for this. And I was also not ready to lose him as a friend. If he asked me now, I would have to let him down. It felt like our new friendship was screaming down a dead-end street.

"I just want to reiterate," he continued, "that that's not what this is. I'm not ready to date again yet, and I don't think you are either, from what you've told me. But I really enjoy spending time with you. I like how easy our conversations are. So if you're happy to continue having non-dates with me, I'd really like that."

I almost sagged with relief, and I was sure he could tell. "Non-dates are perfect. And I really enjoy spending time with you too." He was still holding my hand, so I gave his fingers a squeeze. "Thank you. I'm glad we're on the same page."

He smiled beautifully. "Me too."

My phone buzzed in my pocket, and I let go of his hand so I could check the message.

I'm at the corner.

"It's Mrs Landon," I said out loud for Peter's benefit. "She's parked up at the corner, so I better get going. Thank you for a great afternoon."

"My pleasure. Have fun checking out your new house tomorrow. You'll have to text me and let me know how it goes."

Oh, I'd forgotten about that. "I will. We'll talk soon though, okay?"

He had a peaceful look about him, his lips upturned in a slight smile, his eyes bright and happy. He gave me a nod, and I turned and raced to Mrs Landon's car. When I climbed in, she gave me a knowing look. "You've had a good day."

"I have!" Then I proceeded to give her a rundown of the movie, my mini meltdown, our conversation that followed, and how good Peter was about the whole thing. I told her about his non-date speech, how despite our age differences, we were both kind of at the same place. We valued our friendship, as new as it was, because we just clicked.

"He asked me to go to the theater with him. It's during the week," I explained. "So if it's okay with you, we're going to work out the details later."

"That's wonderful," she said. "He sounds very nice."

"He is. He's just a normal guy who happens to like old movies and theater, just like me."

"Are you comfortable going out at nighttime with him?"

I snorted. "I asked myself that very question. And I am comfortable with him. He's confident, but not in an arrogant, horrible way. More like, he knows himself well enough not to apologize for anything. My ex was the arrogant kind." A cold shiver ran through me. "The horrible kind. But Peter isn't like that. And I know I don't know him that well, but I feel safe around him. I never felt like that with… *him*."

"I'm really glad to hear that." Mrs Landon gave me an eye-crinkling smile. "Are you looking forward to seeing your new house tomorrow?"

"Yes!" And I was excited. It felt so unreal to be finally getting my own place, given that not so long ago, I was officially homeless and standing in line for a cot in a shelter. It was kind of hard to get my head around. "You know, I was telling Patrice that I was frustrated with how long this road to recovery would take. Because some days it feels like I'm not moving forward fast enough. I want to be better, and I want to be able to put this behind me right now. But then I remember that only last month I was on the streets. And before that I was still… I was still living with… *him*. And I realize things are moving faster than what they might seem."

Mrs Landon looked so proud that she just might burst. Her eyes grew misty, but she shook it off. "No making me cry while I'm driving."

But when we got out of the car, she gave me a squeezy kind of hug. "There's no right or wrong on the road to recovery. You go as fast or as slow as you need, and we'll be with you every step of the way."

Then it was my turn to cry.

THE HOUSE I was going to be moving into was a two story, semi-detached. It had white walls and a terracotta roof, and from the outside, it looked like a happy place. Built in the 40s, it was probably once a huge single house but had since been converted into two separate places. There were four bedrooms upstairs with one shared bathroom. Downstairs was the kitchen and a living room. I could tell by the décor it had been remodeled in the 80s, but it was bright and had a good feeling about it.

I had a quick peek inside the room that would be mine, but considering the girl I was replacing was still living there, I didn't want to intrude. Her name was Merry; she was short, had a bun on either side of her head, and wore a huge smile. She gave Mrs Landon a sweeping hug, which Mrs Landon seemed used to getting from her, then she pulled me into the room by the hand. "Don't be silly! Of course you can see it. This will be your room soon. The bed is super comfy. I wish I could take it with me. The closet is small, but not the worst I've come out of." She winked at me. "The hot water is best early mornings or late at night. There's a Vietnamese store, like two blocks down; they have the best produce. And the bakery half a block up makes the best cinnamon rolls, if you do carbs. Laundromat half a block west. And there are about ten coffee shops in a three-block radius, so take your pick." She used her hands as she spoke wildly about the area, and I wished she was staying.

"Have you met everyone else yet?" She didn't wait for me to answer. "They're all great. Skylar is awesome, and she makes the best spaghetti Provençale. We're all supposed to cook for ourselves, you know, learn to be independent, how to shop on a budget, et cetera." She waved her hand. "But if you sling her a few bucks, she'll make you some, and it's cheaper than takeout, right?"

I found myself smiling at her. "Right."

"Jordan's kinda quiet, and she keeps to herself. She's okay, just strictly not a people person, and that's okay. No loud noises or yelling around her and you're golden."

"I don't like loud noises or yelling either," I offered

lamely, wondering if this Jordan had been through something similar to me. I hoped like hell she hadn't.

Merry tilted her head and gave me a smiley-frown. "You poor thing. You'll be good here. This place will fix you. It's like the best thing ever."

I felt a wave of emotion come over me, and I let out a nervous laugh so I wouldn't cry.

"Then there's George." Merry gave me a wink. "He's totally goth, and he looks kinda grumpy, but he's a big ol' softie. You'll love him."

Wow. This was a lot to take in.

"So, um, so where are you going?" I regretted my personal question as soon as I'd asked it.

"I'm moving into a place with some college friends. My time here is done. I'm ready to move on and let someone else move in."

"How long were you here for?"

She gave me another one of those frowny-smiles. I wasn't really asking how long she'd lived here. I was asking how long it took her to get better. "Twelve months. Some are here longer, some just a few months. Everyone's different. Don't rush it."

I needed to change the subject before my heart clawed its way out of my throat. "Nice room, though. Thanks for showing me."

She linked our arms and led me out and showed me the bathroom quickly, then bypassing a smiling Mrs Landon, she dragged me down the stairs and into the kitchen, where three other people stood, who had very clearly been talking about me because their conversation stopped cold. "Oh good, we're all here," Merry announced. "This is Yanni. He'll be taking my room." She made introductions. "Jordan, George, and Skylar."

They each looked about twenty years old. Skylar smiled and gave a bit of a wave. Jordan crossed her arms and tried to make herself smaller, but she gave me a nod. And George, dressed in all black with black hair masking half his face and black lipstick, murmured the only word. "Cool."

Merry turned to me triumphantly. "Right, then. I have to go or I'll be late for my shift. See you guys later tonight." And with that, she was gone.

I looked at my three soon-to-be roommates. "Thanks for letting me have a look around," I said, not sure where I found the courage to speak.

Mrs Landon walked in, thankfully taking the attention off me, and quickly got herself hugs from each of them. They were all so happy to see her. Skylar was the most vocal. "It's so good to see you again," she said. George's goth demeanor cracked a little when he smiled as he took his turn, and Jordan hugged Mrs Landon fiercely, and Mrs Landon held on to her the longest.

It was pretty hard to ignore that the four of us were all so very different, yet not that different at all. Something had happened to each of us that had brought us here.

We were only there for a few minutes after that, and by the time we got back into the car, I was feeling very positive. I was nervous, but in a good way.

"Like it?" Mrs Landon asked, though I was pretty sure she already knew my answer.

I nodded. "They seem pretty cool."

"How did you feel about the house? It has a good energy, right?"

"Yes! I knew it would be good before I even walked in. It looks happy even from the street. Though I kind of wish Merry was staying. I really liked her."

"She's great, isn't she?" Mrs Landon pulled the car out onto the street. "But the others are great too."

"They're all pretty different," I admitted.

"Individual," she corrected me gently. "Different would imply outside the norm."

"Sorry. Individual."

She gave me a warm smile. "You're gonna do great there. I just know it."

LATER THAT AFTERNOON, I was lying on my bed looking at random stuff on the internet, waiting for my washing to be done, when my phone rang in my hand. Startled, I almost dropped it. It hadn't ever rung before—only ever beeped with an incoming message.

Peter-Charlie-Chaplin's name flashed on screen, and I smiled before I answered. "Hello?"

"Hello to you too." His voice was deep and smooth. "Is it okay if I call? I wasn't sure if you preferred messaging, but I was just wondering how your house inspection went this morning?"

My blood warmed, knowing he'd remembered but also that he'd thought of me. "It was great. It's just a shared house, but I met the other three I'll be living with, and they all seem pretty cool."

"That's really good, Yanni. I'm glad it went well."

I smiled at the ceiling. "Yeah, me too. I was worried it wouldn't be the right place for me. But I think it'll be good."

"Excellent! So what did you do this afternoon?"

"Laundry."

He laughed. "Glamorous."

I snorted. "Oh so glamorous. Though to be honest, it'll be more glamorous than the laundromat I'll be using in a few weeks."

"Ah, I remember those days."

"Like the olden days?"

He gasped. "I'm not that old."

I laughed. "I'm just kidding. What did you do this afternoon?"

"Fixed a wheel on the wagon, sent a telegram, listened to the gramaphone. You know, olden-day stuff."

I laughed again, letting my free hand fall from my hair to the bed. I couldn't remember feeling this relaxed. "So tell me, when's *West Side Story* showing again?"

"It shows on Tuesdays and Wednesdays. The theater hosts other things on weekends, like bands and other live shows, apparently. So is during the week okay?"

"Yeah, it's fine. Is Tuesday okay with you?"

"Sure."

I didn't want to have to explain that I had therapy on Wednesdays and it usually left me drained.

"This week or next?"

"This week," I answered, probably a little too quickly. I knew I sounded eager, and while part of me cringed inside, the other part of me wanted him to know I was looking forward to it.

"Perfect. I can come pick you up if you'd like. It's no big deal."

My stomach clenched. The truth was, yes, I trusted Peter. And while I thought of the Landons' house as my security fort, I would be moving out in under three weeks and I needed to get used to being a little more exposed. "Can I let you know about that?" Then, because I sounded like a school kid needing his parents' permission, I added, "It's just, I don't know what the Landons are doing on Tuesday night, and given I'm staying with them, I need to respect their house rules, that's all."

"It's fine, Yanni. You don't need to explain anything."

I sighed, then I remembered something. "Oh, what are you doing on Sunday in two weeks from now?"

"Um, I'm not sure. I'll have to check. Why?"

"Well, the Landons are hosting some fancy lunch thing, and I'd really like to not be here. I can't do crowds that size, especially of famous people."

Peter snorted. "I'll check my calendar and get back to you. If I'm free, I'm yours. We can grab some lunch and go to a museum or something. I haven't done that in a while."

I wanted to hug my phone. "Sounds perfect."

"Excellent! Okay then, well, I'll let you get back to your laundry. And let me know if you need a ride on Tuesday night."

"I will. Thanks."

"Anytime." There was a pause, then, "Bye, Yanni."

"Bye, Peter."

When he ended the call, I put my phone to my chest and smiled. It was ridiculous that so much of my happiness rested on Peter's shoulders, and I made a mental note to ask Patrice about that, but for now, I let myself bask in this moment. For the first time in a long time, I was happy and felt I was really getting my shit together.

I rolled off the bed and went and finished my laundry.

I'D DECIDED that having Peter pick me up on Tuesday evening was a good idea. A test of sorts. It played on my nerves a little, or maybe it was anticipation.

Getting ready, I'd done and redone my hair twenty times, though my curls refused to be tamed. I had a love-hate relationship with my hair. I thought the floppy curls made me look younger, which I hated. But I couldn't bear to wear it short.

Once, after my ex had grabbed handfuls of my hair and yanked me to the floor, I took clippers to it and gave myself a buzz cut. Needless to say, it hadn't gone over well, and I'd never been sorrier...

Every time I looked in the mirror for the two weeks after that, I looked at my shorn hair and would forever associate it with the black eye and cut lip that came with it.

So I've worn it longer, like a halo of dark black curls, ever since.

Tonight, because we were going to the theater, even if it was for an amateur show with student-priced tickets, Mr Landon insisted I wear a vest over my shirt. I was sure it was part of his three-piece Armani suit, though I refused to look at the label. It was gray, and with simple black pants and a teal shirt that Mrs Landon swore matched my eyes perfectly, I felt pretty good.

When Peter arrived, he spoke through the intercom at the gate. Mr Landon gave him a code, then much to my horror, he met him at the front door. "Please, come in," Mr Landon said.

If Peter was shocked, he certainly didn't show it. "Thank you. You have a very beautiful home."

Mr Landon extended his hand. "Please, call me Allan."

"Peter." They shook hands, and Peter shot me an amused look.

"I'm sorry," I mouthed silently, and it only made him smile wider.

Mr Landon then proceeded to give Peter a rundown of rules and expectations, ending with, "Now, I know this isn't a date, per se, but you're taking our Yanni out at night, and I need you to know that we take his safety very seriously."

I couldn't even be mortified. He'd said *our Yanni*...

"Of course," Peter said earnestly. "And I appreciate your concern for him." He took his wallet out and found a business card. "This has all my contact details. If you need."

Mr Landon seemed pleased with this, and they discussed our plans for the evening and approximately what time we'd be returning while I took a minute to get my thoughts together. Mr Landon had called me *our Yanni*, as in, I belonged to them. With them. My heart ballooned in my chest, and I'd lost track of their conversation, suddenly realizing they'd stopped talking and were both watching me.

"Oh, pardon?"

"Nothing," Mr Landon said with a smile. "You have a good night. I want to hear all about the performance, okay?"

I nodded and said my goodbyes, but before I got out the door, I turned and gave Mr Landon a crushing hug. "Thank you."

"Call me if you need anything, okay?"

He let go of me, and I gave him a nod before I turned back to Peter. "We ready?"

I was pretty sure Peter knew he'd just witnessed a bit of a moment between Mr Landon and me. He gave me a warm smile. "If you are?"

I nodded quickly and opened the door. "It was a plea-sure to meet you," Peter said to Mr Landon.

"Same," he replied. "Have a fun evening, gentlemen."

We walked to Peter's car. Now, I knew very little about cars, but I knew his was sleek, black, and sexy. He opened my door for me, which was surprising and very sweet, though his smile was telling. When he got into the car, he had to bite his lip so he wouldn't grin.

"I'm so sorry," I said quickly. "I had no idea he was going to give you the third degree."

Peter slid the gearstick into first, the car purred, and we slowly made our way down the drive. The security gate opened automatically, and we made our way down the darkening street. "It's really no problem, Yanni. It's just been a long time since I've had to meet the parents before a non-date."

I cringed. "Well, they're not my parents," I offered lamely.

Peter reached over and took my hand. "I know, and I didn't mean anything by it, sorry. And Allan might not be your actual father, but I'm pretty sure he thinks of you as one of his kids."

"He called me 'our Yanni.'"

Peter's smile was huge and warm. "I know."

My heart did that balloon thing again, and I didn't even try to hide how happy it made me. "He's really nice. They both are. I'm very lucky."

Peter squeezed my hand. "And you look very handsome tonight."

"Oh." Flattery was something I didn't wear well. Like I expected an insult to follow swiftly after it. Of course, there was no insult, only another gentle squeeze of my hand. It was then I remembered my manners. "You too! I mean, you look great." And he did. He wore a blue blazer over a plain white shirt and dark pants; his graying hair was short, a little spiky, and styled perfectly. Though I was sure he managed the stylish, modern fortyish man look without even trying. "Do you even try for sophisticated and polished, or does it come natural?"

Peter laughed as he drove. "I'm… perceptive… when it comes to fashion, and I spend hours in the gym a week."

"Perceptive?"

"This is LA. I just look around to see what the latest trends are. The social pages of the papers, that kind of thing."

"The papers? As in newspapers? Are they still a thing?"

He shot me a playful glare. "I'm not that old."

Now I squeezed his hand. "No, you're absolutely not. I'm just kidding."

He glanced at his dash. "So, did you want to eat first? We have some time, and I'm sure there are a few restaurants close to the theater."

"Uh, sure. Sounds good."

By some kind of miracle, we found a parking spot close by, and walking into the restaurant, Peter held the door for me and put his hand on my lower back. He was a gentleman, thoughtful and kind, and I liked the way he maneuvered himself to be protective of me. I felt… treasured.

I tried not to read too much into it, and I tried not to let dangerous things like hope and anticipation take root. We ordered tapas and lime sodas. "Did you want a glass of wine?" I asked. "You'd be more than fine to drive after the show."

Peter inhaled through his nose, like he was steeling himself. "I don't drink. My uh, my father was a drinker."

"Oh."

He tried to smile. "Sorry. It's not something I make a habit of sharing, but you've been honest with me when I'm sure it hasn't been easy for you."

"Honesty is important to me, so thank you for telling me. But there's a difference between simply divulging all you're comfortable with and lying."

One corner of his lip curled up. "True."

"So it's probably fairer to say that while I appreciate honesty, my true issue is with deceit."

Peter studied me for a moment, as he toyed with his

glass with his long thick fingers. "You're wiser than your age suggests."

I raised one eyebrow. "Is that a dig at my intelligence or my age?"

He laughed, just as the waiter arrived with our tapas. He placed the platter in the middle of the table and a small plate in front of each of us, and I instinctively slid my hands under my thighs. Peter served himself, then stopped. "Aren't you hungry?"

Oh, God. "Oh, yes, sorry. Habit." I set about serving myself some stuffed olives and shaved pancetta while ignoring Peter's gaze. I knew I'd said the wrong thing so I changed tack. I took a mouthful of bread, olive oil, and balsamic vinegar. "This is good."

Peter chose the pancetta instead and hummed thoughtfully. "It's very delicate."

I pretended not to acknowledge that he was referring to me.

He frowned. "You can veto me at any time, but may I ask you a question?"

I sipped my soda and took my time to answer. He was giving me an out if I chose it, but he'd also been honest with me. "You want to know why I said the word habit."

Peter wiped his mouth with his napkin and never broke eye contact. It wasn't a look that bored into me. It was a gentle gaze that encouraged and reassured. Well, this was one way to ruin the mood of our non-date.

"I wasn't allowed to eat unless I was told to. For a long time."

He stared, unfaltering, like he was trying to be strong for me, and his only tell was the flare of his nostrils. "Your parents did that to you?"

I shook my head. "No. All my parents did was disown

me and kick me out. It was my ex who played the mind games."

Peter looked like he'd swallowed something particularly unpleasant, and his eyes flinched. "I'm sorry."

"Deciding if I was allowed to eat was probably one of the nicest things he did." I swallowed hard. "Sorry for bringing it up, but in light of my speech on honesty earlier…"

"Please, don't apologize. I was the one who asked."

I gave him the best smile I could manage. "Mr and Mrs Landon have been working with me on the food thing. Trying to help me not wait for permission, and I'd been doing well. I guess I forgot tonight, given I'm a little out of my comfort zone."

Peter started to stand. "Do you want to leave?"

I grabbed his hand. "No. I want to finish this tapas, then go to the theater. I want to take back what that bastard took from me and start living my life again."

Peter's eyes flashed with emotion, and for a brief, frightening moment, I thought he might shed a tear. But he laughed. "Oh, Yanni, you are something special."

THE SHOW WAS WONDERFUL. Raw, unpolished, and completely authentic. When we left, it felt utterly natural for me to slip my arm through Peter's as we walked back to his car. Growing up, I used to be such a touchy-feely person, always throwing my arms around someone, holding their hands, sitting on their laps. But I hadn't been that way in a long time, and I did it now with Peter, almost without thinking, like it was something we did all the time. He didn't seem to mind; in fact, from his smile, I thought he liked it.

"What did you think of it?" Peter asked.

"The performance? Yeah, it was great! It just makes me more determined to do it, you know? Getting my shit together, get through college, then who knows, one day that might be me up there on stage."

"You'll get there, I know you will." He seemed so adamant. "How much longer do you have in college?"

"I got through two years, so I have one year left. Hopefully I'll finish at LASPA."

"You're enrolled to start already?"

"Yep. Classes start in three weeks. Mr Landon's been really busy getting schedules and subjects organized. Mrs Landon helps him too, of course. In between the school and her job at the Acacia Foundation, she's been helping me put together a list of things I'll need when I move out."

"So you'll be moving out, then a few days later starting school? You will be busy."

"I know, right? I'm actually looking forward to it. It's a bit scary, but it feels right." Then I thought of something. Disappointment sunk in my belly like a stone. "Oh. I have to find other work, probably at a coffee shop or restaurant, and that usually means Saturday shifts. But I still want to see the Charlie Chaplin matinees with you, so I'm not sure how that will work out."

Peter smiled serenely. "I'm sure we'll figure something out. If we can't do the weekend matinee, then I might have to buy the entire DVD collection and a lot of popcorn."

I grinned, my excitement showing on my face. "I'd really like that."

We arrived at Peter's car, and he opened my door, waiting for me to climb in before closing it behind me. A moment later he slid in behind the wheel, and we chatted as he drove me home. When he passed through the security gate, I was suddenly nervous. I wasn't sure what non-date protocol was. He kissed me on the cheek once before, and tonight I'd linked my arm with his. Was a thank you kiss proper etiquette? What were the rules for non-dates? For friends even? Did I want to kiss him?

Yes, a voice answered from somewhere in my subconscious.

Jesus, do I want to kiss him?

Of course I do.

Okay, this ship was sailing into dangerous waters.

"Yanni, you okay?" Peter's voice startled me. He brought the car to a stop at the front of the house.

"Oh, yes." I chuckled, embarrassed, nervous. I couldn't see Mr or Mrs Landon in the doorway or looking out any of the windows and was relieved I didn't have an audience. "I had a really lovely time, thank you."

"Me too. We should do this again."

I nodded. "We should." Then, before my nerves got the better of me, I leaned over and quickly kissed his cheek. "Thank you," I said, before scrambling out of the car. I waved him off, trying not to smile too much, just as Mrs Landon met me at the front door. She waved Peter off as well, then pulled me into a hug.

"How was it?"

I tried not to flail, but my answering grin told her all she needed to know.

"The show was great! A small, honest production. I really love the small theaters; they're more intimate, like you're almost on stage with them."

Mrs Landon beamed. "And how was Peter?"

"A true gentleman. I had a small hiccup at the restaurant—I waited for him to give me permission…" I grimaced. "He was honest with me about something else before, so I was honest with him about why I sometimes don't eat until I'm told, and he was really good about it.

He asked if I wanted to leave if I wasn't comfortable, and I told him I wanted to stay and take my life back!" I finished with a flourish, and Mrs Landon clapped and cheered.

"So we watched the show and it was great. He said we should do it again."

Mrs Landon sighed dreamily. "He sounds wonderful."

"He is." Then I noticed the house was quiet. "Is Mr Landon in bed already? I didn't know you'd be waiting up for me."

She patted my hand. "It's fine, sweetie. I'm off to bed now myself."

"Yeah, I should probably go too. Early start tomorrow."

We said goodnight, and after getting ready for bed, I lay there staring at the ceiling with a stupid smile on my face. Sure, I still slept with the light on, but I didn't remember ever being this happy.

CHAPTER NINE

MY SESSION with Patrice started well when she recognized the week before had been hard for me, but talking about my parents was crucial in understanding, accepting, and moving on.

Or so she said.

I told her about my week: my job, my two non-dates with Peter, and shared the joke of me telling Peter she might think I have daddy issues given my taste in older men. I told her about seeing my new house and meeting the people I'd be living with. We talked about that for a little while, but then she reminded me of the words I'd used to describe how being disowned made me feel—failure, shame, regret, pain. Then she asked me to recount for her the time my parents kicked me out of their house and their lives.

"I can't do this right now," I said weakly. "I've had such a good week. I feel positive about where I am right now. And it's the first time in a long time I've been able to say that. So can we please not do this right now?"

Patrice stared at me for a long moment before relenting. "Okay, Yanni. Fair enough. But here's what I want you to do… I want you to write it down for me. Think of it as practice before school starts again. But I want you to write it as a screenplay."

"A what?"

She obviously saw where my mind went because she raised one hand. "No one will ever see it but me, I promise you. It won't go outside this office."

"A screenplay?"

"Yes. I want you to cast actors who you could see as family members. Give me character descriptions on temper, attitude, how they dress. Exactly like a director would give their cast and crew."

"Can I ask why?"

"Because you can detach yourself from it but still give a detailed account. It doesn't have to be perfect, Yanni. There's no pass or fail. This is simply for me to learn about you within a process that you can identify with, in a time-frame you're comfortable with. You've read screenplays before, yes?"

"Yes, of course."

"So, describe what music would play when your father's on screen. Describe the way he speaks. Describe how your character reacts."

I nodded. That sounded reasonable.

Patrice gave me a pained smile. "It allows you to detach yourself from the moment. Look through the lens as though you're watching it happen, not having it happen to you all over again. Okay? Are you comfortable doing it this way?"

I tried to answer yes or no but couldn't. "I'm not sure. I don't like to think about it. I'm not repressing memories or trying to pretend it didn't happen. I'm trying to move on, and reliving it over and over again seems counterproductive to me. I trust your methods, but I'm not sure what you need to know other than it was horrible and I was made to feel like garbage, good for nothing but the trash pile. Unloved, unwanted. Is dredging all that up again really going to help me or just pour salt on wounds that are trying to heal? Because truly, it's what happened *after* my parents kicked me out that is the reason I'm here today."

She seemed to consider this for a moment. "Okay, Yanni, I'll tell you what. Do the screenplay or don't do it. I'll leave it up to you. But I want you to consider something for me. Why don't you ever use Lance's name? Why don't you ever call your parents Mom and Dad?"

"For the same reason, they no longer call me a son. Because they're not my mom and dad," I shot back angrily. "They're my biological parents; they birthed me. Oh, they raised and loved me, but only until the second they knew I was gay. Then suddenly there were terms and conditions: change who you are, or leave and don't ever come back. 'Mom and Dad' is a term for parents who love unconditionally, so my *parents* don't deserve those titles."

"And Lance?"

"He deserves nothing." I spat the words. "I won't ever call him by name. He's a piece of shit who doesn't deserve that from me." I was so angry, I could almost feel my blood boiling in my veins. I clenched and unclenched my jaw and tried to calm my thumping heart. I glared at Patrice. "If you tell me that anger is a valid emotion, I'll scream."

She fought a smile but had the decency to look sorry. "Okay, so without mentioning the validity of certain emotions, I think we've covered a few unexpected things today."

I was still angry. I could barely speak. "Right."

"Yanni, you *should* be angry. You should be livid that

these people you trusted hurt you and betrayed you in unspeakable ways."

"I *am* angry."

"Good."

"And I'm frustrated."

"Why?"

"Because I can't change what they did. I have no control over what's in my past. I can only control my future, and I want to be fixed *now*. I don't want to waste any more time on them. They've taken enough from me. I waited for Peter to give me permission to eat, for fuck's sake. And I still sleep with the light on! In a secure house like the Landons'. What the hell am I going to be like in the new house?" I shook my head, and my anger and frustration became tears. "I want to be free of everything they did to me. I want to be happy. I deserve to be happy."

"Yes, you do. And you're taking the right steps."

I let my head fall back and I groaned. "Somedays I think I'm doing okay, then things like this remind me that I'm far from okay."

"Yanni, you're doing more than okay. Last week, you mentioned some key words that I'd like to reflect on. Like fear. Let's explore that…"

And so we did. For the remainder of my session, we discussed the fear I'd felt when my parents kicked me out. By the time the appointment was over, I was exhausted. I felt like I'd swum the Pacific Ocean with weights on my arms and legs.

When I walked out, Mr Landon took one look at me and put his arm around me. "Come on, let's go have some ice cream."

THE SESSION THE FOLLOWING WEEK, Patrice dissected words like failure and regret, leaving me emotionally drained and exposed. Peter was a constant light in my dark. Our non-date on Saturday was lovely. He kissed my cheek hello, and I linked our arms as we walked to the coffee shop afterward where we talked for hours. But even during the week, just a quick text from him to let me know he was thinking of me, or to ask how my day was, or to double check we were still on for our usual Saturday matinee as well as taking me out while the Landons had their annual fancy lunch on Sunday, were highlights of my days. I felt safer knowing he was just a quick message or a call away. And I'd send him a text when I got into bed so I'd fall asleep thinking happy thoughts.

Mrs Landon made time in her busy schedule to help me buy things for when I moved into the new house, and I helped her organize things for her annual luncheon. We did floral arrangements, menu planning, and dealt with cleaners, catering companies, and everything in between.

I kept up with my morning cleaning job at the school, and I even had some time to jot a few things down on Patrice's screenplay. Maybe being busy was a welcome distraction, but thinking about my parents as characters instead of actual people did kind of help. I could compartmentalize and separate myself from it, enough to give the exercise some perspective.

But I was excited for the weekend. I was spending both Saturday and Sunday with Peter. We were doing our usual Charlie Chaplin matinee on Saturday, and Peter wanted to go to the Hammer Museum on Sunday to see an exhibit on Russian art it was currently hosting. I couldn't wait.

I met Peter out in front of the cinema on Saturday. Again, he greeted me with a kiss on the cheek and a strong but gentle hand on my back. "You look great, as always," I said.

"You too. That shirt looks incredible on you."

Oh. It was the teal colored shirt that Mrs Landon had insisted I wear to the theater. It matched my eyes almost exactly, but I still wasn't too comfortable with compliments. "Uh, thanks."

His gaze ran down to where the shirt collar met my neck, and I pretended not to notice the heat in his eyes. "It looks great against your olive skin."

Okay, one compliment I could brush aside but not two. I tried not to cringe, and Peter gave me a saddened smile. "You don't like compliments, do you?"

"Not a fan, no. They make me uncomfortable, like I'm waiting to be the punch line to someone's joke."

Now he frowned. "I wouldn't ever say anything to be mean to you. And if I comment on how beautiful your eyes and skin are, it's because it's the truth."

"Beautiful?" I barked out a laugh. "Again with the compliments."

This time Peter linked his arm with mine, and we walked very casually toward the cinema doors. "I don't mean to make you uncomfortable, but it is the truth. One day, Yanni, you will see yourself clearly." He opened the door for me. "Do you want popcorn?"

Glad for the change of subject, I nodded. "You know I'm starting to fill out all the clothes that Mr Landon gave me. If I keep eating like I have been, I'll have none that fit me."

Peter laughed. "There's nothing of you!"

"Well, I wouldn't exactly call me skinny."

"Slender is the word I'd use. You're perfect just the way you are."

I cleared my throat. "Perfect is a pretty big word."

"Like I said, it's not a compliment if it's the truth."

"What can I get you gentlemen?" the cashier asked.

Peter bought our tickets and a large popcorn for us to share. I offered him a twenty, but he waved me off. "You can buy coffee after."

"Okay." I don't know what I liked more, the fact that he treated me as an equal, that we would both contribute, or that coffee and hours of conversation had become a weekly thing. Our thing.

It was a double feature this week. *The Immigrant* followed by *The Adventurer*. Both were only half an hour long, so it wasn't long before we found ourselves at the coffee shop.

I ordered and paid and we found a table at the back. We settled into easy conversation about the two films we just watched, which then became conversations about Peter's week at work, my up and coming classes, and how I now had a few boxes of things to call my own in my new house.

And I could talk about how simple kitchen utensils and my own coffee cups made me feel good about myself, and Peter never once looked down on me. Here he was, a well-established professional man, who had his own house and a fancy car, but he was excited for me to get new bath towels and bed sheets.

"Mrs Landon helped me choose them, but I paid for them," I explained. "The money I get paid isn't much, but it's mine. I'm saving as much as I can for school, but I'll need to find work closer to the house."

"Have you got a résumé?" Peter asked. "I can help you draft something if you need."

"Mrs Landon has already taken care of that, but thank you."

"We could do the rounds of all the local cafés and drop

them off tomorrow before we go to the museum, if you want."

"Really?"

"Sure!"

"That would be really helpful, thank you." I smiled at him. "Want another coffee? My treat."

Which was subtext for *want to stay and chat some more?* I didn't want our time together to end just yet.

Peter smiled in a way that made my insides tumble. "Sure."

I went to the counter and, like an independent adult took for granted, ordered two more coffees. I paid with the little cash I had, again taken aback at the importance of something other people didn't think twice about.

The cashier was an older lady with a gray bun and a kind smile. "Can I just say how lovely it is to see a father and son spend some quality time together? I've seen you the last few weekends, talking and laughing like it should be. None of this staring into a phone screen."

Father and son? Oh my God. She thought we were father and son.

"Uh, thanks," I mumbled and went back to our table.

"What's so funny?" Peter asked.

"She thinks we're father and son." A smile started to spread across my face, which became a chuckle.

"It's not that funny," he said, though his smile soon became a grin. "How to bruise a man's ego!"

I put my hand over my mouth so I wouldn't laugh. "I'm sorry, what did you say earlier? It's not a compliment if it's the truth."

"It wasn't a compliment!"

"Yes, it was."

"Maybe for you…"

"She said it was sweet to see a boy spend time with his

daddy. And believe me, you'd make a smokin' hot daddy. It was definitely a compliment."

Peter chewed on the inside of his lip, whether to stop his smile or to contemplate what I just said, I wasn't sure. "A smoking hot daddy, huh?"

Just then, the barista called my name, but Peter shot out of his seat. "I'll grab them," he said before I could argue. Not that I would have. This interaction was the most fun I'd had in so long. It felt good—normal—to be playful, so when he sat back down and put my coffee in front of me, I pushed the sugar bowl toward Peter. "Sugar, Daddy?"

I was expecting him to laugh, but the look he gave me was sexy and sultry. It made my insides curl in a delicious way that I wasn't expecting. "Oh, you like that," I said in a rush, not really meaning to say it out loud. I felt my face flame with embarrassment while butterflies stormed my stomach.

Peter took a deep breath, let it out slowly, and broke eye contact with me to look around the coffee shop. He looked flushed, and dare I say it, sexy? I'd never thought of him in that way before. Sure, he was strikingly handsome and confident, intelligent and kind. We'd joked about our dates that weren't dates, and we'd established from the very beginning that neither of us was ready for anything other than friendship. But as skewed as my experience was with relationships, I knew attraction when I saw it.

And the look in Peter's eyes was attraction. Was he attracted to me? Or was he attracted to the idea of being someone's daddy?

He very obviously had the daddy vibe, but I certainly wasn't ready to be the young guy he needed... But the thought of him being with someone else clawed at my insides. And it was selfish of me to hold him back from what he wanted or needed because I needed him to be my friend.

God, this was getting far too complicated.

I sipped my coffee, trying to get my scattered thoughts and thumping heart under control.

"Yanni?"

I looked up, startled. "Yeah?"

"You okay?"

And there it was. Did I owe him honesty? Or did I need to pretend I was clueless?

He cleared his throat. He was still a little flushed, but there was a determined spark in his eyes. "Can I tell you something?"

Oh God. "Yes, of course."

"I want to be completely honest with you. I've told you I like younger men. That's no surprise. A moment ago you said I liked being a sugar daddy, and I won't lie to you. I do. For me it's rewarding to provide and care for a younger man. I like knowing their every need is met, and that I'm all they need. I won't justify that."

"You don't have to. Not to me. I get it." I really did. I liked and was attracted to older men. I couldn't help what I liked any more than he could. And I certainly wouldn't judge him for it.

One corner of his lips pulled up. "I know you do. Thank you. And you have been a breath of fresh air for me. You're gorgeous." He waved his hand in my general area. "But you're so much more than that. You're gifted, driven, stronger than I can even imagine. And somehow, you and I have more in common than anyone else I've met—I'm sure we could talk for days and never get bored.

"But Yanni, I'm not ready for that kind of relationship, and I'm sure you're not either."

The relief I felt was like a whoosh of air. "I'm not

ready, so thank you for saying that." Then, because he'd been so brazenly honest with me, I felt I owed him the same. "Can I be honest with you?"

"Please."

"I want to be. Ready, that is. But above all that, I don't want to lose our friendship. I know I might rely on you more than I should. I haven't really had the chance to meet many people, so my branching out with new friends kind of came down to you. I know I'll make more friends when I move and when I start school, but I don't want to lose what we have. That's probably selfish of me and something I should probably talk to Patrice about."

"Why?"

"Because I feel entitled, or hopeful at least, and that's new for me."

Peter gave me a patient smile. "I don't want to lose our friendship either. And you will be ready again, one day. When it's right for you, Yanni. And it's not selfish. It's human."

I let out a deep breath. "I'm really glad we talked this out. I feel better knowing we're on the same page."

Peter's grin was warm and wide. "Me too."

PETER PICKED me up at ten o'clock on Sunday morning. I was armed with a dozen photocopies of my résumé, courtesy of Mrs Landon, and Peter and I set off to hand deliver them to coffee shops and restaurants close to where I'd be living.

It was a beautiful day. The sun was warm, people were out having coffee, walking dogs, just enjoying a typical LA summer's day. Peter found a parking spot on a side street, and together we walked up and down, doing the rounds.

There were even a few shops with help wanted signs in the front window. I introduced myself, handing over my résumé, and after an hour, I had no copies left and a very positive feeling.

We grabbed lunch from a taco truck, and all in all had one of the best mornings I could remember having for a very long time.

I felt normal. I felt like the old me, the Yanni I used to be before *him*.

We made our way to the museum, and once inside, I linked my arm through Peter's and we studied, appreciated, discussed, and debated the exhibits. He was so worldly, experienced and educated when it came to things like art and culture, history, and anthropology.

He explained some exhibition pieces to me and wanted my interpretation. He listened as I explained my thoughts, and he gently clarified when I needed him to. Not in a demeaning way, but in a helpful way. He was teaching me things I didn't know, in a way that didn't even feel like a lesson. By the time we left the museum, I knew more about the history of Russian art than I ever thought I'd need to know.

I also knew more about Peter.

And I had to admit, as much as it frightened me, the better I knew him, the more I liked him.

And because it was such a beautiful day, when we were done, instead of going straight back home, I suggested another walk in the afternoon sun. We barely made it a few yards when I heard my name.

"Yanni? Is that you?"

I recognized the voice and turned around. "Christopher!"

He approached us, now walking with a cane and a smile. "What are you doing here?"

"We've been to the museum." Then I introduced him. "This is my friend Peter. This is Christopher. He very kindly let me do his job for four weeks, until his leg is better."

Christopher held up the cane. "No crutches anymore."

"You'll be back at work in no time."

Christopher grinned, then nodded back toward the museum entrance where some people were waiting for him. "I better get going. I'll see you at work tomorrow. I'm allowed to do light duties. The doctor said I could."

"Excellent. I'll see you then."

We watched him leave, then I could feel Peter's eyes on me. "He's a nice guy," I explained.

"He's not the only one." Peter seemed happy, proud even.

"Thank you for today. Especially through the exhibitions, for opening my eyes and helping me learn."

"I could thank you for the same thing. You teach me things too."

I scoffed. "Hardly. Like what?"

"Like how to be a better person."

Oh. There he was again with the compliments. He looked at me like those words were as hard for him to say as they were for me to hear. But then, instead of apologizing, he chuckled and threw his arm around my shoulders, pulling me into his side as we walked to the closest café.

We ordered coffee and a slice of pie to share, and Peter talked and talked of his family's Russian traditions that his mother still did, handed down from generations before. How Easter was very important to her, and how he still made time every year to help with hand-dyed eggs and traditional Easter breads.

He was obviously close with his mom but rarely

mentioned his father. I didn't push, for the same reason he trod carefully around me on the same subject.

"What Greek traditions did you do as a boy?" he asked.

"We would paint eggs also," I said, smiling at the fond memories. "My mom and yaya would make *koulouria*, which is an Easter cake, and *tsourekia*, which is a traditional Easter bread. We would have roast lamb, and there was always lots of family, lots of food."

Peter seemed pleased with this. "What was your favorite food?"

"The *kourabiedes*, of course! Sweet cookies. I loved them."

"We should make them!"

I almost laughed. "Why?"

"Because you just said you loved them. And just because your circumstances have changed, doesn't mean you should stop celebrating your traditions. It's who you are. The only thing that's different now is the people who choose to celebrate with you."

I found myself smiling at him. I liked the idea, but Easter was months away, and I was still doing one day at a time. "Maybe."

I realized then that the server had only given us one fork for our shared pie. We hadn't touched it because we'd been so busy talking, so I went to the counter to grab one when the front door to the coffee shop opened. A man was yelling, screaming obscenities. He was dirty and disheveled, probably homeless, and frightening. He shoved an empty table so it skidded across the floor.

Everything happened so fast, but in slow motion at the same time.

Staff was trying to get rid of him, and someone had called the cops, but I was stuck. Frozen in fear. I couldn't move, my feet were bolted to the floor, my heart was stricken, squeezed beyond beating, and the fork started to shake in my hands.

Then Peter was in front of me. His face, his smell, his warmth.

"Yanni, look at me." His voice, distant and detached, sounded so far away, but like it was whispered in my ear at the same time. "Yanni, look at me."

I met his eyes then. The purest blue. Soft, worried, and cautious. He stared into me, like he filled the empty spaces of my soul. I was lost in that moment, those memories, and I was lost in the sea of hurt and fear. But then I felt his hands on mine, anchoring me to his safe harbor. He'd put himself between me and the angry, screaming man.

"Can you hear me?" Peter put his hands to my face. Warm, reassuring, and gentle. "Yanni?"

I nodded so he'd know I could hear him. I just couldn't speak.

"I've got you," he whispered. "Breathe for me."

I sucked back a breath, not realizing I'd stopped breathing. My head spun, and there was noise, the scraping of chairs on the floor, and people yelling. There was chaos all around me, but all I could see was Peter.

"I've got you," he said again. Above all the noise, all I could hear was him.

Then the man was gone, thrown out or removed, I didn't know. All that was left was a resounding silence that felt too enclosed, too constricting.

Peter pulled me against him, into the safety of his arms. I went willingly, sagging with longing and relief. "You're safe with me," he whispered against the side of my head.

And I was. I'd never felt that protected. I couldn't explain it. I knew then, in that moment, I would be safe with him always. He would never hurt me, never yell, threaten, or punch me. He would never humiliate me. He would never demean me, beat me.

And with that came the tears.

He never told me to shush; he never told me to stop crying. He simply stood there in the middle of the coffee shop with my head on his chest, his arms wound tight around me, and he let me cry. He waved some poor concerned staff member off, telling them I was fine now, just that I didn't do too well with yelling. He simply stood, like a mountain of strength with all the patience in the world, and held me until I could speak.

"Please take me home."

I felt him nod against my head and only then did he let me go. He took the fork from my hand, threw a twenty onto the table, and led me out to his car.

I felt terrible. Now that the adrenaline was wearing off, sickness and shame settled in. "I'm so sorry" was all I could say.

He took my hand over the console. "Yanni, it was unexpected, and your reaction was completely warranted. Don't be sorry."

He kept saying the right things, and part of me wanted him to tell me I was a head case, or a mental fucking loon, because I'd agree with that more. I just wanted to get home, back to the safety net of the Landons' house, though I wanted Peter to stay with me. When we drove up to the gate, I remembered that the Landons were having a huge party. God, the very last thing I wanted was to face a hundred strangers, but when Peter punched in his security code, I could see no cars were there. In fact, *no* cars were there. When I'd left, it had been buzzing. Now it looked deserted.

I frowned. "I don't think anyone's home."

Peter glanced out the windshield, then back to me. "Are they supposed to be?"

"Yes. Mr Landon said Andrew and Spencer and Sarah would be here this afternoon."

"I'll come in with you. Maybe they caught a cab."

But the house was empty. In fact, there were still things spread over the kitchen counter and furniture pushed aside in the living room, like something horrible happened and they left in a hurry.

"Something's wrong," I said, and from Peter's worried face, I knew he agreed with me. Dread clawed at my stomach, and I took out my phone, scrolling for Mrs Landon's number. She answered on the second ring. "Yanni?"

"Is everything okay?" I asked. "No one's here and it looks like you left in a hurry."

"Spencer's been taken to the hospital."

I leaned against the kitchen counter. "Oh my God, is he all right?"

Peter was quickly in front of me, his hand reassuringly on my arm.

"Yes, well, he is now." She spoke to someone off the phone, then came back to me. "We're just leaving the hospital. We'll be home soon and I'll explain everything."

"Okay."

"Yanni, are you okay?"

"Um, I think so."

She paused, and I knew she was trying to decipher my words. "Are you alone?"

"No, Peter's with me."

"Do you feel safe?"

I knew she was asking me closed questions, to which I would only have to reply yes or no, so if I were in danger, the unwanted person listening wouldn't know what we were talking about. *Did I feel safe with Peter?* I took in Peter's face, the kindness in his eyes, the warmth of his touch. "Yes."

"Okay then, we'll be home soon."

I clicked off the call and slid my phone onto the counter. "Spencer's in the hospital. I don't know any more than that," I said. "Mr and Mrs Landon are on their way home."

Peter slid the hand that was on my arm to my shoulder, then rested it against my neck. "You look exhausted," he said softly.

"I feel it." The emotional day now weighed on me like a wet blanket. I sagged a little and leaned against his touch. He responded kindly by stepping closer and letting me fall against him. I sighed as he put his arms around me. His touch—even just his presence—had healing properties. I could feel the tension slacken in my shoulders. My anxiety slowly ebbed away.

I don't know how long we stood there like that. Ages, yet not long enough. Mr and Mrs Landon came home, and it was only then I peeled myself out of his arms. I missed his warmth immediately. Mrs Landon came into the kitchen and took one look at me. "Yanni, what happened?"

"I had a meltdown in public."

Peter spoke beside me. "There was an incident at the coffee shop near the museum. A drug-affected man walked in screaming and hurling tables. Yanni was scared. He wasn't the only one."

Mr and Mrs Landon looked horrified, and Mrs Landon's hands went to my face. "Oh my word. Were you hurt?"

I shook my head. "Peter saved me. He protected me and talked me through it. If he hadn't been there…"

Mr Landon clapped Peter on the back in a sign of

thanks. "Can I get you a drink? I think we all could use a drink."

"Uh, no, thank you," Peter respectfully declined. "I don't drink."

"How about I make us all hot chocolate," Mrs Landon offered instead. "And I can tell you the story of how Spencer almost died on our living room floor."

———

THE FOLLOWING WEDNESDAY, I walked into Patrice's office and sat down. Before she could ask me how my week was, I spoke first. "I need to apologize."

She stared at me but waited for me to continue.

"I was frustrated with my progress because I thought I was getting better. I thought I was further ahead than what I am. But I'm not. I'm nowhere near it. I thought I was ready to move out into the world. I thought I was ready to run, but the truth is, I can't even walk."

She gave me a sad smile. "Oh, Yanni, you've already been walking all this time. It's okay to stumble at the first hurdle. Wanna know why? You pick yourself up, regroup, dust yourself off, because you, believe it or not, Yanni, are now ready to run."

ACT TWO

LEARNING TO RUN

CHAPTER TEN

I SAT on my new bed, in my new room, in my new house, trying to take it all in.

Mr and Mrs Landon were both here with me. We brought everything I owned from their place to here in one car trip. Actually, it fit in one box and two bags. Mrs Landon had helped me make the bed. Mr Landon put my kitchen utensils in my drawer, my food in my cupboard and on my shelf in the fridge.

Skylar, Jordan, and George were all here but were giving me some time to settle in.

I was excited about this new chapter in my life, but after the incident last week in the coffee shop, I was also a little nervous. It had knocked my confidence down a peg or two, though Patrice reassured me I could use it as a positive experience, to trust my instincts and to learn about my reactions so I could process the steps if and when it were to happen again.

"We can't take responsibility for other people's actions," she'd said. "We can only be responsible for how we react. How we learn, how we process situations and experience moving forward is completely up to us."

I told her I didn't think I was ready to move out. She told me I was stronger than I gave myself credit for.

So there I sat, trying to get my bearings in my new life.

Mr Landon put a heavy-looking box on my desk. "A little housewarming gift from me," he said.

"A gift?" I shook my head. "But you've already given me enough. Too much, actually." I waved my hand at the clothes, the new bedding, the whole room in general. It was all because of them.

He waved his hand like it was nothing. "Ah, don't mention it. Just a few things you'll need for school on Monday."

I opened the box to find a pile of books, papers, pens, and what looked like a few second-hand textbooks. "Oh, wow." I got choked up. "Thank you. I don't know what to say."

He gave me a fatherly smile. "Say you'll go to every class and do your best."

"I will. I promise."

Then it was Mrs Landon's turn. She handed me a smaller, rectangular box. It looked like it might've been a box a business shirt came in. "You might want to open that later," she said with a wink.

Mr Landon took his cue. "I'll just be downstairs," he said, quickly darting out of the room.

Mrs Landon giggled at her husband and nodded toward the box. "It's nothing too risqué or embarrassing, don't worry. But I thought you might like to have it."

I sat on the bed and gently pulled the lid off the box. In there, folded beautifully, was the purple silk gown I'd appreciated when we were going through their bag of clothes for Goodwill. "Oh, Mrs Landon…"

"You don't have to keep it," she said quietly. "It's just that your eyes kept going back to it when we were finding you clothes. I knew you liked it, but you thought it wasn't…"

"Appropriate to wear in your house," I finished for her.

She laughed. "Yes. Well, now you're in your own house, in your own room with a lockable door. You can wear whatever you please."

My heart was thumping erratically. "I've always wanted to own something like this. Something extravagant and… feminine."

"Well, now you can." She lifted the fabric out of the box and handed it to me. It felt like cool water as it draped over my hand. "It's yours."

"Thank you. For this. For everything. For everything you've done. I don't even want to know where I'd be if it weren't for you and Mr Landon."

Mrs Landon looked at me fondly. "You're more than welcome, Yanni. You've been an absolute joy to have around." She blinked back tears and took my hand. "Come on then, let's go find Allan."

Saying goodbye to them was hard, and it seemed like I wasn't the only one who thought so. Mrs Landon was teary again. "You've got our numbers?"

"Yes."

"And you promise you'll call if you need anything?"

"Yes."

"And you'll still have dinner with us once a week?"

"You can come home with me after class on Wednesdays or something," Mr Landon added.

"Sure." I couldn't help but smile. "I'd really like that."

"And you've got Andrew and Sarah's numbers. You can call them for anything too. I've told them."

I chuckled, pretending not to be embarrassed. "Yes, thank you."

"Okay, I think we've covered everything," Mr Landon said with a wink. He tried pulling Mrs Landon toward the door. "Don't forget. Class starts at nine."

"I'll be there."

Mrs Landon broke free from Mr Landon's hand and she quickly hugged me again. "You'll be fine."

"And so will you," I said with a laugh.

She was crying now, and Mr Landon came and put his arm around her. "She cries when all the kids leave home."

And that got me right in the heart. I gave them both another hug, as tight as I dared, and stood at the door as they walked to their car. I turned to face my three new roommates, who were all watching me. I wanted to hide upstairs in my room but figured I needed to be brave, or at least pretend to be.

"Come in and sit down with us," Skylar said, patting the sofa. "*Jeopardy*'s about to start."

So, I sat in the living room with them as they tried to outdo each other with answers. I only answered one or two questions toward the end when I felt more comfortable, but it was a lot of fun. Skylar was the loudest, George was the funniest with his random answers, but Jordan was by far the smartest. She was the quietest too and sat on the single sofa like she was trying to make herself smaller, but she was there being sociable and I was pretty sure she was putting in such an effort on my behalf. Given it was my first day, her effort for me was very touching. I caught her looking at me a few times, and I gave her a smile that hopefully told her I understood.

As afternoon became evening, we moved into the kitchen and each cooked our own dinners. I made a simple pasta with tomatoes, olives, and basil, which Jordan was jealous over. She was having grilled cheese and tomato soup, which looked just fine to me, but I took this opportunity to return the goodwill and I promised to make my pasta dish for her one day. She rewarded me with a smile and a nod, and I knew we'd be okay.

After the kitchen was clean and we'd all done our bit, I was looking forward to spending some time in my room. I needed to let it all sink in, to decompress. I closed the door behind me and leaned against it, taking a moment to just breathe.

I was smiling. I felt good. Positive. I had a real good feeling about being here. I know it was only early and scary as hell, but I started to think that I actually had a future.

I noticed the box on the bed and the purple fabric that spilled over the side. I went to it, running my fingertips over the cool silk just as my phone buzzed in my pocket. I startled like I'd been caught with the gown. Realizing I was still very much alone, I pulled my phone out and grinned when I saw who had messaged me.

Peter.

Settling in okay?

I threw myself on the bed, lay on my back, and replied. *Yes, thank you. Watched TV and had dinner with my roommates. Just in my room now.*

Sounds good. I'm really happy for you.

Thanks. I feel good about it.

Still up for a visitor tomorrow?

Can you talk?

Yes.

I called his number. "Hello?"

"Yanni, everything okay?" He sounded concerned.

"Yeah, I just wanted to let you know, there are house rules."

"House rules?" His concern now sounded amused.

"Well, yes. For the safety of everyone."

"Oh."

"Visitors are allowed, but only briefly and not overnight." Then I realized how that sounded. "Ah, not that we're… not that you're…"

"I get it, Yanni."

"It's just that everyone here has… some issues, and this place is their safe space. If someone was just to turn up and make someone else feel uncomfortable in their safe place, that wouldn't be right. Know what I mean?"

He was quiet for a moment. "I'm sorry if I sounded mocking before. I didn't mean to sound insensitive."

"I know. It takes some getting used to. Everyone here is pretty cool, but I don't want to upset anyone."

"No, of course not."

"I still want you to come here though. Just for a quick look, and then maybe we can grab coffee somewhere?"

"Sounds great."

"I'm sorry I missed our movie date today."

"Date?"

"Non-date," I corrected quickly.

Peter chuckled. "There will be other days."

"So, is eleven o'clock tomorrow okay?"

"Perfect."

"You remember the address?"

I'm sure he found that amusing. "Yes, of course."

"See you then."

"I'll look forward to it."

He disconnected the call, and I put my phone to my chest and smiled. I was looking forward to it too.

I let my hand fall to the box with the silk gown so my fingers could traipse over it. I allowed myself to pick it up and brought it to my face. It was light and cool and smelled fresh and clean, floral. I didn't dare try it on, not yet. I would. But not yet. I rolled off the bed and slipped the silk gown into a drawer.

I got myself ready for bed and passed George in the hall. "Goodnight," he said, as cheerfully as a goth could say.

I smiled nervously. "Night."

I closed my door behind me, then locked it as quietly as I could. I checked and double-checked that the window was locked. I knew I was safe here. There was a great alarm system on the front and back doors, and I trusted my new roommates. But I pulled my backpack into bed with me, and like always, slept with the light on.

CHAPTER ELEVEN

PETER WAS RIGHT ON TIME. I found it reassuring that he was punctual, like in all things—he means what he says. The sound of the doorbell sent a thrill through me, and when I opened the door, my smile became a grin.

He looked like summer, warm and amazing. He wore shorts that, from their cut and design, I could tell were expensive. His polo shirt clung to him in all the right places, his sunglasses perched on top of his head, and his whole face smiled when he saw me.

He held a potted orchid out to me. "A housewarming gift."

"Oh, wow! Thank you. You didn't have to do that." I took the plant. The purple flowers reminded me of the silk gown I now owned, and I was thankful I didn't blush. I leaned in and kissed his cheek. "Please, come in."

I showed him the living room and kitchen. Skylar and George were there, so I introduced them. I was pretty sure they were shocked that Peter was older, and before it could get awkward, I looked at Peter and said, "Come upstairs. I'll put this in my room, then we can go."

Peter followed me wordlessly up the stairs and I opened the door to my room. "This is me."

He stepped inside and looked around. "Nice. Reminds me of my college days. You'll have a lot of fun here."

"I hope so." I put the plant on the dresser. "I like it."

"Did you sleep okay on your first night?"

I nodded. "Yeah, I guess." The truth was, it was a long night. I listened to the sounds of the house, the creaks and the sounds the wind and traffic made outside, familiarizing myself. But it was peaceful enough and I eventually fell asleep sometime after two. I also left out the part where I hid my backpack in my bed and slept with the light on. There were some things he didn't need to know.

I took a deep breath. "Do you like it?"

Peter nodded slowly. "I do."

I exhaled finally. "I'm glad. I wanted you to like it. I don't know why."

Peter slid his hand into mine. "You're gonna do great here. I'm proud of you for doing this. I know you were unsure after last week."

"I was. But I feel good about it."

His smile was pure joy. "Let me buy us an early lunch to celebrate."

I squeezed his hand, not ready to let it go, but knowing I had to. "Okay."

We went back downstairs and I stuck my head into the kitchen. "I'm heading out for a few hours. Anyone need anything?"

No one did, so I walked Peter to the door, then out into the beautiful LA morning. "You look really good today," I said as we got to the sidewalk. "Very summery."

"Thanks. You do too." He did this weird cringey kind of smile. "Sorry. I'm trying not to compliment you because

I know you don't like it. It's just hard when you look the way you do."

"What do you mean 'look the way I do'?"

"Well, I could say gorgeous or stunning, but today I'm going to go with happy."

I shook my head and let out a disbelieving laugh. "I will accept the *happy* because today it's true."

We got to the corner, and instead of waiting for the lights to change, I grabbed Peter's hand and together we ran across the street. One car had to slow down, so Peter gave them a wave, and I laughed as we got to the sidewalk. "Are you trying to get us killed?" He might have sounded mad if he wasn't smiling.

"That was my cardio session for the day." Letting go of his hand, I linked my arm with his. I liked walking with him like this and was pretty sure Peter didn't mind either. We found a 1950s retro diner, which looked like fun. We sat in a booth facing each other across the table, and when Peter's foot bumped mine, he didn't move it. It made my heart bloom with warmth, or maybe it was Peter's smile. We ordered burgers and milkshakes while Chuck Berry played on a neon lit jukebox.

Peter joked about how much cardio he'd be doing this week at the gym to work off the burger and milkshake, I thanked him again for the housewarming orchid he gave me, and we talked about my new roommates and about school starting tomorrow. He had a busy week at work ahead, something to do with quarterly analytics, which I didn't exactly understand, but it was pretty clear to see he loved his job.

In all the weeks we'd been having these non-dates, our conversations tended to center on me. So today I wanted to make it about him. I asked him to explain quarterly analytics to me, and I asked him about his colleagues, the company he worked for, and about his friends.

After the waitress had offered us another refill on coffee, we figured it was our cue to leave. Half a block up, I found a thrift store, and taking Peter's hand, I dragged him inside. It was very obviously not his kind of shop, but it was very much mine. Well, my kind of budget anyway. He could've looked down at me or turned his nose up in disgust, but he didn't. He laughed when I slouched a beret on my head and butchered the French language and again when I wore the bright orange fake fur coat and did a Muppet impersonation.

He shook his head when I'd paired up a maroon scarf with a brown tweed jacket, complete with elbow patches, but did a double take when I tried it on for him. "That actually looks really good."

"Um, thanks?"

He laughed. "I've never thought of tweed as fashionable, but clearly you can pull it off."

"I can pull anything off." Then I realized how that sounded. "I mean, I can wear anything. I didn't mean pulling off. Oh God." I buried my face in my hands and only looked up when I felt a hat being put on my head.

Peter was right in front of me, smiling. "I knew what you meant. Though I won't lie, I do like where your mind went." I felt my face flame twenty different degrees of red, the heat curled right down to my belly. He looked at me with a spark of something I couldn't quite identify, then changing topics, he looked at the top of my head. "I like that hat on you."

Needing to clear my mind, I turned to face the mirror to find he'd chosen a Fedora. It didn't sit very well with my curly hair, so I took it off and put it on Peter's head instead. "Suits you more."

He took the hat off and threw it back onto the pile. "No, I look like a try hard mafia boss." Then he came up with a maroon beanie. "Here, what about this one?" He put it on my head and fixed it until it was just so. "Perfect."

I looked in the mirror and had to admit, it suited me. I turned, checking out the ensemble from all angles. "It's a shame I have to wait until winter to wear it."

"Then let's look for some summer clothes," Peter suggested.

I found some jeans I could cut off for shorts and two cute button-down short-sleeve shirts. I'm sure they were someone's grandfather's at some point. One was faded lime green with pinstripes, and the other was a light blue with little dark blue palm trees on it. Peter thought they were hideous on the hanger, but when I tried them on for him, he loved them.

Happy with my find, and even happier that all of it came to a grand total of twenty-two dollars, we went to the counter. Before I could pull out the cash, Peter stopped me. "Please let me buy these for you."

"I have the money."

"I know you do. But you're starting classes tomorrow, and you might need it. And this is my way of helping out."

The little old lady behind the counter took Peter's card. She wore really thick glasses and spoke loudly. "Listen to your daddy, son. You youngins need all the help you can get these days, with them student debts and all."

Oh my God. She thought he was my daddy.

Peter stared, then blinked slowly, and his cheeks turned pink. Peter took back his card and I took the bag of clothes, holding in my laughter until we made it outside. "That was so funny!"

He groaned. "That's the second time that's happened."

"We must give off the daddy/son vibe." I grinned right

at him and bit my bottom lip. "Thank you for the clothes, *Daddy*."

His nostrils flared and his eyes focused on my mouth before meeting my eyes again. It was a look that sent a shiver down my spine. Maybe it was wrong to tease him.

Maybe I wasn't teasing.

My phone rang in my pocket, breaking the spell between us. I fished it out, but the number was unknown. My happy, playful mood was gone. Cold dread was in its place. "I don't know who that is," I whispered. "What if it's… what if he somehow got my number?"

Peter took my phone and answered the call. His voice was strong and direct. "Hello… No, this is Peter." Whoever had called spoke for a second. Then Peter said, "May I ask who's calling?" Another brief pause, then Peter smiled and said, "One moment, please." He handed the phone to me. "It's one of the coffeehouses you put your name down at. They're calling about a job."

Relief detonated through me. I let out my breath and took the phone. "Hello, this is Yanni."

As it turned out, it was a coffeehouse two blocks from home, and the owner, a lady by the name of Vonna, wanted to know if I could drop by to meet her. "I can be there in ten minutes," I said.

Her response was short and sweet. "Perfect. See you soon."

Peter was already smiling when I ended the call. "She wants to see you now?"

I nodded. "Yes. No time to get nervous, I suppose. And thank you for answering my phone. I guess I forgot when I applied for jobs that I'd be getting calls from unknown numbers."

"Anytime." He looked up and down the street. "Which way are we going?"

I pointed to the block across. "That way."

I wasn't wrong about not having time to get nervous. Peter talked about buying the Charlie Chaplin box set of DVDs nonstop for the entire ten minutes it took to walk there. When he stopped me just outside the café, I realized it was his attempt at distracting me and not letting me overthink anything. He took my bag of clothes. "I'll wait out here."

"Okay. I don't know how long I'll be."

"It's fine." I looked at the café door and let out a slow, nervous breath.

"Yanni?"

I turned to Peter to find courage and conviction in his eyes. He smiled so easily. "Just be yourself."

Bolstered by his confidence, I went inside. The coffee-house itself looked recently renovated, with dark timber paneling and highlighted color around the space in warm grays and blues. A quick glance at the menu board told me it specialized in Italian coffees, and the front cabinet was full of Italian cakes and pastries. The staff behind the counter all wore a uniform of black pants, long-sleeved white shirt, a black vest, and tie, with a short black waist apron. They looked impeccable and busy, but most impor-tantly, they looked happy to work there.

A lady at the till smiled at me. She was in her thirties, maybe, and her name tag declared her to be Charise. "Can I help you?"

Swallowing my nerves, I tried to appear calm. "My name is Yanni. Vonna called me for an interview."

"I'll just get her for you." She smiled and disappeared through a staff-only door, and from the corner of my eye, I noticed a few of the other staff look in my direction.

Vonna was a short, thin, middle-aged woman with black hair in a bob style and a round, kind face. She came in through the door, looked up at me, and smiled. "Come this way," she said, waving me around the counter.

I followed her past a cold storeroom, a dry storeroom, to a door with an Office plaque. The room was small, barely big enough to fit a desk, two chairs, filing cabinets, and not much else. The state of her desk told me she tried to be organized but was too busy to make it happen. "Take a seat," she said, edging her way around to her side of the desk. I was grateful she was tiny because anyone bigger would have struggled. "You dropped your details off at the right time. One of the boys finished school and moved on." She had my résumé in front of her. "You have experience, yes? I called your last place of employment. He said you were very good, but you left with no notice."

Don't panic. Don't panic. Take a breath and explain.

"My circumstances changed. I was going to school and working part-time. But I had to leave… an abusive relationship." The words felt surreal to say out loud, but I couldn't very well lie to her. Not if she was to hire me.

She put her hand to her heart. "Oh my."

I gave her the best smile I could manage. "I'm on my feet again now. New place, new school, and now I just need the work."

She paused a moment, like she forgot her train of thought, then asked me a few questions about which point of sale systems I'd used, what hours my schooling would be, when I was available to work. "And you live ten minutes away?"

"Yes, two blocks."

She seemed happy with that. "Can you make me a coffee?"

"Right now?"

Vonna nodded. "Yes, now. Come with me." She got up and edged her way back around the desk, dodging my long legs and making it out the door. I followed her into the dry storage room, where she pulled a black waist apron off a hook and handed it to me. And for the next ten minutes, I got to play barista.

"I'll have a ristretto," Vonna said.

Thankfully, the coffee machine wasn't too different from the one I was used to. This was bigger and looked ten times more expensive but still functioned the same. So I made Vonna her coffee, then someone ordered a cappuccino, so I made that. Then a double vanilla latte, a soy long macchiato, and a decaf cappuccino, so I made those too.

Charise stood at the machine with me making her order, and she gave me a smile. "Doing good," she whispered, and I was certain I saw her give Vonna a nod. When my time was up, Vonna waved me over toward the end of the counter. I took my apron off, folded it neatly, and placed it on the counter. She smiled and had to crane her neck to look up at me. "Can you start this week?"

And just like that, another part of my life was back on track.

We sorted out some details, she gave me some forms to take home and fill out, and I walked out into the sunshine to find Peter leaning against a street pole holding my bag of new clothes across his thighs. He must have known from my smile. "Yes?"

"I start Tuesday."

Peter's grin was instantaneous; excitement and happiness for me just beamed right out of him. "That's excellent!" He gave me a hug and his warmth enveloped me and pulled me in in more than just a physical way. Something in my blood, in my bones, in my soul was drawn in, like the light in him not only kept me safe but also healed me.

I couldn't really explain it. I couldn't find the words,

and I also couldn't find it in me to let go of him. "You okay?" he asked. I felt his voice through his chest more than I heard it.

"Yeah." I pulled back reluctantly. "Thank you, for before. On the way here, you kept me distracted so I didn't overthink everything and bail out before I got here."

He laughed, not even trying to hide the fact he'd done it. "Anytime." He looked down the street toward my house. "Well, I should get going. Or move my car, at least, before they tow it."

"Oh, shoot!" I'd forgotten about his car. But that also meant our time together was almost over.

He seemed unsure for a moment. Like he didn't want our time to be over either but not sure how to prolong it. "We could take a drive to the beach if you want?"

I slid my arm through his and sidled up close as we started the walk home. "Sounds perfect."

BY THE TIME he dropped me home, I was warmed through from the sun and had a belly full of food and gelato. It had been such an amazing day. I felt like I was buzzing.

Everyone was in the living room. Skylar and George were watching a cooking show, and Jordan had her legs curled up under her with her nose in a book. "Look at you!" Skylar said. "All glowing and shit."

George raised the one eyebrow that wasn't hidden by a curtain of black hair. "Dude, you look far too happy. Cut it out."

I laughed and plonked myself onto the end of the sofa Jordan was sitting on. I was still holding my bag from the thrift store, so I kind of held it up awkwardly. "Shopping at the second-hand store. Scored six things for twenty bucks. Ate far too much, twice, but the gelato was too good to say no to. Oh, and I got a job!"

"Awesome!" Skylar said.

George nodded slowly. "Cool."

Jordan closed her book and gave me a timid smile. "That's really great."

"Thanks. It's a coffee shop, probably four shifts a week, which is all I need right now."

We sat in silence for a beat. George played with the silver ring in his lip. "So, that Peter guy… is he your dad or something?"

I snorted, ignoring the burn I could feel across my cheeks. "Uh, no. He's not my dad. Just a friend." I was about to explain that neither of us was ready for anything more than friendship just yet but figured these new friends might not need *all* the details, and so an awkward pause filled the room instead.

"Show us what clothes you got," Skylar said, saving us all from dying of awkwardness.

So I did that, showing each piece and telling how much each one cost. Not that they were probably too interested…

"Is that the thrift shop on San Pedro?" George asked. "They have some pretty cool stuff."

"Yeah, I got my purple cardigan there," Skylar added.

Jordan held her arm out and pointed to the long sleeve of her floral shirt. "I got this from there. Two bucks."

We fell into an easy conversation about bargain shopping until Skylar declared she was going to make her dinner. George soon followed, but Jordan and I stayed on the sofa.

She spoke quietly, timidly, and I would always remember

how Mrs Landon hugged her the longest. Whatever she'd been through was rough, and I didn't know why, but it was important to me that Jordan knew I was on her side.

I sank back into the sofa and gave her a smile. "What's the book?"

"*Economies of the Waking World*," she replied. "It's about financial ramifications of globalization in the twenty-first century."

"So," I deadpanned, "just a bit of light reading."

She smiled. "Yeah. It's not bad."

"What are you studying? I mean, is it for class?"

"No, I'm just reading it. I'm studying psychology."

"Oh." God, I couldn't even imagine… "That's a tough one. I have enough trouble dealing with my own messed-up head. Not sure I could cope with studying anyone else's as well."

I wondered briefly if that was the wrong thing to say, but she smiled. "I'm opposite. I want to study why people do messed-up things to other people. Why the people who treat others terribly do what they do."

I ran my hand over my face, trying to process that. Did I ever want to know why someone assaulted another person? Did I want to humanize them, empathize with them, sympathize with them? No, no I didn't. "Well, you're stronger than me. I don't think I could do that."

Her smile had an edge of sadness now. "I'm sure I'm not. We just deal differently. That's all."

And I could see it in her eyes then. A familiarity, a survivor's tell. *I've been through it. I've been where you are.*

I swallowed hard. "What year are you in? With your classes?"

"This is my third year."

"Me too. Well, I'm starting my third year. I've been to

two different schools before now. But I start my third year tomorrow."

"Are you excited?"

I nodded. "New school, new job, new house. New me."

Jordan smiled and nodded in that familiar "I've been where you are" kind of way. "Sorry I missed meeting your friend earlier." She shrugged, going for nonchalance, but the death grip on her book told me otherwise. "I don't do well meeting strangers. I hope you understand."

"It's fine, really it is." I waited for her eyes to meet mine. "I do understand. I don't do well meeting new people. It's damn hard, and some people don't get that, but I do. So don't apologize. It's all cool."

"I don't do well in crowds or with loud noises."

Yep. She understood. She'd definitely been where I've been. I frowned. "Me either."

She grimaced. "You went out today though."

"Because I was with Peter. I trust him. I had a freak-out in a café last week. Some drugged-out guy came in and started yelling and throwing furniture and stuff, and I had like an anxiety attack. It wasn't pretty, but Peter was there. He talked me through it."

Jordan looked horrified. She clutched her book with both hands to her chest. "I would have died."

"If Peter wasn't there, it would've been a whole lot worse. I can do controlled environments," I explained. "Like classes or go to the movies because I know what to expect. I find headphones are a good way to drown out the loud noises, and it usually stops people from trying to talk to you."

Jordan nodded and gave me a weak smile. "Yeah, I can do controlled environments. And headphones do deter some people, but not always."

"If you ever need me to come to the store with you, please just ask. Safety in numbers kind of thing."

She gave me a relieved huff followed by a brief smile. "Thanks." Then she said, "I'm getting better. And I don't mean to dump all this on you on day one, but it's probably best if you know from the beginning."

"I'm glad you told me." I felt a bit more relaxed with her now. "Have you got a cell? I can give you my number and you can text me if you need. But only if you want to, that is. If you want someone to walk home with you or to school or the store." I shrugged again, feeling a little foolish for suggesting it.

Jordan looked unsure, but in the end she nodded. "Ah, yeah, sure. That'd be great."

I gave her my number, and after she had put her phone away, an easy silence fell between us. "So," I started, "what's a normal Sunday night here?"

"Depends. Sometimes a movie, sometimes study. Sometimes we all hang out here, sometimes we're all in our own rooms."

On this particular Sunday night, the four of us sat in the living room watching *101 Dalmatians* on TV. It was relaxed, and all in all a nice way to spend the night.

When the movie was done, knowing I had my first day of school in the morning, I said goodnight and went upstairs. I called Mr and Mrs Landon quickly, to let them know I'd gotten a job.

"Oh, Yanni, that's such good news!" Mrs Landon said. "When do you start?"

"Tuesday, after class." I lay back on my bed and smiled at the ceiling. "I told them Wednesday afternoons are out. I have my appointment with Patrice, and I was hoping we were still doing Wednesday night dinners."

"Oh yes, of course! That's a wonderful idea!" She sounded about ready to burst. "Takeout or home-cooked?"

"I don't mind." I didn't want to be an inconvenience, but I had loved the times we had spent in the kitchen together. And given that my appointments with my therapist usually left me feeling a little vulnerable, I suggested one thing that had been such a comfort to me. "Actually, maybe the three of us can prepare and cook dinner like we used to."

She was quiet for a moment before she sniffled into the phone. "Perfect! That's so perfect!"

"Tell Mr Landon I'll see him at school in the morning."

"I will. Thank you for calling."

"Anytime."

I disconnected the call and went through all the school things that Mr Landon had given me. I sorted out books and pens and put together what I hoped I'd need for my first day and put them in my backpack.

I sorted out what clothes I wanted to wear, jotted down some notes in my diary for class, and marked on my daily calendar things like work, Patrice, dinner at the Landons' on Wednesdays, and school hours. I marked what day I would have free to do laundry and chores, and I wrote Peter's name with a question mark on Saturday and Sunday afternoon.

It was such a simple thing to do, really. Like filling in a weekly to-do list. But for me, it was about taking back control and having direction and purpose. It truly felt like I was getting my life back.

I felt positive, excited at the possibilities, and I finally, finally, felt hope for my future.

When I was ready for bed, I gave Peter's orchid a drink of water, then I made sure the window and door were both locked, and I climbed into bed. I shoved my backpack, with my few schoolbooks in it, under the blankets beside me, and settled in for the night.

As my thoughts wandered back over the day, I inevitably thought of Peter. I reached over for my phone and quickly thumbed out a message.

Thank you for a wonderful day.

His reply came straight back. *I could say the same to you. I enjoyed every minute.*

I smiled at my phone. *Looking at my schedule, I think I only have Saturday and Sunday afternoons free this week. Is that okay?*

Are you offering me both?

I laughed. *If you want…*

I want.

I finish work at two on Saturday.

I'll pick you up. We can do something fun.

Like what?

I'll think of something.

Sounds good.

First day of class tomorrow. Are you nervous?

A little. Mostly excited. I'm in bed, trying to sleep, but I'm all keyed up.

That was probably a little too much information—that I was in bed and excited—but I was sure Peter wouldn't take it like that. Until I watched the dots in the bubble on screen appear, disappear, appear again, then disappear again. He was either writing me a novel, or he kept starting then deleting what he was trying to say. In the end I thought I should put him out of his misery, and I hit Call.

His deep, soothing voice crooned in my ear. "Hello."

"Hi. You seemed a little stuck for words."

Peter laughed. "I was trying to reply without a double meaning or an innuendo."

"I didn't realize how it sounded until after I'd hit Send. Sorry about that."

He chuckled, a deep, throaty sound. It resonated in my chest, pooled a warmth around my heart that felt... a lot like something I longed for but wasn't ready for yet. I didn't want to get ahead of myself, but I also didn't want to let it go. I wanted to grab it with both hands and hold onto it forever.

No matter how much it terrified me. Thrilled me.

"Can I call you tomorrow night? To ask about your first day at class?"

That warm feeling got a little warmer. "Of course you can. I'd really like that."

"I won't get home till a little later this week."

"Oh, your quarterly analytics."

"You remembered?"

"Yeah, of course." A rush of pride ran through me. "And you can tell me all about your day too. Reports and analytics, all that data stuff, office gossip, that kind of thing."

Peter made a happy sound. "I will."

I yawned. "Sorry. I'm more tired than I thought."

"I didn't mean to bore you," he replied, a smile in his voice.

"Hardly. More like you put me at ease."

"I'll take that as a compliment?"

I snorted a laugh. "You should. I meant it as one."

"Sweet dreams, Yanni."

"You too."

CHAPTER TWELVE

———————————

I WAS EARLY TO CLASS, nervous, excited, and eager to make my dreams a reality. I walked with Jordan to her bus stop, then walked to my new school. I was early, yes. But I wasn't the first one there. Christopher was mopping the foyer, and his surprise to see me became a smile. "Yanni. You're a student now," he declared.

"I am. Is your leg better?"

"Much better, thank you." He lifted his leg off the ground, bending it at the knee, as though proving it and showing me was important to him.

"That's really good." I gave him a grin. "I'm glad. I start my new job tomorrow, but if you ever need some help, you come find me or ask Mr Landon to call me. I'll help you, no problem."

Christopher smiled and kept mopping the floor. "I will."

Mr Landon's voice sounded behind me. "Yanni! You're early."

I spun to face him, and he crossed the floor and gave

me a bit of a hug. Christopher looked at the floor, then to Mr Landon. "You walked on my floor."

Mr Landon looked shocked and apologetic. "I'm sorry." He took my arm and dragged me toward his office. "Sorry, Christopher."

When we were in his office, he shut the door. "So, you found work already? Helen told me you called."

"Yeah, first shift tomorrow. It's an Italian coffee shop. I have to wear a tie and vest as the uniform."

He laughed. "Sounds fancy. Looking forward to today?"

"So much."

"Me too!" He clapped his hands together. "I love the beginning of term. Everyone's fresh and new; there's excitement in the air."

His energy was contagious. "I've been awake since five," I admitted. "I've been ready for hours."

"You're ready for this," he said, his tone now soft and serious. "You're gonna nail it. But!" He put up his pointer finger. "Even though you are clearly our favorite student, we don't have favorites. You'll have to work hard."

"I know."

He gave me a smirk. "I know you do. And I know you're gonna give everything you've got."

"I will."

"If things get too much, you need to come to me, okay? If you need to take a step back at any time, you only have to say."

I nodded.

"Helen would say something award-winning like 'being strong is the ability to ask for help, not trying to shoulder everything alone,' but I'll just say this: if you feel like you're struggling, with anything, you come find me, okay?"

"I will. Thank you. Right now, I feel great. I'm in a real

good place, mentally. I'm not expecting this to be easy, but I *want* this. And I know I can do it. Everyone has helped me get here, and I want to prove to them that I can. Not just for everyone else, but for me too. I want this, and I'll do anything to make it happen."

He smiled and nodded slowly. Proud, even. "And that's why you'll make it."

We spoke for a while about how I found my new living arrangements, but it wasn't long before he noticed the time. "Oh wow," he said, shooting to his feet. "We're gonna be late."

We'd lost track of time, and when we went out into the halls, we found them buzzing with students. Mr Landon pointed me in the direction of the classroom I was supposed to be in, while he went off in another direction saying hellos and high-fiving people as he went.

The morning of the first day was spent going through introductions, class schedules, expectations, and the syllabi we'd be studying this year. The afternoon was spent intro-ducing ourselves to our classmates, and ad-libbing short scenes. It was daunting, frantic, and the most fun I'd had in ages. I loved every minute.

I met tons of new people, some of whom I liked imme-diately—the kind of people who you know you'll be friends with—and some who were possibly a little too loud for my liking. But everyone was friendly, at least, and we were all there for one thing: to learn from the best.

And by the time the day was done, I was so excited, I couldn't wait to tell Peter all about it. I knew he was hours away from finishing his workday, but I was too happy to wait, so on the walk home, I sent him a selfie of my biggest grin and followed with a quick message. *Best first day ever.*

I got a reply a few minutes later. *Looks like it. Great photo, made my day. Can't wait to hear all about it.*

I almost skipped the rest of the way home. I was the first home, and given my mood, I decided I'd make good on my promise to Jordan to fix her my Greek pasta and made enough for all of us. If someone didn't want it, I'd have enough for my dinner tomorrow night after work.

"You didn't have to do that," Skylar said kindly as I served it up. "But I'll never say no."

I laughed. "I had a really good day, and I have these fresh ingredients from shopping with Mrs Landon, and I figured I won't always have the opportunity to make it. So, voilà!"

George nodded approvingly as he ate his. "This is good, man. Thanks."

"No problem."

I was sitting next to Jordan on the sofa as we ate, and she gave me a gentle elbow nudge and a smile. I think she liked the fact I was making an effort to fit in. I guessed she'd been nervous when learning someone new would be moving in, and she didn't know what to expect. But we were a lot alike, and I think she found comfort in that.

"I have homework to do," I announced. "Who the hell gets homework on their first day?"

They each put their hands up, and we all laughed. I nodded and swallowed down the last of my dinner. "Fair enough," I agreed. We discussed practice versus theory in our classes while we cleaned up the kitchen, and my phone rang in my pocket just as we were done.

I fished it out of my pocket to find Peter's name on screen. It made me smile. I didn't even have to say anything. Skylar took one look at me and waved me off. "Go on, answer it." Then she added, "Goodnight, Yanni," as I took the stairs two at a time.

I answered the call with a laugh as I got to my room. "Hello."

"Did you run for the phone?" Peter asked. "You sound out of breath."

I chuckled and closed my door, sliding the lock into place, and flopped onto my bed. "Just ran upstairs. We just finished dinner. I cooked for everyone."

"Sounds like you've had a great day."

"I have!"

"So, tell me about your classes."

"Well, I'm in my last year of a three-year program," I started. "So this year we'll be doing more voice and movement, complex text and language with things like classical dramatic, verse and prose, that kind of thing. There's also physicality, voice, and speech for things like accents and dialects. So that's kind of fun. Then we choose our electives, which is more about discipline and control."

"What electives will you choose?"

"Applied Theatre and Classical Acting for the Contemporary Stage. I think they're best suited for me."

"Sounds great, Yanni."

"It's really exciting. Though I have homework already."

Peter laughed. "Ah, so do I."

"You have homework?"

"Well, work I brought home with me. Spreadsheets, data collation, analysis. Most exciting stuff."

"I'll never complain about the integration of technical facility and creative expression to reveal character again."

Peter barked out a laugh. "That sounds intense actually."

"It's a subject we're doing this semester. We're supposed to write a short essay on our interpretation and expectations of what we *think* it means."

Peter groaned. "I think I'll stick with my spreadsheets."

"How was your day? You sound a bit stressed, actually. Do you always bring work home with you?"

"Not always. Sometimes. I live alone, well, apart from Neenish, but she doesn't mind."

"Neenish?"

"My cat."

His cat? "I never knew you had a cat."

"Didn't I mention her before?"

"No." Not that it really mattered, and to be fair, we had spent most of our time together talking about me. But I was a little disappointed that I didn't know this about him. "What's she like?"

"She's a tortoiseshell. She thinks rather highly of herself."

I chuckled. "Why Neenish?"

"Like a neenish tart. When I was traveling around Australia, they had these small tarts that were half-pink, half-brown."

"You traveled to Australia?"

"After college. I spent two months backpacking around Australia, and two months through Europe."

Wow. Disappointment pecked at me. "There's so much about you I don't know."

"Give us time, Yanni," he said gently. "We'll get there."

I smiled at his sincerity. And the fact he saw a future—of some kind—for us. I also couldn't expect to know everything about him when I'd not told him everything about me. "So, why does a half-pink, half-brown tart remind you of your cat?"

"Her feet. Well, her paws, to be exact. Her toe pads are pink, brown, pink, brown, like a neenish tart."

Now I laughed. "That's cute."

"I'll send you a photo. Right now, she has chosen me to be a suitable seat. I should feel lucky, I suppose. Sometimes she won't speak to me, but she's rather purry tonight."

If I was sitting on Peter's lap, I'd probably purr too.

That thought stopped me cold. Well, more importantly, stopped that warm, seeping heat spreading through my belly. Jesus. I was really thinking of him like that. I held the phone to my chest, took a deep breath, and shook my head. God, he was my friend. I wasn't ready for him to be anything more than that.

I heard a muffled voice from the phone and quickly put it to my ear. "Sorry, I missed what you said," I said lamely.

"I just asked if you were okay."

"Yeah, yeah, I'm fine."

We chatted for a bit longer, well, Peter did most of the talking. His voice was soft and melodic, safe and strong. But soon, he claimed he had work to do and it was time to say goodbye. "Will you call me after your shift at the coffeehouse tomorrow? Let me know how it goes."

"Yes, of course. It'll probably just be boring, but I'll tell you all about it."

"Are you right to walk home at night by yourself?"

"Yeah, it's not far." His concern squeezed around my heart. "Thank you."

"That's okay. Have a good day tomorrow. And remember, if you need, you can call me and I'll come pick you up and drive you home."

"It would take you thirty minutes to get there for a two-minute drive."

"I don't care. If you don't feel safe, call me."

Again, his protective nature felt like a warm blanket. "I will. Though I'm sure it'll be fine."

"Have fun writing your essay."

I snorted. "Fun and essay don't belong in the same sentence."

Peter laughed. "Goodnight, Yanni."

"Night. Give Neenish a pat for me."

"I will."

Two minutes after we'd hung up, I was at my desk contemplating the opening line of my essay when my phone buzzed with a message. It was a photo, followed quickly by another one. The first picture was of a cat's foot, and there were the cutest little pink and brown toe pads I'd ever seen.

The second photo was of Peter's torso and legs, dressed in checkered pajama bottoms and a gray tee, and he was sitting on his sofa with his feet on the coffee table. On his stomach was a pretty cat with her eyes closed and a contented look on her face, and Peter's hand was scratching her behind the ear. There was a caption. *She says thanks for the pat.*

I stared at the photo for a long time. How an image portrayed such warmth, I'll never know. But there was contentment and affection, tenderness and a sense of home that made my insides ache.

But I didn't long for what I'd lost.

This was different. I wanted to be there with him, curled into his side while his cat purred on his lap. He would put his strong arm around me, kiss the top of my head, and keep me safe and warm.

Like a good daddy should.

I put my phone on my desk, like it was suddenly too hot to hold, and took a deep breath. And then another.

Oh God. The lines between us were starting to blur. No, correction. My lines between Peter and I were starting to blur. He'd told me several times he wasn't ready for a relationship, and I'd said I wasn't either. But my brain and heart seemed to be on different pages. In different books, even.

I wasn't ready for another relationship. Not yet. I needed time to be myself before I could be part of someone else's life. Yet, I wanted him. I wanted to be his boy. For him to protect me always, keep me safe.

Like a good daddy should.

I had to reply to Peter's photo. He wasn't to know I was having an internal crisis… So I thumbed out a quick reply. I typed out *Lucky cat*, and almost hit Send, but changed my mind. I deleted that and wrote *Gorgeous* instead. I hit Send before I could change my mind again. I turned my phone on silent and threw it onto my bed.

I made a mental note to ask Patrice what she thought of this development, then started my essay.

Expectations and Realities: an essay on what happens when they merge.

SCHOOL WAS MUCH the same the next day, exciting, fun, new. And my first shift at the *Il Chicco di Caffè* went as I hoped it would. I found my feet easily enough, working out where everything was, how the cashier point of sale system worked, and when I wasn't serving, I was cleaning, cleaning, cleaning. Typical barista work. But there was a comfort in the consistency.

I worked the closing shift, getting on well with Charise as she showed me how it was expected to be done. When we'd done everything—the chairs stood on the tables, the floor drying from being mopped, security lights on— Charise locked the door behind us. "You all right to get home?" she asked, looking up the darkened street.

"Yeah, it's just a ten-minute walk."

"Come on, I'll give you lift. It's on my way."

I got into her car, kinda annoyed that no one trusted

me to walk home by myself but kinda grateful for the lift. The rational part of my brain knew it wasn't always safe to walk home alone at ten o'clock at night in LA, and yes, I was jumpy at sudden noises and would probably crap myself if a couple of guys appeared out of nowhere. But I'd also spent weeks living rough before Spencer found me and months after my parents had kicked me out before I moved in with *him*. For too many nights, these very streets were my home. I wasn't some street-savvy thug, by any stretch of the imagination, but I also wasn't useless. I'd survived far more than a ten-minute walk in the dark.

It literally took Charise two minutes to drive down my street. "This is me."

She pulled up at the corner. "You have a good night. When are you working again?"

"Thursday."

"See you then."

"Thanks for the ride." I got out and waved her off, quickly making it to my front door and letting myself in. I reset the alarm and found the living room empty, a lone light on in the kitchen. There was a note stuck to the fridge door. *Yanni, there's a slice of my pizza leftover. It's yours if you want it.* It was signed by Skylar, and I assumed a thank you for cooking dinner the night before.

It made me smile. I took out the pizza and inspected it. It looked like a vegetarian, with a stack of veggies thrown on top, and even cold, it smelled good. I nuked it and quickly scarfed it down. I took the note and wrote *Thanks* with a smiley face on it, in case I didn't see her in the morning, then carried my tired bones up to my room.

I got changed into pajamas, then made a quick stop to the bathroom, and got back to my room just in time to hear my phone buzz. It was a message from Peter.

Everything okay?

I sat on my bed and wondered how to reply. I liked that he cared, and his concern was somehow different than Charise's, or even the way the Landons cared for me. When and if my ex ever showed concern for me, it was belittling and humiliating—it was never concern for me at all. But Peter's concern was genuine and from a good place, and it felt different. I could just picture him staring at his phone, waiting for me to reply, wondering if he should get in his car and come find me. I sent a quick reply.

Everything's fine. Just got home, ate a quick dinner, am ready for bed. Was going to text you but you beat me to it.

I've been worried.

I lived on the streets, you know. I'm okay walking home in the dark.

He didn't reply for a beat too long. *Sorry. Can I call you?*

Sure.

My phone rang half a second later. He didn't bother with greetings. "I'm sorry. I didn't mean to sound like I was chastising you."

His voice made me feel as if I'd sunk down into a warm bath. Everything about it soothed me. "It's fine. I like that you care. I do. It means a lot to me. Anyway, Charise gave me a lift home. Apparently she doesn't like the idea of me walking home either, but I can manage just fine. I managed just fine on the streets for weeks on my own."

Silence. "I hate that you went through that."

"That was far from the worst I've been through."

It sounded like he ran his hand over his face. Then his voice was quiet, wistful. "He should have treated you like a king. Worshipped you."

I wondered if he *worshipped* his ex. The one who left him. From what I knew, Peter had given him everything, adorned him with time and love, and his ex had thrown it back in his face. "Did you worship your ex?"

My question clearly surprised him and threw him off. "Oh, um…" He cleared his throat. More silence, followed by a quiet, "Yes. Too much, probably. I thought I was enough for him. I gave him everything I thought he needed, but…"

"You were enough. You *are* enough, more than enough," I said, climbing under the covers and settling down in bed. "You would have been perfect. It was his loss. Any inadequacies fall on him, not you."

I could imagine how attentive he'd be, how caring and thoughtful he'd be to the lucky guy he chose next.

"He didn't think so."

"Then he wasn't right for you. He was a fool, Peter."

He sighed. "I'm over him now. I did love him. Well, I thought I did. But maybe I was projecting too much on him."

"Projecting what?"

"My needs."

I swallowed hard. This conversation had gone down a path I wasn't expecting, but one I didn't want to get off. My words were almost a whisper. "And what are your needs?"

I heard him lick his lips. "I want… someone to share my life with."

"Someone younger than you."

"Yes."

"Someone you can keep safe, someone you can care for… be a father figure to."

It took him a moment, and his voice was rough when he answered, "Yes."

My heart was pounding so hard, my rib cage felt too small, and I wondered if he could somehow hear it. My voice was a strangled whisper. "You'll find someone else. Someone who wants those things."

He let out a long, unsteady breath. "Maybe. Maybe we should have this conversation another time, perhaps. Not over the phone."

I cleared my throat and tried to calm my hammering heart. He was right. I needed to change topics. "Sorry. How was work today?"

"Busy. Too many meetings that should've been emails."

I laughed. "School was busy too. We had to read in front of the class, passages with different emotions. It was fun."

"I can stand in front of crowds and give reports and speeches on financial findings, but I'm not sure I could stand up and bare my soul like that."

"Ah, it's easy. It's not my soul I'm baring. It's a character's, not mine."

"I guess that's true."

I couldn't hold back my yawn any longer. "Sorry."

"You're tired, and it's late. I should let you go."

"I am tired. It's been a long day. But I'm lying in bed, super comfortable, and your voice is soothing to me." I didn't know what made me say that out loud, so I added, "I could listen to you talk for ages."

He hummed, a low, rough sound. He didn't speak for a little while, and I wondered if I'd admitted too much. "I'm in bed too," he said eventually. "And I like the sound of your voice as well."

I smiled. "Goodnight, Peter."

"Night, Yanni."

———

"I'M STARTING to think of Peter in ways I probably

shouldn't," I admitted to Patrice. We'd discussed my move into the house and the start of school and my job. She was pleased with the progress but knew something else was bothering me.

"In what ways?"

"You know... *Those* kinds of thoughts." God, did I need to spell it out for her? "More-than-friends kind of thoughts."

"Well, that's not too surprising. You've been spending a lot of time with him." She gave me a motherly smile. "Why are you worried about this? Do you not think he feels the same?"

"Well, am I ready for that? Because right now, I think his friendship is more important than what anything physical might be." My stomach knotted, and not in a good way. "God, I'm not sure I can deal with anything sexual right now. I mean, the last time I had sex with... my ex, it wasn't exactly pleasant..."

Patrice frowned. "Was it consensual?"

I shook my head. "Not for me." I took in and let out a deep breath, trying not to remember that night. "I'm not ready for anything physical. I mean, my brain knows that, but my body... well, it's not thinking clearly."

Patrice talked for a while about broken trust and emotional and physical trauma that went with it. Her voice was calming, almost hypnotic. She told me I would know when I was ready to take any next steps, if at all, and not to be pressured until then.

"Peter would never pressure me."

"You trust him." It wasn't a question.

"Yes." My answer was immediate. "I feel very safe with him."

"Is there something you're not telling me, Yanni?"

"Well, it's about Peter, and I don't want him to think I was talking about him behind his back."

"Nothing leaves this room," she reassured me. "Does it involve you in any way?"

I nodded. "Yeah. Well, it could, I guess. I think I want it to."

She frowned but waited for me to explain.

"He's what I'd call a daddy. In that he's older—forty-three, to be exact—and he likes guys my age. He likes to provide and care for them. It sounds creepy when I say it like that, but it's not. He's more like a mentor or a father-figure, who just happens to like being protective…" I cringed. "I'm not saying this right."

"I know what a daddy is," Patrice said gently. She looked at the folder in front of her like she was choosing her next words carefully. "Is that what you want?"

I swallowed hard and gave a slight nod. "I like older guys. My ex was older. It was what attracted me to him in the beginning." I sighed. "They're just more confident, they have their shit together, and they know what they want. I like knowing that they're more… experienced." I looked out the window. "I like the idea of being cared for, loved by an older man. Treated properly, protected and adored. And the other night when I was thinking about Peter, and how I imagined it would feel like to be his boy… That he'd treat me like, and the exact words I thought were 'like a good daddy should.'"

Patrice blinked.

"I know, right?" I said with a laugh. I scrubbed my hands over my face. "I just added another few years to my therapy schedule because I have daddy issues, didn't I?"

Patrice chuckled. "Oh, Yanni."

But then she didn't disagree with me, and we spoke some more about my father.

MR LANDON PICKED me up from outside Patrice's office. I slid into the front passenger seat. "How was it?" he asked.

I sighed, trying to smile. "Good."

Whether he believed me or not was a different matter. "Excellent. I hope you're hungry because Helen is planning a huge dinner."

I smiled and sank back in my seat. "Sounds perfect."

CHAPTER THIRTEEN

THE REST of the first week of school flew by. I worked again on Thursday evening, and Charise gave me a lift home. She simply claimed she drove right past my house so it made sense, and I was grateful. But I didn't work with her on Friday night, and after closing up, I had a very uneventful walk home by myself. I had a morning shift on Saturday, which went by in a busy blur, but all I was looking forward to was spending the afternoon with Peter.

We'd spoken every night on the phone. But we'd never gone back to the conversation we'd had about the whole daddy-needs, and to be truthful, I hadn't given it another thought. Peter was more to me than an older guy who liked his men younger. He was so much more than that. It wasn't all there was to him. It didn't define him, as much as what I'd been through didn't define me.

Just after two, I'd showered after work and came downstairs just as the doorbell rang. Peter, wearing dress shorts again with a polo shirt and looking incredible, greeted me with a smile and a kiss on my cheek that made my heart skip a beat. "You ready?" he asked.

"Sure! What did you have planned?"

"Well, seeing as though we've missed the last two Charlie Chaplin matinees, I thought we could go shopping for the DVD collection, grab some snacks, and have dinner. How does that sound?"

"We uh, we don't have a DVD player."

"We can watch it at my place if you want?"

My stomach did a swoony-jittery thing. "That sounds perfect."

"Not too boring?"

"Are you kidding? It would totally be my perfect date. Or *non*-date," I amended. I assumed that's what we were still calling them. Then I stuck my head around the doorway to the living room, where George was watching cartoons. "I'll be back later tonight."

He gave me a peace sign, and I looked back at Peter. "Ready when you are."

We hit Peter's local mall and found a store with wall-to-wall DVDs and CDs. I'd spent a lot of time with Peter, but never in a shopping situation outside of the thrift store, and I thought it would be a good chance for me to see how he reacted and behaved in a retail environment. I highly doubted he was the type to treat a sales person like crap, but it was a true test of character to witness how someone treated people they thought beneath them.

Like my ex had. He thought everyone was beneath him, and maybe if I'd seen how he treated waitstaff, cashiers, or sales staff earlier in our relationship, I could have gotten out sooner. God, I would've run a mile.

I should've never doubted Peter. A girl, maybe seventeen, a little heavyset with pink hair and braces, greeted us. "Can I help you guys with anything?"

"Yes, thank you," Peter said kindly. "We're looking for Charlie Chaplin films or the collection if you have them?"

"Let's have a look," she said, urging him along to a computer at the sales desk. They chatted about classics, and I watched on as Peter listened to her opinions on Hepburn and Grant as they checked the system for what he'd asked for. Then he followed her to one shelf in particular, still chatting away, and he grinned when she found him the box set. "Is that the one you want?"

Peter held it out to me. "Yanni?"

It was the digitally remastered complete collection of Charlie Chaplin. "Perfect!"

"We'll take it," Peter said. Then he turned back to me. "Is there anything else you want?"

Surprised, I shook my head. "No."

He gave the sales girl a smile. "That's it, then." He paid, a crazy amount of money I might add, tipped her, and thanked her again for being so helpful, and we left.

"What are you smiling at?" he asked as we walked to the grocery store.

"You. You were very nice to her."

He made a face and looked at me, confused. "Why wouldn't I be?"

And that right there was why Peter Hannikov was a good man. He was nothing like my ex. *Nothing*. "What snacks do you like?" I asked.

Peter seemed to consider for a moment. "Popcorn is always good. Though truthfully, I should be eating fruit. The gym's killing me."

I laughed. "That's why I don't go."

He chuckled. "You don't go because you don't need to. I, on the other hand, need to. Doctor's orders."

"Really?"

He shrugged. "Proactive health. Heart, blood pressure, blood sugar. That kind of thing."

"Oh. But you look great!"

"Because I slog it out at the gym four days a week."

I slid my arm through his and leaned into him as we walked. "Well, then, we shall get unbuttered popcorn and some fresh fruit for a platter. How does that sound?"

Peter leaned into me too. His smile was shy and thankful, adorable. "Perfect."

It was fun in the market with him. He held the basket and I smelled the fruit before choosing the very best. When I said I didn't need to smell the bananas because I picked the biggest and firmest, then blushed every shade of red, he laughed and put his arm around me. He picked some yogurt and I found the popcorn, and we were soon on our way to his place.

I was a little nervous about going to his house. I knew we'd be alone and isolated. If I found myself in a situation I didn't want to be in, I'd be in trouble. But this nervousness was a pleasant feeling. I've known dread, that curdling weight in the pit of my stomach, and this was far from that. This was anticipation.

I tried to tamp it down, but of course, Peter noticed something was off.

"You okay?" He'd parked his car in front and we'd walked to his portico, carrying our bags of movies and snacks, and he'd eyed me cautiously as he opened the door. "You're a little quiet."

"I'm fine." I smiled nervously.

He frowned briefly before opening his door and holding it for me. His house was very nice. Furnished like some magazine, everything was perfectly neat. There was a dark leather sofa facing a huge flat screen TV, one of those fancy chaise lounge with cushions that matched those on the sofa. A coffee table on a rug and expensive-looking art completed the room. There was a dining table with an orchid in the center, high-backed chairs all neatly in place, and his kitchen was marble and stainless steel.

I suddenly felt very out of my depth. He was a bright and shiny million dollars, and I was a dirty nickel.

Peter put his bags on the kitchen counter and waited for me to do the same before he took my hands. My breath caught, and I was sure I looked like a deer in headlights.

"Yanni, you're not stuck here. If you want to leave, you just say and I'll take you."

I licked my lips and swallowed. "It's not that. I do trust you. If that's what you mean. I feel safe with you. It's just…"

"It's just what?"

"Your house is very nice. Very fancy. Everything is so lovely." I looked around me. "And I'm wearing second-hand clothes."

Peter's mouth fell open before he thought to close it. He blinked, then shook his head. "No. No, that's not true. You're… this house is just full of material things. At the end of the day, they're meaningless, not important. But you… Yanni, you're worth more than words can describe. Everything in this house can be replaced, but not you." He put his hands to my face, and I thought for a second he was going to kiss me. I hoped he would. I wanted him to. I wanted to feel the warmth of his lips… He caressed my cheekbone with his thumb, and I licked my lips again. His eyes caught the flick of my tongue and his nostrils flared. He took a deep breath, slowly dropped his hands, and took a small step back. His voice was gruff and warm. "You are perfect exactly as you are."

When I realized he wasn't going to kiss me, embarrassment seeped through me. I chuckled to cover my rejection. "I have a therapist who would disagree with that."

Peter smiled, though it was more sad than happy. He

ignored my mention of therapy. "Can I show you the rest of my house? And you can see it's just a house."

Realizing my words had hurt him, which was never my intention, I gave a nod. He took my hand and led me through the kitchen. It was a single-story bungalow-style home. "Two bedrooms. Mine is the farthest down the hall, the spare room is here," he said, waving to the open door. "It only gets used if one of the guys has too much to drink after poker night. Bathroom is here and laundry."

"I miss Mrs Landon's laundry."

Peter chuckled. "Yes. If you want to bring your laundry over, you can do it here while we watch a movie."

He took me back to the kitchen and opened the pantry door, then the fridge. "Food, fridge. You can just help yourself. You don't need to ask for anything."

He really was the very opposite of my ex.

"It's just a house," Peter said sadly. "It's just a fridge. But they're just *things*. You are worth so much more than that."

I squeezed his hand. "I'm sorry if I hurt you by what I said."

"If I've ever made you feel anything less than you are——"

I shook my head. "No, no. You've always been so good to me. What I said before was a reflection of me, not you. I'm sorry I said it."

"Don't apologize for telling me how you feel."

I closed my eyes and breathed in deep. "I'm still sorry. I ruined our perfect day."

"Did you want to go home?"

My eyes shot to his. Panic struck at my chest. "No. Do you want me to leave?"

He shook his head slowly. "No."

"I want to watch a movie with you and eat fruit and

popcorn." I realized then that I was still holding his hand, so I gave it another squeeze. "If that's okay?"

He let go of my hand and put his fingers to my hair, softly brushing a wayward curl off my forehead. He seemed to take in my whole face before he spoke. "Why don't you go in and unpack the DVDs, pick one, and get it started, and I'll sort out the snacks."

His gaze, his gentle touch, left me warm all over. I nodded and did as he asked. The box of DVDs had a cellophane cover, and by the time I had that pulled off, I had a supervisor. A cat sat near the coffee table watching my every move. "Oh, hello. You must be Neenish."

She stared at me, and Peter chuckled from the kitchen. "She sits on the windowsill in the sun. It's like she's solar powered."

I smiled at her, and after long consideration, she deemed the crinkling sound of the cellophane paper worthy of a closer inspection. She hopped up onto the coffee table and sniffed. "Is she allowed on the coffee table?" I asked Peter.

He scoffed. "Well, we've discussed boundaries. I set them; she disregards them."

That made me laugh. I let Neenish smell the back of my hand before giving her a pat, which she didn't object to. I picked a movie and fed it into the DVD player just as Peter came into the room with a plate and a bowl. He set them on the coffee table and scooped up Neenish, gave her a quick scratch behind the ear, and set her down on the floor. "No snacks for you," he told her before walking back into the kitchen. "I'll just grab drinks. Which one are we watching?"

"*The Circus*. Is that okay?"

"Perfect. Water okay or soda?"

"Water, please."

I sat on the sofa, leaving a spot for Peter, and he came back in and handed me a bottle of water before he sat back down. We were close enough that our shoulders were almost touching. But as the movie rolled on, we ate our platter of fruit and handfuls of popcorn, laughing at Chaplin's comedic grace, and soon our shoulders and arms were touching.

We'd somehow leaned into each other and Peter didn't seem to mind. I certainly didn't. I leaned forward to put the bowl back on the coffee table and settled back into my spot, just as Neenish decided to jump up onto Peter's lap. But she didn't stop on him. She walked over him to get to me. She simply walked onto my lap and plonked herself down.

"Oh, I see how it is," Peter said with a disbelieving laugh. "Traitor."

"Leave her alone," I joked, giving her a pat. "She knows a quality seat when she sees one."

Peter's cheeks went pink. "Mmm." He got up quickly, taking the empty plate and bowl back to the kitchen. I had to think about what I'd said, then I wondered if he liked the idea of sitting on me... or being seated in me.

My blood warmed at that thought. I knew which I'd prefer. Or using him as a seat...

Jesus.

It had been so long since I'd had sexual thoughts. It had been so long since I'd wanted anything physical. My sexual appetite had been taken away from me, replaced with unpleasant things I tried not to think about.

I knew in my heart, I was a long way off from actually being ready to be sexual again, but the fact my brain was making these leaps and my body was reacting to them was a sure sign that every day I was a little more ready than the day before.

I was healing.

"Would you like another drink?" Peter called out.

I let out a slow and steady breath. "Yes, thank you."

We watched another movie, one that Peter had to choose and put on because—I pointed to my lap with the still-purring cat—I was stuck. And after that, we stayed on the couch and talked. I asked him about his travels. He'd mentioned it before, so I listened, smiling along with him as he recalled the months he spent backpacking after college before coming back to work his ass off.

Neenish had long ago decided my usefulness had expired, and now I sat with one leg tucked up under my ass, facing him. Peter sat side on to me, with one arm along the back of the sofa, the other resting in his lap. I don't know why or where I got the courage from, but I took his hand from the back of the sofa and held it between us.

I liked to touch him. It felt natural to be close to him. If it was crossing boundaries, I wasn't sure. Peter didn't seem to mind at all.

When he mentioned dinner, I hadn't even realized it had grown dark outside. "What do you feel like?" he asked. "We can order in from anywhere."

I thought about all the possibilities… "You know what I feel like? And this is strange, so you'll probably laugh. But I feel like scrambled eggs on toast."

Laugh, he did. "We can make that here." He got up from the couch and, still holding my hand, pulled me to my feet. "You can be on toast duties."

He whisked some eggs in a bowl and slid them into a frying pan. I popped some bread into the toaster, and soon enough we were sitting at his dining table eating scrambled eggs. I told him what I was doing in classes, what shifts I was working, and as we cleaned up afterward, he spoke of some big account he had to work on this week as well.

When everything was clean and there was nothing else to do, we both stood in the kitchen. The air was suddenly electric, for me at least. It was like this was it, all pretenses were over, and I had no other reason to be there alone with him except for…

"I should probably get you home," he said. His voice was rough, and he fidgeted with his hands like he wanted to touch me but couldn't, and I was pretty sure taking me home was the last thing he wanted to do. "I'm supposed to be at the gym at seven in the morning."

I nodded, partly relieved that he was setting limits, partly disappointed. "You really do take the whole healthy heart thing seriously."

He half-nodded, half-shrugged. "My father died at forty-four of a heart attack."

Oh shit. "God, I'm sorry. That was a callous thing for me to say."

He raised his hand. "No, heart disease was the least of his worries. He drank a lot and he… was an angry man. I was seventeen."

A rush of understanding washed over me, and I stepped closer to him, putting my hand on his arm. "I'm sorry."

"It's okay."

"That's why you don't drink," I said. It wasn't a question.

Peter gave me a sad smile. "Yeah. I knew pretty early on I would be nothing like him."

Now it was me who reached up and ran my fingers through his hair. He didn't have to paint me a picture: a father who was an angry drunk didn't need explaining. "You're the kindest, gentlest man I've ever met."

He studied me for a long moment, his eyes exploring mine, seeing into my very soul. I felt exposed but somehow not vulnerable. I felt a security with him I'd not felt in a long, long time. Suddenly there was an electric static in the air, the room felt too small, and the distance between us was far too wide. I almost stepped in close. I almost told him to kiss me…

He looked away, breaking the intense moment between us, before looking back to me. "What are you doing tomorrow?"

"Laundry."

"You can bring it here if you like?"

"Well, I already told Jordan I'd go to the laundromat with her. But I'm free in the afternoon, by twelve-ish?"

He grimaced. "Shit. I just remembered. I'm meeting the guys to watch the game tomorrow night. We usually get there a little early. But there's probably an hour or two where I could come over."

"It's fine," I said, trying not to sound too disappointed. "I should probably get some prep work done for school anyway."

"Are you sure?"

I nodded. He seemed as disappointed as me, which was a comfort. "An afternoon at the library won't hurt me."

"Why the library? Isn't everything online?"

"I don't have a computer."

"Oh." He made a face, then brightened like he just thought of something. "I have an old laptop you can have."

A laptop? "No, I can't take that."

"Seriously, it's four years old and has sat in the bottom of my closet for two years. I get updated every two years through work, and I always meant to give it to those refurbish places that take old technology and clean them up to sell or give away or whatever." He put his hand on my arm. "I'll go grab it, and you can take a look."

He darted out of the room and came back a moment later with a black satchel. He slid the bag onto the kitchen counter and took out the laptop. It was, just as he'd said, an older model laptop, and a little dusty. He opened the laptop and blew on the keyboard. "It hasn't been switched on or charged in years, so I don't even know if it still works. It should. The hard drive has been cleaned, all my work has been taken off it, and it's basically back to factory settings. It's yours if you want it."

"Oh. I can't just take a laptop…"

"I was just gonna give it away. I'd prefer you took it." He slid the laptop back into the carry bag and dusted it off a bit. He seemed pleased that he could do this for me, but his smile died when he saw the look on my face. "You don't have to take it. It was just an idea."

"I appreciate it. I really do, and it would be really helpful." I couldn't deny that. "But you've already given me so much, and the Landons have given me everything, including my phone. I feel a bit like a charity case."

Hurt crossed his face and he frowned. "You're not a charity case. I offered it because you need one and I have one that literally just sits unused. It's not anything new or flashy. It's just practical." His eyebrows knit together. "You're not a charity case, Yanni."

Great. Now I'd made him feel bad. I hated that I'd put that on him. He was just trying to be helpful, and I'd thrown it back in his face. "Hey." I stepped in close and put my hand over his. "Thank you. I know you meant well, and I'm grateful. A laptop would be a great help. I don't have Wi-Fi at home, but if I need to do research, I can take it to a café or something, but I can type up my assessments on it."

"So you'll take it?"

I leaned against him and kissed his cheek. "Yes,

thank you."

His breath caught, and when I pulled back, there was something in his eyes I couldn't put a name to. Want? Fear? Both?

"I should get you home," he whispered.

I nodded. "Okay."

The drive to my place was kinda quiet. I wouldn't call it awkward, but something between us had changed. I was pretty sure he felt what I felt. Though where I had feared putting myself out there again, his was more than likely unease at getting close to someone with so much baggage. Like he was warring between want and trepidation.

I was, after all, damaged goods.

He pulled up out front of my place. "Thank you," I said. "For the laptop, but also for today. I had a great day with you."

The crinkles at the corners of his eyes when he looked at me and smiled were more pronounced by the dashboard light. "I did too." He did that peaceful staring-at-me thing. "When will I see you again?"

"Well, I work Tuesday, have my therapy appointment, then dinner with the Landons on Wednesday, then work again on Thursday and Friday nights. So, next Saturday?" God, it seemed so far away.

He sighed. "Okay."

"I'll call you, though, and text. And you can call me whenever."

He smiled again and gave me a nod before he leaned over the console. I leaned in too, meeting him halfway, and he kissed my cheek. Soft lips and hard stubble made my insides swoop, and scorching hot butterflies took flight.

"Goodnight," he murmured.

Not trusting myself to speak, I nodded and got out of his car. Not until I had my front door open and waved did he drive away. I shut the door behind me and leaned against it, smiling. "Is that you, Yanni?" Jordan asked from inside.

"Yep." I set the alarm and went into the living room. Jordan was sitting on the edge of the sofa with her legs curled up, and I joined her. "Hey. How was your night?"

"Not as good as yours." She raised a questioning eyebrow, her lips curled upwards.

I laughed. "I had a good day."

"So… Peter, huh?"

"Nothing's happened. Well, a lot of static and butter-flies. He kissed my cheek, and I thought I was going to die."

Jordan's smile widened. "But you want it to happen?"

"Yes, eventually. I'm not ready, I don't think. I mean, I get the nerves and heart palpitations when he looks at me, but I'm pretty sure if things were to go… *there*… I'd freak out."

She nodded like she got it. And who knew, maybe she understood completely. She nodded toward the carry bag I'd put at my feet. "What have you got there?"

"Oh, Peter had an old laptop stored away. He gave it to me. I don't even know if it works, but he wanted me to have it." I pulled the laptop out of the bag and flipped the lid. "Do you know much about laptops?"

She smiled. "Uh, a bit."

"Should we see if it works?"

"Sure."

I pulled out the cord and plugged it in and waited for it to boot up. After a lot of whirring and thinking, the home screen blinked on.

I snorted. "Well, that was easier than I thought."

Jordan laughed. "It looks good. It's a few years old, but it's a good model. And he just gave it to you?"

"Yeah."

"You're lucky."

"I know." I shrugged. "I kinda feel bad, like a bit of a charity case, but I know that's not what he meant."

"Don't feel bad." Jordan looked at me like I was crazy. "Jeez. I wish I had a sugar daddy who gave me stuff. Well," she frowned. "A sugar momma."

I snorted, and she blushed. I gently nudged her with my elbow. "Still on for laundry duty tomorrow?"

"Yeah."

"Cool." I closed the laptop, unplugged the cord, and shoved it back into the bag. "Then I'll see you after breakfast. Night."

She nodded, and I left her to watch her movie in peace. I climbed the stairs, got ready for bed, and locked my door. I plugged the laptop back in so it could charge overnight, double-checked the window was locked, and climbed into bed. I considered pulling my backpack into bed with me but left it on the wall side of the bed.

It was a small step, but I felt good about it.

I sighed at the ceiling and my thoughts soon turned to Peter. My stomach felt all jittery, and even though the conflicting thoughts battled with each other, I smiled. I rolled over and plugged my phone into the charger, hesitated, then quickly sent him a text.

Thank you for today. And thank you for the laptop. It works just fine :) Have fun tomorrow.

His reply came through a few moments later. *You're more than welcome. Sweet dreams.*

I slid my phone onto my bedside table, and just like he said, for the first time in a long time, I had the sweetest dreams. Of laughter and sunshine, and safe arms and sure hands, and eyes that crinkled at the corners when he smiled.

CHAPTER FOURTEEN

I BEGAN my appointment with Patrice asking about my week. How school went, how work had been going, how I was getting on with my roommates. It had been a few weeks of transitions, and all things considered, I thought it was going great.

"School's good. I've done three assessments and my grades were good. Mr Landon was pleased. We're starting ad libs next week, where we have to do solos in front of the whole class. It'll be fun. Work is good too! It's just coffee, but I think my boss is happy with me. I like my coworkers. Charise, and my boss, Vonna, have taken me under their wings." I snorted. "I seem to have that effect on people."

Patrice smiled. "And how're you enjoying the living arrangements? You've been there almost three weeks now."

"Oh, great. I love it. They're all cool, different in their own way, but we get along well, laugh a lot, watch TV together, *Jeopardy*, that kind of thing. I really like Skylar and George, but I definitely get on with Jordan more. I walk her to the bus stop every morning, and we did our laundry together as well. I think she likes the company, but she also likes having someone with her when she's out. She doesn't do crowds very well, or strangers."

"And how are things with Peter?"

"Things with Peter are great. Better than great, actually. We spent all day Saturday together, but we did our own thing on Sunday… and I missed him. He missed me too. I think."

"You think?"

"Well, he was out with his friends to watch football but called me on his way home and we talked for hours. It was almost midnight by the time I went to sleep."

"It sounds like he missed you."

I tried not to smile and failed. "He really is very nice."

"Do you see him during the week?"

"No. His job is demanding, but with my classes and work, it's just not possible. But we talk or text."

"It sounds like it's getting serious."

And that was the crux. "How soon is too soon? I mean, after everything I've been through, how soon is too soon before I'm ready for… something? Anything? I don't even know."

"You keep asking, and I understand and can sympathize with your impatience. You want your life back. But these things are different for everyone. Some people can move forward quicker than others; some take years. But each person moves at the speed that is best for them. There's no wrong or right." Patrice put her pen down and straightened the folder in front of her. "But you need to make sure your motives are your own."

"What do you mean?"

"Don't use Peter as the reason. The only reason you should be ready is because you want it, for you. Not for anyone else."

"Peter would never pressure me," I said, quickly defending him. "But I do want it for me." So I finished with a question that had weighed on my mind for days. "It's not just about moving forward with my life. I guess I want to know how will I know when I'm ready to be intimate with someone, mentally and physically?"

"With Peter?"

"Well, yeah." I chewed on my bottom lip for a while. "It's like my body is reacting to him. I get butterflies and I want to touch him all the time. He looks at me like he's interested, but then he pulls back like he's worried I'll break. And sometimes I think I might, ya know? I don't want to take the next step with him and then freak out because I'm not ready for anyone to touch me like that."

"Do you want him to touch you like that?"

I nodded. "Well, yeah. I think so. I just want to crawl into his arms where it's safe and warm. Which I'm sure would lead to other things…"

"Do you think about him when you pleasure yourself?"

I blinked.

"How does it play out in your mind? Are you comfortable with the idea?"

Jesus. "Um, I haven't done that… not in a long time."

Now Patrice blinked. "Okay, then that's a good place to start."

I'm sure the smile she fought was from the horrified look on my face. God, it was like talking about masturbating with my mother.

She gave me a sympathetic look. "You've been through sexually traumatic experiences. There are no rules or guidelines for recovering. Some people can eventually resume an active sex life; some people never can. Everyone is different. There is no right or wrong. The only reason I'm even suggesting this to you is because you brought it up, and it's a safer option for you to find what you're comfortable with when you're by yourself rather than with a partner. You don't have to do anything if you don't want. It is always up to you."

I wiped my sweaty palms on my thighs.

"But my advice for any sexual assault survivor is this: you should discuss this with your partner. They need to know your limits, what's acceptable, and most definitely what not to do. Anything off limits, any trigger words or touches."

"I have to tell him what happened to me?"

Patrice nodded slowly. "I would recommend being honest with him, yes."

She talked for a little longer about the importance of open communication and how it eliminates any confusion and assumptions, and all I kept thinking about was the fact I had to admit my shame.

And if that was a hurdle I had to get over before I could have a relationship with Peter, then I wasn't sure I could.

I snorted out a laugh, and Patrice's eyes narrowed with concern. "What's funny?"

"Well, here I am having this existential crisis about the fact I want, or might possibly want, a relationship with him, and he's not even aware."

She tilted her head in that reassuring, knowing way she usually did. "Then maybe that's where you need to start."

———

THE REST of the week passed in a blur of classes and work. I closed up late on Friday night, and when I got home, I fell onto the sofa and pulled off my shoes. "I'm beat."

George, who was watching cartoons, snorted. "Such a party animal."

I laughed at that. "Says the guy wearing a death metal shirt and watching *Phineas and Ferb*."

He tongued the ring in his lip. "I'll have you know, this is a perfect example of how capitalism tries to impede science and intellectualism believing control over the public serves the hierarchy best. I'm writing a paper on how it's a subliminal political statement aimed at children."

I stared at him for a long moment, then at the TV, just in time to watch Phineas and Ferb foil the bad guy's plans using science, and the moral that good guys always win, with the help of a secret agent spy platypus, of course.

"Right." I nodded slowly. "How clueless are their parents? I mean, how can they be so oblivious?"

"Don't all generations think they're better than the one before it?"

I considered that. "It might be true, to some degree, but not always."

George looked at me and smirked. "Because you happen to have a thing for the older generation. Mr Hottie Gen X." I threw a cushion at him, and he laughed. "Speaking of *friends*," he said, clearing his throat. "I'm having a friend over tomorrow. If that's okay with you? He'll be here for a few hours before we head out. I just wanted to pre-warn, that's all."

"Oh, yeah. That's fine. Peter'll be here after two-ish, but we're not staying here. We'll go out and probably go back to his place." Then I thought I'd pry for a bit of info. "Your friend, do they have a name?"

George hesitated for a moment, then blushed a little. "His name is Ajit."

Then because I couldn't help myself, "And is Ajit a Gen-X hottie or a Gen-Y hottie?"

He tossed the cushion back at me, which I caught with a laugh. "Gen Y. Definitely Gen Y."

My tired chuckle became a sigh. "I gotta get to bed. I need my beauty sleep." I trudged upstairs, got ready for bed, did my nightly routine of window and door checking, and fell onto the mattress.

Then my phone beeped. I blinked sleepily at the screen. It was a message from Peter. *How was your night?*

I smiled as I replied. *Busy, but good. How was your day?*

Can I call you?

Yep.

I hit Answer as soon as my phone rang. "Hey, you."

There was a smile in his voice. "Hey, you, too."

His deep, rough voice felt like a warm caress and I hummed. "I've missed your voice." He was quiet, and I realized I'd said that out loud, so I covered quickly with, "I mean, texts are nice and all, but it's not the same."

"Are you in your room? I can't hear the TV."

"Yeah, in bed. I'm tired."

"Oh. I can call back in the morning."

"No, it's all good. I like that you called. How was work?"

"Good. Productive week, which is always nice. Are we still on for tomorrow?"

"Yeah. I'm looking forward to it. I finish at two. What were you thinking we should do?"

"There's a music festival thing on at Venice Beach. We could go have a look?"

Sunshine, music, and Peter. "Sounds perfect."

"I'll see you at your place at about two-thirty."

"Okay."

"You sound sleepy. I should let you go."

The truth was, his voice, soft and low in my ear, was lulling me to sleep. "'Kay. See you tomorrow."

"Sweet dreams, Yanni."

"Sweet dreams, Peter."

I clicked off the call, plugged my phone into the charger, aimed at my bedside table with a too-tired hope for the best throw, and fell asleep.

———

I'D BEEN SO busy all week, I hadn't given Patrice's advice much thought. I certainly hadn't taken her suggestion of self-servicing too seriously either. But with a quick shower after work on Saturday, my dick was certainly open to suggestions.

I hadn't had one inkling of sexual awakening since... *him*. My ex. Sex was certainly something I hadn't enjoyed, given pleasure was something he only took for himself. Whenever he wanted it, whether I did or not.

So no, my libido had gone to ground, and that was perfectly fine with me. But for the first time in a long time, I was half-hard. In the shower and drying myself off there was a warmth and twinge of anticipation.

And maybe my body was ready, but I wasn't sure my mind was. So I ignored it, for now, got dressed, and went downstairs. George was in the kitchen with his friend. They were arguing playfully over adding chili sauce to homemade nachos and how Ajit's Sri Lankan grandparents would think George's definition of spicy was funny. "Oh, hey," I said, going for casual as I opened the fridge.

"Yanni, this is Ajit. Ajit, my roommate Yanni."

Ajit was not what I was expecting, at all. I assumed, with George being goth, that someone he was interested in would be too, but Ajit was anything but. He looked like he just came from math club, wearing tan pants and a striped T-shirt tucked in. He was tall, thin, had gorgeous dark skin, light brown eyes, and the longest eyelashes I had ever seen on another human being. He was cute.

"Nice to meet you," he said.

"Likewise." I smiled at him and George. "What are you guys up to today?" I asked, grabbing my yogurt out of the fridge.

"We're studying," George replied.

"The cartoon capitalism thing?"

Ajit laughed. "Something like that."

"I'm being kicked off the TV," Jordan said. I hadn't even realized she was sitting on the sofa.

"Hey!" I grabbed a spoon and took my yogurt, plonking myself right beside her. "Didn't see you there."

She smiled. Her long hair was in a braid today, and it looked pretty. She hid herself away in her baggy clothes, wore long-sleeve shirts and pants, and a long cardigan, which she often wrapped around herself. It was a self-protective thing, which I understood. I never commented on her clothes or appearance, not only because it made her self-conscious but because, well, she was more than just fabric, and I didn't give a shit what she wore.

"What are you doing today?" I asked.

"I have an assignment due Monday."

"Ugh."

"Yeah. So that's my weekend. We still doing laundry tomorrow morning?"

"Yep. Have to. I'm out of clothes." I looked down at my blue shirt with the little palm trees on it and my red denim shorts.

"You look great. Anyway, I'm sure Peter won't care what you wear."

I took a mouthful of yogurt and gave her a nudge. "He'll be here soon. Wanna meet him?"

We'd talked so much about him, but she still hadn't met him. And that was fine. I would ask but would never push.

And just then, the doorbell rang. "That'll be him." I shot up off the couch and got to the door before I looked back at Jordan and gave her a questioning look, which asked her *yes or no*. She took a deep breath and gave the slightest nod.

I shoved my spoon in my mouth, so I could unlock the front door, and grinned when I saw him. I had to take the spoon out so I could speak. "Good afternoon."

He chuckled. "Hello."

"Come in. I'll just put this away and we can get going."

He followed me in and stood at the living room entrance, which opened up to the kitchen. "Peter, this is Jordan," I said. She had her legs pulled up and her knees tucked into her cardigan, but she gave a small wave. Then taking the emphasis off her, I waved toward the kitchen. "You've met George before, but this is Ajit."

Peter smiled but didn't walk in any closer. "Hi."

I threw my yogurt in the fridge and quickly washed and dried the spoon. Meeting Peter back at the hall, I took his hand and pulled him out the front door. "I'll be back later tonight. Don't wait up, kids."

There were muffled laughs as I shut the door and found myself bathed in the warm LA sun and a huge smile from Peter. We drove to Venice and walked the boardwalk, listening to all kinds of music, and enjoyed a lunch of pita wraps from a Greek takeout truck. Peter insisted we eat Greek food "because it's who you are," he'd said. He made me order for him, so I chose beef *kefta*, *tzatziki*, piccalilli mustard, tomato pitas.

And he was right. I loved my heritage, and I did miss food like we'd have at family get togethers. Like he'd said before, I couldn't do much about being kicked out of my family, but that didn't mean I had to give up my traditions. So I ordered a small *bougatsa* for us each as well.

"I know you're watching your diet," I said, "but you must try this. It's vanilla bean custard with sugar and cinnamon pastry. It's amazing, and it's only small."

He bit into it and groaned, letting his head fall back. "Oh wow. That is so good!"

"I know!" I cried. I shoved mine into my mouth. "And tonight, we totally order Russian food for dinner."

Peter's smile almost outshone the sun. "Deal."

We strolled with our arms linked, walking slowly, talking and laughing, listening to music, and all too soon, the afternoon sun began to get lower and lower. And whether it was my busy week, the hours in the sun, or all the walking and food we ate, by the time we got back to his place, I was sleepy. We were on his couch watching another Charlie Chaplin silent movie and my blinks were getting longer, my eyelids heavier. I hadn't realized I was leaning into him until my head fell onto his shoulder.

I startled and sat up, but Peter simply pulled a cushion against his arm for my neck, then dragged the throw blanket over me. "Comfy now?" he asked.

"Very."

He extended his long legs out onto the coffee table, and for the next hour, we sat like that. Even Neenish joined us, curling up on top of the blanket, purring loudly. I was suddenly wide awake; weariness was no match for my hammering heart and adrenaline.

Leaning on him, being so comfortable with him felt so good, so unbelievably right.

I wasn't sure where things were between Peter and me, but I was pretty certain where they were headed. We were crossing the 'just friends' line, inch by incredible inch. There was no rushing, no pressure. *Thank God he didn't pres-*

sure me. And with that thought came the realization that what Patrice had said was true.

I had to tell him everything. I had to admit to what I'd been through and the shame and embarrassment that went with it.

But I didn't want him to think differently of me. I didn't want him to realize the depth of my problems.

I didn't want to lose him.

When the film ended, I reluctantly sat up, missing his warmth immediately. I couldn't bring myself to even start the conversation I knew we had to have. I wasn't ready. And if I wasn't ready to even talk about it, then surely I wasn't ready for an intimate relationship either.

"You hungry?" he asked.

"Yes, though I don't know how." I fought a yawn. "All that walking today must have burned off all the food we ate at lunch."

"Stay here," he said, peeling himself off the couch.

I looked at Neenish, who was somewhat disgruntled that I'd changed positions, and she gave me the stink eye. "Not sure your cat is giving me any alternative."

"If she's annoying you, just move her," he called out from the kitchen.

I gave her a scratch under the chin and her purr told me I was forgiven. "Nah, she's fine."

Peter came with a takeout menu. "Russian still okay?"

"Yes! But I want you to order for me! Pick something you know I'll like."

"Beet soup, duck liver, and beef tongue it is then."

"Uh…" I grimaced.

He burst out laughing. "Just kidding."

In the end, he ordered some lamb dish with rice, marinated peppers, and fresh vegetable salad to be delivered. "This is delicious!" I said as we tucked into it.

"My babushka would make something similar to this," he said with a wistful smile. "It reminds me of visiting her when I was young."

He told me a story of when he stayed with his grandparents when he was nine. His father had been arrested; his mother admitted to the hospital. He remembered the stories his grandmother told him of when she lived in Russia, looking at photographs and touching the ornaments they'd brought with them.

Even though the memory wasn't strictly pleasant, he recalled it fondly. "I loved spending time with them. They were very kind and very generous. Their son, my father, wasn't like them at all, and I remember my dedulya, my grandfather, telling me he didn't know why my father was so angry. I think he blamed himself. I don't know."

I slid my hand across the table and gave his fingers a squeeze.

Tonight was about Peter's past. Mine could wait.

IT DIDN'T HAPPEN the next weekend either. Maybe there were plenty of opportunities. Maybe I was putting it off. But I was more focused on enjoying my time with him, the small touches, the lingering looks, and the laughter.

I didn't want to ruin any of it. School was great, work was good, but Peter was the absolute highlight of my days. A text, a phone call at bed time, a photo of the piles of folders and papers on his desk along with a crying emoticon. The fun we had on Saturday, the lazy hours on Sunday afternoon after I'd done my weekly laundromat trip with Jordan.

On Wednesday, I had dinner with the Landons, including Andrew, who told us all about his trip to

Australia with Spencer, and before that, I had my usual appointment with Patrice, which went fine. I'd explained that I was resigned to telling Peter everything, but I wasn't sure when the right time was, and even though I wanted him to know everything so we could possibly move forward, I was afraid. She talked of patience and listening to my heart, and I understood completely.

But the next weekend, reality came to a crashing halt.

Work went fine. I walked home on Friday night without incident, crawled into bed exhausted from a busy week at school, then spoke to Peter until I fell asleep. Saturday was work in the morning, then Peter and I went to the Getty Center in the afternoon. We walked around, our arms linked, taking it all in. It was incredible, and he knew so much, and I hung onto every word like a kid in awe. We had a late dinner, he dropped me home, I kissed his cheek and said goodnight. I fell into bed, exhausted but never happier.

Sunday morning saw Jordan and me sorting our laundry and talking about our week. She'd had an exam, and she was happy with how it went, and she'd even gone for coffee with one of the girls in her class. She tried to hide the way her cheeks blushed, but it was pretty obvious she liked her. "Did you get her number?" I asked.

"I did, but just for study group. We're doing a project together…"

I buzzed with excitement and she finally laughed. Then she mumbled, "She asked me out for coffee again."

"And what is this young lady's name?" I asked, pretending to be serious.

"Hayley."

"And you said yes to another coffee date, yes?"

"It's not a date. Honestly, it's not. It's just school."

"Uh, yes, it is. It's totally a date."

"Like you spending hours with Peter," she countered. "You keep saying they're not dates, but they totally are."

I opened my mouth to argue but promptly shut it again. "That's different."

"Of course it is." Jordan laughed, and we pulled our wet clothes out of the machines and threw them into the dryers.

Two hours later, I met Peter at the front door and kissed his cheek. "Hello."

He smelled like heaven on earth and smiled much the same. "Afternoon."

"What did you want to do today?"

"We missed our movie date… or non-date, yesterday," I said. Jordan laughed from the living room. I ignored her and the embarrassment that crept over my cheeks. "We could go back to your place and spend a lazy afternoon watching movies?"

"Perfect!"

I called out goodbye to Jordan and to Skylar, who I thought was still in the kitchen, and closed the door behind me.

Peter opened the door to his car but looked at me over the top. "I haven't had lunch yet. You hungry?"

"Always."

Peter chuckled. "How does wood-fired pizza sound?"

I slid into the passenger side. "That sounds so good."

We ate our gourmet pizzas on the couch while Charlie Chaplin's *Tramp* made us laugh on the TV, and when that was done and we were cleaning up the mess we'd made, my phone rang.

As soon as I saw Jordan's name on my screen, I knew something was wrong. Frowning, I hit Answer. "Jordan? Are you okay?"

She let out a sob. "I'm at the store…" There was more

sobbing. She sounded distraught. "You said to call you if I needed... There was a man...."

My blood ran cold. "Which store? Jordan, where are you?" By this time Peter was in front of me, his eyes wide. I was trying not to panic. "We'll come get you."

There was muffled noise in the background, then she sniffled. "At the greengrocer's with the yogurt bar."

"I'll be there in fifteen minutes."

Peter had already grabbed his keys and wallet, and we were out the door. I gave directions and Peter drove a little too fast, but I didn't mind.

"Is she okay?" he asked, clearly concerned.

"I don't know." She didn't sound very okay, and the fact that she called me... "I told her to call me if she ever needed someone. She doesn't like crowds. She's afraid of men. When we walk to the bus or go to the laundromat, she tenses when there's a guy. I've never asked her for details, but I can guess."

Peter frowned and drove a little bit faster.

When we arrived at the grocer's, I didn't need to ask where she was. There was a bit of a crowd toward the end of the store, and a manager ushered us through. "There was a guy who pestered her, but he took off when she freaked out," the lady said, as if that explained everything.

I stopped when I saw her.

Jordan was sitting on the floor, up against the dairy fridge in the corner, with her knees pulled up against her chest. Her long hair hid her red, puffy eyes and tear-streaked, pale face. I could see she was shaking from where I stood. I knelt down beside her and didn't know if I should touch her, but needing to comfort her, I slid my hand over hers. "Jordan, it's me, Yanni."

She looked up at me, and that wild, frightened look in

her eyes was one I recognized. "How about I get you home?"

It took her a second to process my words, but eventually she nodded. I took her hand and helped her to her feet, put my arm around her, and walked her out. I ignored the way people stared, like there was something wrong with her, like she was crazy or a freak. I helped her into the backseat of Peter's car and climbed in beside her.

Just like Spencer did with me that day he found me. He'd sat in the backseat of a car and held my hand while they drove me to safety. I gripped Jordan's hand, and she tried to crawl into the smallest ball she could make. "We'll get you home, huh?" I said soothingly.

Jordan never said a word, but Peter's eyes kept watching me in the rearview mirror, and a minute or two later, we pulled up in front of our place. I got her inside, and Peter hesitated at the door. "Want me to go?" he asked quietly.

"No, please stay." I needed him, selfish or not. I needed him with me.

We got Jordan settled on the couch, and I pulled the throw blanket over her. She stared blankly into the in-between space, where memories and the present sometimes lived.

"I'll make something," Peter mumbled, walking into the kitchen, and I sat down with Jordan.

"It was so bad," she mumbled, crying. "There was a man, he tried to talk to me, but I had my earphones in. I didn't want to talk to anyone so I ignored him at first, but he... he followed me around the aisle. I told him I wasn't interested." She looked at me with wide eyes. "I was polite, but he grabbed my arm. I said no, Yanni. I said no, but he wouldn't let go."

"He had no right to touch you."

She scrubbed her hands over her face, smearing her tears. "I dropped my basket, and he called me names and I kicked and screamed." She sobbed again.

"He was wrong," I murmured, fighting my own tears. "He had no right to speak to you or touch you. You did nothing wrong."

Peter came in, then, holding a coffee cup. "It's lemon and honey," he said softly.

I took it first, then waited for Jordan to unwrap her hands from the blanket so she could hold it. Peter stepped back and sat on the other sofa.

Then Jordan told us her story, of how she ended up under the care of the Acacia Foundation and in this house. Her face was pale. Her voice was detached, resigned. "I grew up in a religious home. We lived on a property with other families in the same religion. It was remote. We lived with and did homeschool with the other kids, and were self-sufficient, mostly. Never saw anyone outside of our own."

Oh, God. A cult. She grew up in a religious cult.

"I knew I was in trouble when I was little. I never liked boys. I tried to because it was a sin not to. When I was sixteen, I was supposed to get married to a man my father chose and have babies and be a good woman in the eyes of the Lord." Jordan sniffled and shivered. "But I told my father I didn't want to. I begged him to give me more time. I wasn't ready. I never would be ready."

She took a deep breath, and I braced myself to hear what was coming.

"The men took turns… in *converting* me. Said they'd drive out the demons and I'd have their babies. It would be the Lord's will, and I'd be cured."

Oh, fucking hell.

"The pastoral leader, my father, my brother, the other men…"

I felt like I was going to be sick. Tears rolled down my cheeks. I didn't even try to stop them. "Oh, Jordan. I'm so sorry."

"After… I tried to kill myself, even though I knew it was eternal damnation, but that couldn't be any worse, right?" A shiver ran through her whole body. "One of the grandmothers took me to a hospital. They saved my life. But the police went in and arrested the men and disbanded the commune. I had nowhere to go. Not that I would have gone back there, but I had nothing, no one. I ended up on Skid Row, ya know, where all the homeless go?"

I nodded. "I went there too."

Jordan stared at me, then frowned. "That's where I heard about the Acacia Foundation. I met Helen Landon, and she changed my life."

I pulled my legs up underneath me and leaned my head on the sofa. "She changed mine too."

Jordan took a sip from the cup and gave Peter a weak smile. "Thank you. This tastes nice."

I glanced at him then. He looked like hearing Jordan's story had scrubbed him raw. I knew that feeling well.

"I'm sorry for calling you," Jordan said to me.

I shook my head. "No, you did the right thing. You can call me anytime. It's what friends are for."

Her eyes watered again. "Thank you. I feel a bit better now. Sorry for dumping it all on you."

"Don't apologize." I gave her a sad smile. "I'm glad we could help."

A while later, Jordan went up to her room. She was exhausted, emotionally, physically. She'd thanked us again and again, and I thought she was a little embarrassed, but she needed some time to herself. Skylar was home by then and promised to keep an eye on her. And I was left alone with Peter. I knew what I had to do.

"Can we go to your place?" I asked him. George and Ajit had come back, so doing this here wasn't an option.

"Of course."

He never asked questions. He never hesitated. He just did as I asked. I spent the drive to his house trying to get my thoughts in order, and by the time we walked into his house, I figured I should start at the beginning.

I sat him on the couch. "I need to tell you something."

He frowned. "Okay."

"I've been talking about us with Patrice, my therapist, and she suggested I be honest with you. If I want more with you, and if what we have is going to become something more, then there are things you need to know." I took a deep breath. "And I do want more with you. When I'm ready. But there are things about me you should know before we go any further."

He took my hand. "I want more with you too."

I felt a brief rush of relief before the reality of what I was about to tell him took its place.

"I came out to my parents when I was nineteen. I knew they wouldn't like it, but I thought… well, I didn't think they'd kick me out. But they did. I'd just finished my first year of college. I had a bag of clothes and nothing else. My entire family shunned me. Grandparents, aunts, uncles. Everyone. Told me I was an abomination to their faith. And I found myself on the streets of LA. It wasn't easy, and I was scared as hell. Like Jordan, I ended up on Skid Row. There are shelters and soup kitchens. But I didn't hear about the Acacia Foundation. Not then. What I did hear about was boys like me who made money…" I let out a breath and took another to steel myself. "They made money selling themselves. And believe me, after having nothing for so long, the idea of money for food when you don't have two dimes is hard to ignore. So I thought I could try it…"

Peter never looked away. There was no judgment in his eyes, only concern.

"On my very first night, I went to a bar like I was told to. But I didn't hook up with some random stranger or a john. I met a guy who had an expensive suit and sharp eyes, and he promised me the world."

"Your ex."

I nodded. "And you know, the first few months weren't too bad. I mean, I had a place to stay, a warm bed, showers, food. He would make me… do things… in bed. I put up with it because it was better than living rough." I shook my head and barked out a laugh. "I was a virgin when I met him. Can you believe that? I had *no* clue what I was getting myself into."

Peter squeezed my hand. "Oh, Yanni."

"He was older and more experienced, and he knew what he was doing and I didn't have a clue what I was doing and I thought… I mean, I thought I'd struck gold, ya know? He bought me things. He paid for my school." I frowned. "But then he got possessive and angry. The first time he hit me, he said he was sorry, and I believed him."

Peter's eyes closed slowly, and when he looked up at me again, there was something alight inside him. Anger for what I'd been through? He put his hand to my face and gently caressed my cheek. "I'm sorry he did that to you."

"That was the least of it." I sighed, and now resigned to him hearing everything, I let it out. "He became very mean and controlling. He'd tell me I was just worthless ass to him, for him to treat as he wanted. He'd decide when I could eat. He once put my plate on the floor beside his chair at the table like a dog."

Peter's jaw clenched, his nostrils flared. The anger in his eyes burned.

"He would hit me, then he'd go out and get drunk and come back and he would force himself on me. He raped me often. In the end, it hurt less if I didn't fight him."

Now Peter's eyes welled with tears, though the fire behind his eyes raged on.

"That last time, he left me on the bathroom floor. I had a black eye, cut lip, swollen cheek. He never used to hit my face. Always body blows, but he was getting worse. And I didn't want to wait around to see how bad the next one was gonna be. I mean, if he did end up killing me, no one would miss me."

Peter blinked and a tear rolled down his cheek. He made no attempt to hide it or apologize.

"I was so scared of him, but I couldn't leave. I had no one, nothing. Over time, he'd cut me off from my friends. I was totally dependent on him. I didn't want to go back to the streets, I really didn't. But I had to. The very last time he hit me, I swore never again. So I left everything. None of it was mine anyway. I had the backpack and the few clothes I went there with, and that was it. I had no clue where to go, so I went to the hospital to get my face looked at, and they called the police and took me downtown with them. I figured I'd be safe there, at least. I made a report, which I think they just laughed at. You know, a gay lovers' tiff." My eyes blurred with tears. "And I walked out of that police station and went back to living rough."

I took a deep breath, feeling a weight lift off my shoulders now that I'd told him the truth. I wiped my face with the back of my hand. "That's my story. Not as horrific as Jordan's, but still not sunshine and roses."

Peter stared at me for the longest time. It had grown

dark outside, the only light was from the kitchen behind us, and I couldn't really read his eyes anymore.

I shrugged, trying to be brave. "It's okay if you need to take a step back. I understand. People come with all kinds of baggage, but not *this* kind of baggage. I don't even know if I can be intimate with anyone. I don't know if I'll ever have sex again. I think I want to, but I don't know if I'll ever be ready. He took so much from me, and it doesn't just end because I left him. I live with this. I've only just stopped sleeping with my backpack in bed with me, and I still sleep with the light on." I laughed right out loud. "God, I can't believe I'm telling you this."

Peter's face crumpled, and he slowly slid his fingers along my jaw. When I leaned into his touch, like it was some kind of permission, he pulled me against his chest and held me.

"Is this okay?" he asked gruffly.

I nodded against him. "Yes."

Then he wrapped his arms around me: strong, warm, safe arms. And for the longest time, he just held me. The beat of his heart in my ear was his rhetoric. It was all I needed to hear.

Eventually he kissed the top of my head and whispered, "Thank you for telling me."

I never wanted to move. He rubbed my back and kept me warm. The feel of his stubbly jaw resting on my head felt like home to me.

I had said so much and he so little. It was a lot to process, but I couldn't escape the feeling of rejection looming over me. Then I realized maybe he was trying to think of a way to let me down gently, so I decided to help him out. "It's a lot to take in. I don't expect an answer straight away."

"An answer to what?"

"If you want to take a step back. We've been spending a lot of time together, and if you need time—"

He shook his head. "I'm not giving up on you, if that's what you're asking."

I sat up then and almost fell off the couch, so Peter pulled me onto his lap and put his arms around me. To anyone else, it might have been weird, but with him, it felt like where I was supposed to be. Like I was his boy and he was comforting me. I found myself smiling, despite the somber mood of the evening. "Do you think any less of me?"

"Never. I hate what you went through. I hate that he did those things to you, that he hurt you like that. He should have worshipped you." He frowned, our faces just a few inches apart. "I think you're strong and brave. You're kind and funny and more resilient than you realize."

I wasn't sure I totally agreed with that, but whatever.

He smiled. "It's true. And I would never think any less of you. If anything, I think more of you now, knowing what you've been through, what you survived. You're very remarkable, Yanni."

I swallowed down my heart and put my hand to his cheek. "I meant what I said about wanting more with you."

He smiled under my palm. "And I meant what I said about wanting more with you too."

"Even after everything I told you?"

"Nothing can change what I feel about you."

His words struck my blood like lightning. My heart thundered. "And what do you feel about me?"

"Well, I feel that we could have something special."

There was hesitation and a hint of doubt in his voice, and even in the darkening room, I could see it on his face.

He was scared of pushing me, forcing me. "You know, I've spoken to my therapist about you."

The corner of his lip curled up. "So you said."

"And I mentioned how you like being the daddy, and I told her I like the idea of being your boy…"

His eyes widened. "You said that?"

I nodded. "She asked me what I liked about it. I told her that you make me feel safe. That I trust you to be in control, and how you know what's best for me, to keep me, well, safe. It's the best word for it."

Peter swallowed hard. "Yanni."

"It's okay. I think she was worried I'd gone from one controlling relationship to another. But it's not like that at all. It's so different. The difference being you protect me from people like him."

"I will."

I broke out a smile. "Like a good daddy should."

Peter made a sound that could only be described as a growly whimper. "Yanni, I would never hurt you."

"I know. But can we talk about how I'm not ready for anything sexual? Because it's true, I'm not. As much as I might want to, I think I'd freak out, to be honest. But sitting here with you like this, in your lap and in your arms, feels so right." I shrugged one shoulder. "Can you be patient with me while I figure this whole sex thing out?"

He put his big warm hand to my cheek. "I will give you all the time in the world. Anything you need."

I kissed his palm, then met his gaze. "So, we're doing this?"

Peter smiled. "Completely at your pace."

I leaned in closer, our noses almost touching. "So if I wanted to kiss you right now, that'd be okay?"

His breath caught. "Very."

God, this is it. With my hand still at his cheek, I slid my fingers into his hair and slowly, oh so slowly pressed my lips to his. It was soft lips, hard stubble, electric and perfect. I pulled back an inch, only to kiss him again, opening my mouth a little, tasting him on my tongue. There was a promise in his kiss, of purpose and patience.

I pulled back to see his face in the dark, his eyes heavy-lidded and his lips wet. He looked sexy as hell. Something that spoke to my insides, like I couldn't have done anything else, and I kissed him again.

Still soft, still testing my boundaries, but deeper. I tilted my head and I slowly let my tongue taste his. He groaned, and the sound shot flames through my body. Just the barest of touches, a slight caress of our tongues, and I melted in his arms. I kissed him deeper still.

Peter let me lead, taking my cues and never rushing, never pushing. Until he put his hands to my face, big but gentle, and he slowed the kiss before pulling away. He swept his thumb across my lip, his eyes trained on my mouth. "You are the sweetest thing," he murmured. Then he shifted me on his lap, adjusting my weight.

It took me a kiss-drunk moment to realize why. He was turned on. "Oh, sorry."

He let his forehead fall onto my shoulder, and he chuckled through his embarrassment. "Don't apologize."

I stroked my fingers through his hair, from his temples to the nape of his neck. "I should probably go home."

He looked up then. "Are you hungry?"

I made a so-so face. "I can eat at home."

"Or we can get disgustingly greasy burgers and fries on the way."

I snorted. "I thought you were supposed to cut back on saturated fats."

He grinned at that. "I'll hit the gym early."

I climbed off his lap and stood up, giving him room to

do the same. I followed him into the kitchen, deliberately keeping my eyes above his belt at all times. I wasn't sure what I'd do if I saw his bulge. I liked that I was the reason he was turned on, but I didn't want to push him.

He refilled Neenish's bowl with cat biscuits and grabbed his wallet and keys. "You ready?"

"Yeah."

We found a burger joint, and I convinced Peter to let me pay. It was the least I could do, and now that I'd been working for a few weeks, I had a little cash. We didn't talk about us or my past while we ate. Instead, we talked about what movies we would watch after we'd gone through the Chaplin box set. I suggested classics like *Moby Dick* and Peter suggested classic black and white spaghetti westerns, then we somehow ended up debating the difference between classic Clark Gable and Humphrey Bogart.

It was so effortless with him, and now that we'd agreed to take our relationship one step further, it seemed even easier. There was no pretense, no wondering *what if?* There was no doubt. We just slotted into this new phase.

When we pulled up in front of my place, he shut off the engine. "When can I see you again?"

"I have tomorrow night off work, but I work on Tuesday night, therapy then dinner with the Landons on Wednesday, and work on Thursday and Friday night."

"I can pick you up from work on Friday night?" He sounded so hopeful, it was hard not to smile.

"Sure. Sounds good." Then I thought of something. "What about our usual Saturday afternoons, though?"

"I'll think of something fun for us to do."

I sighed, truly happy for the first time in a long time. I stared at him for a moment, hoping he could see how happy I was. "Thank you for everything. For helping me with Jordan. You were great today, driving me to her and then driving her home. Then taking me back to your place, where I dropped a helluva bombshell on you, and you didn't even run away screaming."

Peter chuckled. "No running, no screaming."

"And you're really prepared to be patient with me?" I didn't know why I asked again. I guess a part of me expected rejection, expected to be hurt.

"I am. I was a little speechless before when you told me. I wasn't sure what to say, but I want you to know I will wait until you're ready. I like you, Yanni."

"And if I'm not ever ready?"

Peter took my hand. "It's not all about sex. I'd like to think we'd have more of a relationship than what happens —or doesn't happen—in the bedroom."

"Thank you. But just so you know, I do want to be. Ready, that is. I want to get my life back."

"You're doing great. There's no rush."

"You're kinda perfect, ya know that?"

He barked out a laugh. "Ah, no I'm not."

"You know how you told me that you have needs, regarding the whole daddy thing?"

He nodded. "Yeah?"

"Will you tell me the details of what you meant by that? Not tonight, but soon?"

He studied me for a moment. "Of course."

"Because this isn't just about me. I mean, I have... issues... that means I have needs." I cringed at how lame I sounded. "But that doesn't mean your needs aren't as important..." I let my words die off.

He squeezed my hand. "Thank you. I'll tell you every-thing you want to know. It's nothing sinister, just so you know. Though I do prefer to be upfront about it, that's all."

I let out a nervous breath and nodded. "Okay."

"I'll text you when I get home."

"Or call. I like the sound of your voice when I'm sleepy."

Peter's eyes went wide. "Oh. Okay, call it is."

I took my hand from his so I could cover my face. "That was kind of embarrassing."

He laughed. "No, not at all. I'm glad you told me!"

"I should go." He surprised me by taking the keys from the ignition. "What are you doing?"

He grinned and took off his seatbelt. "I'm walking you to your door."

I walked in front of him and stopped on the top step. I turned to face him and he was two steps down, smiling up at me. "Thank you for today," he said. "Thank you for telling me you want to get to know me. I understand that's a huge step for you, and I'm really glad you did."

"Me too."

He took one more step up, making butterflies swarm in my stomach. "Tell Jordan I said hi, and I hope she's feeling better."

"I will."

"Can I kiss you goodnight?"

I nodded, and he gently cupped my face and brought my lips to his. It was a warm kiss, with open lips and just the barest hint of his tongue. It took my breath away.

"Goodnight, Yanni."

I couldn't speak, so I giggled instead, making him laugh as he walked back to his car. I bumbled getting my key into the lock but managed to wave when he started the engine. "Night."

And with the stupidest grin and a thumping heart, I went inside.

CHAPTER FIFTEEN

SKYLAR WAS WAITING up for me when I walked into the living room, and a stab of fear went through me. "Is Jordan okay?" I asked, my hand pressed to my heart.

Her smile was illuminated from the TV. "Yeah. She made some soup for dinner and we talked. She's really embarrassed."

I sat down. "She has nothing to be embarrassed about."

"I know. I just wanted to thank you for what you did today. You really came through for her, and that means a lot."

"I told her she can call me anytime. If she ever needs someone, I'll be there."

"She said Peter was very kind."

I smiled at the mere mention of his name. "He's kinda great."

Skylar tilted her head. "Well, look at you."

"What?"

"That smile!"

I tried to pull my lips into a flat line, a pout even, but no, I couldn't. "Tonight's been a good night."

Now she raised one very surprised eyebrow. "Really?"

Realizing what she assumed, I balked. "No, not that kind of good! God, no. We just talked about stuff. Like expectations and how we both want… more."

"Oooh." She clapped her hands together. "Exciting!"

"It is. He's promised to be patient with me, but I did kiss him. Is that TMI?"

Skylar laughed and waved her hand at me. "Not at all." Then she leaned in, "So, how was it?"

"The kiss?" I swooned and fell back onto the sofa. "So good."

She chuckled. "I think George and his man had a good night too."

"Oh, really? Is Ajit still here?"

"No, he left a little while ago. George is in his room, but he was wearing a smile similar to yours."

I pressed my lips together. "And Jordan's okay?"

"Yeah, she's okay. Thanks again. It's good to know you've got her back. Know what I mean?"

I nodded. "Same goes for you and George." I shrugged. "If you ever need someone to walk to the store with you, or whatever. Just call me. I mean, I'm not tough or anything, and seriously, if some guy grabbed me like they did Jordan today, I'd freak out too. But sometimes there's safety in numbers, ya know?"

She nodded. "Thanks, man."

I looked at the TV. "What are you watching?"

"*Jumanji*. I've only seen it a hundred times, and it only has ten minutes to go, but I still have to stay till the end."

"Okay, then I'll leave you to it. I better call it a night."

"Night."

I walked upstairs and got changed, locked my door,

checked the window, and climbed into bed. I plugged my phone into the charger but kept it on my chest, knowing Peter would call soon. He was all I could think about. Our kiss on the sofa, how warm he felt, how strong and gentle he was, and how he let me lead. Then our kiss at the front door. He took the lead that time, tilting my face just so, and God, the memory of the combination of his soft kiss and rough stubble, of how he kissed me so sweetly, sent a flush of warmth through me.

Then I remembered how turned on he was when I kissed him on the couch.

The warmth pooled low in my belly, in my balls.

I let my hand creep over my dick to find it half-hard. I bent one knee so I could reach lower and lower still. I cupped my balls, squeezing just a little. My cock throbbed and I bit back a groan. It had been so long since anything had felt good.

And this felt so good.

Then my phone rang and scared the shit out of me. It was Peter, of course, and I laughed when I answered it. "Hello."

"Something funny."

"Oh, nothing." I cleared my throat. "How was your drive home? Uneventful, I hope."

"Yeah."

"Thank you for driving me around so much. You know, I can Lyft or Uber it if you need. I have some money now."

"It's fine. I don't mind at all. But if it would make you feel any better, you can buy me coffee next Saturday."

"Deal. Though it seems forever away. I know our weeks are busy, but still."

"It'll go quickly. And I'll call you at night. You like the sound of my voice when you're sleepy, apparently."

I put my free hand over my eyes. "I can't believe I told you that."

His deep, rumbling chuckle seeped into my chest. "Are you in your room?"

"In bed."

"Me too."

My heart rate spiked. God, was I supposed to respond with something suggestive? Something flirty?

"Um, well, that makes two of us." I slapped my hand over my eyes again. *Good one, Yanni. You idiot.*

Peter chuckled. "It does. Are you tired?"

"I am. It's been a crazy day, huh?"

"Yeah. A good day. Well, it ended pretty damn good."

I bit my lip, trying not to smile. "It did."

"The way you kissed me…" His voice was gruff. "You can kiss me like that any time you like."

Oh God, he was going to talk about it? "I like how you kissed me, too, at my door."

"You're very welcome."

I let my hand wander down my belly, down farther to my cock. This awakening was new and wonderful, and a little scary. I tried not to overthink it and just go with what felt good. And it did feel really good.

He talked more about going to the gym before work and what he had scheduled for work this week, and the soft melodic tune of his voice was like a lullaby.

"You're sleepy, aren't you?" he asked quietly.

"Mmmm." I let go of my dick, not wanting more, just enjoying the buzz of these new sensations without pushing myself. I didn't need to bring myself to climax. I didn't want to either. I was feeling pretty good as it was. "I told you your voice comforts me."

I was sure I heard a quiet groan, as though he liked my words. I could just imagine lying in bed with him, safe in his arms and listening to the lull of his voice until I fell asleep, and I wondered if he was imagining the same thing.

"I should let you go," Peter said softly. "Have a good day at school tomorrow."

"Mmm, 'kay. Have fun at the gym in the morning."

"I'll try."

"Don't work too hard."

"Sweet dreams, Yanni."

I was almost asleep already. "Hmm. You too."

JORDAN APOLOGIZED five times before breakfast, and after I reassured her six times that it was more than fine, we walked to the bus stop. I went to school a little early. Christopher was happily mopping the hall. "Hello, Christopher."

He looked up and smiled when he saw it was me. "Hello, Yanni!"

"How's your morning been?"

"Very good."

"Is Mr Landon here?"

Christopher nodded to the first corridor. "In his office."

"Thanks." I waved as I walked away, then knocked on Mr Landon's office door.

"Come in."

I opened the door and stuck my head around. "How's my favorite teacher?"

He brightened, eyes and smile wide. "Hey, how's my favorite student?"

I came in and sat opposite him at his desk. We chatted about how my classes were going, how much I was loving it, and how happy he was with my grades so far. But time got away from us and we were soon both running to class.

I spent Monday night getting a head start on my next assessment and listened to Peter talk about statistics and percentages until I almost fell asleep. He chuckled warmly down the phone when I mumbled the wrong response. "I'll take it as a compliment that my voice calms you, and it's not my boring day that puts you to sleep."

I chuckled. "I'm tired."

"I'll speak to you tomorrow night."

"Yes please."

He chuckled again. "Sweet dreams."

"You too."

MY APPOINTMENT on Wednesday with Patrice was probably my most productive since I started with her. I talked about how I helped Jordan and how Peter and I discussed our expectations. I told her I was saving some money, slowly but surely, and how my grades were good. She asked questions here and there and gave me advice on transitions and transference and cognitive appraisal, and she wanted me to think about and recognize how my mental fortitude had improved. She reminded me there would be bad days like Jordan had had, but even with a stumble, she was still moving forward.

As was I.

So maybe it wasn't this one session that was productive. Maybe it was all of them combined that led to this. I wasn't sure.

Before our appointment was over, she asked me if I'd taken her advice about self-pleasure. I cringed and laughed at the same time. "Not really. Kind of. I've had some good sensations, but I haven't pushed myself… to finish, if you know what I mean?"

"Orgasm is a heightened experience. Your mind might take you to pleasant places, or it might bring back some unpleasant memories. You don't need to rush anything. But you've told Peter of your concerns, and that's a really important step. Now, if things progress physically, he'll be better prepared. And you can be more relaxed."

"You make it sound like a dentist appointment."

Patrice grinned. "Not that I judge anyone, but I'm sure if it involves dentistry, you're either doing it wrong or we need to address that."

I laughed. "I'll keep that in mind."

"I'm very proud of you, Yanni," she said as our session drew to a close. "You've made great strides this week."

"Thanks. One day at a time, right?"

She smiled until her eyes squinted. "Right. Are you having dinner with the Landons again tonight?"

"Every Wednesday."

"Enjoy your evening."

"See you next week."

And dinner with the Landons was as it always was: lovely and a lot of fun.

Sarah joined us this time, and the four of us ate and laughed, and when Mrs Landon drove me home, I got the feeling she wanted to speak to me alone. We hadn't gotten to the end of their street before I was proven right.

"You look happy, Yanni," she started. "I take it the house was a great match."

"Yes. I love it. The others are pretty cool, and we all understand where we're at. But school is good too. I just love it. Even the homework!" She snorted at that. "I know, it's crazy, right?"

"I'm glad you're loving it," she said. "I just wanted to ask you, without an audience, if everything was okay?"

"Everything's kinda great right now. I don't want to jinx myself, but yeah, I'm happy."

"And Peter?"

"Peter's awesome."

She looked from the road, to me, then back to the traffic. "I can tell by the smile."

I laughed. "We've been spending a lot of time together, and we've talked about… certain things… but he knows I'm not ready, and he knows why. He's being very patient with me."

"Oh, love," Mrs Landon said with a smiley frown. "I'm so happy for you! And I'm glad he understands. He sounds wonderful."

"He really is. I worried that it might be happening too fast. I mean, it's been what, four or five months since I left… my ex? So I know it's all happening fast, and I need time to be, well, me. I get that."

"I moved in with Alan the day I left my ex," she said simply. "I had nowhere else to go, and he had the room, so it made sense." Her gaze shot to mine. "Things didn't progress between us for a while. That certainly didn't happen the day I moved in with him. But what happens when you meet the right person at the wrong time?"

"You wait?"

She gave a hard nod. "You wait. And if he's not prepared to wait, then he's not the right one."

"He said he has no problem waiting. He even said it's not about… the physical stuff." I cringed at that. "God, this is just as embarrassing to talk to you about as it is Patrice."

Mrs Landon laughed. "Oh, don't be embarrassed. I'm glad you're talking about it." She released a happy sigh.

"All that aside, if Peter knows your history and he's prepared to take things at your pace, then don't worry about the timing. There's no right or wrong. There's no gauge. You just do what feels right."

I found myself thinking about that later that night. When I got home, I'd spent time watching some stupid reality TV show with Jordan, Skylar, and George before calling it a night.

I got ready for bed, watered the orchid Peter gave me, and was admiring the pretty flower when the color reminded me of the silk gown Mrs Landon had given me. I'd forgotten all about it…

I took it out of the drawer, feeling the cool fabric slide under my fingertips. I sat down on my bed with it, just as Peter called.

"Hey," I said as I answered.

"Hey, yourself. How was your day?"

God, the sound of his voice made something warm ache in my chest. It felt a lot like longing. "I had a great day, but I didn't realize I missed you until you spoke just now."

"Oh. Well, thanks. I thought about you today."

"You did?"

"I quite often do. I wonder what you're doing in class. If you're happy. I always picture you happy. Your smile is something special."

I sighed happily. "How was your day?"

"It was good. I just said I thought of you, so it had to be good, right?" There was a smile in his voice.

"I just watered the orchid you gave me. It's very pretty." I stroked the folded gown. "Such a lovely color."

"Are you in bed?"

"Almost. Gimme one sec." I threw the phone down and pulled back my covers, slipping in between the sheets.

I picked up the phone and the gown and lay down with both. "Now I am."

He laughed. "Me too. It's been a long week. And it's only Wednesday."

"I'm looking forward to Friday. Are you sure it's not a hassle for you to pick me up and drop me back at work in the morning?"

"No hassle at all. I'm looking forward to seeing you."

"Me too." I picked up the silk gown and held it, rubbing the fabric between my fingers. Then a thought occurred to me. "I could... well, I could stay at your place on Friday night. I can sleep in the spare room, can't I?"

"Of course you can. I'd really like that. I can make you breakfast!"

The happiness in his voice squashed any doubts I had about my staying there being way too soon for me. I wanted to take my life back, and Patrice said I was making strides. I trusted Peter. I could do this. "It would be easier than you dropping me home then picking me up again, right?" I knew I was trying to justify my asking.

"I'll tell you what, I'll pick you up from work on Friday night. If you want to go home, I'll drop you home. If you want to come to my place, we can do that. No pressure."

I really liked how he gave me options. He let me control my comfort levels. And strangely enough, it only made me want to try harder for him. "Sounds good."

"How was your dinner tonight with the Landons?"

"Lovely. Sarah was there tonight. All we did was laugh. I'm very lucky to have them. They've become like a surrogate family in a lot of ways."

"That's really great."

"Well, apart from the awkward sex talk."

"The what?"

I dropped the silk gown so it fell on my chest. "Oh, I

wasn't... I didn't mean to say that. See what being tired and talking to you does? It relaxes me so much my brain doesn't work. Was that TMI?"

Peter chuckled. "No, definitely not TMI. You can talk to me about the awkward sex stuff if you want."

"Well, it'd probably be just as horrifying talking to you about it as it would be with Mrs Landon or Patrice, given you're part of the conversa—" I slapped my free hand across my eyes. "You know what, let's forget I said anything."

Peter let out a surprised laugh, a deep rumble in my ear that resonated in my chest. I moved my hand from my face down to my heart but instead of feeling my cotton shirt, I felt silk.

And I liked it.

"I'm part of the awkward sex conversation with Patrice, am I?" There was humor in his voice. Thank God.

"Yes." There was no point in lying about it. I rubbed the silk gown, feeling it slide over my chest, between my shirt and my hand. "I talk about you often. About what I want to be comfortable with and where I want to be emotionally... physically."

I heard him swallow, and when he spoke, his voice was rough and smooth at the same time. "And that involves me? Emotionally and physically?"

I lifted my shirt and put the silk directly on my chest. It was cool and warm, smooth like oil but tangible. My breath hitched. "Yes."

"Jesus, Yanni, are you touching yourself?"

I chuckled, embarrassed but not. This was such a bizarre conversation to be having, and how could I begin to describe the silk? "Kind of."

Another brief pause. "Kind of?"

"I'm taking it slow, this whole self-service thing Patrice suggested." *God, did I just say that out loud?*

"She suggested what?"

Now I *had* to fess up. "That I... *take care of myself*, if you know what I mean, before I get too far with you. So I can see how my body reacts and where my mind goes. I didn't want to be with you *in that way* and freak out on you. If you know what I mean."

"I get it. Like I said, I'll be as patient as you need."

I smiled despite my embarrassment. "Thank you." I moved my hand in circles over my chest, over my nipple, and bam! A shot of electricity jolted through me, and I groaned.

"Okay, Jesus, Yanni, I'm gonna leave you to finish doing whatever it is you're doing." He barked out a strained laugh. "You're killing me here, and as much as I want to join you over the phone, I don't think you're ready for that."

"Sorry." I wanted to ask him if he was touching himself, but I knew that wouldn't be fair. He was right. I wasn't ready to hear him pant and groan in my ear. I knew one day soon I would be, but not tonight. "Promise you'll call me tomorrow night."

His reply was husky, and it made my dick pulse. "Promise."

"Sweet dreams, Peter," I murmured.

A groaned laugh was his response before I disconnected the call. I dropped my phone to the bed and used that hand to reach down and grip my dick. I was hard. Rock hard. I was too far gone to let it subside on its own, so I stroked myself and rubbed the silk over my chest with my other hand.

But my mind went to Peter. And I imagined him on his bed, jerking his own cock with me on his mind, my name on his lips. I pictured him as he came, tweaked my nipple with the silk, and the pleasure in my balls exploded. My orgasm rocketed through me so fast, so pure, and I came in spurts on my belly.

I slumped back onto the mattress, boneless and spent. I lay there for a while in a daze and waited for memories and shame to creep in.

They never did.

BY THE TIME I finished work on Friday, I was exhausted. I was also ridiculously excited about seeing Peter. It was a little after ten when we closed the coffee shop, and his car was waiting right out front. I waved goodbye to my coworkers and slid into the passenger seat. I shoved my backpack down at my feet, closed my door, and finally looked at Peter.

He was brutally handsome. The inside of his car smelled of him, and it was heavenly to be surrounded by his scent. Any stress or worries from my week simply melted away. "Hey."

"Hi." He leaned over the center console toward me for a greeting kiss, but instead of kissing his cheek, I aimed for his mouth instead. It was warm and all too brief. Not that he seemed to mind, if his smile was anything to go by. "Okay, so am I taking you to my place or yours?"

There was no way I was going home alone tonight. "Yours."

He grinned. "Have you eaten?"

"Yeah. We sell these vegetable tarts at work that are amazing. Roasted peppers, marinated artichokes, eggplant. I swear, working in an Italian coffeehouse has its perks."

"Sounds like it."

"Have you eaten? Did you want to get something on the way?"

"I'm good. I made dinner and cooked enough for you because I wasn't sure if you would have eaten or not."

I reached out and put my hand on his arm. "Aww, thank you. I wish I had known."

"It's fine. Nothing to worry about." He turned his palm upwards in a hold-my-hand kind of way. I gladly threaded our fingers and was rewarded with an eye-crinkling smile.

He really was the very opposite to my ex. There were times when I would have been punished for not eating offered food or if I ate too much or not enough. Yet Peter truly couldn't have cared less. I loved that he thought about me.

"What did you have?" I asked.

"Stroganoff."

"Mmm, maybe I could have a little bit," I reasoned.

Peter chuckled and the sound warmed my heart. We talked about our days for the rest of the drive to his house. It was a good way to keep my mind from over-thinking, and maybe that was his intention. But when I walked into his house, the realization truly dawned on me.

I was alone with him. I was spending the night at his house. I was at his mercy.

The sound of the front door locking made me jump. Something Peter did not miss. "Are you okay?"

"Yeah." I swallowed hard and kept my backpack in front of me. "I'm fine."

But he knew I was lying. He saw straight through me. A frown pulled at his lips; concern marred his eyes. "You can leave whenever you want. If you want to go home—"

"No." I shook my head. *I could do this*.

"Okay, so tell me what to do. Do I give you some space

right now? Or do I give you a hug?" He shrugged. "I don't want to get it wrong."

I didn't know how to answer. "Um, what do you want to do?"

"I want to hold you and tell you it will be okay, but I don't want to scare you off."

All I could do was nod, and in two long strides, Peter pulled me into his arms. He was a pillar of warmth and strength and everything my soul craved. He was safety and comfort, holding me close and rubbing my back. I let my backpack fall to our feet so I could put my arms around his waist, and I melted into him.

"You're safe here," he whispered and planted a kiss on the top of my head.

I nodded against his chest. "I know. I just had a little freakout, but I'm good now."

He tried to pull away, but I kept my arms tightened around him. "I said I'm good now, not done with the hug."

He folded his arms around me again and his chuckle reverberated through his chest to my ear. "Feels good, huh?"

He had no idea how good he felt. A hug from him filled every void in me. "Very."

Eventually, reluctantly, I pulled away and he let me go. "You good now?" he asked.

I nodded. "Yes, thank you."

"Did you want some more dinner? Or just a drink?"

"I'm fine for the moment, thank you."

He relaxed a bit now, too, and looked me up and down. "I have to say, I like your work uniform."

I looked down at myself. I was wearing what I always wore to work: black dress pants, black vest, long-sleeved white shirt rolled to my elbows, and a black tie. It was my uniform. "They supply it, so I have to wear it. It's kinda fun, though, to get dressed up."

Peter gently straightened my tie. "It's sexy as hell."

"Oh." A blush crept up my neck and stole across my cheeks.

He put his fingers under my chin and lifted my face. "I've missed you this week."

"Me too. I didn't realize how much until I got into your car." I looked into his eyes and my knees went weak. "If you'd like to kiss me right now, that would be more than okay with me."

He laughed. "You are a surprise at every turn." He ran his thumb over my cheek. "One minute you look like a scared rabbit, then you're a fox the next."

"I don't mean to be."

"I know you don't. That's the surprising part."

"You still haven't kissed me."

He held my face in both hands now, gently angled my face up to his, closed his eyes, and brought his lips to mine. Soft, open, warm, and wet, it was perfect. It was the first time we'd kissed standing up, and his few inches advantage was more evident now. So was his size. His broad shoulders towered over me, his huge hands cradled my face, holding me there, yet I felt completely safe.

Adored. I felt adored.

I opened my mouth for him and tilted my head, giving him all the access he wanted. My whole body hummed when his tongue touched mine, and he made a strangled groaning sound that buckled my knees. I melted into him again and he held me up, kissing me with a tenderness and passion I'd never known.

He was hard against me, in all the right places. God, he made my body sing. I couldn't ever remember feeling this good.

Peter eventually slowed the kiss and ended by resting his forehead on mine. We were both breathless and smiling. "Wow," I whispered.

He looked dazed. "Wow, indeed."

I wanted to grab him and make him kiss me like that all night long, but I knew if I did, it would escalate to more. So I took a small step back and breathed in deep. I knew I was grinning but couldn't make myself stop. My dick was aching, and without thinking, I palmed myself.

Peter's nostrils flared, and he closed his eyes slowly before taking a step back. "How about I fix you a little dinner?"

I nodded, thinking the space would do us good. "Yeah, okay, thanks. Actually, I need to wash out my shirt so I can wear it again tomorrow, if that's okay?"

"Yes, of course. If you go change, I can wash your whole uniform and put it in the dryer, if you like."

"That'd be great." I picked up my backpack as Peter was dishing up a plate of stroganoff to reheat, and I took myself to the bathroom. I changed out of my uniform and into my pajamas and freshened up a bit. I needed to take a moment to catch my breath and to get rid of the stupid smile. I barely recognized the guy in the mirror. The light in his eyes and his grin was something I hadn't seen in years.

I needed to get a grip on myself. I needed to set some boundaries so I could stay comfortable. It was clear what my body wanted, but my head needed to catch up. So, folding up my uniform, I made my way back out to the kitchen.

Peter looked me up and down again, this time smiling at my pajamas. They were just old sweatpants and a faded T-shirt, both hand-me-downs from Mr Landon. I suddenly felt very self-conscious. "I wasn't sure what pajamas to wear…"

"You look great. Very relaxed and comfortable, which is how I want you to be, so it's perfect."

Ignoring his compliment, I held up my clothes. "Um."

We threw my uniform into the washer and were back just in time for the microwave to beep at us. I ended up sitting on the sofa with Peter, my legs curled up underneath me, and my bowl of stroganoff on my lap. Neenish sat in Peter's lap, and we watched the end of *The Godfather*. Which led to a discussion on Al Pacino, which became a critique of his best work, and we'd have probably talked until morning if the washer hadn't beeped at us to signal its work was done.

It was late and I was tired, so when Peter suggested we call it a night, I agreed. He put my clothes into the dryer and turned the lights off and showed me to the spare room. I put my backpack next to the bed and gave him a smile.

"Will you be all right?"

I nodded, not feeling as brave as I tried to be. "Sure."

"Okay. Well, I'm just across the hall if you need anything."

I walked over to him, and leaning up on my toes, I kissed him. "Thank you."

"Goodnight," he said softly, closing the door behind him.

I looked around the room. It was decorated in blacks and browns, and the bedding and furniture probably cost a small fortune. It was warm and cozy, and rationally, I knew I was safe. But something was off. The light was still on, of course, and I quickly double-checked the window was locked and everything was peaceful. I climbed into bed with my backpack and settled in but stared at the ceiling for what felt like hours.

I couldn't sleep, and the longer I lay there, the worse my insecurities became. Panic crept in like a mist, and even as tiredness became exhaustion, there was no way I was sleeping. Not here.

I had two choices: I could wake Peter and ask him to drive me home, or I could wake Peter and... what? Ask him to talk to me until I fell asleep? I almost laughed because surely he'd think I was crazy...

My heart was hammering and I was beginning to really freak out. Before it became a full-blown episode, I grabbed my backpack and ran to the door. The hall was pitch black, save the light coming from behind me. Peter's bedroom door was ajar but there was only darkness inside.

I hesitated at his door. Did I wake him? Or did I just leave? I could call a cab. I had some cash.

"Yanni?" Peter's voice startled me. I pushed on the door and could make out his silhouette. He was sitting up in bed. "What's wrong?"

"I can't sleep," I answered quickly. My voice was pitchy, my panic barely contained.

Peter reached over and switched on his bedside lamp. He'd been asleep and I felt bad for waking him. But he didn't hesitate. He flipped back the covers to his bed in invitation.

Did I want to do that? Did I want to be wrapped in his arms where I felt safe and warm? Did I want him to hold me until my heart wasn't trying to beat out of my chest? I didn't even need to answer. I simply dropped my backpack at the door and ran to his bed, sliding in beside him. And I didn't stop there. I curled right into his side. "Sorry. I didn't mean to wake you."

"It's okay. I'd rather you did than be scared by yourself." His voice was rough with sleep, and his arm settled around me. The weight of it made me feel better already.

"Is this okay?"

He shuffled a little so he was more on his side, and his arm wrapped tighter around me. I buried my face into his bare chest, breathing in his smell, and his soft chest hair felt amazing. He brushed my curly hair down and rested his face against the top of my head. "This is perfect," he murmured. "Did you want me to talk until you fall asleep? You always said it helps calm you."

I was already out like a light.

CHAPTER SIXTEEN

I WOKE up and it took me a moment to get my bearings. I was in Peter's bed, but I was alone. My heart sank when I realized he must have woken up and bolted.

But then I heard his voice, and from what I could tell, he was telling Neenish she couldn't have "any." I had no idea what the *any* was, but then I got a whiff of toast… no, not toast. Pancakes.

He was making me pancakes.

I smiled into his pillow and rolled out of bed. I had no clue what time it was, but after a quick bathroom stop, I wandered out to the kitchen.

"Good morning," I said.

"Morning," he said brightly. "You slept okay."

Was he asking me or telling me I did? I wasn't sure. "Yeah, sorry about that. I didn't mean to freak out."

He flipped a pancake and gave me a kind smile. "It was no problem. Actually, it was kinda nice. And you were asleep in no time."

I pretended I wasn't blushing but figured the best way to hide my embarrassment was to hide my face. In his chest. So I sidled up to him and slid one arm around his waist and leaned my face against his shirt. He'd showered and smelled divine. He was warm, and when he put his arm around my shoulders, it made me sigh.

"How long have you been up?" I asked.

"Since six. I'm always up at that time."

"Sorry I woke you in the middle of the night."

"Don't apologize. I'm glad you came to me." He kissed the top of my head. "I hung your uniform up in the spare room."

Work? "Oh crap! What time is it?"

Peter chuckled. "It's just after eight. You have plenty of time."

I leaned over and inspected the pancakes. "I thought you were supposed to be eating healthy?"

He chuckled again and rubbed my back before letting me go. He took those pancakes from the pan and poured in three more perfect circles of batter. "Well, I thought you might like pancakes, so I compromised. These are made from buckwheat and sweetened with honey."

"They smell great."

"Why don't you grab a shower, and by the time you get out, they'll be done."

Given my body was responding to being so close to him and I was wearing unforgiving track pants, I agreed. "Good idea."

A quick shower later, I dressed for work, minus the vest and tie, and found Peter just finished setting the table. There was coffee and juice, pancakes and sliced fruit, and yogurt. "Um, wow. You know, I'm equally good with toast."

Peter smiled and looked me over for a split second, then looked away like he didn't trust himself to not say what was on his mind. I'd washed my hair so my curls were damp and wild. I'd also used his soap and body wash. Whether he was appreciating me freshly showered or smelling like him, or the fact the top two buttons on my shirt were undone, I wasn't sure. "Feel better?" he asked, taking a seat at the head of the table.

I sat in the seat closest to his right. "Much more awake."

Peter dished up some pancakes on my plate and told me to help myself to berries and yogurt. I sipped coffee first, then piled on strawberries and blueberries, added a dollop of plain yogurt, and practically inhaled the best breakfast I'd ever had.

"I take it you liked it?" Peter asked, wiping his mouth with his napkin.

I washed it down with my coffee and leaned back to give my belly some room. "That was so good."

Peter seemed pleased that I'd liked it. Pleased that he'd provided for me, and I wanted to thank him for being everything I didn't know I needed. I got up from my seat and brazenly sat on his lap. It surprised him, but he looked up at me, happy. And that filled me with something that felt a lot like pride. Wrapping my arms around his neck, I scraped my fingers through the hair at the back of his neck. "I just wanted to say thank you."

He rubbed one hand on my back, the other sat on my knee. His eyes were a sparkling blue. "You're more than welcome."

I leaned down and kissed him, opening his lips with my own and sweeping my tongue into his mouth. He let me kiss him like that, always letting me set the pace. He could have easily picked me up and carried me to the sofa or to his bedroom—and part of me wanted him to. A pleasant ache pooled in my belly at the thought—but he ever so patiently let me take charge.

When I pulled back, his pupils were blown and he licked his bottom lip. I put my hand to his cheek and kissed him again, chastely this time. "I thought a proper thank you was in order."

He chuckled and shifted in his seat. I wondered if he was turned on. I couldn't feel anything from how I was sitting, but I secretly, selfishly hoped he was. Like I was.

This was all so new to me. Part of me felt like I was careening out of control, and part of me loved every second.

He looked up at me like I was a puzzle to be solved. "You're doing the rabbit/fox thing again. Timid one minute, bold the next."

"Is it confusing you?" I asked. "Because it's confusing me. I have *never* been so brave. If you'd have seen me a year ago, you'd never believe..." I stopped that train of thought and shook it out of my head. "But with you, it feels right. I can't explain it. I want to make you happy because it makes me happy." I searched his eyes. "If it's too much, if *I'm* being too much, please tell me."

Now he put his hand to my jaw, gentle and reassuring. "Everything you're doing is right. I don't want to push you. I want to let you lead. I'm perfectly happy with where we're at. If anything, we're moving a little faster than I thought you would. If you want to explore, that's fine, but I'm okay with slowing down if you need."

"I don't know what I'm doing. I'm just going with what feels right. I don't want you to think I'm being a tease."

He smiled. "You're not a tease. I understand where you're coming from. And I'm very glad this feels right for you. You can crawl into my lap anytime you like."

I let my cheek rest against the top of his head and just enjoyed the moment for what it was: me needing comfort and him giving it. *Like a good daddy should.*

I spoke into his hair so he couldn't see my face. "Will you tell me about what a good daddy does? What it means?"

I felt him freeze for a second, so I quickly added, "You said you would. And I keep thinking about it and how you do everything for me like a good daddy should, but I don't even know if I'm on the right page."

Peter pulled back, making me look at him. "I'll explain everything. We can talk about it tonight if you want?"

I needed to know. "Yeah."

"But this right here," he said, meaning me on his lap, "makes me very happy. You coming to me last night because you were scared, makes me very happy."

I kissed his temple. "Makes me happy too."

"I better get you to work, though, or you'll be late. And we can talk about everything tonight. Is that okay?"

I smiled and kissed his lips. "Yep." I jumped off his lap and took some plates to the kitchen before grabbing my backpack from Peter's room. I did the buttons up on my shirt, took my necktie, and popped my collar up, but before I could get started, Peter gently took over.

"Let me." With all the care and devotion in the world, he made the perfect knot. His big hands carefully folded the material with finesse, his eyes trained on what he was doing. It was such a beautiful moment between us. He turned my collar back down, and looking rather pleased with himself, he smiled. "All done."

I put my vest on and buttoned it up. "Look okay?"

"Incredible."

I looked at the light in his eyes, then to his lips. "Can you kiss me now before we get in the car? Because that center console gets in the way."

He certainly didn't need to be asked twice. With one

hand around my jaw and the other around my waist, he pulled me to him and crushed his mouth to mine.

Jesus, he could kiss.

When his body pressed against me and I felt the hardness of his erection, I groaned, he grunted, and my entire brain stopped working. Short-circuited, zero transmissions. My reactions were instinct only, purely motivated by what my body wanted.

I raked my hands up his sides so I could hold his face. I gave him my tongue and he took it gratefully. But all too soon, he pulled away. He put his hands on my hips and put a noticeable distance between us. He was breathing heavily, his lips were red and wet, and he looked crazed with want.

"We better cool it," he said breathily. "Or it's going to get out of hand."

"I want to climb you like a tree."

He blinked, then snorted. "Right."

"Sorry. My brain's not working right now." I took some deep breaths and hoped my work pants hid my hard-on. "But yes, I'm glad you stopped. Or there would likely be tree climbing."

Peter laughed but took in a deep breath. "Okay, we better get going."

The drive to my work was pretty quiet. It had been such a good night and morning. I think we were both happy with our progress. We held hands over the console, and when he pulled up near my work, we made plans for him to come past my place around three that afternoon.

And work was good. Busy and fun, and I loved chatting with my coworkers and with customers, but all I could really think about was Peter. He was going to tell me tonight about what being a daddy meant for him and therefore, what he kind of expected of me.

If sitting on his lap and sleeping in his arms made him happy, then holy hell, we were golden. Because it made me really freaking happy. And if he wanted to kiss me like that all day long, I'd happily oblige.

I couldn't help but notice, though, his fascination with my tie, and I wondered if that leaked into some schoolboy fantasy, and I had to admit... I didn't like that.

It was a little niggle in the back of my mind that crossed underage-consent lines, and that wasn't a good thing. I needed to wait to see what he divulged tonight, and I needed to ask the right questions.

I was also very aware that things between us, physically, were moving pretty fast. I mean, it was my pace. I knew that. And I wanted it. I wanted more. And I knew tonight, all things going well, there was a very good chance there would be more.

Which was why, when the doorbell rang at three o'clock, I was a bundle of nerves.

I opened the door and my stomach did that swoopy thing it did every time I saw him. "Hi," I said breathily. I gave him a quick peck on the lips and welcomed him inside.

"How was work?" he asked.

I grabbed his hand and led him into the living room. "Good. How was your day?"

"Fine." Then he noticed Skylar and Jordan sitting on the sofa. "Oh, hello!"

They each waved and said, "Hi." Then Skylar grinned at me. "So, Yanni, can we expect you home tonight?"

My face flamed. "Uh, yeah. I'll be home tonight." I glanced at Peter. "Jordan and I have laundry duty in the morning."

Jordan gave me a smile, and Skylar brightened. "Oh, I could go too. I have some laundry to do."

"Cool," I said. I turned to Peter. "We ready?"

He gave a nod, then waved to the girls. "See you later."

We drove to Peter's place, our hands joined on his thigh. "So, what do you have planned for us today?" I asked.

"I found a Shakespeare in the Park I thought looked good, but it's on tomorrow. So today, I wondered if our usual Charlie Chaplin movie thing would be okay? I bought some fish and thought we could grill some dinner."

"Sounds great. I hope you didn't mind me saying I can't stay tonight. I don't want Jordan to think I'm bailing on her."

"No, it's fine. As much as I want to monopolize your time, you shouldn't ignore your friends."

"Jordan, in particular. I don't want her to feel abandoned."

Peter squeezed my hand and gave me a smile. "You're a good friend. Though she and Skylar looked cozy together."

I shot him a look. "As in… cozy?"

He chuckled. "Yes."

"Oh." I hadn't thought of that, but now that he mentioned it, since Jordan's little episode last weekend, Skylar had been very present around Jordan. Actually, even before then, but since last weekend in particular. They ate dinner together, watched TV together, and I'd noticed them talking more. The idea made me smile. "I hope so."

We pulled up at Peter's house, and he said, "And I haven't forgotten your request. I thought, if you want, I could show you a few things."

"Show me?"

"Online," he added quickly. I must've looked as shocked as I sounded. "Just online. Not me personally."

"Oh." I relaxed a little.

He pulled our joined hands up to his lips and kissed my knuckles. "Trust me, Yanni. I would never throw you into a situation you're not comfortable with."

"I do trust you. I'm just a little nervous."

"Don't be." He got out of the car and waited for me to do the same, and he showed me to his front door. Neenish met us inside, and Peter quickly scooped her up. I gave her a pat and a scratch, and Peter put Neenish down so he could dump his keys and wallet on the kitchen counter. "What did you want to do first? Movie? Something to eat or drink? Or did you want to get this talk over with?"

My nerves were going to get the better of me. "Um…"

Peter came over and took both my hands. "It's nothing scary, I promise. But if you don't want to do it now, or today, or this week, then that's fine. We'll watch a movie, cook dinner, whatever. There's no pressure."

"I want to."

"But?"

"No buts. I want to. I want to learn what makes you happy, and what you might expect of me. I'm just nervous. And I do trust you. It's my reaction I don't trust."

He frowned. "What do you mean?"

"Well, it's that rabbit or fox thing. I'm thinking I'll either want to go home or I'll want to do the tree-climbing thing."

Peter chuckled, but his smile soon became a frown. "I don't want to lose you over this. If anything worries you, we'll talk about it." He sighed heavily and took my hand. "Come on, let's get this all out in the open."

He led me to the sofa and sat me down. He grabbed his laptop off the dining table, sat down with me, and put it between us but didn't open it. "I thought it might be easier to show you some pictures or videos that might help so you can see visually, but I want to explain a few things first."

God, here we go. "Okay."

"I need you to understand that the daddy lifestyle is a whole spectrum, and what I particularly enjoy is just a very small part of that. Some are hard-core, and that's fine for them. But that's not for me. What we've been doing already is perfect for me. There are things I'd like to be a part of our relationship, but they aren't necessary. It's not a Master-slave dynamic. You would be on equal footing with me, always. Everything must always be consensual, and that goes both ways."

I nodded slowly. "Okay, so what things would you like to have part of our relationship?"

"There are things that I do want, and things that I don't want. And I'm sure you're exactly the same." Peter frowned, and he wrung his hands in his lap. He was clearly trying to choose his words carefully to get this right. "It's probably easier if we said what our ideal relationship would be. Bearing in mind not many people get their ideal relationship. There's always compromise; there has to be."

He took a deep breath and let it out slowly. "My ideal partner would be younger than me. And he would need me." He frowned at that. "I like to provide and care for. I would make sure you're looked after, that your needs are met."

I was confused. "What's the catch? I keep waiting for the horrible part, but that all sounds pretty good to me."

Peter laughed quietly and shook his head. "Well, some twenty-one-year-olds don't like the idea. I'm a homebody. I don't drink or go clubbing. They just turned twenty-one and find the idea of monogamy... well, they might find it too restrictive or confining. They want freedom, and I totally understand that."

I thought about that for a moment. "You know, my therapist asked me what I found so appealing about older guys, and you know what I told her? That sometimes when you find someone who takes care of you the right way and they take charge and look after you like a good daddy should, that's where the freedom is." I swallowed hard. "For me, when I'm with you, I trust you to take care of me, and I feel… free."

Peter searched my eyes for the longest moment. He seemed to get a little choked up, and it took him a while to speak. "That's all I could ever ask for."

"Can I ask some questions?"

"Please."

"Your ex, did you have that with him?"

He shook his head. "Not really. I think he thought it was fun in the beginning, but it wasn't what he wanted. I was blind to it because I wanted it so badly."

"You wanted him so badly?"

"No. I wanted the kind of relationship that we have. That's what I wanted badly. His name was Duncan, but he never understood. Not like you do."

"Next question. When you say you like young men, how young are we talking?" I cringed, but I needed to ask this. "My age? Or school age?"

Peter looked… aghast. There really was no other word for it. Possibly horrified, a little offended.

"I only ask because you seemed quite fixated on my tie, and I wondered whether it was a preppy schoolboy fetish, and I don't want you to be upset, but this is something I have to ask because that is not okay with me."

He took a minute, probably to get the words right in his head before he said them out loud. "I have only ever been attracted to men. When I was eighteen, I dated eighteen-year-olds. When I was twenty-one, I dated twenty-one-year-olds. But as I got older, the guys who caught my eye were still twenty-one. I liked twinks, guys with boyish looks, but still men. Men who prey on young boys are sick and should be institutionalized where they can't hurt anyone."

I relaxed, but then something occurred to me. "Will there come a time when I'm too old? I won't always be twenty-one."

Peter gave me a half smile and shook his head. "It's not all about age. It's about the relationship and how you would need me to care for you and how I'd look after you."

I let that mull over in my mind for a minute. "Sorry for all the questions."

"Please, don't apologize. You asking questions means that you're not taking this lightly. That you're not going into this blindly. I want you to be aware, and I want you to ask questions."

"Thank you."

"And for the record, the reason I was so fixated on your tie, or your whole work uniform, really, is because it's sexy as hell."

"Oh." I felt my cheeks heat, and he smiled. "It's just a vest and necktie."

"Well, to you, maybe. But those pants hug your ass perfectly. The vest highlights your tiny waist, and the tie makes you look sharp. The black matches your hair, and the white shirt contrasts with your skin."

It was suddenly very warm, and I figured now was a good time as any to ask. "Which brings me to my next question. What's the sex side of it?"

"It's not just sex. There's a whole physical component. And like I said before, if you're not ready for anything sexual, that's okay."

"But your ideal relationship, in a perfect world, would include sex?"

His eyes flinched a little, but he looked me right in the eye when he answered. "It would. I won't lie to you. But I can also honestly say that sitting with you here the other day, with you curled up in my lap, was satisfying to me too. On a different level. An emotional level more than a physical one. But I enjoyed it very much."

"I liked it too. It was the first time I'd ever done that, ever. But it felt… right."

He gave me a shy smile. "I think you get the dynamics more than you realize."

"I don't know about that, but I know what makes me feel safe." Which was all good and well, but I needed to know more. "I know I said I'm not ready for sex, and at the moment, that still stands. But I think it's fair to admit that I'm really liking the physical side of what we've done so far, and I'd like to do more. So I need to know… what about sex?"

His cheeks flushed a little. "Okay, so I thought you might ask this. Well, I hoped you would. And I thought it might be easier to show you rather than tell you." He picked up his laptop and opened it. "There are some sites dedicated to dads and sons. They're a safe space, with forums where dads can talk and sons can talk with other sons. But there's also pictures or viewing galleries."

"Porn?"

"Not all of it. Some are, some aren't. You don't have to click on any videos if you don't want."

Oh, God. I was pretty sure I was blushing from my head to my toes.

"Then there are some other sites which are strictly photos and videos. Some are… well, some are strictly porn, but some are more focused on the relationship side of it."

He clicked on a few things and opened up a few different tabs, then handed his laptop over to me. "Scroll through, take a look. And remember, don't click on anything you don't want to." He stood up. "I'll be in the kitchen making a start on dinner." He leaned down and kissed my forehead before he left me to it. "If you have any questions, just ask."

Part of me was very curious to see, and I was grateful he was giving me some privacy and some time to do this at my own pace. The first page was, as Peter had said, a dads and sons site. There were tabs for forums and other stuff, but I clicked on the gallery tab and was immediately privy to all sorts of photos. There were happy, smiling selfie photos of couples at landmarks, cuddled up on sofas, in bed. Some were clothed, some were shirtless, some, from what I could tell, possibly completely naked. But each couple consisted of one older guy and one younger. They each signed their names and age. *Hugh 46 & Scott 27. Ahmad 39 & Bijan 24. Colin 62 & Than 48.*

They all looked so fucking happy, it made my heart happy and ache at the same time.

I scrolled further down and my eyes almost bugged out. It was a photo of a couple having sex. The younger guy was on his stomach, on a bed, with his legs spread, and his partner lying over him between his thighs. Both were naked, and from the expression of ecstasy on the older man's face, it was very obvious he was mid-climax. But it was the expression on the younger man's face that struck me. It was a look of pure bliss. Not even bliss. Maybe fulfillment was a better word. He looked utterly serene.

The caption read, *My boy knows his place and he loves it. Wayne 45 & Kirk 36.*

Well, I wasn't entirely sure what Wayne meant by "my boy knows his place" but Kirk certainly was loving it.

I kept scrolling. There were more couple photos. One couple on a beach, shirtless and grinning in the tropical sunshine with the caption, *Daddy treats me so good! Holiday in Spain for my birthday! Albert 51 & Roberto 36.*

Another couple was at a bar, another at a restaurant. One more where an older guy sat on a recliner and his boy lay curled up on his lap, his smile peaceful. *My Daddy loves me*, the caption read.

Further down, there was a photo of a man leaning over the edge of a bed. His feet were on the floor, he wore underpants that were pulled to one side, and he looked back to the camera, his smile playful and coy. The caption read, *Waiting for Daddy. Marcello 29 & Brett 46.*

There were comments, so I clicked on them. *Such a good boy. Lucky Daddy. How all sons should greet their dads. My Daddy loves me like this.*

The list went on.

I went back to scrolling the pictures and found more and more sex shots. A hairy torso with a view down to the pale ass he was buried in. *Such a good boy. Keith 53 & Piers 24.*

A close up of a guy's face, his eyes wide and serene, his lips around a cock, all the way to the pubic hair, deep-throating. *Keeping Daddy happy. Tyrone 24 & Ken 38.*

A close-up selfie of a couple in bed. The younger guy was sound asleep, his face buried in a pillow of chest hair. *My boy works so hard. Love him to bits. Patrick 49 & Jin 27.*

Another photo of a younger guy, wearing nothing but a towel around his waist, a face full of shaving cream, and a huge grin. He was laughing at something, and the mirror behind him showed the reflection of the photographer. An older guy was holding a phone camera with a razor in his hand. They looked ridiculously happy. *Another day in paradise. Victor 42 & Tito 25.*

I leaned back on the sofa and took a moment to process what I'd seen. They were clearly all very happy. Some had large age gaps, some didn't. Peter was right. It wasn't about age. They all varied; there was no right or wrong. It was more about body size; some of the daddies were bears, some weren't, but they were all bigger than their partners. The younger men were slight, smaller in stature. They looked young, had little to no body hair, youthful faces.

Like me.

And I was now aware of one thing.

I really liked it. I had a warm-all-over feeling that felt like familiarity, like finding my people.

I clicked on the forum tab, and there were topics like General Discussions for both older and younger guys, but then more select topics like Keeping Your Daddy Happy or What Your Boy Needs.

I would need a week to read through those, so I memorized the URL address and selected the next site tab Peter left open for me. It was a Tumblr blog with a terrible name, but the pictures… well, they weren't terrible at all.

Mostly sexual, mostly explicit. "Uh, do you visit this site often?"

Peter chuckled from the kitchen. "I take it you found the second tab?"

"Mmm." I wasn't ignorant of porn. Before I was thrown out of my childhood home, I'd spent a lot of my teen years mastering free porn sites and deleting my browser history. But this was different. This was specialized like it was made just for me.

Holy hell, it was hot.

There weren't just men in various sexual situations,

they were daddy/son couples, and they were fucking and sucking, gripping and kissing. Faces of pleasure, surrender, giving and taking. There were corded necks and white knuckles, lips parted and eyes rolled closed. And if the photos weren't hot enough, there was thumbnail after thumbnail of videos waiting to be clicked on.

I picked the first one and suddenly loud moaning, grunting, and bodies slapping together came blaring out of the laptop. "Jesus, make it stop!" I stabbed a few buttons in a panic and thankfully manage to hit pause.

Peter's laughter followed. "Watch whatever you want, Yanni," he called out. He didn't come out of the kitchen.

I found the volume button and turned it down real low before I hit Play again. The scene started to roll, and warmth pooled in my groin. *God help me.* The younger guy was bent over the back of a sofa; his daddy was taking him, taking what he wanted. The smaller guy's back was arched, and huge, strong arms wrapped around his chest while the bigger guy impaled his lover with his cock. The smaller man's feet barely touched the floor. His cock hung limp and heavy. "Been a good boy?" the bigger man grunted as he fucked him.

"Yes," the younger man said desperately.

The older man thrust hard. "Do you deserve your reward?"

"Yes, Daddy, please give it to me."

The daddy roared as he came, filling his boy with his reward. The younger man cried out, not coming, but his pleasure was very real.

Jesus, Lord have mercy.

My own cock throbbed and my mouth was dry. I wanted what they had. When I was ready, and if Peter would do it. If my balls had any say in it, I was ready right now.

So I clicked on the next one.

And my blood ran cold. On screen was a twink getting fucked savagely; the top was brutal. Holding him down, slapping him, punishing him. "You'll take my fucking cock," the top growled, then spat at him. "And you'll learn your fucking place, boy."

"Peter!" I pushed the laptop off me. Cold dread filled me. "Peter!"

I heard something drop into the sink, and Peter came running. He took one look at the screen, of the boy being beaten and raped, and quickly shut the computer. He sat beside me and pulled me into his lap. "No, no," he whispered. He held my face to his neck and rocked back and forth a little. "I'm sorry you saw that. I should have screened those first. That's not what I want. That's not what I meant to show you."

We stayed like that then, quiet and soothing, until my heart calmed. "Why would he do that to him?" I asked.

Peter kissed the side of my head. "Sometimes the younger man wants domination. Sometimes the older man wants to give it."

I looked up at him and shook my head. He no doubt saw the fear in my eyes. "No."

He caressed my cheek with the softest touch. "No, not all of them. Not me." He kissed my forehead. "Not you, my beautiful boy."

I put my head back to his chest. "I can't go through that again."

He stroked my hair, comforting me, reassuring me. "I would never hurt you. I will never. I promise you that."

I took a deep breath and let the sound of his heart in my ear calm me. Peter rubbed my back, his voice was soft and warm. "I just wanted you to see the couples having dinner, on vacation, watching TV. I wanted you to see how natural it can be. I'm sorry you saw that video. That site is normally pretty clean. I'm sorry."

I shivered, and he tightened his arms around me. It wasn't his fault, and admittedly I felt better just being in his arms. "It's confusing."

"What is?"

"That something like that can scare me so much, yet you make me feel safe."

"What you saw in that video is not what I'm asking of you. That is not us. This right here," he said, kissing the top of my head again, "this is us. You said I make you feel safe?"

I nodded against his neck.

"That's all I want for you. We don't need to be any more physical than we are right now."

I thought about that for a moment. "I liked everything I saw before that last video," I admitted. He gave me a bit of a squeeze but waited for me to continue. "I saw how it wasn't an age thing. Some boys were in their forties, their daddies were just older."

He replied with a kiss to my hair and kept rubbing my back.

"It was more of a body stature thing. The younger guys were always smaller."

"Most of the time, yes. Sometimes they're bigger. There's a whole spectrum, many different aspects."

"Including that dominance thing?"

He held me tight for a while. "If it's what they want, if it's consensual… Sometimes it's the boy who will dominate the dad. But I don't truly understand that psychological need. It's not my thing."

"It's not mine either." I shuddered. "But this is nice."

Peter huffed a bit of a laugh. "It is."

I looked up at him. "Sorry for freaking out."

He frowned. "Please don't apologize. It's me who's sorry. I put you in a situation that wasn't good for you, and I feel horrible."

I kissed his lips softly. "You're making me feel better already."

Neenish chose that exact moment to jump up on me and plonked herself on my lap. I was curled up on Peter; I guessed it was only fair she curled up on me. "I guess we'll just have to stay like this for a while now."

Peter hummed contentedly and gave me a squeeze. "If you say so."

CHAPTER SEVENTEEN

PETER DROVE me home after dinner. He didn't mention the video again, except to say sorry for the twentieth time as he drove. I waited for him to pull up before I leaned over and gave him a kiss. "Can you call me when you get home?" I asked.

He looked at the steering wheel, resigned. "If you don't want to see me anymore, you can just tell me."

"What?"

"After tonight—"

"After you helped me because I freaked out after seeing some random post on the internet?"

He tilted his head, his eyebrows knit together. "After I gave you material to watch that was harmful."

"I could have easily looked that up on my own and freaked out by myself. But you were there and talked me down. I want you to call me because it helps me fall asleep."

He smiled now, still a little sadly, though, and that made my heart hurt. "And tomorrow?"

"Are we still going to watch Shakespeare in the Park? I'd really love to see it."

"Anything you want."

I leaned over and kissed him again. "I want to spend the day with you. Well, after laundry duty."

He smiled more genuinely now. "Okay."

JORDAN and I took our usual trip to the laundromat after breakfast, though this time Skylar came too. And the more I saw them together, the more I was convinced that I was witnessing the budding of something beautiful.

If Jordan was like me, then Skylar was like Peter.

She gave Jordan a safe place to be herself, a place of understanding and comfort, and Jordan's smiles were becoming more and more frequent.

They asked me how things with Peter were going, and I told them all about last night. I explained how I'd wanted to know more about the daddy/son relationships and he offered me some websites. They were more about couples, and I wasn't even embarrassed to admit there was some porn. "Most of it was gentle and loving, but there was one that wasn't. And I totally freaked out."

Jordan put her hand on my arm. "God. Are you okay?"

"Yeah, I'm fine. He totally talked me through it and calmed me down."

"Oh, God," Skylar said, concerned. "How awful."

"Yeah, the video was pretty graphic, and a bit too real. If you know what I mean…" I frowned, remembering. "He blames himself for me seeing it."

"You really like him, don't you?" Jordan asked.

I nodded. "I do." I fought a smile. "He's kinda great."

Skylar and Jordan both smiled at me, and we finished our laundry talking happily about school and friends and what our plans for the week were. We headed home and hadn't been there long when Peter arrived. I welcomed him with a kiss, he came in, and I continued my conversation with Jordan and Skylar about dinner and recipes, and Peter slotted in easily. There was nothing false, nothing forced, just a simple chat between friends.

Then there was a knock at the door. "It's me, George. I forgot my keys."

"I'll get it," I said, frowning. That wasn't like him. I opened the door and he came in, his dark hair a curtain over his face. He looked at the floor.

He spoke to the floor. "Thanks."

He made for the stairs, but I stopped him. "George, wait?" He stopped but wouldn't look up. "Everything okay?" I waited for him to raise his face, and I half expected to see a black eye or a cut lip. Old habits, I guess.

But he wasn't hurt. He was crying. His mascara ran in lines down his cheeks.

I held his arm. "God, what happened?"

He took a sharp breath, and I thought he was going to dismiss me and race upstairs, but he let out a sob. "Ajit... He introduced me to his family." He shook his head. "But they said no."

Oh no.

"I'm not Sri Lankan enough apparently." He snorted through his tears. "Or at all, really? But can you believe that? It's not bad enough I get disowned by my own family for not being the right sexuality, and now I'm thrown out of his because I'm not the right nationality. Now being gay is fine!" He threw up his hands. "But I'm still not good enough!"

By this time, Jordan and Skylar were both standing behind me, and Peter was standing behind them.

George scrubbed at his face and let his head fall back. He groaned at the ceiling. "Fuck them!"

"Come and sit with us," I urged. "Don't be alone right now."

He allowed himself to be led to the sofa, and we all sat down. George told us how he'd been so excited to meet Ajit's family. They'd been doing so well. They were together six months and things were good between them. Ajit understood him, he said. He thought they were long-term. "Ajit was nervous. He said his mother might not be too happy, but she'd deal, ya know? I even cut back on the eyeliner, took one ring out." He tongued his lip. "I wanted them to like me."

No one spoke for a moment because we'd all been there. We'd all experienced the disappointment and heart-break of not having unconditional love from our families. Peter had his hand low on my back, his thumb reassuring me that he was hearing what wasn't being said.

"Where's Ajit now?" Skylar asked.

George frowned. "He was in a screaming match with his mother, and I had to bail. I couldn't be there." He looked at each of us, his eyes red, sadness etched on his face. "I won't be the reason he loses them. I can't… I won't let him go through what I went through."

It was then I noticed that Skylar and Jordan were sitting very closely on the sofa together, just as there was a knock on the door.

We all looked at each other, wondering who it could be. "I'll get it," Peter said, standing up.

He opened the front door, and I heard a quiet mumble before Ajit appeared in the doorway, Peter behind him. Poor Ajit looked a wreck. He was a wild mess; his eyes were puffy and his hair looked like he'd run the whole way here.

George slowly stood up.

"I'm sorry for what happened," Ajit said, his eyes watering. "If they say they can accept me, they can accept all of me. And that includes you."

George shook his head. "You can't lose your parents."

"I won't. I'm as stubborn as my mother. Dad was already okay when I left, and I know he'll talk her 'round," he said quickly. "George, I love you."

George crossed the floor and hugged Ajit in a crushing embrace, both of them crying.

"Awwww," Skylar said, wiping her eyes with her sleeve. "Goddammit."

George and Ajit broke apart with a bit of a laugh, embarrassed they'd had an audience for the whole thing. "Thanks, guys," George said, looking at us. "But we might —" He looked up the stairs and at Ajit, whose hands were fisted in George's shirt, and giggled. "We ah, we need to talk about stuff…" And they raced upstairs.

"Talk about stuff?" I snorted. "Is that what they're calling it these days?"

Jordan laughed. "That was so sweet!"

"It really was," Skylar agreed.

Peter was standing back a bit, but he was smiling sweetly. "That was a privilege to witness."

I walked over to him and slid my hand around his waist, sinking into half a hug. That instant contented feeling washed over me. I hummed at the contact, not caring that Jordan and Skylar were watching.

Peter breathed in deep like my touch soothed him too. "Did you want to go to the outdoor theater or stay here?"

I looked up at him. "The theater. Do we still have time?"

He gave a nod. "But we'd better go soon."

"I'm ready to go." I broke away and turned to face our audience. Jordan and Skylar were both watching, smiling. "I won't be home too late."

Jordan gave me a smile. "Have fun."

Skylar grinned. "Not too much fun." She gave me a wink, and I stuck my tongue out at her. I grabbed my keys and they were already discussing what they were going to cook for dinner as we left.

The outdoor theater was incredible. It was basically a massive picnic in front of a small stage with curtained wings. Everyone had blankets laid out, some fold-up chairs toward the back, and Peter found us a lovely spot to the side. Of course he'd come prepared. A blanket for us to sit on, a picnic basket full of crackers, grapes, cheese, and figs.

"Wow," I said, duly impressed. "You spoil me."

"I aim to, yes."

The stage director announced the play was about to start, and we sat shoulder to shoulder with our legs outstretched. We ate our picnic and sipped on sparkling water and watched the first act of *The Merchant of Venice*.

It was incredible.

For the second act, I maneuvered myself to sit between his legs, leaning against his chest. "You all right now?" he asked, his smile was the eye-crinkling kind.

"I am now."

His deep chuckle vibrated on my back. And it turned into one of the best afternoons of my life. The play was perfection, the company even more so. When the last curtain call was done, other people were packing up, but I didn't want to move.

"Ah, Yanni. Did you want to get up?"

"No, actually. I'd rather stay just here."

Peter laughed and kissed the side of my head. "I'm not

terribly opposed to staying like this either, but maybe we should do it at home instead."

People were eyeing us as they walked past, but I somehow didn't mind. After one particularly nosey woman walked past, staring, I waited until she'd gone, then said, "I think they're trying to guess if we're related or if we're a couple."

I left the daddy and son aspect unsaid.

"Let them guess." Peter shifted underneath me. "My butt's gone to sleep."

"Oh." I got up and held out my hand, helping him to his feet. "Poor Daddy. Are you all right to drive, or should we walk it off for a while?"

Smiling, Peter rolled his eyes. "Help me pack up."

When we got everything packed away and we got into the car, I took Peter's hand and rested it on my knee and entwined our fingers. I had no intention of letting it go. "I've had the very best afternoon, thank you."

"It was great, wasn't it? And the play was fantastic."

"We should make that our new thing," I said. "Given our Chaplin movies are running out, we should do this on a Sunday instead."

Peter seemed very happy with that idea.

He was also very happy with my idea of cozying up on the couch when we got back to his place. In my defense, we had started to watch TV, but it was some stupid reality show and I was much more interested in my own reality. I was snuggled in under his arm and he was warm and smelled really good, and we still had so much to work out. I know I'd said I needed to take things slow, but it was also killing me. So, plucking up the courage, I lifted his arm off my shoulder, swung my leg around, and straddled him. He was obviously surprised but smiling, so I assumed it was okay. I kissed him softly. "Can we talk about what happened yesterday?"

We hadn't discussed yesterday's freak out today at all, and I thought we should.

"I really am sorry you saw that. I should have screened the first few pages——"

"No." I shook my head. "I want to talk about the photos and videos I watched before that one."

"Oh." His eyebrows knit together. "Did you have questions? I should have asked, sorry."

"I needed some time to process it." That was very true. I'd thought about everything I'd seen and read, and when I was in bed this morning, I searched the site with the forums and read a lot of the posts where other young guys had asked questions about their older partners. It was a very insightful look into the daddy/son dynamics. Sure, there were questions and some posts were a bit too bizarre for me, but the majority of sons just wanted to make their daddy happy. They yearned to please him, the satisfaction coming from someplace deep within, and the more I read, the more I related.

No, I didn't fully understand it. But I identified with it.

"I'm sure I'll have questions at some point, but I think it's more a case of us finding our feet as we go along. But the photos I saw, I liked very much. The few videos I watched, I liked very much." I wriggled on his lap, grinding down a little, just to prove my point.

He let his head fall onto the back of the sofa and he laughed. "Oh, if you were unclear at all, about the fox and rabbit analogy I used to describe you, you should know this is definitely a fox moment."

I kissed him with smiling lips. "And I can't promise when the next rabbit moment will be, but I'm definitely feeling the fox moment." I kissed him again, harder and deeper, and rolled my hips into him.

We kissed like that until I was rubbing on him shamelessly. It felt so damn good. He kept his hands gentle, holding my hips, my back, my thighs. And when he cupped my face and slowed the kiss to a stop, he held me still while he caught his breath. I could feel his erection when I rubbed against him, and I was so incredibly turned on.

"God, Yanni. You're killing me." He closed his eyes. "Just give me a second."

I climbed off him, and lying back, I slowly pulled him with me. To his credit, he kept his weight off me, our faces just a few inches apart. "This is not helping."

"I want to feel your body on top of mine," I told him. "I want to take these next steps. I can't guarantee I won't ask you to stop, though."

"If you tell me to stop, I will stop." He looked at me with such honesty in his eyes. "I promise."

"I want to feel how strong and safe you are."

He crushed his mouth to mine, and ever so slowly, he lowered himself onto me. And sweet Mary, mother of God, it felt good.

He slid his arms under my shoulders, holding me while devouring me with his kiss. I spread my legs as wide as the sofa allowed, and Peter fit snug and perfect. I could feel how turned on he was. He could no doubt feel my erection too. I ground my hips against his and a shudder rolled through him.

He pulled his mouth from mine, only to kiss my ear. "Is this okay?"

"Yes."

Then down my neck. "Is this okay?"

"God yes."

The truth was, it all felt good. Everything Peter did felt

right. He was nothing like my ex. If I was waiting for bad memories to pummel me if Peter touched me a certain way, it never happened.

I bucked my hips, searching for that elusive pleasure that was building and building. With my hands on Peter's face, I brought his lips back to mine. "I need to… I want you to…" God, I thought I'd die if I had to say this out loud.

Still with his arm under my shoulders, his warm hands cupped my face. His eyes were the darkest blue, an ocean of lust and worry, his lips red and wet. "Do you want to stop?"

"No."

"Then tell me," he urged gently. "What do you want?"

"I'm close, and I want you to not stop."

"Do you want to come like this? Or do you want me to touch you?"

Oh God.

"Touch me."

He kissed me first, soft and open-mouthed, gentle. Then he leaned off me, making room, and he watched my eyes as he lowered his hand, down, down. He expertly popped my jeans button with one hand, kissing tenderly and still watching my every reaction. Then he undid my fly, and I thought I might die if he didn't move any faster.

Then he palmed me, over my briefs, and I bucked into his touch. "Oh my God."

"Feel good?"

"So good."

He kissed me deeper at that, slowly slid his fingers beneath my briefs, and wrapped his fingers around my cock. He watched my eyes, waiting for any flicker of doubt or fear.

There wasn't any.

I closed my eyes and let bliss take me. I gave myself away to the feel of his hand, to the pleasure coiled tight and the heat pooling in my belly. "God, Peter."

"Oh, Yanni, you're so beautiful," he murmured against my lips while he gently pumped my cock.

And with that, I came. My orgasm barreled through me, arching and trembling with ecstasy. My cock surged and spilled onto my stomach and shirt, but I couldn't bring myself to care.

There was nothing in that moment but Peter.

He crushed his mouth back to mine in a searing kiss and he fumbled with his jeans button, quickly shoving his hand down his pants.

I wasn't in any coherent state to help or to even act really, but a few strokes of his hand and he came as well. He was a glorious sight; the way his neck corded and how his whole body shook was proof of his restraint.

I was pretty sure he would've preferred something more than masturbating, but his only concern was for me.

"Oh, Jesus." He sagged on me. "I'm sorry. God, that was intense and came from nowhere, and I only meant to get you off, but then you came, and holy hell, Yanni, it was the most beautiful thing I've ever seen…"

I was going to say something profound, but he pretty much nailed it. "Ditto."

He frowned. "Are you okay?"

"I'm so much better than okay."

"You sure? Because that didn't quite go to plan. I got carried away and that was reckless."

"I'm sure. I'm sure. And it wasn't reckless. It was hot. I wasn't expecting to want to… you know, finish. But everything felt so right."

"No regrets?"

"None. Well, except the fact that I just did laundry today and now this whole outfit needs washing."

Peter chuckled. "I can fix that. A quick wash and a tumble dry."

"For me or my clothes?"

His smile made his eyes glisten. "Both, if you want."

"I want." I put my hand to his face. "Thank you for getting me past this first hurdle. It's a pretty big step for me."

He searched my eyes and touched my face like I was the most precious thing he'd ever seen. "Anything for you." Then he peeled himself off me and got to his feet. "Come on, let's get cleaned up."

"NO, we had separate showers and he gave me some sleep pants and a T-shirt to wear while my clothes got clean and dry."

"He was very much a gentleman," Patrice added.

"Yes."

I'd just told her everything that had happened in the last week. Everything. Including my first sexual encounter since... well, since *him*.

"And you were comfortable with everything?"

"Uh, more than comfortable."

She smiled. "That's good, Yanni."

"I think talking about it, before and after, helped a lot. For both of us."

"What did you talk about afterward?"

"After we'd showered and were dressed, we made salad for dinner and we basically sat on the sofa and discussed limits. He wanted to know what was a no-go for me. I think he worries he's going to do the wrong thing. Like when we were… well, he kept asking me if I was okay with what he was doing."

"What did you tell him?"

"Not to ever tie me up. I can't be restrained like that. Not to even hold my hands down, and never to hit me. That was it. Just those two."

"And he was fine with that?"

"Yes, of course. He looked horrified as to why or how I even knew what being restrained and beaten was like. I think it shocks him every time I say something like that."

"And what did he tell you were his limits?"

"No sharing, no cheating. No lying. Basically all things I probably should have added to my list. Oh, and I also told him no punishment. When I'd read those forums and watched those videos, there were some guys who wanted their daddy to punish them. I said no way."

"And what did he say?"

"That if he had any issues with anything I'd done, that we'd sit down and talk it out like adults."

This seemed to please her a great deal, and so she changed subjects. "What have you got on at school this week? How are you handling the pressure of assignments with work?"

"Ugh. I have two assessments due in the next three weeks. They're quite in-depth, and I want to ace them. I don't want to let Mr Landon down."

"You'll need to find a balance between work and Peter. I know everything's very exciting with him right now, and time with him is important. But so is school."

"I know." And truly, I did. "I might have to take my books to his place on the weekend."

And that's exactly what I did.

For the next three weeks, I spent my Saturdays and Sunday afternoons at Peter's, on his couch with my theory

assessments spread out all around me. Peter would sit on
the chaise with a book or his laptop. He'd cook me dinner,
and when I couldn't deal with the history of theater
anymore, I'd toss my homework aside and go pounce on
him. It always started with laughing and making out and
ended with mutual orgasms. He never pushed for more.
He said what we had was perfect. But I couldn't help but
think he was just telling me what I needed to hear.

I kept thinking about what he needed.

The sites he'd shown me definitely featured sex. He'd
once told me, in the very beginning, that he enjoyed sex,
but he wasn't ready. Well, surely he was ready now. The
question was, was I?

The next Friday night, after our exams were done, I
was invited to go out with a group of my classmates. They
were all excited to celebrate, and I wanted to be part of it
with them, so after work, instead of going to Peter's, I was
going out.

For the first time in a long time, I was going out to a
bar, where there would be crowds, drinking, loud music,
and men. I would undoubtedly get jostled and pushed in
the crowds of dancers, and there would definitely be
people in my personal space. But I was ready for this.

And yes, the music was so loud I couldn't hear myself
think, and the crowds were bumping and a little overwhelming. My friends all drank until assessments and
exams were well and truly forgotten, though I stuck to
soda. I laughed with them, told stories, and it felt good to
be social…

But it wasn't what I craved.

I wanted to be on Peter's sofa with our legs curled up,
watching reruns of BBC Shakespearean plays. I wanted
peace and quiet and warm kisses, and I wanted more.

If surviving a pumping nightclub, drunk guys, shouting, and jostling was a test of how far I'd come, then surely I passed. Surely I was ready for more...

I said goodbye to my friends, leaving them to their shots of tequila, and making my way outside the club, I called Peter.

"Yanni?" He sounded alarmed. "Oh my God, is everything okay?"

I checked my phone to find it was almost two a.m. Shit. "Sorry, I didn't realize it was so late."

"Are you okay?"

"Yeah, I'm fine. Can I come over?"

"I'll come get you. Where are you?"

"No, I can Uber it. Stay in bed. Keep it warm for when I get there."

"Are you sure you're okay?"

I smiled. "Yes, Daddy."

Silence.

I wondered if I'd overstepped. I scrambled for something else to say, but he cleared his throat and made a humming sound that made my stomach clench. Yeah, I was really ready for more. "See you when you get here," he said gruffly.

Twenty minutes later, and after a slightly terrifying Uber ride at warp speed, I walked up Peter's steps. He opened the door before I could knock and pulled me inside. "Are you okay?"

"Yes, I'm more than fine. I don't know if that driver was trying to break land speed records, or if it just seemed like it because there's no traffic at half past two in the morning, but—" I leaned in and kissed him. "—I wanted to be here."

"Did you not have a good night with your friends?"

"I did. It was great, actually, but it's not where I belong."

Peter's eyes darkened. "Where do you belong?"

"Here with you."

He put his hand to my cheek and brought his lips to almost touch mine. "I like the sound of that."

I said the words before I lost my nerve. "I want you to take me to bed. I want you to have me, Peter."

He put his forehead to mine. "Oh, Yanni. My sweet boy."

Oh God. He was going to say no. "I'm ready." Then it dawned on me that maybe he wasn't. "Are you? Do you want that with me?"

He kept my face cradled in his hands and he kissed my forehead, my eyelids. "I want it, but only when you're ready."

"I'm ready. It's all I've thought about."

He grimaced like he was pained. "I don't think you are, and I don't want to rush you."

"Please, Peter."

With that, he took my hand and led me to his room. He took total control, and I gladly let him. He undressed me with tender hands and soft kisses, then he was naked and he laid me on the bed. I'd never been fully naked with him before this. He crawled over me, his weight, his erection…

It's okay, I told myself. *It's Peter. This is Peter. I want this.*

He was between my legs, gentle as ever, but fear and panic struck me like a sledgehammer.

No, it's Peter. It's not Lance. Peter would never hurt me. Not like Lance did.

Lance.

Fear gripped my heart, and I froze. I tried to speak, I tried to say stop, but I was stuck. I was screaming in my head, but no sound would come out of my mouth. Anxiety slithered over me like a hundred cold snakes holding me down. I couldn't breathe.

I couldn't breathe.

Peter seemed to realize what was going on because he was then off me. "Jesus, Yanni," he mumbled. And the next thing I knew, I was wrapped up in his bed covers, in his arms, being rocked. He kept one hand on my head, holding me to his chest. "I got you. You're safe. Breathe for me, love."

Yes, breathing. Breathing would be good. I took in the deepest breath I could manage, then another and another. The pounding in my ears dulled to a roar, followed by shame, grief, and rage, all in the form of tears.

I couldn't stop them. I cried and Peter held me, gently rocking and soothing me, and my endless tears fell.

"I'm not ready. I thought I could be," I sobbed. "I wanted to be. But I thought of him. Lance. I thought his name and I couldn't breathe."

Peter kissed my head and rocked me some more.

"I'm so sorry. I'm so sorry." It was all I could seem to say.

"Don't apologize, love." He stroked my hair for a while. "Do you want to take a shower or just sleep?"

I was exhausted, but a hot shower sounded really good. "Shower."

Peter slid out and disappeared. I heard the water start a moment later, and then he was back. He sat me up, unwrapped me from his comforter, and took my hand. He'd put on his pajama bottoms, though I was still naked. He never looked at my body; he never took advantage. He simply led me to the bathroom where the water was steaming.

I stepped under the spray and felt my fright from earlier wash away. It certainly wasn't a fix, but it sure was a good start. When I shut the water off and stepped out, Peter had put a neatly folded pile of clothes on the bathroom counter for me. I put on the pair of sleep pants and T-shirt and found Peter sitting on the end of his bed.

He'd quickly remade the bed like nothing had happened.

But it certainly had.

He stood up and walked to me, sliding his hand along my jaw and pulling me into his arms. "I'm so sorry," I mumbled.

"Apology accepted," he whispered. I guess he'd learned telling me not to be sorry wasn't going to work. He rubbed my back. "Did you want to sleep in here or in the guest room?"

If I was being brutally honest, I wanted to crawl into a hole. But I knew I wouldn't be able to sleep in the guest room. I answered with a shrug. "With you."

He took my hand and we crawled into bed. He immediately pulled me against him, my head on his chest, his arm tight around me. I was so exhausted, my aching heart felt almost too heavy to bear.

I had so much to say, so much to apologize for, but my words fell in the form of silent tears instead.

CHAPTER EIGHTEEN

THE NEXT MORNING, I woke up with the same heavy feeling in my chest. I was alone, unsurprisingly. I half expected to find Peter sitting at his kitchen counter with a "we need to have a chat" look on his face.

I stood at the entrance to his kitchen and waited. He was standing at his coffee machine, had his back to me. I didn't want to have this conversation. I didn't want him to tell me that last night was a mistake, that being with me was a mistake.

He turned, and seeing the look on my face, he quickly walked over to me. "No, no," he murmured, pulling me into his arms. "What's that look for? You look heartbroken."

I blinked back tears. "If you don't want to see me anymore because I'm too much work, I'll understand."

"What?" He pulled back and lifted my face so he could look me in the eye. "Yanni, no. Last night was just a hiccup." He studied me for a long moment before sadness crossed his face. "Please don't shut me out because of what happened last night. It's not your fault. I certainly don't blame you, if that's what you're worried about."

God, he was so good to me. I snuggled back into his chest, holding on to him tightly as he rubbed his strong, warm hands over my back. "I'm so embarrassed," I mumbled. "And ashamed. I hate that I… that he fucked me up. You tried to tell me, and I didn't listen. I'm sorry I put you through that."

Peter kissed the top of my head. "You have nothing to be ashamed about."

"I want to be ready. I want to be the boy that you need."

"You already are."

"I want to be more. I want to be every single thing that you need."

"Yanni," he rebuked me gently. He kissed the top of my head and rubbed my back some more. "You already are."

He didn't get it. I pulled back so he could see the seriousness in my eyes. "I want to have sex with you. I want you to make love to me, so badly it burns me in here," I put my hand to my breastbone. "I want to get my life back, and I want to share it with you. I want you inside me so much I can't stand it. I ache with need when I think about it, and I think about it a lot, but there is some part of my brain that won't let me."

"If it's what you want—"

"It is."

"Then we can work towards it. Slow steps, baby steps, okay? I'm not in any rush. We can take as long as it needs. There's a whole bunch of stuff we haven't done yet." He gave me a cheeky smile. "And believe me when I say, taking my time with you is no hardship."

I fell back into his chest and slid my arms around him. "I don't know what I ever did to deserve you."

"If I remember correctly, you asked me if I wanted to see a Charlie Chaplin film. It was fate."

I smiled into his shirt, then remembered I had to work this morning. I straightened up quickly. "What time is it?"

"Eight thirty."

"Shoot, I have to get going."

"If you'd rather not go, I can call in sick for you."

"I can't let them down."

"I figured you'd say as much." He went back to his coffee machine and held a cup out for me. "That's why I made you a double shot. You can drink it in the car."

I took the coffee and kissed him softly on the lips. "Thank you, for everything."

"Anytime. It's what boyfriends do."

That stopped me. "Boyfriends?"

"Well, I was thinking it was about time we called this what it is. Is that okay with you?"

I think my slow spreading grin was enough answer. "Very okay." Then I thought about it. "Are we still daddy and son? Can we be both?"

Peter made a choked-off groaning sound. "Oh, yeah."

NEEDLESS TO SAY, my appointment with Patrice on Wednesday wasn't an easy one.

As soon as I'd walked into her office and sat down, she knew something was wrong. "What happened?"

I told her everything. How I'd begged Peter to take me to bed, how he'd tried to tell me I wasn't ready, how I'd *begged* him. Then how I had freaked out, and how he took care of me. How he told me I was already everything he needed, and how I still asked him for more.

"I want to be normal."

Patrice was quick to respond. "Normal is subjective. Normal is a dangerous word. Normal is a label——"

"Sorry, wrong word choice." I tried again. "I want my life back. I want to take back what *he* took from me. I want to be who I would have been if I'd never met *him*."

"He?"

I sagged. "You know who. It was me thinking his name the other night in bed with Peter that caused me to freak out. I had a panic attack because I thought of his name. I don't want to give him that power anymore."

"Saying his name doesn't give him power."

"Maybe not. But it takes power away from me."

"Control?" She frowned. "Saying his name takes away your control?"

"Yes. Somehow. I don't know how. It just does."

"Then we need to work on reclaiming your control. We're going to start right now." She picked up her pen and wrote three separate sentences on her notepad, then turned it around so it faced me. "Read those out loud."

Lance has no control of my life.

Lance has no power over me.

Lance is a total jerk whose karma will find him.

I shot her a look, and she shrugged and said, "I ran out of ideas and it seemed appropriate." I snorted out a laugh. She nodded toward the notepad. "Read them to me."

I read them to her.

"Again. Read them over and over until I tell you to stop."

So I did. I must have read them twenty times before she put up a hand to stop me. "Who has no control of your life?"

I really didn't want to say this but I knew what she was vying for. "Lance."

"Who has no power over you?"

"Lance."

"Who is a total jerk whose karma will find him?"

I almost smiled. "Lance."

"It's just a name. A word, a noun. It has no power unless you give it power." She pulled the piece of paper from her notepad, folded it neatly in half, and gave it to me. "Take it home, read it a thousand times. Practice your vocal coaching with it, read it in different accents, impersonate different actors. Add your own lines if you want."

I looked at her skeptically. "This will cure me?"

"It's not a miracle cure, no. There is no miracle cure."

I sighed. "You know what the worst part is? That my life is forever changed because of someone else. I'm living with the consequences, the ramifications, the damage. And he just walks away."

"You know, as a doctor and a lover of science and all things provable, it's probably unreasonable for me to believe in karma. But I think the universe has a way of righting wrongs, in an action/reaction kind of way."

"You think karma is physics?"

Patrice laughed. "I don't know what it is. But I strongly believe people like Lance get what they deserve. Sometimes it's instant. Sometimes it takes years. If it makes you feel any better, he will be sorry."

I sighed. "Maybe. But how many more guys like me have to go through hell before the universe stops them?"

It was a rhetorical question, one Patrice didn't even attempt to answer. But I thought all week about everything we talked about, and even for my session the week after. She started straight back on the Lance-desensitization strategy, asking if I'd continued saying those sentences out loud. Asking if I felt any different when saying it out loud or even thinking about his name.

"I can say it or think it without having an anxiety attack so I guess we would call that progress. But I still don't like it. I don't want any part of him in my life, including just his name."

She was pleased with my progress and gave me some suggestions to get past the mental images, the awful memories of the things Lance did to me when and if I found myself in an intimate situation with Peter. She said it was common for name association and senses like smell and touch to bring back powerful memories.

"Peter and I haven't tried it again," I admitted. "Though we did have a phone sex session during the week. We didn't plan it, but we just kinda went there. It was hot. And last weekend, we made out on the couch that ended… happily." I cringed. "If you know what I mean."

"We're you naked together? On the couch?"

I shook my head. "No."

"But you were naked with him in bed when you needed to stop?"

"Yes." I frowned. "Is the clothing significant?"

"Being naked can make you highly vulnerable and exposed. I think that's very reasonable." She went on to give some suggestions for sexual acts that didn't require full nudity. Not that I really needed suggestions. Lord knew in the last two weeks, I'd done my fair share of research on internet porn. I was just warier of what I clicked on now.

We finished the session, and like every other Wednesday night, I went to the Landons' for dinner. It was just myself and Mr and Mrs Landon. Maybe they picked up on my solemn mood. Even though I tried to hide it, I should have known better.

"Everything okay, sweetheart?" Mrs Landon asked.

"Just something Patrice said to me last week. I've been thinking about it. She spoke of karma and how the universe clears old debts. I mean, I like the idea of that…" I shook my head and shrugged. "But then she also told me that he, Lance—I can say his name now without wanting to vomit—doesn't have power over me unless I give it to him. I'm the only one who can take back control of my life."

Mrs Landon gave a small nod. "That's very true."

"I can't help but think they're connected," I admitted. "I've been trying to make sense of it for a week."

Mr Landon's brow furrowed. "You think that karma and you taking back control are connected? Yanni, you're not thinking of some revenge plot, are you? Some crazy plan to make him pay?"

I balked. "God, no!" I snorted at that ridiculous idea. "I'm not brave or crazy enough to do that."

Mr Landon put his hands to his heart and exhaled with relief. "Oh, thank God. Getting yourself a role on TV is one thing, but *America's Most Wanted* is not the way to do that."

I laughed, and Mrs Landon fought a smile. "What do you mean, Yanni?" she asked.

"That's just it. I don't know." I let out a long sigh. "I hate that I'm stuck trying to fix myself, and he got away with it. I hate that the most. He just walked away without looking back, and I'm left with a path of destruction in his wake."

I half expected her to launch into a speech on the steps of grief and how anger and resentment are a part of healing, but she didn't. She reached across the table and squeezed my hand. "Me too, honey. Me too."

ON FRIDAY AFTER WORK, I said goodbye to my coworkers and headed home. It was late, and I hadn't seen Peter since Sunday night. We'd spoken over the phone, of course, and texted and had phone sex again, but it wasn't the same. I missed him. So I pulled out my phone to talk to him for the ten-minute walk home.

He asked every single week if I wanted him to drive me home, but it was literally a ten-minute walk. I'd worked at the coffee house for four months now and had never had an issue with walking home on Friday nights.

And this night was no different. He was asking me how George and Ajit were doing. "Oh, they are so good," I answered happily. "Ajit is over all the time, and they're really working hard at proving Ajit's family wrong. They're fighting to stay together, so it's kind of sweet."

"And how about Skylar and Jordan?"

"Well, since you mentioned that they were kind of cozy, I've been noticing them more and more now. Something is happening between them, but I haven't asked. I don't want to push."

I walked around the corner, half a block from my house, and stopped cold.

There was a cop car out front. The lights weren't flashing, but there was a uniform standing on our stoop. "Oh my God."

"Yanni, what is it?"

"The cops are at my place," I said. "I gotta go."

I clicked off the call so I could run, and I raced home. It was crazy how many wild and horrible thoughts could go through your mind in a split second. Was Jordan okay? Had something happened to freak her out again? Was George okay? Had Ajit's family asked the police to intervene? Was Skylar okay? What time was she working tonight?

God, I ran straight up to where the policeman stood, and I saw a familiar cop just inside the door. I brushed past, and Jordan, Skylar, George, and Ajit were all standing in the living room, pale and wary. "What's wrong?" I asked, out of breath. "Everyone okay?" I studied Jordan, checking to see if she needed help, but Skylar had her arm around her just fine.

"It's you," Jordan said quietly. "They're here for you."

I spun to the police officer. "Me?"

"Yanni Tomaras?" she asked.

"Yes."

"Do you remember me?" She looked familiar, and it took a second for me to place her. She was the cop who took my statement about Lance hiring Spencer to find me.

"Yeah." She was Officer Serena Hernandez. Her name badge confirmed it. "What are you doing here? I haven't done anything wrong."

"We know. Yanni, you're not in trouble. But I need you to come downtown. There's been another incident involving Lance Nader."

"Is he dead?" I asked, kind of morbidly hoping he was.

"No. He's in custody."

And it hit me like a freight train. "Oh God. He's hurt someone else?"

Serena gave a hard nod. "Unfortunately, yes." She explained there was a guy in the hospital who wasn't too willing to talk, but if they could just get his statement in conjunction with mine, they could put Lance away for a long time. "Will you help us? He's scared as hell, and I figured if anyone understood, it'd be you. Can you talk to him? The hospital can't hold him for much longer."

Too shocked to do anything else, I nodded. In a daze, I got into the patrol car with the two officers, and they drove me downtown.

THE GOOD SAMARITAN HOSPITAL was renowned for treating homeless people. I should know. I'd been admitted here. The smell of hospital food, disease, and disinfectant would be forever etched into my memory. It made my stomach turn.

The walls were scuff-marked, the waiting room full to bursting, the staff inhumanely busy. Nurses scurried from bed to bed and didn't even blink at seeing me walk in with two cops. It was just another day for them. We were waved through the ER, and Serena led the way to a cubicle at the far end, where she stopped and turned to me. She spoke in a serious whisper. "His name is Tyler Smedley. He's nineteen, no fixed address." She paused. "He's taken a beating, so you should be prepared."

I felt cold, like I was in a dream, a memory. I told myself I was ready to do this, but when the curtain was pulled back, I totally wasn't ready at all.

Serena walked in first, standing near the bed. I stood back, trying to breathe, trying not to be sick.

My brain was screaming at me to leave, my stomach felt like it was on a rollercoaster, and my heart squeezed.

Tyler was lying there, so thin the blanket covering him barely made a lump on the bed. His blond hair was dirty, unwashed, as was his shirt. But his face... his eye was swollen shut. A cut had opened his cheek. A blotch of purple colored his jaw. His lip was split.

He wouldn't look at us.

Serena put a manila folder on the tray table and wheeled it over the bed so it was right in front of him. "Tyler, this is Yanni Tomaras. Lance Nader, the man who did this to you, did the same to him."

She opened the folder, and it was only then I realized it

was my case file. Inside were two photos of me taken on my twenty-first birthday. I almost didn't recognize myself. But there I was, looking very much how Tyler looked now.

Beaten. Forgotten. Alone and scared to fucking death.

Serena left us but didn't go too far. I could see her legs underneath the cubicle curtain. I wiped my hands on my thighs and took a shaky breath. "Hey." I swallowed hard. "So, that's me in the photographs."

Tyler's only reaction was the flare of his nostrils.

"I know what you're going through. I've been where you are." When he didn't speak or even look at me, I figured I'd be doing all the talking.

"I was homeless. My parents disowned me because I'm gay; they threw me out," I said. Something flashed in his eye and I guessed his story was similar to mine. So I kept on going. "I was living rough. Trying to survive, ya know?"

He swallowed hard.

"I'd heard other guys talking about making some money, just for spending twenty minutes with a guy, you know, so I thought I could do that. I hadn't eaten in a while, and money's money, right?" God, this would never be easy to talk about. "Anyway, I met Lance on my first night. He had a lot of money, he made a lot of promises, and he wanted me. I thought I'd struck gold. One night became one weekend, and when he realized I didn't have anywhere else to go, he offered me a deal, of sorts. I could stay at his place. He could have whatever he wanted, whenever he wanted. It was something straight out of *Pretty Woman*, and I should have known it was too good to be true. Even in the beginning, I didn't like everything that he did to me, but I put up with it because I had food and showers with hot water and a bed. I mean, I'd gone from homeless to living in a luxury apartment almost overnight.

"But he got rougher and meaner as time went on. It

started during sex. He'd squeeze my neck, hit me, and hold me down and… make me do things I didn't want to do." A cold shiver ran through me. "I begged for him to stop, but he just hit me harder."

A single tear ran from the corner of his eye down his cheek, but still, he said nothing.

"I lived with him for about a year. In fear, every day. He'd isolated me, secluded me, beaten me, raped me."

Tyler looked at me then. "You lived with him?"

I nodded. "I thought I didn't have a choice. But after the last time"—I tapped the photograph of me with my finger—"I knew I had to get out. I left with nothing and went straight to the police. I told them what had happened, but he denied it. Then he hired someone to find me."

Tyler shot me a look of fear that made my heart ache. "Oh God…"

I shook my head quickly and put my hand on his arm. It was then I noticed the scrapes on his knuckles. "We have to stop him. Together, you and me. My report alone wasn't enough, but they can't ignore two of us. I don't want him to do what he did to us to anyone else."

Another tear ran a solitary trail down his face. "I don't think I can."

"You won't be alone, and you're stronger than you know. You're a fighter," I said, nodding to his banged-up knuckles. "You fought back. I never did."

He stared at his hands for a while. "I only met him on weekends, in the bars off Skid Row. Quick cash, you know? He paid well, more than the other johns. So I kept going back. He was so rough, it was always painful. He'd slap and choke me, but this time was different. I could tell by the look in his eyes that he was angry."

I knew that look all too well.

"And it really hurt. He'd always insisted on wearing a condom—and most johns don't, so it was kinda weird—but then I realized why. No DNA, no proof. So when he hit me and kept hitting me, I fought back. I'd seen enough crime shows on TV, and I knew that if he wouldn't leave me any DNA, I'd have to take it. So I scratched him."

"You're very smart."

He shook his head and didn't say anything for a while. "You've done all right for yourself, though," he said, looking at my clothes.

"This is my work uniform. Looks kinda fancy, but it's just a coffee shop. I'm back at school now, and I have a place to live. I can help you do the same. The people who helped me, they'll help you too."

"But only if I agree to the police report, right?" His defensive wall was back up, and I couldn't blame him. "There's always a catch with you do-gooders."

"No, there's no catch. There's a place called the Acacia Foundation, and it's what they do. They help people like you and me, who have been kicked out of our home because we're not straight enough. They find you somewhere to live, they have work placement programs if you need it, they can get you back into college if that's what you want."

He didn't move. Didn't speak. I sighed. "I'll help you, regardless. Do the police report, or don't do the police report. It's up to you. I won't not help you because of that. People like Lance Nader get away with it because they know their victims are scared, broke, and don't have the means to fight back. But we do. And we can. We can stop him. The police out there will take your statement, and that's it. It won't go to trial. Lance will take a deal before it goes that far. Even if he doesn't go to jail, he'll have a criminal record of physical and sexual assault. With a bit of luck, he'll lose his job, and he'll know what it's like to have things taken away from him."

Tyler was still quiet and not looking at me again, and I thought our conversation was over. But then he nodded quickly, and more tears fell. "Will you stay? While I talk to them?"

I gave his hand a squeeze. "Yeah, of course."

Serena came back in then; she'd obviously heard every word. I sat in the corner while he recounted his story and the detective dutifully took notes. His story was so familiar to mine, and although my heart broke for him, it somehow bolstered me as well. I didn't want another person to ever go through what I went through, and most certainly not at the hands of Lance Nader.

When Tyler was almost done, a nurse came to talk to the other officer who had been standing outside the curtain. They disappeared together for a moment, then the officer came back and poked his head around the curtain. "Mr Tomaras, there's a Mr Hannikov here. Says you'll want him here with you?"

Peter. "Yes. God, yes." I stood up, and the officer waved at someone at the end of the hall. I walked to the curtain and followed his line of sight just in time to see Peter walk in. He took one look at me and visibly sagged. He put his hand to his forehead and through his hair as he walked toward me, relief and pain in his eyes.

I put my arms out and he walked right into them, holding me so, so tight. He buried his face into my neck. "I was so scared for you," he mumbled.

"I'm sorry. I should have called or texted. I was kinda busy and not thinking..."

He put his hands to my face and pulled back to get a better look at me. "Are you okay?"

I nodded, but then tears burned in my eyes, and he

pulled me back against his chest. "I raced over to your place," he said softly. "They told me the police took you. Luckily George remembered the officer's name. He said someone was hurt and they needed your help. I tried three police stations, two hospitals. I tried calling…"

I took out my phone, and there were several missed calls. "It was on silent, sorry. I switch it off when I'm at work, and I forgot to switch it back." I then realized it was also three in the morning. God, had it been that long? "I'm so sorry."

He planted a kiss on my forehead, then searched my eyes. "Is everyone okay?"

I shook my head. "Lance hurt someone else."

Peter's nostrils flared, but before he could say anything, Serena announced the report was done, and Tyler was free to leave, given the doctor signed him out. I knew what that meant, though. It meant Tyler was going back out onto the streets. I stepped back around the curtain, so both Serena and Tyler could see me. "Where will you go?" I asked him.

He shrugged, exhausted and a hundred miles past done. "Doesn't matter."

"Of course it matters," I told him. "You can't go back out there, not tonight, not like this," I motioned to his face. "I have a couch. You can sleep on it, and after breakfast, I'll make some calls and we'll get you a place to live."

I hadn't noticed Peter standing beside me, but when I looked at him, I saw that he was staring at the still-open folder on the table. At the photos of me: black eye, swollen and bleeding lip, cut cheek. How gaunt I was, how dirty I was. How utterly broken I was.

I rushed over to close the file and hand it to Serena, but in my panic, the photos and papers fell to the floor. Like it happened in slow-motion, Peter picked up a photograph and stared at it. His frown was deep and his eyes shone with unshed tears. I gently took the picture from him. "That's not who I am anymore," I whispered.

Peter nodded, and Serena took the photo from me and shoved it back in the file. She thanked me, apologized quietly, told us she'd be in touch, and they left. The doctor came in, gave Tyler some pain medication, and discharged him. He gingerly got off the bed and stood up. He was much smaller than I'd realized and so thin. "You don't have to worry. I'll be fine," he mumbled.

"Tyler, I'd really like to help," I said. "It's just a couch and a blanket. A safe place to sleep tonight, breakfast and a hot shower in the morning."

He searched my eyes. "Why?"

"Because good people helped me. I hate to think where I'd be if they hadn't. And I'd like to pay it forward. If you'll let me."

He eyed Peter then, so I introduced them. "This is Peter."

Tyler frowned. "Thought you said your old man kicked you out."

I snorted out a laugh. "Well, he's not my daddy in that sense of the word. He's my boyfriend." It was the first time I'd ever called him that.

"Daddy, huh?" Tyler said.

Peter cleared his throat. "Should we be leaving?"

I nodded and we walked at Tyler's pace out into the cool early morning. We drove to my place and went inside. The house was dark and quiet, everyone obviously sound asleep at half past three in the morning. I made Tyler a pastrami and cheese sandwich while Peter pulled some blankets out of the closet. Tyler inhaled the food, but his one good eye was blinking slower and slower. He curled up on the single chair, his small frame somehow fitting, and I threw a blanket over him. I don't know if it was the meds the doc gave him or pure exhaustion, but he was already asleep.

Peter patted the seat next to him on the three-seater. I fell in beside him, and he laid us down so he was the big spoon, but I rolled over so I could face him. "I'm sorry about tonight. I made you worry, and that must have been horrible."

"I thought something bad had happened to you."

I kissed him softly. "Thank you for looking for me."

He brushed the hair back from my forehead. "You're doing the right thing helping him."

I smiled sadly. "It's the least I could do. His face will be sore as hell tomorrow."

Peter frowned. "That photograph…"

"I'm sorry you saw that."

"I'm sorry you went through that." His eyebrows knit together. "I'd like just five minutes alone with that asshole. I swear, he'd never touch another person again."

I shook my head. "No, you're better than him."

He closed his eyes. "I'm sorry. I just want him to pay for what he does."

"I want to make him pay, too. And I'm going to. But the right way. The police seem to think they'll have enough to stick. I'm ready to take him on now. If that's what's been holding me back, I don't know. He holds no power over me anymore, and I'm going to make sure he pays."

He kissed me. "You're stronger than me."

I scoffed at that. "I'm strong because of you."

He cradled my face. "No, my sweet boy. You're strong because of you. You're a survivor." He searched my eyes. "You are the sweetest thing and so very precious to me."

I snuggled into his chest and his arms wound tight around me. "I called you my boyfriend tonight, and my daddy. The one who keeps me safe."

He kissed the side of my head. "I love you, Yanni."

My heart burst at his declaration, and I pulled back to look into his eyes. "You do?"

He smiled and slow-blinked. "Wholly and completely. With everything I am."

Happy tears sprang to my eyes, and with my hand on his cheek, I kissed him. Then I snuggled back into his chest so the sound of his heart could lull me to sleep.

CHAPTER NINETEEN

I WOKE up to the feeling of being watched. It took me a minute to remember where I was… on the couch with Peter. He was being the big spoon and I was his little spoon, and George, Ajit, Skylar, and Jordan all stood near the kitchen. Not watching me and Peter, but staring at the single seater.

Oh, shit. Tyler.

I sat up. "Hey, guys," I whispered, craning my neck to see if Tyler was still there. He was, and still sound asleep. I stood up and walked over to my roommates, where I turned to look at our sleeping guest as well.

"I'm sorry I brought him back here without asking, but it was half past three in the morning. He had nowhere else to go."

They were all still staring at him, at his banged-up face. I couldn't tell if his eye was better or worse, but his cheek and jaw definitely had more color.

"It's fine," George said, clapping me on the shoulder. "He looks like he needed somewhere safe."

I nodded. "Yeah. I'm gonna call Mrs Landon this morning. She'll find him somewhere more permanent."

"I'll start cooking breakfast," Skylar said.

"I have some bacon left," I said.

"I've got enough eggs," Jordan said.

"I'll make toast," George added, and Ajit started the coffee.

Man, I loved these guys.

I went back to the sofa and sat down next to Peter. He was just starting to wake up. He double-blinked and took a second to get his bearings, then his eyes refocused on me and he smiled. I put my hand to his face and traced my thumb across his eyebrow. "You're so handsome," I whispered.

"Good morning to you too."

"Sleep okay?"

"Yeah." He shuffled a bit so he was more on his back and groaned. "But my back will never forgive me."

I gave him a sad, frowny face. "Here, let me help you up."

He sat up first, then got to his feet, ironing out the kinks in his back, then looked toward the stairs. "Uh, bathroom?"

I'd shown him where it was before, so he knew where it was. "Sure. We're making coffee. Want some?"

"Yes, please."

Two minutes later, he was back with a coffee cup in hand. We all worked around the kitchen as quietly as possible so as not to wake Tyler. He was sound asleep. I doubted he'd even stirred once during the night. I knew what that kind of exhaustion felt like, and I wondered when he'd last had a proper night's sleep.

The first thing I did was call Mrs Landon. I gave her a

very brief rundown of what had happened, and within twenty minutes, they were on their way here.

I didn't know if it was the noise of breakfast being dished up or if it was the smell of cooked food, but Tyler woke up. He woke with a start, jolting upright, and immediately recoiled in pain. I hadn't seen him without a shirt on, but knowing Lance as well as I did, I wouldn't have been at all surprised if Tyler had bruised ribs.

I knelt down in front of him. "Hey. It's all good. Everyone here is cool. They've just cooked you up some breakfast. Hungry?"

He looked around the room and at the people in it, much the same way a frightened animal does. But then he looked at the plates of food. "Yeah, I could eat."

The other four opted to eat theirs in front of the TV, but Peter and I sat with Tyler at the small table. He devoured everything on his plate and two cups of coffee. His eye was a little bit better, still swollen, but not swollen shut. His bruises definitely had more color. When he was done eating, I asked, "Wanna take a shower?"

He nodded timidly, as though he was embarrassed. "Sure."

I took him upstairs and grabbed him a towel. Then I took in the state of his clothes. "Hang on. Wait here, I might have something that'll fit you." I rummaged through the clothes that Mr Landon had kindly given me. I was certain there was a pair of pants that were a bit short in the leg for me. I found them, grabbed an old T-shirt Mr Landon had also given me that I'd only ever worn once, and handed them to Tyler. "Try them on for size. I think they'll be a mile too big, but they're clean and they're yours if you want them."

He took the offered clothes with his head down. "Hey," I said gently. "I get it. Everyone in this house gets it. You don't need to be embarrassed here." He nodded slowly and looked towards the bathroom door. So I added, "The green shampoo and conditioner is mine; use whatever soap you can find. No one here will care," and left him to it.

I went back downstairs to find Peter still sitting at the table, his breakfast barely touched. He gave me a tired smile, and instead of sitting on the chair next to him, I sat on his knee instead. I put my arms around him and fingered the soft hair at the nape of his neck. "You okay?"

He gave me a sad smile. "Yeah."

I knew all the things he wasn't quite ready to say, especially when the others would hear. *It's hard to look at someone when their face is black and blue. What are you supposed to say to someone who's just been assaulted? How do you stomach food when they're eating like they haven't in days?* "I know." I kissed the side of his head. "I know."

He leaned his face against my shoulder and tightened his arms around me.

"Aw, look at you two being all cute," Skylar said from the sofa.

I poked my tongue out at her, making Jordan smile, just as there was a knock at the door. "That'll be the Landons." I raced over to let them in. Mrs Landon looked as glamorous as always. Even in simple tan slacks and a white cardigan, she looked like a million dollars. Mr Landon was his usual, stylish self, understated yet classy. Though today they both looked concerned. "Tyler's just upstairs having a shower. He might be a while. You know that first shower is always the best."

Mrs Landon squeezed my arm, then noticed everyone else in the living room. Like a mother hen and her clutch, she huddled them in for a chat while Mr Landon made a beeline for Peter. "Long night, huh?"

"You could say that," Peter answered with a smile. I

started to collect plates and clean up after breakfast. It was the least I could do after they'd all cooked it. I made more coffee, and by the time I sat back down with Peter, I caught the tail end of their conversation.

"I don't know how they do it. These kids just pick themselves up and keep moving forward," Peter said. "They have such resilience, and I'm always telling Yanni he's much stronger than I would ever be."

I reached over and squeezed his hand. Mr Landon smiled right at me. "Yeah, they're pretty remarkable."

Peter sighed. "I guess I don't know what drives someone or makes them want to hurt another human being. I'll never understand it."

"Because you're a good person," I said simply. "And good people don't inflict harm on others. People like Lance are not good or even half-way decent."

Mrs Landon sat gracefully at the table, picked up her coffee with her pinky finger extended, put the cup to her lips, and said, "Lance Nader is a monster's asshole, and I hope he rots in jail."

Everyone laughed, and Mr Landon looked at his wife fondly. "Such elegance."

She smiled beautifully, just as Tyler came downstairs. He was dressed in the clothes I'd given him; they were miles too big, but at least they were clean. His hair was washed, still wet and slicked back, his dirty clothes rolled into a ball under his arm. I stood up and offered him my seat next to Mrs Landon. "Tyler, this is Mr and Mrs Landon. They run the Acacia Foundation I was telling you about. They helped me find this place to live and got me back into college."

"And me," Skylar said, putting her hand up.

Jordan did the same. "And me."

George gave a salute. "And me."

Ajit just waved. "I'm just the moral support." Everyone chuckled.

Knowing the Landons and Tyler were about to have a difficult conversation, and knowing Tyler would probably prefer not to have an audience, they all cleared out and went upstairs, and I took that as mine and Peter's cue to leave as well. I held out my hand, which he took and got to his feet. "I have to get ready for work, so we'll just be upstairs. Call out when you're done."

Still holding Peter's hand, I led the way into my bedroom and closed the door behind us. Sure, he'd been in my room before, but this was the first time we'd had the door closed. I felt a little nervous and strangely empowered. Maybe I was just exhausted after a ridiculously stressful night.

"Are you sure you're all right to work today?" Peter asked. "You didn't get much sleep."

"Yeah, I don't want to let them down. It's only four hours, and I'll be so busy I won't have time to think. And then we can spend the afternoon doing absolutely nothing on the sofa." Then I amended, "Well, not absolutely nothing. I'm sure there'll be a make-out session or two."

Peter smiled at that. "I'm sure there will be."

I started to throw some clothes into my backpack to take to his place. "You can go home and have a snooze, or you can lie down on my bed and sleep for four hours if you like."

He looked at my bed like it was a serious contender. "Tempting, but I probably should go home. I'll drop you at work first, though, save you the walk."

I walked back to him and kissed him soundly on the lips. "Thank you. For last night, for this morning, being here for me. It means a lot."

"You're welcome."

"I need to have a shower and get dressed for work. I need to shave." I scratched at my barely-there three whiskers of stubble, then I gently scratched at his full, rough growth. "I could get used to this."

Peter laughed. "Go and have your shower."

I grabbed a clean shirt, some briefs, and my last pair of clean work pants. "Make yourself at home," I said, before heading to the bathroom. I had the quickest shower and shave ever before heading back to my room with my hairbrush in my hand.

Peter was sitting on the end of my newly made bed. "Hope you don't mind," he said. "Thought I may as well be useful. But I wasn't sure what you wanted me to do with that." He nodded toward my pillow, where my purple silk gown now laid neatly folded.

I almost dropped the brush. "Oh, I uh, I um... that's not mine. Well, it is mine, but I... oh God."

In two long strides, Peter stood in front of me. He pushed my door closed, took my hand, and sat me down on the bed. "Yanni, it's fine. You don't need to hide any part of you from me."

I picked up the gown and held it in my lap. "I like the way it feels on my skin. I only wear it to bed. It's smooth and sensual, that's all. I don't make a habit of wearing women's clothes, if that's what you're worried about."

"I'm not worried about anything," he answered gently. "You can wear all the women's clothes you want. I wouldn't care one bit. If you want to wear this"—he touched the gown—"then you wear it."

I looked up into his eyes, seeing only understanding there. "Are you sure?"

"Yes, I'm sure." He looked at the purple silk, then back to my eyes. "I bet you're as hot as hell in this. And you wear it to bed?"

I nodded. "When we talk on the phone… and have phone sex."

Peter swallowed hard and his eyes were smoldering. "Will you wear it for me?"

"Would you like me to?"

His nostrils flared. "Oh yeah."

Oh. He *really* liked the idea of it. I bit my lip to hide my smile. "Okay." I stuffed it into my backpack, figuring I'd work on my courage to actually wear it for him later.

"Yanni?" Mrs Landon called from downstairs.

"Coming!"

I heard George laugh from his room. I rolled my eyes and Peter chuckled, but we went downstairs. The Landons stood with Tyler, who looked like he'd been crying. "We're heading out now," Mrs Landon said. "Tyler's comfortable coming with us, and I have the perfect place in mind for him, so we'll go and see what he thinks."

"Awesome!" I said, dropping my backpack near the door.

"Are you going to work?" Mr Landon asked.

"Yeah." I looked down at my uniform. "It's just a short lunch shift."

Mrs Landon put her hands on my shoulders. "You did a wonderful thing."

I felt my face warm, as did my heart. "Thank you."

She gave a serious nod. "I'll be contacting the police and getting report numbers. I want to be kept informed about Lance, and I want to know what lawyer he hires, and if and when he makes bail." She rubbed my arms. "We're not letting this go, and I'll happily make it my mission in life to ensure Mr Nader never lays another finger on another human being."

"Me too," I said. "I'm ready to stand up to him now. I wasn't before, but I am now."

Mrs Landon's eyes watered and she hugged me again. "I'm really proud of you."

"Thank you," I whispered. I'd never had a parent tell me they were proud of me for anything, so her words meant more than I could ever say. But she seemed to understand. They made their way to the door, and I said goodbye to Tyler. "Mrs Landon can give you my number. Let me know where you end up."

"Thanks," he said quietly.

We watched them leave, and Peter gave me a hug and kissed my temple. "You ready to go?"

It was almost ten. "Yeah."

He dropped me off at work, saying he had every intention of going home for a nap before he'd be back to pick me up. I kissed him in the car and went to work. And everything was going great: people were chatty, tips were good, and I'd been so busy I hadn't had any time to think about last night. I had brief moments, when frothing milk or wiping tables, and wondered how Tyler was getting on, or if Lance was still sitting in a holding cell, hopefully with a few homicidal ice addicts. And it was close to my finishing time, the lunch hour rush was over; I was putting plates away when I remembered something…

Peter told me he loved me.

The plates fell back onto the stack with a clatter, and thankfully nothing broke. Charise was quickly beside me. "Yanni, what is it?"

I couldn't have wiped the grin off my face if I tried. "Oh, nothing. I just remembered something."

"Something special, by the look on your face."

I covered my mouth with my hand. "I can't believe I forgot! I'll have some making up to do tonight."

She waggled her eyebrows and bumped her hip with mine. "Oooooh."

"No, not like that!" I swatted her away to hide the fact I blushed right down to my toes.

She laughed, and just a few minutes later, she nodded toward the front of the shop where Peter's car was pulling up. She winked and said, "Have fun, Yanni!"

I was still laughing when I got in the car. This man loved me. This gorgeous, gentle, and kind man was in love with me. "Well, look at you," he said, leaning over for a kiss. "Work was good, I take it?"

"Work was fine." I was still grinning, but I didn't want to have this conversation in his car. I wanted to be able to throw my arms around him and feel him against me. "I'll tell you all about it when we get home."

"My place or yours?"

"Your place."

"Okay, then." He eyed me curiously, smiled, but said nothing.

But when we walked into his house, he took my hand. "Okay, it's killing me. What did you want to tell me?"

"I remembered something. Actually, I can't believe I forgot." No, that wasn't right. "I didn't forget. We just got sidetracked this morning with Tyler."

"Yanni, please."

I put my arms around him. "I remembered what you said to me last night."

"Oh."

"You told me you loved me."

"I did." He wasn't smiling.

"Did you mean it?"

"Yes, very much. I won't ever lie to you. I just worried it wasn't the right time."

"It was the perfect time." I kissed him, then surprising the crap out of him, I put my arms around his neck and hoisted myself up so I could wrap my legs around his waist. He quickly grabbed me, holding me right where I wanted to be.

Surprised, yes, but smiling too. "Yanni, what are you doing?"

"Climbing you like a tree. Now take me to bed. I have a theory I want to test out."

He blinked, his eyes dark and wary. "Are you sure?"

"Never been surer."

So he carried me, too easily, like I weighed next to nothing, and laid me down on his bed. "Tell me what to do," he whispered.

"Well, my theory is technically Patrice's theory, that maybe I won't feel so vulnerable or exposed if we're not completely naked. And there's still plenty we can do with our clothes on. Or mostly on, if you get what I mean."

"And you'd like to try?"

"I'd love to try." With my hands cupping his face, I brought his mouth to mine and kissed him. I tilted my head and opened my lips, inviting him in. I spread my legs and he oh-so slowly settled his weight on my body. It made me groan, and he kissed me harder.

In no time at all, he was hard, and so was I. Our erections rubbed together, the fabric of our clothes between us as we kissed and touched, rocked and bucked. I'd been this far with him before, on the couch, but I was certain I was ready for more.

I took a second to evaluate my sensory overload. I searched every nerve for fear or anxiety, but there was none to be found. Only a whole lot of fire, lust, and want. The tightening in my belly was something new and wonderful, and it felt so good.

So I reached between us and fumbled with my belt. Peter lifted his body weight onto his elbows, giving me more room. I undid my belt, and his eyes, a crashing ocean of desire, searched mine. "Feels good?"

I nodded and popped the button and slowly pulled the zipper down. The sound made his breath catch, and I slid my hand beneath the elastic of my briefs and freed my cock. "Feels so good."

Then I went for his jeans. I managed to get the button undone and I undid the zipper without fumbling too much. I palmed him through his briefs, and he shuddered, his breath hitched.

Could I do this?

Did I feel vulnerable? Not at all. Did I feel safe? Very.

Peter was letting me lead, letting me set the pace, letting me explore. I wasn't pressured, I wasn't cornered, I wasn't doing anything against my will.

Oh no, I wanted this very much. I wanted to have this with him. I wanted to make him happy. That ache in my chest, that desire to make him—my safe harbor, my Daddy—happy, burned.

I slid my hand under his briefs and gripped his cock. He was hard and hot and really big. Something at the base of my spine uncurled at the thought of taking him inside my body. Not yet, but one day. One day soon, I would know what it felt like to have him.

"Oh God, Yanni." Peter's breaths were strangled, his face strained, though he never took his eyes off mine. "Oh, my sweet boy."

Letting go of him, I pushed my briefs down under my balls and let our cocks touch. Lightning set fire to my blood. I gripped us both, gasping at the sensation. Peter looked down between us then, and his whole body jerked. "Fuck," he whined.

I'd never heard him swear, and to know I made him curse with pleasure thrilled me. I looked down at our cocks too, and oh, my God... his big cock pressing against my smaller one, our shafts sliding, our cockheads alternating through my fist... it was so hot.

"Peter," I panted. "I'm going to come."

He groaned and bucked his hips. "Come for Daddy."

And I did. White-hot pleasure ripped through me, and my cock pumped come onto my stomach. It was blinding and all-encompassing and it would have been a little frightening, but Peter wrapped me in his arms, keeping me safe, and rocked into me. I'd let go of his cock but he came anyway, his orgasm spilling between us. Even through my own orgasm haze, I could feel his cock pulse and jerk as he came.

I held onto him as tight as I could, and then the emotions dumped on me like a wave. I let out a shaky sob, and Peter immediately pulled back. "Yanni?"

I laughed at my own stupid reaction. "Happy tears," I cried, covering my eyes with my hand.

Peter peeled back my fingers, concern and love in his eyes. "Are you sure?"

I nodded. "Very happy. Too much emotion. Or something." More tears came, and I felt so foolish. "I've never felt anything so powerful."

"Oh, love," he crooned and kissed me softly. He wiped a stray tear that rolled to my temple. "That was the most incredible thing. You were incredible."

He kissed me soft and sweet for a few minutes before he took me into the shower. He washed me like I was the most precious thing, and strangely enough, being naked with him in the shower was fine. Maybe it was because it wasn't sexual. It was tender and loving, but never sexual.

He offered me some of his old comfy track pants and an old college sweater and even a pair of socks. He got dressed too, wearing sweats and a T-shirt, and we cozied up on the couch. He was lying back on the chaise and I was between his legs, my face against his chest, and we spent the entire afternoon as I promised we would, doing not very much at all. We snoozed and he kissed the top of my head every so often and rubbed circles on my back.

I had this feeling, though, that my heart was too big and hot for my chest. Like Peter had taken up all the room there was. Now, I'd known a lot of hate in my life—I'd experienced it firsthand. But I also knew what love was. I wasn't stupid. I'd had crushes in high school and had fooled around a bit in my first year at college, and even in the early days with Lance, I'd been infatuated, but that didn't last very long, and it was certainly never love.

But this was. And Peter telling me he loved me was what made it more real. I leaned up on his chest and looked him in the eyes. This gentle, perfect man loved me. He never once treated me like I was broken beyond repair. Instead, he found beauty in my fault lines, like the cracks in my life were what made me strong.

I smiled at him, overwhelmed by emotion. "I love you too."

His smile was eye-crinkling and a little teary too, but he hooked his hands under my arms and pulled me up to kiss him. He never pushed for more. He never did. He just kissed me until we were all kissed out, then I buried my face into his neck. He wrapped his arms around me, and we snoozed some more.

Later that night when we were getting ready for bed, I grabbed my backpack to pull out my pajamas and found the silk gown stuffed in on top. Butterflies exploded in my belly as I warred with myself.

Can I wear it for him?

Am I brave enough to share this part of myself with him?

I knew he'd never ridicule me. In fact, he'd seemed to

like the idea… So with that in mind, I left my PJ bottoms on, but instead of wearing a T-shirt, I slid the gown on instead. It gave me goose bumps. *Oh yes, I could definitely wear it for him.*

But it looked ridiculous with the pajama pants on, so I pulled them off and just left my briefs on. I tied the sash off at my waist, and taking a deep breath, I went back to his room. He was pulling back the bed covers and asking me what time I'd told Jordan we were doing laundry tomorrow when he looked up at me and stopped.

And stared.

I stood there in the doorway, wearing nothing but underpants and a flimsy silk gown, feeling equal parts scared and brave.

"Oh wow," he murmured. "You're so beautiful."

I held out one arm so he could see how it draped. "It was Mrs Landon's. She was giving it away, but I was too scared to take it, even though I loved it. She gave it to me as a housewarming gift when I moved out." I was rambling, nervous. Then I swallowed down the lump in my throat. "Do you like it?"

"Love it," he said, his voice gruff. "You look incredible." He walked over to me, slowly. He put his fingers to my chin and lifted my face to his. "How does it make you feel?"

"Sexy," I breathed.

He crushed his lips to mine, and I could feel his half-hard erection against my belly. Oh yes, he liked it. When he broke the kiss, I could see the war in his eyes. He wanted to take me to bed and make me his, I could see it. But he couldn't. Not yet.

I didn't feel bad or guilty for that. I felt empowered, encouraged by his self-control. There was intensity in his restraint that made me bolder than I ever thought possible. So I took his hand and led him to bed.

"Uh, Yanni," he said weakly. He swallowed hard. "Are you sure this is a good idea?"

So maybe his restraint wasn't as herculean as I thought. I probably should have given him a few moments, or maybe I should have opted for the spare room. But I yearned to take care of him. I ached to make him happy.

"Lie down," I whispered.

Warily, he did as I asked. I crawled on top of him and he rubbed the silk on my arm, making us both moan. God, it felt even better under his hand.

I straddled his hips, rubbing against his erection. He still wore pajama pants. I was still wearing briefs. I was in total control. Peter would never hurt me. I could do this.

I sat up on him so he rubbed the silk across my chest, and I let his cock press against my balls and near my ass, still with our clothes between us.

Then he let his hands slide the silk over my ribs and down to my hips, my thighs, and I ground against him, letting his pajama-clad cock rub against my balls. "Fuck, Yanni," he groaned.

I leaned down so my mouth was almost touching his. "One day soon, I promise." Then I lifted my hips and he whined at the loss of contact. "I want to take care of you," I whispered, kissing him. "With my mouth."

Peter moaned and a shiver ran through him.

"I don't know if I can, but I want to try," I said, shuffling down a bit. "I want to make my Daddy happy."

Peter's eyes rolled closed and his dick twitched in his pants. He put his hand to his forehead. "You're going to kill me."

Smiling, I pulled the elastic of his sleep pants and briefs down to his balls, freeing his cock completely. God, he was beautiful. He was big and cut; his mushroom head was flushed purple and leaking precome at the tip.

I'd only ever given head before when Lance made me. But sometimes Lance had done it to me when he was trying to apologize for hurting me, trying to counter the pain with pleasure. So I knew how good this could be.

I paused for a moment because I'd just thought of Lance and a memory that wasn't a particularly good one. But there was still no panic; there was no anxiety, no fear.

This was Peter, and I was in control. I wanted to do this for him. For me.

Confidence, fortified with a deep desire to be a good boy for Daddy, I took his cock into my mouth.

And the pride and satisfaction I felt when he came onto his belly a few minutes later were like nothing I'd ever felt. Peter pulled his shirt off, wiped himself clean, then scooped me into his arms and held me tight. "Are you okay?"

I was so much better than okay. "Yes, Daddy," I mumbled.

With that, he lifted my chin and kissed me until my eyes rolled into the back of my head. Yes, Daddy was very happy with his boy, indeed.

ON WEDNESDAY, I sat across from Patrice and grinned. "Well, you've clearly had a good week," she observed.

"I have. I passed all my exams with high grades, I helped a stranger get some help through the Acacia Foundation. Lance Nader has been officially charged with five counts of aggravated sexual assault, plus a string of other related offenses, and the sex-while-still-clothed with Peter worked very well."

Patrice chuckled proudly. "A great week then."

"The best. I told Peter I loved him."

Her eyes went wide. "And Peter?"

I laughed, that warm surge filled my chest every time I thought of him. "Oh boy. Just thinking about him makes me fly."

ACT THREE

LEARNING TO FLY

CHAPTER TWENTY

THE AUDIENCE CHEERED, and for the final curtain call, we got a standing ovation. I stood with my classmates in a line of smiling actors, relief at having our first live production over with and proud as hell.

Our semester's final production was a modern take on *A Midsummer Night's Dream*, where Fairyland was Los Angeles, and Theseus and Hippolyta were television directors, and the mechanicals were six actors on a famed sitcom, manipulated by their own characters' personas. I, of course, was given the role of Puck, a spritely manifestation of their egos, who got to tease and taunt as he saw fit.

In the audience, I saw Peter next to Mr and Mrs Landon, all of them standing, grinning, and clapping. But Peter looked so proud he could burst. I wanted to leap from the stage into his arms but decided everyone had seen enough theatrics for one night.

Peter had endured months of me practicing lines over and over, and I was sure he knew the entire play by heart. It had been three months since I'd told him I'd loved him, three months of getting a little more physical with him, a little braver. Three months of falling deeper in love, three months of absolute perfection. It had also been three months of hard work getting this play flawless, and between my appointments with Patrice, my shifts at the coffee house, school, making time for my roommates—who I now called friends—and spending time with Peter, not one minute of the last three months had been wasted.

Now that the production was over, I was certain I'd sleep the entire weekend.

Backstage, we all hugged and high-fived. We had planned to go out afterward to celebrate, which I was looking forward to. We could bring partners, so Peter wouldn't be the only tagalong, thankfully, because I really wanted him there.

Instead of going straight to the dressing rooms, I snuck out through the wings to the auditorium, still in full costume, to where Peter and the Landons were chatting. I was too buzzed to wait. Peter saw me and put his arms out, whether he knew I wanted to hug him or if he wanted to hug me, I wasn't sure. I just launched myself at him. I took the Landons by surprise, but Peter caught me easily.

"You were so great!" he said against my ear. "I'm so proud of you."

I pulled back and looked to Mr and Mrs Landon. I was still grinning. "That was such a high!"

They both laughed and hugged me, congratulating me. "You were brilliant," Mr Landon said. "Timing was perfect, delivery en pointe."

"You were hilarious!" Mrs Landon said. "Oh, Yanni, I'm so proud of you!" She put her hands to my face. "You were born for the stage."

A rush of pride bloomed through me. "I couldn't have done this without you, without any of you." I included Peter.

"Yanni, hurry up, man," someone yelled from the wings.

Too excited to keep still, I kissed Mrs and Mr Landon on the cheek, paused long enough to look Peter in the eye before I kissed him, then raced off to join the others. Ten very rushed minutes later, we were walking out of the college auditorium to the nearest bar.

As fun as it was, I didn't want to hang out all night. We laughed and told stories and joked about rehearsals, and Peter was very much included, but after a few hours, I'd had enough.

He was sitting on a stool, and I stood between his legs. "Let's go home," I suggested.

"You sure?"

I gave him a nod. "Yeah, this has been fun, but it's not my scene."

Peter rubbed his thumb on my hip. "Okay, then. Let's go."

We said our goodbyes with a few hugs and walked back to his car. The weather was cooler now and I shivered, so Peter put his arm around me to keep me warm. "Your place or mine?" he asked as he opened the passenger door of his car for me.

I rolled my eyes. There was a no-sleepover rule at my house. "Uh, yours."

"I have a gift for you at home," he said when he'd gotten in.

"A gift? What for?"

"For tonight. A celebratory gift for all the hard work you put into the play." He smiled serenely. "You were so good on stage. Like you really come alive up there."

"I love it," I said simply.

"And your friends are great."

"They are. Thank you for hanging out with them tonight."

"I um, I'd really like you to meet my friends," he said nervously. He talked about how he'd spoken to his friends about their monthly poker night, and how it was scheduled for the weekend after next. He'd hesitated about missing time with me, which of course opened the floodgates of a hundred questions. "Oh, they gave me hell," he said happily. "And now they want to know when they can meet you. Apparently I might have mentioned you one time too many, and they're ribbing me."

"Oh," I said, blinking. "Yes, I'd love to meet them." And I would. He'd spoken of them a lot and I wanted to be a part of his entire life, but I wasn't sure about meeting two strange men in close quarters where there would be alcohol involved. I needed to be mentally prepared for this. "Would it be at your house or out somewhere?"

"We usually meet at my house, though, only because they're both married with kids, and my house is like their man-cave. We put a game on the TV, play poker at the dining table, and talk crap all night. It's nothing like…" He took a deep breath. "I get it, though. If you're not comfortable, I don't want to push you."

"No, that sounds okay. I don't play poker, though."

"It doesn't have to be poker. We can have our poker night anytime, really. How about we do dinner one time instead? It doesn't have to be anytime soon, but you and I can cook dinner and they can bring their wives, and we'll make a proper night out of it?"

"That sounds great." Much more my kind of thing.

He eyed me cautiously. "Are you sure you're okay with it?"

I knew he'd see through me. "What if they don't like me?"

Peter laughed and lifted our joined hands to kiss the back of my hand. "Impossible. You know what fascinates me about you?"

"No, what?"

"Tonight, you were on that stage and you owned it. Demanding presence and loud voice. Yet off stage you're the opposite."

"That's just playing a role," I replied. "Like I've said before. That's not me up there. That's a character. This here"—I waved between us—"this is the real me."

He pulled the car up at a stoplight and gave me that eye-crinkling smile I loved so much. "Well, then," he started nervously, "how would you feel about meeting my mother?"

I stared at him. "For real? Your actual mother?"

He chuckled. "I do only have one."

Oh, God. Goose bumps crawled over my skin, and not in a very pleasant way. "Um." I let out a breath and tried to loosen the coil of fear that squeezed my heart.

Peter gave me a tight smile that was more sad than happy. "It's okay if you're not ready for that."

I didn't want to hurt him in any way. How could he not see this wasn't about him? "What if she doesn't like me? What if she thinks I'm too young? Or not good enough? I don't have any money or a career or anything, really. Oh God, what if she thinks I'm some gold digger? I'd be horrified."

Peter pulled the car to a stop at his house and shut the engine off. He turned in his seat to face me and squeezed my hand. "Yanni, my sweetest boy."

A flush of warmth at his term of endearment for me eased the panic a little.

"She will see that I am happy, and she will see that I am hopelessly head over heels in love with you. That's all she'll see. And she'll love you too. I promise." The look in his eyes was pure strength and certainty. "If anything, she'll probably say you're too thin and will offer you enough food to feed an army. She's not happy unless she's feeding someone."

I felt a bit more comfortable with the idea. Not about her liking me, but the whole feeding people was familiar. My mother and grandmother were always trying to feed people. Well, unless they were gay... "She knows we're a couple, right? She'll know that I'm... you know, gay."

Peter pursed his lips together, fighting a smile until he saw my question was a serious one. "She knows, and she will love you. Because I do. That's the only reason she needs."

"Oh."

He finally smiled. "Come on, let's get inside. You have a gift waiting, remember?"

I followed him inside and scooped up a rather peeved Neenish. I gave her a cuddle. "Oh, baby girl, did Daddy forget to feed you?"

"No, Daddy didn't forget," Peter said. "Her food bowl is still half-full."

I gave Neenish a scratch. "Did you just miss your daddy then?" I asked her.

Peter was holding a large, white rectangular box with a black ribbon: my gift. "Here. I'll swap you. I'll take Miss Crankypuss, you take this."

I handed over Neenish, and Peter gave me the box. We sat on the sofa, Neenish now purring on Peter's lap, the box sitting on mine. "You didn't have to get me anything," I said.

"I wanted to."

"You spoil me."

Peter smiled proudly. "I like spoiling you."

I pulled at the ribbon and it fell away. Even the ribbon felt expensive, and the box was thick, embossed cardboard. Whatever was inside was clearly lavish. I pulled the top of the box off to find out.

A swathe of neatly folded purple and pink silk lay inside the box. God, I didn't even have to touch it to know it was expensive. "Oh, Peter."

"I know how much you love the one you have, and I certainly know how much I love it."

I smiled at that.

"So I thought you could leave this one here, or leave the other one here, and have one to wear at your place. For when we talk on the phone at night."

My cheeks heated. "Well, it would save me bringing it here on the weekends."

Peter was beaming. "It would."

"Should I try it on?"

"Yes, please."

I stood up and slowly unbuttoned my shirt, and he clearly enjoyed the show. The cooler air chilled my skin; my nipples were hard. I lifted the silk out of the box, feeling the cool, luxurious fabric in my fingers. I found the collar of the garment and let it drape to its full length. It was another overshirt, or gown as I called it. Thigh length, with long, flowing sleeves, and a sash to tie it off around the waist. The purple and pink were mottled swirls, like an abstract watercolor art piece.

It was exquisite.

I slid one arm through the sleeve, then the next, and I'd never felt anything so delicate, so utterly, so utterly…

"How does it feel?"

"Opulent."

Peter's eyebrows shot up. "Opulent. I like that."

"Peter, it's incredible. And the color is beautiful."

"Purple suits you. It brings out the tone of your skin."

I ran my hand up my arm, caressing the silk over my skin. And as much as I liked the feel of it, Peter loved the show I was putting on for him. Hmm. I put my booted foot near his thigh. "Could you take that off for me?"

The corner of his lip pulled upward; lust flickered in his eyes. He undid the laces on my boot and pulled it off gently. So I gave him my other foot. He removed that boot too, and I stood in front of him and undid my belt.

He picked up Neenish and put her on the couch, shifted in his seat a little, and spread his legs. His eyes were dark now, urging me on.

I popped the button on my jeans and slowly let the zipper down. He licked his bottom lip. I pulled my jeans down, letting them pool at my feet, and I kicked them off. I stood there, wearing nothing but my briefs and the silk gown.

Then I straddled him.

Peter's chest rose and fell with harsh breaths, and I lifted his chin so I could kiss him. "It's beautiful," I murmured.

"So are you." He skimmed his hands over my hips, up my sides, caressing the silk on my skin. "I bought it at a lingerie store. The sales clerk told me the lady I was buying it for was very lucky, indeed. I told her she was wrong. It was a man, and *I* was the lucky one."

I kissed him again, softer, slower, grinding on him a little. "I'm the lucky one." I kissed him harder then, and Peter let his head fall back onto the back of the sofa, giving me full control.

I ground down on him, feeling his erection through his trousers. He reached between us and freed his cock, then with his hands on my hips, he directed our bodies to move together. I was braver with him now, and he read all my cues so well. He could take more control, hold me, roll me over, lie on top of me. There was always still clothing involved, like I was less vulnerable or he was less threatening if he wasn't completely naked. Which was ludicrous, because Peter was never threatening. And we could shower naked together, and he could get undressed in front of me, and me in front of him.

I was braver now. And I wanted him to take me.

As I straddled his hips and he rubbed our cocks together as we kissed, I imagined he was inside me. I would picture it to the point where I could almost feel it, and that ache of longing, of wanting him buried inside me was getting stronger, and I couldn't deny it anymore.

Peter came and I followed a few heartbeats after. We got cleaned up and climbed into bed. I wore the silk shirt. Peter wore only sleep pants, leaving his pillow of chest hair for me to cuddle into. He pulled the covers up over us and rubbed my back and planted soft kisses to the top of my head.

"Peter?"

"Hmm?"

"I want to try again."

A pause. "Try what again?"

"Sex."

He chuckled. "We just finished ten minutes ago. I'll need longer——"

He misunderstood what I meant. "No, sorry, I mean anal sex." I kept my face to his chest. "I want to have you inside my body."

He was silent and still. "Tonight?"

"No, not tonight, but soon."

"Will you look at me please?"

I leaned up so I could see his face. The room was dark, but I could still make out the seriousness in his eyes.

He put his hand to my face and pushed my wayward curls off my forehead. "Do you feel something is lacking between us? Because I don't. If you want to do this because you think it's something I want, then please know, what we have is perfectly enough for me."

"No," I started, then I sighed. "Well, yes, a little. I feel like something is lacking a bit. I mean, I love what we have, but when we have sex now, I imagine you inside me and it's better. Does that sound bad, because I don't mean for it to?"

"It doesn't sound bad at all," he said gruffly.

"I can't describe it really, but it's like an ache, a longing. I want you to have me, to truly make me yours."

He grunted and rolled us over, crushing his mouth to mine. Even when he manhandled me, there was still a gentleness, an awareness of my comfort levels. He broke the kiss, panting heavily. "Yanni, my sweet boy."

"Yes, Daddy?"

He groaned and leaned his forehead to mine, letting out a strained laugh. "You're killing me."

"Will you try again with me?"

He kissed me softly, and even in the darkness, I could see the promise in his eyes. "Yes. Of course." He rolled us onto our sides and cradled me in his arms. "We can talk about it more tomorrow. It's late and we should sleep."

I felt better having asked him, and I felt even better that he agreed. I snuggled into his neck and smiled. "Night, Daddy."

He groaned again and I chuckled, but he tightened his arms around me, and that was how we woke up the next morning.

WORK ON SATURDAY was the longest four-hour shift ever. The customers were pleasant, tips were good, coworkers were chatty, and all in all, it was a good day, but I longed to be home with Peter.

I longed to be in bed with Peter.

I raced home, changed clothes, packed a bag, and met him at the door with a slow kiss. "Well, that's one hell of a welcome," he said, smiling.

I reminded Jordan and Skylar that I'd be home for our usual Sunday morning laundry date, and I all but dragged Peter to his car. But my plans for spending the afternoon in bed with Peter came to a screeching halt when he started the engine.

"Speaking of tomorrow," he said. He pulled the car out into traffic. "I spoke to my mom, and instead of meeting her for brunch, I thought we could do afternoon tea instead. Or a late lunch. Whatever you'd prefer."

I stared. "I'm meeting your mom tomorrow?" My voice squeaked.

He reached over and took my hand. "Is that okay?"

I put my free hand to my forehead. "I'm not prepared."

"What do you need to be prepared about?"

"I can't turn up empty-handed!" I stared at him like he'd lost his mind. "Does she like flowers? I should totally bring her flowers. What are her favorites? Or chocolate? Or wine? Jesus, Peter, I need more time!"

"Yanni, it'll be fine."

"No, I need her to like me, and I was raised to know that when you're meeting family, you take something, usually food. It's a Greek thing... well, actually, it's not even Greek. It's just a good manners thing."

Peter chuckled and kissed the back of my hand. "Then we can make her something." He changed lanes and turned at the next intersection. "It'll mean more if it comes from the heart."

He took some more turns, very obviously familiar with wherever we were going, and a short time later, pulled up at a small Russian market.

I didn't know why, but when he'd suggested making something, I'd assumed Greek. He'd obviously assumed Russian. "Um, I can't cook Russian food," I hissed at him. God, this was going to be a disaster. "I'm going to butcher some family favorite recipe, and your mother will banish me from the house!"

Peter just laughed, got out of the car, and walked around to open my door. "Please, trust me," he said, still smiling.

Okay, trusting myself not to make a mess of everything was one thing, but trusting him, I could do. So into the market we went, with the full intention of buying ingredients to make something from scratch. But inside the tiny store, as well as aisles of groceries, were selections of freshly baked cakes and sweets, hot meals, and cold selections of all kinds of fish and caviar.

Peter collected a basket and went for the cake selections first. "I thought we were going to bring something homemade?" I asked quietly.

He pointed to the display counter of different pastries and breads. "These are homemade. They bake everything here."

A stout lady behind the counter scowled at us until Peter looked up and said something in Russian. Her expression changed immediately, breaking out into a handsome grin. I gaped at Peter. "I didn't know you speak Russian," I whispered so only he could hear.

"Only the basics," he replied. "Do you not know a few Greek phrases?"

I conceded with a nod. "Good point."

He ordered some kind of raisin bread, some honey-berry gingerbread, and some walnut-looking cookie things he called *oreshki*. He looked at me. "Have you eaten lunch?"

The trouble with working ten till two was that no, sometimes I forgot to eat lunch and he knew this. "Nope. Too busy today."

So we moved to the display of hot food. There were a dozen trays of different dishes: creamy potatoes, beef stews, fried cod, stroganoff, and dishes Peter called *golubtsi* and *pelmeni*. He ordered small containers of a few different dishes, and after that, we strolled the aisles looking at all the different items. Some labels he could read, some he couldn't. Some things looked curiously delicious, and some looked downright questionable. But it was fun, and I loved this insight into Peter's history.

He found some Russian cheese in the deli section, grabbed some crackers, selected some kind of fig paste, a few green pears, and we were finally done.

Peter paid for everything—I was too scared to look at the total price and pretended not to be listening as he made small talk with the server in a language I couldn't understand. And he was beaming as we drove back to his place.

"Mom's gonna love it," he said, putting the grocery bag on the kitchen counter. "She only goes to the Russian market for special occasions, so this will be a real treat." He put everything in the fridge, leaving out the hot dishes. He grabbed two forks, and we ate his selections of dishes, picnic style, on his couch.

And truth be told, I forgot about my secret agenda of us attempting to make love all afternoon. Until, that was, we were lazing on the sofa with my face on his chest, my hips snug between his legs, watching one of Charlie Chaplin's "talkie" films and Peter stroking my back. "So, I've been thinking about what you asked last night."

It took me a second or two to catch on. "Oh? Not having second thoughts?"

He laughed. "Ah, no. Far from it."

"Okay, good."

"Are you?"

I looked up at him and shook my head slowly. "No. None."

"And I've been thinking about what might be easier or better for you, position-wise."

"Oh." I hadn't even thought of that. I felt my face flame.

Peter ran his thumb across my blush. "If you straddle me," he whispered gruffly, "you'll be in control."

I nodded, suddenly full of butterflies and anticipation. "When?"

He studied me for a moment. "That's up to you."

"What about tonight?"

He gave a smirk. "Is that too soon?"

"No," I answered probably a little too quickly.

He chuckled. "Well, just remember you can say stop at any time, and I promise you, I'll stop."

"I know you will." I guess now was the right time to bring up something else I'd been thinking about. "And about condoms…"

"I have some," he replied.

I frowned. "Well, how would you feel about not using them?"

Peter blinked and went still. "Um…"

I sat up, and he shuffled a bit so he was sitting up straighter. "It's fine. I shouldn't have asked."

"Yanni, if you've brought it up, then I know there's a reason."

"Well, it's just that all the porn we've watched," and we'd watched a lot more of those short clips on those sites he showed me—only this time, he watched with me and screened which ones weren't suitable. It always led to mutual orgasms. Always. "Well, they don't use them. And I like the idea of it. Having you and nothing else, if you know what I mean. We've both been tested and everything was fine. But I'll understand if you don't want to."

Peter took my hand and took a moment before he spoke. "I've never done that with anyone else."

"Neither have I," I admitted. "Lance always insisted on them. The one thing I'm thankful for."

Peter cocked his head to the side. "Do you not want to use them because he did?"

"No, it's not that."

"What is it then?"

"Well, I just like the idea of it being just you and nothing else between us, like I already said." I was certain my face went bright red, but I had to be truthful with him. "And I like the idea of you coming inside me."

Peter's eyes went wide, and he hissed out a breath. "Oh, Yanni." He said my name like a prayer.

"And in those videos, those guys get their daddy's reward for being a good boy," I mumbled, mortified at saying this out loud. I covered my face with my hands. "I'm so embarrassed."

Gentle fingers peeled my hands away, and Peter's face was so close. His pupils were blown, and his face was flushed. "You want a reward for being a good boy?"

The lust in his voice curled around my insides and made my balls throb. I nodded.

Peter picked me up like I weighed nothing and brought me to his lap. He shuffled to the edge of the sofa, then, with my legs wrapped around his waist, he stood up and I laughed and kissed down his neck as he carried me to his room.

He gently placed me on his bed. I shuffled up and he followed me, crawling over me. "Are you okay with me undressing you?" he asked, kissing the slip of skin above my waistband.

I knew being completely naked with him in bed would have to happen at some point, and I trusted him. "Yes."

He undid my jeans and stripped them off me, only stopping to lick my cock. I fell back against the bed with a moan. Then he knelt up to pull his shirt off and unbutton his pants. He left them on for now, even though I could see the tent of his hard-on, he only ever thought of me.

He took me into his mouth again, sucking and licking like he'd done so many times before. Normally I still had briefs on, but I was more than fine with this. But then he climbed off the bed and found the tube of lube we'd used to stroke each other and threw it on the bed beside me.

And I knew this was going to happen.

I wanted it.

"I need to prepare you," he said softly, kissing his way back up my thighs.

This was the unspoken test. Because if I couldn't handle his gentle fingers, then this would stop right now. I'd done this to myself over the last month or two when I lay in my own bed, talking to him on the phone or just imagining him there. I told myself this was no different. "Okay."

So he worked my cock with his mouth and gently massaged my thighs, my balls, my perineum. "I'm going to lick your balls," he said, doing exactly what he said. Anticipation curled in my belly; he was making my body sing.

Then he licked me lower, and lower, and oh my God. I gripped bed covers and held on, not wanting to fall over the precipice but hoping I did all the same. "Oh God, Peter," I cried out.

Then he stopped, taking a quick suck of my dick again, making me shudder with pleasure. He sucked on my nipples, then kissed up my neck to my jaw. His stubble juxtaposed with the softness of his lips, and he kissed me fiercely, sucking my tongue into his mouth. I had no clue he was holding the lube until I heard the click of the lid... and then his fingers were there, rubbing gently at first, pressing in just a little, then rubbing some more.

I was in sensory overload, and every nerve ending was strung tight with pleasure. He was making love to my body in languid, gentle ebbs and flows. Nothing had ever felt this good.

Then he slipped a finger inside me, and I wanted it. I wanted more. So much more.

This was the ache I felt, needing him to fill every part of me. I needed more of him inside me. "Yes. More," I moaned into his mouth.

So he gave me more. He pushed his finger farther into me, sliding in and out, and I writhed for it. I needed it.

After he'd worked me with a second finger, I couldn't stand it anymore. It wasn't enough. I needed to feel him buried inside me. "I'm ready," I panted. My whole body craved him.

Peter maneuvered himself so he sat up, leaning against the headboard. He lifted his hips and pulled his briefs down to his thighs; his huge cock sprang free. A rush of warmth filled my belly. He was a solid build, broad and thickset, with hair in all the right places. I was lean, skinny even, with sinewy limbs, and mostly hairless. As far as body types go, we were polar opposites, yet mentally, emotion-ally, we were a perfect match.

Peter took the lube and slicked his cock, though his eyes never left mine. "Are you sure you want this?"

Lifting one leg over him, I straddled his legs and nodded. Then, leaning over his cock, I pulled his chin up so I could kiss him. "I want you so bad."

He made a strained humming noise that spurred me on. I could do this. This felt so right. He poured some lube onto my fingers. "For you."

I reached behind me and slicked the lube over my hole, then shuffled up into position. I took hold of his shaft—he felt huge in my hand—and pressed the cockhead against my entrance.

Oh God. This was it.

I pushed against him, just a little, feeling him nudging my hole. I rose up an inch, then back down, letting him nudge in a little farther each time. I hadn't even taken the tip in yet—he was so big. Bigger than I imagined. Bigger than I anticipated. I mean, I knew he was big. I'd held his cock before, felt the size and weight of it. I'd taken it in my mouth, but having it in my ass was a different game altogether.

I pulled off again and writhed so his cock ran along my perineum. I wanted this but wasn't sure if I could.

"Just breathe, my love," Peter murmured. His eyes were imploring, kind and concerned. "Take as much of me as you want."

I crushed my mouth to his, letting him taste the grati-tude on my tongue. He was giving me all the time and patience in the world. Never rushing, never demanding. I sank down on him again, a little farther this time. The head of his cock pushed against the ring of muscle. I sucked back a breath but didn't pull away. I held it and held it until the discomfort passed, and he slipped inside me.

Peter gasped, his huge hands held my thighs, keeping me still, and his eyes were wide. His jaw set with restraint. "Oh, Yanni," he cried. "You're so beautiful."

I slid my hand along his jaw and kissed him, rocking slowly on his cock. I couldn't take any more of him in me. Not yet. Just the tip of him was enough for now.

Peter's whole body went rigid, his muscles tight. "You're gonna make me come," he breathed the words through gritted teeth. He was almost vibrating with self-control. His touches were gentle yet firm, his pleas were soft yet commanding. Just like a good daddy should. "Please, boy. Please."

"Yes, Daddy," I whispered against his mouth.

He convulsed, pleasure wracking through him, then he stilled as his cock pulsed inside me. I could feel him come, swelling and surging, spilling his seed in me. His neck was corded, his head pressed back, and he let out a primal groan as his orgasm left him spent.

But as he softened a little, I could take more of him, and his back arched, and he moaned as I sank down on him.

He wrapped his arms tight around me and rolled us over so he was on top of me, still inside me. "Oh, Yanni, my beautiful boy," he murmured between kisses and slow-rocking hips. He was only half-hard, but he still filled me perfectly. "That was amazing. You are amazing."

He kissed me until my eyes rolled back in my head, but the gentle thrust of his hips, the slick slide of his cock inside me, made me wrap my legs around him. "Oh God, Peter."

Without another word, he understood. He leaned up on one hand and took my cock with his other, pumping me as he stayed buried inside me. I came hard, and he kissed me, swallowing my cries of pleasure.

When my senses came back to me, he had enveloped me in his arms with soft kisses and murmurs of sweet nothings. "I love you, Yanni."

"Mmm." I nuzzled into him, feeling spongy and completely worshipped. "I love you, too."

"Do you feel okay? Sore anywhere?"

I took stock of my body. I knew what pain was like from unprepared sex, and there was definitely nothing like that. "I can't feel anything but bliss right now."

He chuckled and seemed to relax then. I knew we'd have to get cleaned up at some point, but we enjoyed a moment of quiet, unmoving, just savoring what we'd just experienced.

I'd done it. I'd broken through the last shackle that Lance had put on me, and I felt liberated, empowered. I'd taken another part of my life back.

Except for one small detail...

"You have a really big dick," I mumbled into his chest.

Peter barked out a laugh. "Uh, thanks?"

"I couldn't take it all. Well, not to begin with." I pulled back so I could look into his eyes. "After you came it was fine."

He groaned. "That was the hottest thing I've ever done."

"I like that you've never done that with anyone else," I admitted. I kissed him softly. "And I really like that your come is still inside me."

He made a sound that might have been a half growl. "Yanni, you have no idea what that does to me."

I laughed cheekily. I knew exactly what it did to him. "And tomorrow night, we'll do it again. Though this time, I'm pretty sure I'll take all of you."

His head fell back onto the pillow and he groaned. "Jesus. I'm not sure I'll survive you."

I laughed. "Yeah, you will. And you'll love every minute."

He pulled me into his arms and kissed the top of my head. "I already do."

CHAPTER TWENTY-ONE

I DUMPED my laundry bag on the floor next to a machine, and Jordan and Skylar did the same with theirs. This had been our weekly ritual for months, and as silly and as mundane as it was, I enjoyed this time. It used to be just Jordan and me, but Skylar had started to join us, and I was more than fine with that. There was clearly something budding between them. Their friendship had cemented a long time ago, but now the glances and giggles from private conversations were more and more frequent.

We each threw our first loads into our machines and set them going, and this was when our conversations started. We usually talked about school or work or Peter, and after last night, I was still buzzing.

"Okay, Yanni," Skylar said, crossing her arms and smirking. "Give us the details. You haven't stopped smiling yet."

I felt blush burn from my forehead to my toes. But I couldn't deny it. I was sure my smile bordered on ridiculous. "Peter and I had sex last night." They both stopped and stared. "I mean, we've done a lot of sexual things," I whispered, looking around at the other people doing laundry. No one even looked in our direction. "But last night was... *the* night."

Then, surprising even myself, I started to cry. My eyes welled with tears, and I laughed at how stupid it was. "I don't know why I'm crying!"

"Aww," Skylar said, coming in for a hug. "It's okay."

Then Jordan was there, sneaking into the embrace as well. The three of us hugged until I pulled back to wipe my eyes. "I've never been this happy. These tears are stupid!"

"It's a huge deal," Skylar said. She put her hand on my arm and whispered, "Overcoming sexual assault is a huge fucking deal, Yanni. You should be proud of yourself."

"I am." I sniffled, swallowing my tears. "I don't know if I've overcome it. I think it will always be a part of me. My life is forever changed, ya know?" They both nodded sadly. "But I took back control. Lance took it from me, and I took it back! So maybe that is conquering it, I don't know." I shook my head with a teary laugh. "I'm a freaking mess today."

Jordan, holding the cuffs of her long sleeves in her fists, gave me another silent hug, which, for her, was a big deal. I guessed she trusted me, and that realization moved me back to tears. I returned her hug gently, and Skylar looked on with tears in her eyes. "I'm proud of you," Jordan whispered, and when she pulled back, I saw that she was teary too.

"God, I'm making us all cry," I said, trying to laugh off this emotion that came from nowhere. I waved my hands in front of my eyes, fanning them, trying to stem the burn of tears. "And he was so wonderful. I mean, we've been working up to it. It's taken months of tiny steps—you know, two steps forward, one step back—but the timing was right, or the planets aligned, or something cosmic happened anyway. It was perfect."

Skylar giggled. "I'm sure it was cosmic."

"I'm meeting his mom this afternoon."

They both stared again, eyes wide. "His mom?" Jordan asked.

"Yeah. He normally goes to see her when I'm here with you guys, but today we're going after. He wants me to meet her. And his friends, but we're starting with his mom."

"Holy shit," Skylar whispered. "Now *that's* a big deal."

"I know. It's *all* a big deal. Last night, now meeting his mom, then his friends next week or next month or sometime."

"He's really serious about you," Jordan said quietly.

I shrugged one shoulder. "Well, yeah. He tells me he loves me all the time."

Jordan nodded. "Yeah, but still. Saying that is one thing. And it's a very big thing, don't get me wrong. But wanting you to meet everyone is a whole other level."

"It's a whole permanent level," Skylar added. "Like he's thinking permanent. Forever. May as well get married, take his name, have his babies kind of level."

My heart tripped over in my chest. "You think?"

Jordan's smile was slow and knowing. "Look at you. You're not even the slightest bit freaked out."

Skylar snorted. "He's glowing."

I buried my face in my hands to hide my embarrassment, but then I laughed right out loud and did some crazy happy wiggle. "Give me another hug," I said, and they both did.

Only this time, I pulled away and maneuvered their arms so they were hugging each other. "Well, would you look at that," I said. "Happiness is contagious."

Both girls blushed but there was a look shared between them, and for a moment I thought they might kiss. I was disappointed they didn't but happy neither of them pulled apart too soon. I hummed excitedly, back to buzzing and nonstop smiling, just as our washing machines beeped to signal they were done.

We went back to our laundry, the three of us smiling away to ourselves.

I CLIMBED into Peter's car knowing we were heading to his mother's house, and I was nervous. He kissed me over the console, slow and sweet. "I missed you," he whispered. He'd only dropped me off a few hours before, but I understood because I missed him too. "How were Jordan and Skylar? Get all your washing done?"

"Yep, all done. And they're good. I told them we had sex last night."

Peter's eyes went wide with surprise. "You did?"

I nodded. "I had to tell someone. They knew something had happened because I was buzzing, apparently."

"And what did they do?"

"They hugged me." I laughed and shook my head. "In the middle of the laundromat. I might have cried. Just a little."

He was immediately concerned. "You cried?"

"It was so weird. I think I was too happy." I didn't want to explain the whole emotion-dump of overcoming my past. But this was Peter, and he understood me. "And Skylar said something that rang true with me. I conquered a demon last night. With your help, of course. I took back the only remaining thing that Lance stole from me."

He took my hand and put it to his face. His eyes shone fiercely. "I love you."

I leaned my head on the headrest and just stared at him. This wonderful man did love me. I could see it in everything he did. "I love you too."

He leaned over and kissed me. "Ready to meet my mom? She's very excited to meet you."

Nerves stomped all over my good mood. "What if I say something stupid?"

"You do the fox and rabbit thing so well. Slaying demons one minute, timid as a rabbit the next."

"That's me," I said. "A demon-slaying rabbit."

Peter laughed and started the car. "Perfect in every way."

PETER'S MOTHER'S house was an older-style bungalow that had at some point been converted into two smaller houses. They shared the wide front steps and a roof, but there were two front doors and a brick wall that separated each home.

Peter gave me an encouraging smile and opened the driver door. He collected a canvas grocery bag from the backseat and waited for me to join him. Swallowing down my nerves and trying to put on a brave face, I walked up the steps and stood back while Peter rang the doorbell.

The woman who answered was an older, female version of Peter, elegantly dressed in a black tailored pantsuit with a fitted jacket. I suddenly felt underdressed in tan pants and a button-down shirt. She was tall, had short, gray hair, styled nicely, and from her shoulders and arms, she looked very strong and fit. She threw open the door, pulled Peter in for a kiss on the cheek, then putting her hands on my shoulders, she let out a sigh and hugged me.

Yep. She was as strong as she looked.

"Oh, you're a doll," she said. Peter looked on with a grin while holding the door back, and his mother went inside. "Come in, come in."

Peter held the door for me. I stepped inside but waited so I could follow him. There was a short hall that led to an old-fashioned white and yellow kitchen. Peter put the bag on the table that sat in the middle of the room. "How was church?" he asked, pulling out the goods we'd bought yesterday.

She waved her hand dramatically. "Always the same. I just got in, actually. Can you give me a moment to get changed? Peter, be a dear and get that coffee machine going, and when I come back, you can introduce me properly to this gorgeous man of yours."

She disappeared with a smile, and Peter was quick to wrap his arms around me, kissing the side of my head. "She loves you already."

I was more nervous now than before I got here. I noticed a gold-framed picture of Jesus on the wall just off the kitchen... and she just got back from church. I suddenly felt a little lightheaded. "She's religious?"

Peter froze, then pulled back with his hands on my arms. "She is. Russian Orthodox, to be exact. She always has been, but when things with my father got particularly bad, her faith helped her through that."

A wave of guilt washed over me. "Oh."

"Yanni," he said gently, lifting my face. "She accepts me, just as I am. She's not going to shun you because you're gay."

I closed my eyes. "My parents did."

He kissed my eyelids. "I know. But please don't worry. I would never bring you into a situation like that."

I took a deep breath and found comfort from his words. I even managed half a smile. "Thank you."

"I better get this coffee started," he said, walking to the coffee machine.

I finished unpacking the items from the grocery bag on the table as his mom came back out, now wearing a long, flowy navy skirt and a knitted blouse, and she even wore glasses with purple frames. She looked much more comfortable and a little less daunting.

"Now, Peter," she said smiling at me.

"Ah." He shut the lid on the coffee machine and darted over to me. "Mom, this is my boyfriend, Yanni Tomaras. Yanni, my mom, Katia Hannikova."

"Mrs Hannikova," I said. "It's a pleasure to meet you."

"I love your manners, darling," she said with a smile that reminded me of Peter's. "But please, call me Katia." She pulled out a seat at the table, then one for me. "Come, sit with me. Tell me about you."

"Oh, uh," I stammered, sitting nervously beside her. I had no idea what Peter had told her about me, if anything.

She seemed to pick up on my unease. "Peter tells me you're studying to be an actor."

"Yes, at LASPA."

Peter put coffees in front of us, then bringing his own to the table, he sat down next to me and took my hand. In front of his mother. "And he's brilliant," Peter said. "I watched his *Midsummer Night's Dream* portrayal, where he was the most brilliant Puck."

"It was just a class production," I added, downplaying his compliment.

"It was a packed audience," Peter told her. "With a standing ovation."

Katia laughed. "I'm sorry, Yanni. But if Peter says you're brilliant, then I'm inclined to believe him."

I was sure my blush could have been seen from space. Peter laughed, and standing, he kissed my temple, then opened the container of sweets. "Yanni wanted to bring something, so we called into the Russian *rynok*. We got these *Alenka* chocolates for you."

"You thought of these?" Katia asked me.

"Well, Peter suggested them. If I'd been left unsupervised, I'd have probably made *koulourakia*. They're a Greek cookie."

Katia beamed at me. "And I would have loved them!"

Peter went to a cupboard and took out three small plates, then some spoons from a drawer. We ate and talked, and it was clear to me that Peter and Katia were very close. We soon moved to the sitting room, Peter and me on the loveseat and his mom next to me on the single recliner. But when Peter excused himself to go to the bathroom, Katia zeroed in on me.

I was suddenly and apparently very obviously petrified.

"Oh, honey," she said. "Let me tell you something about my boy…"

I stopped breathing.

"I have never, ever seen him this happy."

Oh. "Oh." I could literally feel the color return to my face.

She laughed quietly, and reaching over, she put her hand on my arm. "I always wondered if he'd find someone who he'd give his heart to, and now I know he has."

I put my free hand to my heart. "Oh wow, I thought you were going to tell me I wasn't good enough."

She looked horrified. "Oh, my good Lord, no. I would never!"

I felt instant relief. "Good, because I'm kind of in love with him."

She raised an eyebrow. "Just kind of?"

"Okay, so completely head over heels." I put my hand over my eyes, mortified that I just admitted that to Peter's mother.

She laughed just as Peter came back in, carrying a tray with the cheese, crackers, fig paste, and sliced pears. "Okay, what did I miss?"

He put the tray on the coffee table and sat next to me. "I'm just embarrassing myself," I said, putting my face against his shoulder.

"No, he's not. He's charming me," Katia said. Then she noticed the cheese. "Oh, Peter, is that *Omichka*?"

"Sure is."

"My mother would be proud," she said wistfully. "You spoil me."

"Well, today was a special occasion," he said, taking my hand. So we ate the cheese and crackers, the fig paste was incredible, the pears were too. We drank sparkling mineral water, and Katia told me stories of Peter's high school days, trying to embarrass him. "His school photos are on the mantel."

Smiling, I walked over to the silver frames of a young, blond boy, the younger ones with gappy teeth and spiky hair, an older one with braces, then his college graduation photo where he stood proudly with his mother, certificate in hand. There was no photo of his father, and I was kind of glad.

There was a photo that didn't match the others, though. It was a group of college kids at some outdoor gathering, and there, at the bottom left of the picture, was Peter. He had his arm around some guy and he looked happy. "Is that an ex-boyfriend?"

Peter, now standing next to me, simply shrugged like it was no big deal. "Yeah. We dated for a while in our first year of college. His name was Jimmy Cortez. I have no idea whatever happened to him. We lost touch."

Oh. It struck me as an odd choice of photo to display in his mom's house.

Katia now stood on the other side of me. "Yanni, did Peter ever tell you how he came out to me?"

I shook my head. "No."

Peter leaned into me a little and gave me a smile, but it was Katia who spoke. "He didn't have the best childhood," she said sadly, staring at the photograph. "But he was good at school, happy, at least, and always got good grades. He had lots of friends, and by the time he was in high school… well, suffice it to say, I was so busy with my own problems that I didn't notice anything out of the ordinary."

"You did just fine, Mom," Peter said like they'd had this conversation a hundred times.

"He was an A-student, played football, even worked after school to help me pay the bills. Him having or not having a girlfriend was the least of my worries…" Katia frowned. "Then he started college. He lived in the dorm, but he'd helped set me up in my own place by then, so I wanted him to go out and experience life. He'd always been so serious. I wanted him to have some fun, ya know?"

I swallowed, unsure of where this was going. "Yeah. I know."

Katia was still staring at the photo, and she smiled. "Then before the end of his first year, I was reading the college newspaper, and this photo was in it." She sighed heavily. "So, it wasn't really that he told me he liked boys. It was more that he was outed. It was an article about youth diversity or something like that. I can't even really remember what the article said exactly. But this photo…"

Peter put his arm around me and smiled fondly. "She called me, very upset. And when I came home, I found her sitting at the kitchen table staring at the photo and crying her eyes out."

I couldn't help the sharp breath, but I was quick to put my hand on his back. *How awful.* "Oh."

Katia laughed. "Oh no, it wasn't like that. I cried and cried because I'd never seen my own son as happy as he was in that photo. And after everything we'd been through, it killed me inside that he thought he had to hide that part of himself from me."

Peter leaned into me some more. "It's true. She hugged me and told me she only wanted me to be happy and to be myself."

Katia took the photo frame from the mantel and stared at where Peter was frozen in time, some twenty years ago, laughing in the sun. "Well," she said. "I'd never seen him that happy." She put the frame back in its place and gave us a warm smile. "Until now."

I shrank into Peter, and he laughed, putting his arm around me protectively. "I can't argue with that," he murmured.

"Not even with whatshisname?" Katia said, going back to her seat. "Demetri? Dennis?"

"Duncan," Peter corrected her. Duncan was the guy Peter had hired Spencer to help get back.

Katia all but rolled her eyes. "I never did care much for that boy. And you didn't either, did you Peter?"

"I thought I did," he answered. I looked up at him and he smiled at me. "But I can see now he wasn't the one for me."

The one for him? As in *the one*? Oh my God. I tried to speak, but my heart was doing crazy things in my chest.

"Oh yes," Katia said, collecting the tray and taking it into the kitchen. "We can all see that."

When his mother had left the room, Peter cupped my face and kissed me softly. "Ready to go home now?"

I nodded. "Yeah."

We said our goodbyes, and Katia made Peter promise he'd bring me back or even invite her for dinner—she hinted with a wink. She hugged me again. "It's so lovely to finally meet you, Yanni. He's done nothing but talk about you for months, and now I can see why. You're an absolute treasure. You look after my boy now, won't you?"

I nodded solemnly. "I promise."

She kissed my cheek, then hugged Peter. "And you give this boy everything he needs, you hear?" she told Peter.

The corner of his lip curled up. "I do, Mom."

God, I thought I might possibly die from embarrassment. Oblivious to the innuendo, she walked us out to the car so she could wave us off. It took me a few blocks before I could speak. "You give me everything I need? Did you really just tell your Mom that you give me *everything* I need?"

Peter laughed loudly. "I'm not going to lie to my own mother!"

"Oh God. Is it possible to die from blushing? Can the blood rush to my face be fatal?"

He laughed some more. "Did you like her?"

"She's amazing. You're so alike."

He nodded. "Thank you for meeting her. It meant a lot that you would do that for me."

"I'll do anything for you."

"Including meeting my friends?" He looked hopeful.

"Of course I'll meet them."

"Good, because I might have already made plans?"

I stared at him. "You what?"

"Dinner, next weekend, at my place."

I wasn't a fan of surprises. "Peter…"

He took my hand and kissed from my knuckles up my wrist, as far as he could while he was driving. "Yanni," he said with a wicked smile. "Be a good boy and say yes."

I laughed. "Oh, you're gonna play the Daddy card now?"

He grinned. "Did it work?"

I rolled my eyes. "Of course it did. But you need to make it up to me tonight."

He laughed and wiggled in his seat, happiness beaming out of him. "Oh, I plan to."

SPENDING the afternoon with Peter's mom and hearing Peter's coming out story and the sadness in Katia's voice got me thinking. So when we were back at his place, Peter was in the kitchen fixing salad for dinner and I sat on the counter out of his way, I wanted to know his whole story but wasn't sure how to ask.

"Peter, can I ask you something?"

He continued to slice the avocado. "Of course."

"I don't want to upset you, so you can say no if you want. I don't mean to dredge up bad memories, so if you'd rather not talk about it, that's okay."

"You want to know about my father?"

I nodded. "I know you've said he was an angry drunk, and I know what that means," I said quietly. "I just want to know your story, that's all."

He set the avocado aside and leaned against the counter. "He was an alcoholic. And yes, he was an angry drunk. He would beat my mother. One of my earliest memories, I remember being very young, maybe four or five, and hearing them fight in their room. He was yelling and she was crying, something smashed against the wall, and I hid in my bed."

"Oh, my God."

"It got better for a few years. Well, it didn't get any worse. But when I was nine, he got laid off and would drink all day." Peter frowned. "He was so angry at everything. The world owed him, or so he thought. And he took it out on her. Then when she wasn't enough, he started on me."

"Oh, Peter." I slid off the counter and went to him, putting my arms around him.

"He did a stint in jail after that, and things were good for us. Until he got out. We'd moved, but he found us. I was in high school by then, almost as big as him. He turned up, and I stopped him before he set one foot on the front step."

I squeezed him tight. "I'm sorry. I shouldn't have asked."

"It was a long time ago," he said. "Twenty-five years ago, actually." He kissed the top of my head. "I can talk about it now."

Still, reliving such a horrible time would never be easy, no matter how much time had filled the void between.

"He was rotten drunk, and I launched myself at him from the top step. I'd never hit anyone before or since, but I punched the shit outta him right then and there. I hit him for every time he'd hurt my mom, for every time he'd hit me. And when he was a bloodied mess on the front lawn, I dragged his ass to the curb with the garbage cans and told him to never come back."

I smiled at that. "I'm glad you did."

"We never saw him again. Heard he died a few years after that. Don't know the details; never wanted to find out."

"That's why you don't drink."

"Never touched a drop."

I squeezed him again and breathed his scent, reveling in his warmth. "You're an amazing man, Peter."

He sighed contentedly and rubbed my back. "Are you ready for dinner?"

I nodded. "Let me get it for you." I served it up and carried our plates to the table, then the cutlery and some sparkling mineral water. While we ate, he told me the story of the guy in the photo with him at college, and even though it was funny, there was an edge of sadness in his eyes that I was certain the memories of his father dredged up. I was grateful he told me about his father—I felt closer to him now—but I felt awful that I'd caused him pain in asking.

When he'd put his fork down for the final time, I stood up and swung my leg over him so I could sit on his lap. I draped my arms around his neck and nudged his nose to mine before kissing him slowly. When we drew apart, he hummed. "What was that for?"

"For being you," I replied. "Now, correct me if I'm wrong, but I believe we have some promises to keep."

His eyes flashed with curiosity and questions. "Promises?"

I kissed him again. "Yep. You promised you'd make it up to me tonight for organizing a dinner party next weekend so I could meet your friends without asking me."

He smiled. "Oh, right. Well, that's one. You said promises, as in plural."

"Last night I promised that tonight, when we make

love," I whispered, kissing him again. "That I'd take all of you."

His nostrils flared and his eyes darkened. "Now, that I remember."

"And you told your mom today that you'd give me everything I need."

"I did."

"I need you, Peter." I rolled my hips, feeling his hardening dick pushing against his jeans. It made me whimper.

Peter pulled my mouth to his, and keeping his huge hands on my thighs, he stood up. For a brief moment, I thought he considered laying me on the dining table, but he turned instead and carried me to his room.

"I like carrying you like this," he said.

I tightened my legs and hooked my ankles over his ass. "I like it too."

He took his time undressing me. And he took so long preparing me, stretching me, getting me ready to take him, I was writhing on his fingers, pleading with him that I was ready, but he was adamant. "I don't want to hurt you. Be patient, and I promise I'll make you feel so good…"

I couldn't argue with that.

He kissed me, massaged me, stroked me, caressed me. He ran his hands over every inch of my skin, kissed me some more, murmured sweet nothings in my ear. He didn't just get my ass ready. He got my whole body ready. And when he had me on my back with a pillow shoved under my ass, my legs spread wide, I was so pliable, so relaxed, and so turned on.

He applied lube, and when I thought he was done, he applied some more. Then, leaning over me, sliding his arms under my shoulders, he pressed his cock to my ready hole and slowly, slowly, pushed into me.

He held me tenderly, one arm now under my neck, the

other holding the top of my head. He kissed me, watching my every reaction. My eyes were wide as he breached me, my mouth open, my knees up near my chest as my body succumbed to taking him in. He was so gentle, so patient, every movement was for my benefit, not his.

"God, I love you," I murmured, arching my back and taking more of him inside me until I'd taken every inch. I was so full of him, it felt so good, I cried out, whined and moaned.

He froze. "Yanni?"

"Don't move," I pleaded. If he pulled out of me, I was sure I'd die. I locked my legs around him so he couldn't move. "Please, don't stop."

He rolled his hips and held my face as a long whining noise escaped me. "Oh, good boy," he said before covering my mouth with his. He gave me his tongue and I was lost, completely consumed by him. He owned my ass and my mouth, my heart and soul, and there was something so utterly freeing in giving him my control.

He was my safety, the cage in which I was safe to fly.

Then he started to thrust, slow and deep, my cock pressed between our bodies, sliding, and it was everything I needed. And when he changed his angle and slid into me again, I saw fireworks behind my eyes. "Holy fuck!" I cried out, gripping him with all my strength, digging my fingers into his skin. "More."

Peter groaned and did it again and again. "Feels good when I do that?"

"Yes, Daddy. Please, Daddy." I'd heard of prostate orgasms, but I'd never... I'd never... oh, fuck. I didn't recognize the sound that came out of my throat as I came. A pleasure so blinding exploded inside me, and I shot thick and hot between us, my cock untouched.

Peter cupped my face and held me until my orgasm

subsided, the look on his face one of wonder and love. "Such a good boy," he grated out as my legs splayed out onto the bed. I was completely spent, my bones were nothing but sponge, but he was still buried inside me, and God, he felt so good.

He somehow felt better after I'd come. The sensations were tenfold, yet I was more pliable. He could do whatever he wanted to me in that moment—move me, shape me, shift me—and I'd welcome it. As long as he stayed inside me.

"I want you inside me forever," I whispered, my brain hazy with post-orgasm bliss, my body like a ragdoll.

He leaned back over me so he could kiss me, and he thrust again, slow and long, making me feel every inch over and over. "You're such a good boy," he said, his voice gruff, his breaths ragged. "Do good boys get rewards?"

I nodded desperately. A shiver of a new kind of pleasure rolled through me. "Yes, please, Daddy."

And that was all it took. He thrust deep and groaned as he came inside me. I could feel each pulse, every jerk of his cock as he spilled his load.

He collapsed on top of me, still inside me, exactly where I wanted him. "Stay inside me," I whispered.

He tightened his arms around me, and we fell asleep just like that.

CHAPTER TWENTY-TWO

I SAT across from Patrice and divulged everything about what Peter and I had done in bed. Maybe I would have spared her the details, but what Skylar said to me had stuck. I'd conquered a demon. I'd taken back what was taken from me.

Patrice was happy for me, proud even, but she talked about highs and lows, and how post-traumatic stress disorder came in ebbs and flows. I listened, I learned, I understood. Even though things were flying at the moment, there would be turbulence. And that didn't mean failure. It just meant I needed to pilot cautiously.

"Maybe that would explain why I also felt… I don't know," I picked at my thumbnail. "Guilty, I suppose."

"Guilt, for what?"

"For liking it so much."

"For liking sex?"

I nodded. "Not right after… I think it took me about an hour to come back into my own body." She chuckled and I shrugged. "But the next day, it was like a creeping feeling. Kinda hard to explain, but that I shouldn't have enjoyed it so much. You know, all things considered…"

"Survivor's guilt," she said with an understanding nod. Then she went on to explain that guilt is a reasonable expectation and something that shouldn't be brushed aside. "I wish it was as simple as telling you that you shouldn't feel guilty, but it's not. It's a valid emotion, just one we need to address. But I'll tell you what I think. I think you found someone you have a very deep connection with. A very strong love, and I think it's wonderful that you feel comfortable enough with him to let your inhibitions go. That's never an easy task, even for people who haven't suffered any kind of abuse. So for you to acknowledge this is a good thing. A brave thing." She tilted her head. "You never had any doubts or anxiety while you were making love?"

My cheeks heated. "None. I can't explain it very well, but it's the whole daddy thing." I blushed some more but pushed on. "It's like being in a… I don't want to say cage because that's not the right word."

"A bubble?"

"Yeah, a bubble. That he puts me in and nothing on the outside can hurt me. I'm free to be myself and not have a care in the world because I know he'll take care of me. There's a freedom in that, for me at least." I shrugged again, not knowing if I was explaining this properly. "I give him my absolute trust, and he gives me the world. I dunno, it's hard to explain. I feel so safe with him, like he'll protect me and make decisions that are only in my best interest because he wants me to be happy. But it's not restrictive; it's the opposite. It's a kind of freedom."

"Like a father." Patrice raised her eyebrows and smiled.

"Yes!" Then I made a face. "Just with certain benefits. And without the incest."

Patrice laughed. "I get it, Yanni."

"I also met his mother."

She hid her surprise well. "And how did you feel about that?"

"Peter sprung it on me. In hindsight it was probably a good thing; I had no time to freak out. But she was very welcoming. I was worried she'd take one look at me and say 'no.'"

"Why?"

"Because I'm half his age."

"But she didn't."

"No. She told me she'd never seen him look so happy."

Patrice smiled. "So I assume it went well."

"Yes, I guess." I chewed my lip. "I'm meeting his friends this weekend."

"You're nervous about this?"

"Well, yes! They're professionals, and I'm a student. And an actor. In LA. I'm a cliché, and they're all successful and wealthy." I shrugged. "And I have nothing."

"It's a healthy reaction to be nervous. But if they respect Peter, they'll respect you."

I frowned and sighed. "And if they don't? Respect me, that is? I don't want to come between his friends. He's known them for longer than I've been alive…" My eyes shot to hers. "Oh God. He's known them longer than I've been alive."

"Yanni," she said sternly. "You'll be just fine. You trust Peter not to put you in a situation where you're not comfortable?"

"Yes."

"Then trust him. If he believes in you, then maybe you should too." She smiled. "Be yourself. They'll love you."

MR LANDON PICKED me up from my appointment with Patrice, like every Wednesday, and we headed back to his place for dinner. I smiled when I saw Andrew's car parked in the drive—it had been a while since I'd seen him—but I was even more pleasantly surprised when we found Spencer there as well. He was sitting at the kitchen counter with Andrew, talking animatedly to Mrs Landon when we walked in. Something was cooking and it smelled divine.

"Ah, should have known," Mr Landon joked. "Where there's food, there's Andrew." He threw his arm around his son and gave him half a tackle-hug. Andrew replied with a scissor pinch in his dad's ribs.

Spencer laughed but took one look at me and broke out in a grin. He leaped off his chair and pulled me into a fierce hug. "My God, look at you!"

"Hey," I squeaked.

"Oh." He pulled me back. "You look real good, Yanni."

Andrew poked Spencer in the back. "Hey."

Spencer rolled his eyes. "Not *that* good. But good."

Andrew gave me a clap on the arm with a warm smile. "Nice to see you again, and yes, Spencer's right. You look great. Who wants a drink?"

My God, everything with them was always so much fun. Lots of food, lots of talking over each other, and lots of laughter. It was the closest thing to family I had. Not like my roommates were my new friends-family, and not like how Peter was my boyfriend-family, but like with parents-and-brothers kind of family.

Like a real family.

All throughout dinner, and even when our plates were empty, Spencer was very excited about how he and his brother in Sydney were in the early stages of setting up a foundation for at-risk LGBT kids, much like the Acacia

Foundation here. Mrs Landon was helping, of course, and she and Spencer were discussing all sorts of details. Spencer had obviously been spending more time at the headquarters with her, and it was something that clearly made Andrew very happy.

"And how about you?" Andrew asked me. "How's school?"

"Oh, great! We're just starting prelims for our end-of-year production." I grinned at Mr Landon. "It's going to be epic."

Mr Landon beamed. "Yes, it will."

"It's an adaptation of George Orwell's *1984*," I announced.

"Oooh, like a middle-finger salute to the government," Spencer added. "I like it."

Mr Landon laughed and raised his glass of water in a cheers motion. "To the Arts. For keeping it real since the dawn of time."

We all held up our glasses. "Cheers to that."

Mrs Landon smiled lovingly at me. "And how's Peter doing?"

"Oh." I put my glass down and pretended I wasn't blushing. "He is so great."

Spencer's eyes widened, as did his smile. "Well, look at that," he said proudly. "My greatest matchmaking accomplishment."

Andrew cleared his throat. "Pardon?"

Spencer reluctantly added, "Well, okay, you helped."

"No," Andrew said, squinting at him. "I meant us. Shouldn't we be your best, greatest matchmaking accomplishment?"

"Oh, yeah. Us. Definitely." Spencer shifted in his seat and shot Mrs Landon a look for help.

She held up her hands. "Don't look at me. I don't pick sides."

Mr Landon laughed. "Yeah, you'll need to dig your own way out on that one."

Andrew puffed out his chest and raised his chin, and Spencer started searching around the table. "Anyone have a shrimp cocktail handy?"

Everyone laughed because only Spencer would think dying of anaphylaxis was preferable to arguing with Andrew, and Andrew pulled Spencer over so he could kiss the side of his head. They were so in love, and it made me smile to watch them.

"Oh," Mrs Landon said like she'd just remembered something. "Next month, Yanni, the Acacia Foundation is holding a gala day. Once a year we hit the streets, handing out flyers, cards, posters. You must come! It's such a wonderful day."

"I would love to."

"Bring Peter," Spencer added. "I'd like to catch up with him again."

"I will," I said.

"You should have brought him along tonight," Andrew added.

"Yes," Mrs Landon agreed. "We'll have to have him around for dinner sometime soon, okay?"

I nodded, feeling that warmth flush in my chest. "I'm sure he'd love that."

And it was funny how crystal clear some things become. Of course, Peter would love it. He'd met them all before, he'd met all my friends, and he'd never even batted an eyelid. *Why couldn't I do that for him?* So after Andrew and Spencer dropped me off at home and I was ready for bed, I took my phone and waited for Peter's silken voice to sound in my ear.

"Hello, you," he said huskily.

"You sound sleepy," I noted.

"Sign of old age."

"Nonsense." Then I thought of him lying in his bed, all warm and heavy-lidded. "I wish I was there with you."

He hummed. "Me too. How was your evening?"

"Lovely." I had to ask him about dinner and the Acacia Foundation gala day, but first I had to ask him something else. "This dinner party with your friends this weekend…"

"Yeah?" He sounded unsure, like he was half expecting me to say I wouldn't meet his friends.

"What are we going to cook? We need to plan the menu. What are their wives' names? Does anyone have any dietary requirements? I can swap my Saturday shift so we can spend all day making it perfect."

There was a smile in his voice. "I love you, Yanni."

My heart exploded into a gallop. "I love you too."

TO SAY I was nervous was an understatement. Everything was cooked, the house was sparkling, fresh flowers sat as a centerpiece on the dining table, and I'd stopped looking at my clothes in the mirror because I was pretty sure I would never look good enough.

Peter stopped me, his hands cupping my jaw. "Stop panicking. You're perfect."

Then the doorbell rang. "Oh God." I took a breath, and Peter kissed my lips. "I'll pretend I'm busy in here," I said. "You go let them in."

He disappeared, and I wondered if they'd notice if I spent the night locked in the bathroom. I heard a round of hellos and a slew of greetings, then a second later, Peter appeared in the kitchen with four smiling faces staring back at me. I tried to smile, but I was sure it was akin to a rabbit in a spotlight.

Peter was quick to stand by my side. "This is Rob and Sharon," he introduced the first couple. "And this is Mike and Clara." Then he looked at me. "This is Yanni."

Mike, a strikingly handsome black man who had to be six foot four, offered me his hand to shake first, then Rob. Rob reminded me of my eighth-grade science teacher, with ruddy skin and graying curly hair and glasses. They both wore button-down shirts and jeans and huge smiles.

Sharon, a curvy woman with blonde hair, went straight for a kiss to my cheek. "So nice to finally meet you," she said, giving Peter a sly smile.

Then Clara did the same. She reminded me of Jada Pinkett-Smith, beautiful and lucky to be five feet tall. "And something smells fantastic," she said.

She was holding a bottle of wine. "Here, let me take that for you," I said, remembering my manners.

"Yanni did most of the cooking," Peter said. "I hope you like Greek food."

I shot Peter a look, because what if they didn't? It was too late now, and the whole night would be ruined—

Clara put her hand on my arm. "Of course we do."

Peter rubbed my back and smiled at his guests. "Who wants a drink?"

In the beginning, I felt like a kid sitting at the grown-ups table. They talked politics and interest rates and discussed the growth of the Chinese economy and how the Nasdaq was faring.

I sat with my hands in my lap, not touching any of the canapés we'd put out. Peter slid his hand on my knee, making me jump. "Everything okay?" he asked quietly.

Only then did I realize I'd been sitting there waiting for permission to eat. That hadn't happened in a long time.

Wow. I had no idea where that had come from. I thought I was past that… "Yes, of course," I said, giving him a smile. I shook my head a little and helped myself to a goat cheese and balsamic pastry.

No one else seemed to notice, and if it bothered Peter any, he thankfully let it go. Then they laughed as Mike told about some old friend of theirs who got caught with his pants down in the office supply room, with the CEO's intern daughter no less, then told stories of their own kids' funny antics at high school, and they chatted like the very best of friends. It was great to see Peter in his element. These people meant a lot to him, and I could see very clearly around the table that there was warmth and a deep-rooted history here. If there was any truth to the saying "you are the company you keep," then I was in very good hands. Because his friends were down to earth, smart and funny, and very welcoming, and it somehow made me love Peter just a little bit more.

Peter and I served dinner. Greek-style lamb and pota-toes and Greek salad. It had been my idea because I was familiar with how to make it—I'd helped my mother make it a dozen times—but it also showed them a little of who I was.

"Wow," Rob said. "Yanni, you made this?"

"Peter helped," I said, deflecting his compliment.

Peter put his arm around my shoulder. "I peeled the potatoes. Not sure that qualifies as 'helped.'"

Everyone chuckled, then Mike asked a simple yet horri-fying question. "So Yanni, tell us about you?"

And I froze. *What could I say? Shit. I had to say something.* I sipped my mineral water to give myself a second. "I uh, I'm twenty-one." *Good one, idiot. Point out the fact you're half their age.* "My grandparents are from Greece, which explains the food." Peter took my hand under the table, giving me a reassuring squeeze. Not sure if they wanted that kind of information, but that's what they got.

"You met Peter over silent films?" Rob asked.

"Uh, yeah. Charlie Chaplin, actually."

Mike and Rob both groaned. "Who would have thought there would be two guys under the age of one hundred and fifty that like that crap," Rob said.

Peter rolled his eyes. "Ignore them. They've made fun of me for years."

Mike nudged Rob's arm. "Remember in college, the year Peter went as Charlie Chaplin for Halloween?"

"How can I forget?" Rob replied with a groan.

I looked at Peter. "You went as Charlie Chaplin? You never told me that."

"Sure did. And they're still talking about it, that's how good I was."

I chuckled. "You would have looked awesome."

He gave me an eye-crinkling smile. "Thank you. Though I'll leave the acting up to you."

"Yes," Sharon said. "Peter tells us you're an actor."

"Well, I'm studying at LASPA, second year."

"I've heard good things about that school," Clara said. "Isn't that where Jevon Tibbet went?"

I nodded. "Yeah, I believe so."

Peter smiled proudly. "Tell them what play you're working on?"

I looked at him. Of course I'd told Peter all about it, but I wasn't sure anyone else would be too interested. "Um, we're doing an adaptation of George Orwell's *1984*."

The four of them grinned. "Hell yeah!" Mike clapped.

"Never has dystopian and social science fiction been more relevant," Rob added seriously.

"Yeah, fuck the authoritarian assholes!" Sharon said.

Clara gave her a high five. "Amen, sister."

I laughed, remembering a very similar conversation around the Landons' dining table. And I realized right then and there that maybe I wasn't too different from these people after all.

I held up my glass of mineral water. "I'll drink to that."

LATER THAT NIGHT, when everyone had gone home and Peter and I had cleaned up, we crawled into bed, exhausted but happy.

Peter had on his usual sleep pants, sans shirt, and I wore underpants with the purple silk gown he'd given me, even if there would be no love making tonight. It still made me feel special. I snuggled into my most favorite place in the world: the crook of his arm with my head on his chest and his arms tight around me.

"Your friends are awesome," I said.

"They loved you. Seriously, after that dessert you made, I think Sharon and Clara want to marry you."

It was a simple tart with apple slices, cinnamon, and honey drizzle on a store-bought pastry served with a dollop of Greek yogurt. It was hardly fancy, but that wasn't the point. "Too late. I'm taken."

Peter chuckled and kissed my head. "Yes. Yes, you are."

SO THE NEXT four weeks fell into what had become my routine. School, work, hanging out with my roommates during the week, spending weekends with Peter. And there was a lot to be said about routine. There was a sense of normalcy, but a sense of security also.

I'd somehow managed, after everything I'd been through, to build myself a bubble of complacency.

That was until the Acacia Foundation gala weekend.

I'd been so excited to help out. I'd organized to take the weekend off work so I could spend every minute doing whatever the Landons needed to be done. Myself, Peter, Jordan and Skylar, and George and Ajit were all there, ready to get started.

Spencer and Andrew, and Sarah, and Lola and Emilio—who I didn't exactly remember but was re-introduced to—were there too, with Mrs Landon in full boss mode, and Mr Landon at her side.

Even with the early morning start, I was pumped and excited, and I just loved that Peter was here with me. He understood my need to pay forward all the help I'd been given. I couldn't change the fact I'd once been homeless, I'd once lived rough. It was a part of my past, of who I was, and what made me the man I was today, and Peter got that.

There were hundreds of people, all ages, all races, all religions, all there to help, and it felt so good to be a part of something positive. We were an army, all decked out in the Foundation's bright green T-shirts, armed with information brochures, pamphlets, cards, flyers, and posters. It was going to be fun and rewarding, and I was buzzing.

We hit the streets. The weather was a perfect winter's day in LA, and our first stop was Skid Row. It was where the majority of homeless LGBT folk ended up. It was where I ended up, so it made sense to go there.

But I wasn't prepared for the memories. I wasn't prepared for the dirt and grime or the smell. And despite all of that, it was vacant eyes, the hopelessness, the lost and broken souls that got me.

By ten o'clock, I found myself sitting on some steps

next to a kid—he couldn't have been more than sixteen—named Collin. If that was his real name or not, I didn't know. I doubted it. He was just skin and bone, with dirty, red hair flopped down into his eyes, his pale skin grimy, and had what looked like a faded bruised eye. His filthy clothes might have fit him once, but they swam on him now, and I asked him when the last time he ate was.

"I do all right," he said, shrugging me off without answering.

"How long have you been here?" I asked.

His eyes hardened. "A year."

Jesus. I swallowed hard, and it took me a little while before I could speak. "I used to sleep at the Union," I said quietly. "If I could get a bed."

Collin's eyes shot to mine before he looked away. "You were here?"

I nodded.

"How'd you get out?"

"With the help of some very good people." I handed him a flyer. He snorted like it was something funny or maybe like a joke that wasn't funny at all. "It's not a religion, if that's what you're worried about. They just help people. There's no catch. You just have to want to help yourself, that's it. Nothing else."

"Yeah, well," he said, stuffing the flyer into his pocket. "Like I said, I do all right."

I nodded slowly. He'd been here a year and was still alive, so that meant he could look after himself. "Yeah, you do. Think about it anyway. They can get you a place to live, a job, school, whatever. And they're holding a soup kitchen tonight at the Mission, if you're in the area. Free food."

He never replied, so I stood up, and with each step away, I blinked back tears.

And the next kid after that. And the one after that. And the older lady who wore rainbow feathers in her hair who deserved more human decency than the world had given her, and the girl with scars on one arm, track marks on the other, with hollow eyes and chapped lips.

By the time we were supposed to meet back at the Los Angeles Mission to help out at the soup kitchen, I couldn't hold it in any longer. The second I saw Mrs Landon, I burst into tears and ran into her arms.

"Oh, Yanni," she cooed, patting my hair and rocking me a little. "It's hard, I know." I couldn't even speak. I didn't need to explain myself. She'd been where I'd been. She understood.

"I want to help them all," I mumbled.

"I know you do." She pulled back, and keeping her hands on my shoulders, she said, "You know who's here? Tyler. The guy you helped who reported Lance? He's here helping out. He's doing well because of you." She smiled, then scanned the huge hall-like room. "There he is."

I looked over, and sure enough, there was the blond guy I'd visited in the hospital after Lance had beaten him.

Mrs Landon called out to him, and as soon as he saw me, he broke out into a smile and made his way over. He greeted me with a hug. "I was hoping I'd see you here," he said.

He looked good, healthier, like he'd eaten properly, and all his bruises were long gone. His clothes were clean, his hair cut and washed. I wiped my face. "Sorry, been a hard day."

Tyler nodded. "Yeah, I get that. Hey, I wanted to thank you," he said. "For everything you did. Helen's team was great."

Mrs Landon was now talking to Peter, their heads together, though she looked up and smiled at us.

"Yeah, they're the best," I agreed. I let out a deep breath. "Man, today's been rough."

Tyler smiled sadly. "But it feels good, yeah?"

"Yeah, it does. But also kinda helpless. Like it's overwhelming. I want to help all of them."

He nodded sympathetically. "Hey, I got a job," he said, brightening. "It's just at a grocery store. Nothing too exciting, but it's my own money. And I start business school at the community college next semester."

"That's awesome!" I told him.

"Yeah, it is." He smiled, but it soon faded. "Hey, have you heard any more on Fuckface?"

I assumed Fuckface was Lance. "No, I haven't. Mrs Landon had all the report numbers and they were gonna let her know when or if anything came of it."

Tyler nodded. "Well, fingers crossed, huh?"

"Yeah, for sure. Hey, do you have a phone? If I hear anything, I'll let you know."

He grinned and fished a phone out of his pocket. "Yeah." We exchanged numbers. "And I can let you know how school goes, you know, if you want."

"I'd really like that."

He eyed Peter for a second, then gave me a raised eyebrow. "Your old man's a fox."

I chuckled and swatted his arm. "He is, and he's all mine. So eyes off."

Tyler laughed me off. "Oh, don't worry. I've sworn off *everything* until I get my shit together. If I fail school, I could always try the priesthood."

I laughed at that, and Tyler said goodbye and went back to the group he was with. Peter came over, slid his arm around my waist and nodded toward the door. "Look."

A familiar mop of red hair came in, scanning the room

like a kid ready to bolt. "Collin," I called out, making my way over to him. "Come on in. They're just about to start serving dinner."

He immediately played it cool, stuffing his hands in his pockets and looking around. "Thought I'd check it out, ya know."

"For sure," I said, trying not to smile too hard. "Hey, there's someone I'd like you to meet." I shot a look back toward the kitchen, where Mrs Landon had wandered off to, and I caught her attention. I knew she was flat-out swamped, but I also knew she'd give me a minute. "This is Mrs Landon," I said. "And this is Collin. I met him earlier today and told him to come here tonight."

Mrs Landon beamed at him. "Well, I'm very glad you did, Collin."

Then I saw another face in the kitchen. He had a hairnet on and paper apron, but his beard and tattoos were unmistakable. "Collin, you know how you asked me how I got off the streets? Well, that guy through there"—I pointed to Spencer—"he took me to meet Mrs Landon."

She put her arm around him. "Now, dinner is five minutes away, but first there are some people I'd love you to meet," she said, leading him off to a group of people who I knew to be caseworkers for the Foundation.

Peter put his hand on my back, and I turned to him, giving him a teary smile. He pulled me in for a hug. "I'm so proud of you," he whispered into my hair.

I didn't trust myself to speak, so I held him as tightly as I could instead.

"Are you okay, love?" he asked. "It's been an emotional day."

My eyes burned with unshed tears. "I'm okay. Exhausted but good."

"Want to go home?"

"I think I should stay and help serve dinner," I said with a shrug. "Or something."

He simply nodded and smiled. "Okay."

"If you want to go home, I can catch a cab later."

He kissed my forehead. "There's no place I'd rather be."

I kissed him right on the lips, not caring who saw. "Thank you." Then I quickly called Jordan to see how they'd gotten along, but after a long day, the four of them were safely on a bus homeward bound. I reminded her that I was staying at Peter's and our usual laundry date would have to be postponed because I'd be back at the Mission in the morning. She told me she'd see me there. So, for the next two hours, we served stew with rice or mashed potatoes, until the last person had eaten. Then we helped clean up, right alongside Andrew and Spencer.

When all was said and done, I fell into a seat next to the others with a grunt. "Long day, huh?" Spencer said.

"Yeah." I looked at Andrew and Sarah. "You guys help out every year?"

Sarah nodded. "Keeps it real," Andrew said.

"Yeah, it sure does," I agreed.

Mrs Landon pulled her hairnet off and sagged into her seat. Peter and Mr Landon were slumped in theirs. The three of them looked more exhausted than I felt. Slowly, I got to my feet. "I better get this man home," I said, holding out my hand to Peter. He'd been with me every step of the way without one word of complaint all day.

He stood up wearily. "And we're back tomorrow to do it all again."

"Thank you," Mrs Landon said, her tone heartfelt.

"It's been a pleasure," he answered. Then he amended, "An eye-opening, heart-wrenching pleasure."

Everyone nodded in agreement. "See you all in the morning," I said, waving them off.

The cab ride home was quiet. We sat in the backseat, my head on his shoulder and his arm around me. We both needed a little time to decompress and let our thoughts and emotions settle.

When we walked into Peter's place, he slid his keys and wallet onto the kitchen counter. "You hungry?"

After working with all that food, I really wasn't. "No."

Peter scrubbed his hands over his face. "Me either. I need a shower, though."

"Me too."

Even washing away the dirt and grime of the day didn't lift the heaviness of our hearts. We showered together and helped wash each other's hair and bodies with loving hands and tender touches. We dried off, and Peter got dressed into his usual sleep pants, I wore briefs with my silk gown, and I crawled into his arms in bed, with my head on his chest and his arms around me.

"You were so good today," I said after a long while. "I couldn't have gotten through it without you."

He kissed my forehead. "And you were amazing today."

"I wasn't prepared for how hard it was going to be," I admitted. "I used to live like that. I was one of them."

He squeezed me and nuzzled into my hair. He said nothing, somehow sensing I needed to talk.

"And look at me now. In such a short amount of time, I have everything I ever could've wanted." I let out a sad sigh. "I'm not gloating. Just the opposite, actually. Because I wouldn't have anything if it weren't for Spencer and Andrew or Mr and Mrs Landon. Or you."

"Oh, my sweet boy. You have everything you do because you've worked hard for it. You go to school full time, you work twenty-something hours a week, and go to therapy. You're a good friend to your roommates, and believe me, when it comes to us, I'm the lucky one."

I snuggled into his hairy chest. "I don't ever want to get complacent. I don't ever want to take any of it for granted. I'm so thankful. I really am. And I'm sorry if I don't tell you enough."

"You don't have to apologize, my love." Peter kissed the top of my head. "Today was heartbreaking. Not just for the kids on the street. But for you too. It was hard to watch you struggling. I think we all take some things for granted. Today was a good reminder, huh?"

"You know they're out there right now, in the cold, in alleys, taking drugs, selling their bodies, trying to sleep without being attacked, robbed." A cold shiver ran through me. "You know I slept with my bag in my bed with me, even after I moved into my new house. I still sleep with the light on." I felt ashamed to admit that.

"You don't need the light on when you're here," he murmured.

"No, because I have you."

Peter pulled the blankets up and tucked me into his chest so I was wrapped up safe and sound. I closed my eyes and felt sleep taking me. "And you always will," he whispered. "Always."

THE NEXT MORNING, we arrived at the Acacia headquarters just after nine to find everybody already in full swing. I found Mrs Landon going through boxes of flyers. "Sorry we're a little late," I said. "I had to make a stop. I've ordered three hundred dollars' worth of sandwiches to be delivered here before lunchtime."

Mrs Landon stared at me, then Peter. He put his hands up. "I offered to help pay, but he refused."

"I wanted to do it. I had to do something," I said quickly. "To pay back, or pay it forward, or just put good karma out into the universe. I couldn't help but think of all the people who didn't eat last night, and I had some money saved. I've been working a lot, and I figure some folks might be more inclined to hear what we have to say if it comes with half a sub."

Mrs Landon dropped her handful of flyers back into the box and crushed me in a teary hug. "You are such a sweet boy," she said. "You make me such a proud momma."

And that right there was worth every penny I spent on sandwiches. She called herself my momma and said I made her proud. It squeezed my heart until my eyes welled with tears. "I promised myself no crying today."

Mrs Landon laughed, trying to dry her eyes. "Good luck with that."

We helped her sort the flyers, and soon Jordan and Skylar were there. "George sends his apologies. He's having lunch today with Ajit's family," Skylar said. We all knew that George and Ajit weren't giving up on their hopes of Ajit's mother's acceptance, so a lunch sounded promising.

"God, I hope it goes well," I said.

"Me too," Jordan said. She looked around the bustling room. "So, where do we start?"

Peter held up a rather large box. He was sorting female sanitary products to give to homeless girls and women. He didn't even bat an eyelid when he was given the task, but there were a lot of boxes to get through. "You can help me sort these into bags."

I smiled as the three of them worked together and

continued helping Mrs Landon sort flyers. Just before we were ready to hit the streets, the delivery of sandwiches arrived, then another two. I looked at Mrs Landon, who just shrugged. "It was a great idea."

So we headed back out onto the streets, handing out flyers and food, meeting and talking to some pretty incredible, resilient people, whose only "crime" was being attracted to the same sex.

I was better prepared for it now. Their stories still broke my heart, their circumstances so close to my own. I was one of the lucky ones. I knew it, and so help me God, I'd never forget it.

"I just want them to see there's hope," I said to Peter as we walked back to headquarters. "It doesn't have to be the end."

Peter let go of my hand so he could put his arm around me. "I think you're an inspiration," he said, kissing the side of my head. "I'm pretty sure they see you and see what they can become."

Well, I didn't know about that, but I hoped it was true.

We arrived back just before dinner was ready to be served to the masses, so Peter and I helped out as best we could. So many people from all walks of life came in to eat, so grateful, it made my heart full.

Toward the end of the night, I just happened to be in the wrong place at the wrong time. I was cleaning down tables and collecting used trays when an argument broke out between two men over turf they each claimed as their own.

They both got to their feet, their chairs scraping on the floor, tumbling over, and they grabbed at each other, yelling and trying to punch. It was loud, and people came running to separate them. I was right there. Right in the middle of it.

Peter came running for me, but I noticed a kid, no more than five, watching on in horror, his hands covering his ears. He got jostled, stumbled backward, and almost fell, but I caught him just as a table was upended. I picked him up and carried him to the far wall, out of harm's way, and cuddled him as he started to cry.

His mom was soon there, taking him, thanking me warily. She'd just gone to get him another bread roll, she'd said. She was just gone a second.

"It's okay," I told her. "He's fine now."

"Thank you." She took him and cradled him, and I stood there trying to get my heart rate down.

Jesus. My adrenaline was pumping. My heart was hammering.

Peter's eyes were wide, and he crushed me against him. "Are you okay?" he asked.

I nodded and let out a shaky breath. "Yeah."

The fight was over, both men escorted out, and the room was returning to normal, though I kept my back to the tables being reset, like it protected me, or maybe it was facing Peter that protected me. Mr Landon came over to us, putting his hand on my shoulder. "Everything okay here?" he asked.

"Yeah," I answered, pulling out of Peter's arms. "Just an adrenaline rush."

"You did real good," Mr Landon said. "Getting that kid out of there."

"You really did," Peter said proudly.

The adrenaline was starting to wear off, and my hands began to shake and my eyes started to well with tears. "I still didn't like it," I said lamely. Peter pulled me against him again.

"How about you call it a day," Mr Landon said. "We're

just about done here. We've only got clean up to do and we're done."

Peter rubbed my back. "Want to go home? Or want to stay?"

I glanced around, and Mr Landon was right. It was almost all over, and weariness was starting to settle in. "Home."

We said our goodbyes, and Mrs Landon promised to organize a dinner for us as a thanks for our hard work. I got hugs from Spencer and Andrew, told them we'd see them again soon, and Peter and I headed home.

"My place or yours?" he asked as we climbed into a cab.

"God, your place, please." I wanted to climb into his lap on the sofa and didn't think my roommates would appreciate the show. Jordan and Skylar had gone home during the afternoon and were no doubt planted in front of the TV, and with a bit of luck, cuddled up together. I wondered how George and Ajit's day turned out...

"You okay?" Peter asked.

I was leaning into him, his arm over my shoulder. "Yeah. Today was better, except for that fight at the end."

He rubbed my arm. "You really did save that little boy from getting knocked over, you know. He could have been hurt. *You* could have been hurt."

"I reacted without thinking."

"That's what makes it even better." He kissed the side of my head. "You've come a long way. Remember six months ago when that man was yelling in the coffee shop and you froze?"

I nodded. I remembered, all right. I panicked and freaked the hell out. "Yeah."

"You didn't freeze today. You saved that little kid from

getting hurt, without any thought to your own safety. I think it proves just how far you've come."

I looked up at him to see nothing but pride in his eyes. "I guess I did. I still didn't like it, though. It still scares me."

I put my head back on his shoulder and he gave me a squeeze. "I know it does."

After a while, I broke the silence. "Peter?"

"Yeah?"

"Just so you know, when we get home, even though I'm tired as hell, I'm going to climb you like a tree."

He chuckled. "Is that right?"

"Yep. Hot shower first, then there will be tree climbing. And I might even let you order in Chinese food afterward."

"Sounds good."

"Which part? The food or the tree climbing?

Peter lifted my chin and planted a hard kiss on my lips. "You, on me, will win every time."

A rush of warmth bloomed through me, at his tone, his touch. *Oh yes, there would be tree climbing tonight.*

CHAPTER TWENTY-THREE

I'D STARTED out climbing him like a tree. My legs around his waist, clutching at his broad shoulders, he carried me easily to sit me on the kitchen counter. We kissed frantically, groping hands and open mouths, taking tongues and rolling hips. We began to strip right there in his kitchen but ended up in the shower.

The hot water washed away the grime of the day and eased the muscles in my shoulders, but Peter massaged me everywhere, and I was a puddle of desire on his bed.

I was face down—a position that was new for us—and he was straddling my thighs. He'd massaged me, rubbed me down, lubed me up, stretched me, and lay over me with his cock pressing hot and heavy against my crack.

He whispered in my ear, "Is this okay?"

He'd never had me like this. Normally I was on my back so he could hold me, kiss me, make love to me. Lance had often taken me in this position, so it wasn't a favorite. But this wasn't Lance. This was Peter. And he would never hurt me.

So, like a test to myself, a final test that Peter could

replace all the negative voids in my life with positive light, I nodded. "Yes."

And I did want this. There was not one fiber in my body that didn't.

I was warmed all over, limber and relaxed, waiting for him to bury his cock in me. I raised my hips and spread my legs a little more.

Peter pressed his blunt cockhead against my hole, and lying over my back and kissing my neck, he slipped into me.

God, he felt so good. He was twice my size, and he covered me, weighed me down with his body, and he fit inside me like a missing puzzle piece.

I groaned as I took every inch, and he threaded our fingers together. He was slow, tender, just like always, kissing the back of my neck, my shoulder. "Such a good boy," he whispered.

I whined as he pulled out and pushed back in. "Oh yes, Daddy."

"Does it feel good?" he breathed.

And I understood, I really did, all those forums and comments where guys said their place was to please their daddies. I didn't know why or how, but there was something about making him happy that gave me a thrill, a purpose.

Just like his purpose was to please me. Like a good daddy should.

"So good, Daddy."

He let go of my hand and hooked his arm under my shoulder, lifting my chest, arching my back. If I turned my head, he could kiss me now. So I did, and as soon as his tongue touched mine, I moaned and he bucked.

I cried out and he stilled, so I writhed on his cock. "More, Daddy."

"Roll over," he said, slowly pulling out of me. "I need you to come first."

I did as he asked. Knowing an orgasm was imminent, I didn't need telling twice. I spread my legs wide, lifting my knees to my chest, and he smiled before crashing his mouth to mine as he sank back inside me.

I took him, all of him, and he took my cock in his hand, stroking in time with his thrusts. We'd done this enough over the last few weeks that he knew which buttons to press, and he never failed. His experience and patience were a gift that he gave me every time we made love.

He stroked me as he hit the perfect angle, and I soon unraveled underneath him. But he contained me, held me, strung out every nerve of pleasure as I came. And only when I was a sated mess did he let loose.

I was so much more malleable, so boneless, he bent my legs and took hold of my hips and filled me. "Come in me, Daddy," I urged him.

His eyes shot open, dark galaxies of lust. "God, Yanni," he cried out, stilling and surging deep inside me.

There was nothing like it. Nothing on earth felt like it did when he came inside me. He made me his, in ways no one else ever would. I felt smug knowing he'd never given that to anyone else. Only me.

"God, Yanni," he murmured into my neck. He slid his arms underneath me, around me, and I tightened my legs around him. He shuddered inside me, making both of us groan. "You are so incredible. You're all I will ever need."

I kissed his temple and rocked my hips a little. "And you're it for me," I declared. "You're all I'll ever need too."

He pulled his head back so he could kiss me. "Still want me to order in Chinese food?"

"Yes, Daddy," I said playfully.

"Are you being cheeky?" He asked with a grin. "Naughty boys don't get two rewards in one night."

I laughed. "No, I'm a good boy."

He grinned and kissed me. "Yes, you are."

MY APPOINTMENT with Patrice was pretty full-on. My reaction to the men fighting at the soup kitchen was an important step in my healing process, Patrice had said. Not only did I not freeze in fear, but I acted to protect someone else.

Pair this with my waiting for permission to eat at Peter's dinner party, and Patrice reminded me of the ebbs and flows she'd talked about. There would be huge steps forward and small steps back, and it was okay.

It was okay to stumble, and it was equally important to recognize that it was okay to be happy.

"It's okay to be happy," she'd said. "Repeat that for me."

"It's okay to stumble. And it's okay to be happy," I said.

She smiled like I'd crossed some invisible line of psychological fortitude, and maybe I had. I certainly felt better. Lighter, somehow. I recognized my misstep at Peter's dinner party, that I'd waited for permission to eat, but there was no meltdown, there was no downward spiral, no guilt. I simply saw it for what it was and shook it off, and that, according to Patrice, was kinda huge.

As the appointment drew to a close, she told me to enjoy my dinner with the Landons—as I did every Wednesday night after my session with her—only this time it wasn't Mr Landon waiting. It was Peter. He stood up from his chair in the waiting room and wiped his hands on his thighs. "All done?" he asked.

He was a little nervous about waiting at my appointment, probably unsure if I'd come out quiet or crying or even angry. I guess I'd only spoken to him on the phone a few hours after my appointments, long after I'd had time to decompress, so he wasn't sure what to expect.

But today had been a good session. "It was good. Productive."

He smiled, relieved. "Are you ready to go?"

"Sure." We walked out to his car. "I'm looking forward to tonight. Dinner with the Landons is always entertaining, if not hilarious. And given Spencer and Andrew will be there, it's sure to be fun."

And it was. We were met with hugs and warm hellos and a mountain of food. Mrs Landon said it was thanks for all our help on her gala day, but truthfully, I think she just liked to make sure people were happy and well-fed.

However, I got the distinct feeling that she wasn't telling me something or that she was waiting for the right time. I knew she'd tell me eventually, so I put it to the back of my mind and enjoyed my evening. We talked and laughed through dinner, and when Mrs Landon mentioned dancing and I admitted that Peter and I had never danced, it was decided right then and there that we would.

Mr Landon pushed the coffee table out of the way, and Andrew raced over to the sound system. "I'll choose the music," he said.

"Oh God." Spencer gave us a serious look. "Be prepared for anything."

Andrew shrugged. "Normally I would agree, but given I only have my parents' music selection to choose from…" He waved his hand as the music started to play. "I present ye with the musical score from *The Great Gatsby*."

"Great choice," Mrs Landon said, holding her hand out daintily for Mr Landon to take. He obliged, of course, and soon they were waltzing elegantly across the living room floor.

Spencer held his hand out to Andrew. "Last time we danced right here, I almost died, so please be gentle."

Andrew laughed as he spun Spencer around. "I'd rather never live through the anaphylactic shuffle again, thanks."

Spencer threw his head back and laughed, and they slid against each other seamlessly and began to dance.

Peter held his hand out to me. "May I?"

I place my hand in his. "Well, *you* probably can, but I can't dance. Actually, give me electronic pop and I'll be your personal go-go boy, but classic old-style from the 1920s is not my first choice of dance music."

Peter chuckled. "My own personal go-go boy?" he asked, definitely interested.

I shrugged one shoulder. "I used to like dancing."

"Then we'll have to go sometime." He put my hand on his waist and pulled me close. "But for now, we'll do it old-style. Just feel the beat and follow my lead."

We did some kind of poor attempt at a waltz, which I'm sure I butchered, but no one seemed to care. In fact, Peter seemed to really like it, and I wondered why we hadn't danced before now. "We should do this more often," I said, as I leaned against his neck. "Not clubbing but just dancing. This is nice."

The song changed and the music was a little funkier, and Mr and Mrs Landon started to swing dance. It was awesome!

"Show-offs," Andrew called out. Then he and Spencer interrupted us, and I danced with Andrew for a bit, while Peter and Spencer danced, then Mrs Landon cut in, and I danced with her, tripping over my own feet half the time and laughing.

But then I noticed that Peter was still dancing with Spencer, both talking and smiling, and something stirred inside me. Was it jealousy? Longing? I wasn't sure.

Mrs Landon whispered in my ear, "Go get him," then twirled me off in their direction.

I tapped Spencer on the shoulder. "Excuse me, sir, I believe he's mine."

Spencer grinned and gave me a mock bow, and he stepped aside. Peter quickly pulled me close, closer than he'd danced with Spencer. "Yours, huh?"

I settled my head against his neck again, feeling like all was right with my world. "Yes," I said simply. He replied with a smiling kiss to my head.

But soon the dancing was over and we all fell onto the couches, talking about music, and after Mrs Landon shot Andrew a pointed glare at her watch, Andrew and Spencer declared they had to go. It was a poorly disguised reminder that she needed to speak to us alone.

"Well, we better be off," Andrew said, and they were still arguing over which of Jeff Buckley's songs was the best—after "Hallelujah," of course—as they were leaving. "It has to be 'Eternal Life,'" Spencer said.

"Nope. It's 'Last Goodbye,'" Andrew argued as they walked outside to their car. "Everyone knows that."

"More copies were sold in Australia—"

"But Australia doesn't count."

We all heard Spencer's audible gasp, and we were still laughing at them as Mr Landon closed the door. "Everyone knows it's 'Grace,'" Mr Landon said to us. "But I wasn't getting in the middle of that."

Mrs Landon smiled at him. "How long do you give them?"

"Until they're married?" He sighed. "A year."

She laughed contentedly. "I was going to say living together, but married works."

I settled into the sofa next to Peter and looked at Mrs Landon. "Did you want to speak to me about something?"

She smiled sadly. "Am I that obvious?"

"A little." I took Peter's hand with the feeling that this news wasn't going to be good.

"I had a phone call from Detective Hernandez. Lance's first court hearing is next Monday."

Oh.

"His lawyers kept deferring, but the judge has called it in. The case is pretty solid. They're just trying to buy time, that's all."

I nodded, and I could feel Peter's eyes on me, so I turned to him and gave him a smile before I looked back to Mrs Landon. "Have they said what he's looking at if he's found guilty?"

"The detective said she thought he could get eighteen months to two years. It will depend on the judge though."

"Do I have to be there?" I asked.

"Only if you want. This isn't a trial. If he wants to fight it, or more to the point, if his lawyers think he has a chance, it could go to trial. You'd have to take the stand then, but that's a long time away."

I took a deep breath. Peter squeezed my hand.

"But they're thinking he'll take a deal."

"What does that mean?"

"That he'll plead guilty to a lesser charge."

I nodded slowly. "You know what? I'm okay with it. Whatever the outcome. I mean, I want him to be convicted, and I want the world to know what he did and what kind of man he is. But he's been charged, and that will follow him forever. His friends and family will know, the people he works with will know. If he hasn't been fired already." I shrugged. "I'm okay with whatever happens."

Peter put his arm around my shoulder and pulled me in so he could kiss the side of my head. Mr and Mrs Landon both smiled. "You're a good man, Yanni," Mr Landon said.

"Well, Patrice said I'd turned a corner. But I have to say, I couldn't have done any of it without you three." I looked at them in turn, Mrs Landon, Mr Landon, then finally Peter. "I really am very grateful."

Mrs Landon gave me a teary smile. "Oh, Yanni."

"I keep telling him he's the one doing all the hard work, not us," Peter said with a fond smile. "But he's still not great at taking compliments. We're working on it."

I sighed loudly and deflected his comment. "Well, I'd still be living rough on Skid Row if it weren't for Spencer and Andrew, so…" I shrugged because if weren't for any of these people, I wouldn't be where I am today. Physically or emotionally. "You know, you could have told me in front of Andrew and Spencer," I added. "I wouldn't have cared."

Mrs Landon smiled. "Some things are best heard in private. I'd have hated for the news to upset you in front of anyone else."

I was grateful for her consideration, but I wasn't upset. In fact, I was looking forward to the whole thing being over. Regardless of the outcome, it would be over and I could really move on with my life.

"And," Mrs Landon continued, "speaking of Skid Row, that reminds me. Collin, the red-haired boy you got to come in to meet us, he's now working with the caseworker. And we've found him a place to live."

"Oh, that's excellent!" I cried. "Thank you!"

"Thank *you*, Yanni," she replied.

We chatted a little more but it was getting late, and after a round of hugs and thank yous, Peter drove me home. I leaned over the console in his car so I could kiss him goodnight. "I wish you could stay," I whispered.

"Mmm, me too."

"Call me when you get home."

"Aren't you sick of me yet?"

"Never." I kissed him again. "I'll be in bed waiting."

He groaned. "With that visual, it'll be the longest drive home ever."

I laughed and opened the car door to get out. "Don't speed. I'll wait up, I promise."

He stayed parked until I was safely inside before he drove off. I said a quick hello to George, who was still up watching TV—who told me his persistence with Ajit's mother was beginning to pay off—before I raced upstairs and got ready for bed.

Not long after, my phone rang and Peter's name lit up my screen. "Excuse me, sir," I said. "But if you're already home, that means you exceeded the speed limit."

His throaty chuckle in my ear warmed me all over. "Apologies, officer. But my boy was in bed waiting."

I laughed and snuggled down in bed. "Yes, he is. Though he's cold without his big teddy bear to keep him warm."

"Teddy bear?"

"Daddy bear," I corrected. Then I mimicked a high-pitched voice, pretending to be Goldilocks. "I tried the others, but the Daddy bear was just right."

Peter laughed at that. "Are you really cold?"

"No. Well, a little. My bed's cold when I first get in because you're not in it. I wish it wasn't a house rule that people couldn't sleep over. I mean, I get why not, but still… everyone here likes you." I sighed. "If anyone was even slightly hesitant or uncomfortable around you, I wouldn't even consider it. But everyone here *does* like you, and they trust you. I'm sure if you just happened to fall asleep here one night, no one would care."

"Oh, Yanni. I know, believe me. I wish we could spend more nights together too, but we can't violate their trust like that. Imagine if I got up to pee in the middle of the night and ran into a half-asleep Jordan in the hall. I'd frighten the life out of her. Yanni, I can't do that."

I sighed again, long and loud. He was right and I knew it. I just selfishly wanted him in my bed. "I'm pouting right now, just so you know."

"The image of your lips will be sure to play in my dreams tonight." His voice was husky, the way it croaked when he was tired. I could almost feel his arms around me.

"Tell me what you've got planned tomorrow," I said. My blinks were getting longer and longer, and the sound of his voice, soft and low in my ear, lulled me to sleep just like it did every night without fail.

I WALKED Jordan to the bus stop like always, then sent Tyler a quick text.

Hey, it's Yanni. Not sure if you know already, but the court case starts next Monday.

His reply came through just as I was walking into school. *Will you be there?*

That was a loaded question and one I wasn't sure I was ready to answer. *Not sure I'm ready to see him again. I want to look him in the eye so he knows he didn't beat me in the end, but I'm not sure I'm strong enough.*

I read and re-read what I'd typed out, not sure whether I should hit Send or Delete. I hated admitting fear, but if anyone would understand, it would be Tyler. I let out a breath and hit Send before I could change my mind.

His reply came through five minutes later. *Yeah. I'm hearing ya.* Then another one right after. *I'll go if you do.*

Well, shit. Then I kind of had to go. I couldn't say yes and then bail on him. And being there with Tyler would be better than going alone, but there was no way I could go without Peter.

I checked the time. He would already be at work, and I hoped he didn't mind the interruption. I sent him a message. *Will you come with me to the courthouse for Lance's hearing? I don't know what time it is yet, but will let you know ASAP.*

His reply was immediate. *Of course I will. And don't worry about the time. I'll take the whole day off work.*

Oh God, he was perfect.

Thank you.

Everything okay?

I smiled at my screen. *It is now. I love you.*

Love you, too.

I considered hugging my phone but the other students walking by might think me a bit weird. So I sent Tyler a quick reply instead. *Yes, will be there. Will send you more details when I have them.*

I read his response at lunchtime. *Sweet.*

And the days leading up to the court case were both good and bad. On one hand, I was excited to get it over with, and on the other hand, I was dreading seeing Lance again.

Patrice spent our session talking about the transfer of power and how it was now me who was in charge. Not in charge of him but of myself. He held no power over me. It was okay to be nervous. It was okay to be scared. It was okay to be worried.

Coming face-to-face with my abuser was a scary

thing. A huge thing. I would be sitting in the same room as him, and he could react a number of different ways. He could sneer at me, smile at me, laugh at me. He could plead not guilty. He could call me a liar and tell the judge I asked him to hit me. He could tell the court any number of different things, and I needed to be ready.

I also needed to be prepared for the case to go to trial. I needed to know that the photos of me in my police report could be provided in evidence and that other people might see them.

I needed to be prepared for any possible outcome.

"Abusive people are great manipulators," Patrice said. "They believe the lies they spew because they justify reasons in their own minds. So no matter what he says or does, you sit there with your head held high. You're a survivor, Yanni."

I left that appointment and felt anything but a survivor.

I felt hugely inadequate to deal with what was coming.

Mr Landon took me back to their place, and Mrs Landon took one look at me and gave me a crushing hug. "How about we have pizza and ice cream?"

Mr Landon did a fist pump behind her back, making me almost smile. We watched him race out of the room before Mrs Landon continued with her caring-mom face. "Then I can drive you home or to Peter's. How does that sound?"

Everything in me screamed Peter's, but that came with a wave of guilt. "I rely on him for everything," I mumbled. "Like I rely on you guys."

"Hey," Mrs Landon said softly. She waited for me to look at her. "I know you feel a bit lost and out of your depth."

God, she nailed that.

"But if you need to rely on Peter, then you go right ahead. Something tells me he won't mind one bit."

"He wouldn't mind," I mumbled. "He likes taking care of me." I left out the whole *like a good daddy should* part.

Mrs Landon gave me a look that told me she knew anyway. "You know, when I was going through what you are, Allan was my Peter. And I relied on him for everything. God, some days I swore I couldn't even breathe without him. And there's nothing wrong with that. Some days I could take on the world by myself, then some days I'd want to crawl into his lap and never leave."

My cheeks heated with embarrassment, like she knew how much I loved to do exactly that. "Me too."

"And you know what?" she asked. "There's nothing wrong with that either."

"You sound like Patrice."

"She's a very smart woman."

I finally smiled, feeling a bit better. "Thank you."

"You'll get through this, Yanni. I know you will. And we'll be with you every step of the way."

Mr Landon suddenly appeared, looking very pleased with himself. "Of course Yanni'll get through this," he said, putting his arms around my shoulders and giving me a squeeze. "No matter what happens on Monday, you've still got us, and you've still got Peter. And your roommates, and your friends at school, the people you work with. We're all on your side."

Mrs Landon eyed him for a moment. "You went and ordered pizzas already, didn't you?"

He grinned without shame. "I wasn't letting that opportunity slip me by. You suggested it, dear. I just implemented it."

"Mm hmm," she hummed. "You ordered the healthy-heart option, didn't you?"

"Of course I did," he answered. Then he looked at me, shook his head, and whispered, "Like hell I did."

"What was that?" she asked.

His reply was quick. "It's being delivered."

Mrs Landon sighed and looked at me. "The worst part of marrying an actor. They're so damn good at acting."

I laughed, and the heaviness on my heart let up just a little. We ate our pizza in front of the TV answering *Family Feud* questions, and when it came time to leave, Mrs Landon asked if I wanted to go home or to Peter's.

"Home," I answered. Knowing I'd be calling him as soon as I got in helped. As much as I wanted to be with him, I knew standing on my own two feet, even for just one night, would do me good.

I did feel a bit better, but as soon as I was in bed and called him, the tightness in my chest eased. He'd no sooner said hello than I sighed. "God, it's good to hear your voice."

"Everything okay?"

"I just missed you today, that's all. I had a pretty shit session with Patrice, and I thought about just going straight to your place, but I'm trying not to rely on you for everything."

"Oh, Yanni, you can count on me anytime. Do you need me to come get you?"

I closed my eyes and snuggled down in my bed, rolling onto my side and pulling the blankets up. "No, I'm okay. Just talk to me, please."

And he did. About a funny, long lunch he'd had with Rob and Mike in the city, and how a lady at work was finally having a baby after years of trying, and how Neenish somehow managed to lock herself in the laundry room, and how *that* was a nice mess to clean up when he got home. He spoke about all the little day-to-day things that would have been inconsequential to anyone else, but not to me. I just loved listening to him speak.

"You still awake?" he asked after a moment's silence.

"Yeah. Just listening," I said sleepily. "You have a cadence to the way you speak that I just love. It's melodic and relaxing. I should write my thesis on the power of your voice. I would call it *The Intonation of Peter Hannikov*. I'd get an A+."

He chuckled, low and throaty in my ear, and it felt like he was right here with me. "I would happily be your muse."

"You already are."

"I should let you get some sleep," he murmured.

"Mmm. I can't wait for Friday."

"What's on Friday?"

"You're picking me up from work, and I'm not leaving all weekend."

"Is that so?"

"Yep. Just thought you should know."

He snorted quietly. "Thanks."

"'S okay."

"Yanni?"

"Yeah?"

"I can't wait for Friday either."

I fell asleep and it wasn't until morning that I realized I'd slept with the light off. And I couldn't remember if I'd had the light on or off the night before or if my door was locked or the window... I sat on my bed and stared at the offending lightbulb and door, waiting for panic to crash over me.

It never did.

And just like that, another demon lay dead at my feet.

I WASN'T KIDDING ABOUT NOT LEAVING Peter's place. I'd already explained to Jordan that our usual laundry date would have to be another day. I'd explained I had this goddamn court case on Monday, which I was freaking out about, and she understood. So did my boss, who thankfully got someone to cover my Saturday shift.

So when Peter picked me up from work on Friday night, I had enough clothes for three days and my toothbrush in my backpack, some cash in my pocket, and no intention of leaving his arms.

Peter sat on the sofa and pulled me to him for some daddy/son time, so I crawled into his lap and buried my face into his neck. He wrapped his arms around me, stroking my hair, rubbing my back. "I missed you this week," I mumbled.

"Missed you too," he replied softly. "Did you want to talk about what happened with Patrice?"

"Uh-uh." I shook my head no. "No."

"Okay."

Apparently I *did* want to talk about it. I sat up so I could see his face when I spoke. "She just explained what to expect on Monday. Lance might plead not guilty and fight all charges, which means it could go to trial. Then every single thing he did to me gets told in public and I'd have to testify and I'm not strong enough for that. Or he might not even show up on Monday; just get his lawyers to talk on his behalf. Like he couldn't be bothered because the whole thing, me and Tyler, are nothing but a joke to him."

Peter put his hand to my face. "Oh, my sweet boy. We'll deal with Lance when we know what we're up against. If he's there, if he pleads not guilty, or even if the judge throws the case out or throws the book at him, whatever happens, just remember how I feel about you won't ever change. I love you." He kissed me softly. "And we outnumber him now. You and me together, okay?"

Fighting tears and swallowing past the lump in my throat, I put my hands to his face and kissed him. "Thank you."

"I wish you could see how strong you are," he said, brushing my hair off my forehead. "You say you're not, but Yanni, you're the strongest person I know."

I had nothing to say to that, so I put my face back in his neck and let him hold me. He continued to rub circles on my back, and even though the rise and fall of his chest should have calmed me down, it didn't. I was distracted, antsy, anxious, and stressed.

I kissed his neck. Warm, scented of everything Peter, and it felt like home. "Make me forget," I whispered. "Take me to bed, unravel me, wear me out. I don't want to think of anything but you."

"It's late," he murmured.

"Please, Daddy."

I felt his cock throb under me. *Magic word, that.* He maneuvered me effortlessly so I could wrap my legs around him, and he carried me to bed. He did everything I asked him to do. He devoured me, filled me, until there was nothing but him. Hours of agonizing ecstasy later, we slumped into the mattress, exhausted and spent. Peter simply lifted the blankets over us, and we didn't move again until morning.

THE BEST THING about waking up midmorning as Peter's little spoon was the weight of his morning wood pressed against the cleft of my ass. And the even better part about falling asleep last night without getting cleaned up, was that I was slippery where he'd been inside me the night before.

I wriggled back onto him, and he groaned. "I didn't want to wake you," he said gruffly.

"I'm very awake now." Lifting my top leg, I reached under and behind my balls to my hole, feeling the slickness there. So I squeezed his balls and tugged on his shaft, trying to align him with my entrance. It was awkward, but I got my message across just fine.

Peter's fingers gripped my hip. "You're not ready," he ground out.

"Yes, I am. I'm still covered in lube from last night," I said breathily. "And I'm still full of your come."

Peter's fingers dug into my hip, his forehead rested against the back of my neck, and he rubbed his length through the crack of my ass. "Jesus, Yanni. You shouldn't say those kinds of things to me."

I smiled, loving how I affected him. I pulled my leg higher, giving him all the room he needed, and arched my back. "I want you inside me again. All day, all night." He still seemed hesitant, so I moaned for him. "Have I been a good boy, Daddy?"

He pulled me close so my back was pressed against his front, his lips at my ear. "You know you have."

I writhed against him, trying to press down on his cock. "Good boys get rewards, right?"

"You know they do."

God, yes. I almost had him. His breath was harsh, his cock was hot and swollen, and so, so close to where I needed him. "Then give it to me."

Peter pushed into me, slowly, perfectly. He caged me in his strong arms and held me, whispering sweet nothings in my ear like I was the answer to all his prayers. He was at the perfect angle inside me, brushing against my sweet spot every time he moved. I was helpless, impaled on him and completely at his mercy, yet cradled and secure, loved and adored.

I begged him to never stop.

Peter buried himself to the hilt inside me and stayed there. "Be a good boy and come for Daddy," he said, his voice strained and tight. I stroked myself to climax, full of him in every possible way. And only when I'd sagged, spent and sated, did he start to move again. With his hand on my hip, he thrust into me until he stilled and roared, spilling his seed inside me.

With me still in his arms, him still inside me, we dozed off again. Later we showered and we ate, and when Peter suggested a movie, I crawled straight back into his lap again. We ended up spooning on the sofa, and by the time dinner was delivered, we were almost half-naked again. I made Peter get the door because his jeans hid his arousal. Mine did not.

On Sunday, I didn't even bother with clothes. I just wore the silk gown and briefs around his house all day. And he loved it. He couldn't stop touching me, kissing me, eye-fucking me. I bent over to grab us some water out of the fridge and Peter groaned, palming himself. "You're going to kill me," he said, biting his bottom lip.

I turned around and shut the fridge door behind me. The gown had come open at the front, so he had a great view of the bulge in my briefs. "Exactly how would you like me?"

He let his head fall back with a groan. "I can't decide if you're being a good boy or a naughty boy?"

I laughed and put the bottled waters on the counter, turned, and leaned against the cupboard. "That depends. What prize does a naughty boy get?"

He stepped in front of me, his body almost touching

mine, and looked down at me. "Well, they certainly don't get my reward," he answered gruffly.

I pouted, disappointed. "Oh."

He ran his hand down my stomach to my half-hard dick. "Maybe I should take a reward from you."

I didn't know what he meant, but the tone of his voice and the heat in his eyes made me very interested. "Like I said, exactly how would you like me?"

He spoke against my lips. "On the sofa, feet on the floor, legs spread."

Holy shit. I walked out of the kitchen to the sofa, my legs shaking with anticipation. Things were so different with Peter. *I* was different with Peter. I trusted him. I trusted he would never hurt me, never humiliate me.

And so God help me, he didn't. He loved me. He adored me, worshipped my body, my mind, my soul.

He knelt between my legs, and my heart thundered in my chest. He ran his hands over the silk, caressing my thighs, my stomach, my chest. He pulled my briefs down and licked me from base to tip. "Oh yeah," he said roughly. "I'll take my reward." He took my cock in his mouth, and with his hands under my ass, he lifted me closer, taking me into his throat.

He took his reward all right. He sucked it right out of me.

But if his goal was to keep me distracted all weekend, then he surely succeeded. Because Monday morning came around way too soon, and before I knew it, I was dressed in my fanciest clothes waiting in front of the courthouse, trying not to have an anxiety attack. Or vomit. Or both.

CHAPTER TWENTY-FOUR

EVERYONE WAS AT THE COURTHOUSE. I had no clue they were coming. Not only were Mr and Mrs Landon there, but Spencer and Andrew too. I almost cried when Jordan, Skylar, George, and Ajit turned up. And poor Tyler arrived alone, looking no better than me. He was pale and it appeared like he'd barely slept either. He came with no support, which made me pull him in for a hug, and I kept him close with us while we waited to be let in. He could be part of my *family* for as long as he needed.

And so we waited. And waited some more. Then a guy came out, called some case numbers, and Mrs Landon stood up. She nodded to Tyler and me. "This is us." I stood up and took a shaky breath. She looked Tyler and me in the eye and said, "Keep your chins up, and if that son of a bitch looks at you, stare right back at him." She turned and walked in first, with a fierce determination that I envied.

Peter slid his hand into mine and gave me an encouraging smile. "We got this," he said softly. "Remember, whatever happens…"

I nodded and walked inside.

I sat in the third row with Peter on my right, Tyler on my left. The Landons and Spencer and Andrew sat next to Peter. My roommates sat behind us. Serena Hernandez was there; she gave me a smile and a nod. There were other people there, some uniformed police officers as well, and the court officials were calling out numbers while the judge wrote things down, and for a long while, I had no clue what was going on.

I'd never even watched those law shows on TV, let alone been in an actual courtroom. But there were two tables in the front for counsel, and there were three people sitting at the table on our side. A man and two women, all lawyer-looking. They had files and notepads in front of them, scribbling notes and checking their phones.

Other people filed into the room, people I'd never seen before, and sat at the back of the room. I wondered who they were or whose case they'd come to sit in on, whose side they were on... My stomach was in knots; my knee was bouncing.

Then two men in suits filed in, lawyers obviously, followed by Lance, and another lawyer came in behind them.

I spun around to look at the front of the room, feeling the blood drain from my face. I didn't need to say a word. My death-grip on Peter's hand told him enough. Tyler let out a disgusted sound, and I, very simply, froze.

The three lawyers and Lance took their seats at the other table, and I finally got a good look at Lance. It had been almost a year since I'd seen him. A year since I'd walked out of his apartment clutching hopelessly at the threads that remained of my life.

He looked... smaller... than I remembered.

He looked tired. His skin was pallid; the dark circles

under his eyes made him look ill. His hair was longer than he kept it when I'd known him, slicked back and unwashed. His suit was crinkled and crushed. He looked awful.

Like, *really* awful.

It made me smile.

It was then I noticed Peter's grip on my hand was becoming a vise. I shot him a quick look, but his glare was aimed directly at Lance. Peter's jaw was bulging, ticking, and his eyes were like glass.

I opened my mouth to speak to him, but the judge started proceedings. She cited case numbers and spoke as though she was terribly bored, then looked at Lance's lawyers expectantly. The first lawyer stood up. "Permission to approach the bench."

The judge gave it, and the first lawyer from our side went to the judge's bench with Lance's lawyer. They discussed something inaudible to the rest of us, then she announced a special meeting in her chambers, and the two lead counselors and the judge disappeared through a door to the side.

I leaned past Peter to speak to Mrs Landon. "What's going on?"

"I'm not sure," she answered. "They're either asking for more time, or he's taking a deal."

I leaned back in my seat just as Lance turned around to look at us. It was just a quick glance, but he saw us. Tyler, me, and Peter, all staring back at him. I could feel the anger rolling off Peter, and the look on his face did little to hide his loathing.

Lance spun back around and sank a little lower in his seat.

Tyler nudged me with his elbow and gave me a smirk. "Did you see that?" he whispered. "Low-life fuck can't even look at us." His eyes shot to Peter, then back to me. "Well, your man might've had something to do with that. I'd probably crap myself too if he looked at me like that."

He was right. Peter was vibrating with anger, and the saying "if looks could kill" rang true. "Hey," I said, squeezing his hand. "Hey."

Peter blinked, then looked at me. His eyes took a moment to focus. "Sorry."

Just then, the side door opened and the judge walked in first, followed by the two lawyers. Everyone took their seats, and a silence fell over the room. The judge, with her unimpressed, no-nonsense expression, said, "The state of California versus Mr Lance Nader. Mr Nader—" She looked up then and glared. "Stand when I'm talking to you."

Lance shot to his feet and Tyler snorted.

The judge glared at Lance, not even trying to hide her disdain. "You're pleading guilty to two charges of aggravated assault and two charges of felony sexual battery."

Lance's voice was weak at best. "Yes, your honor."

There was a lot of back and forth, and the judge spieled a lot of legal jargon that I couldn't quite follow... because I was stuck on one word.

Guilty.

He was guilty.

Tyler grabbed my hand and squeezed, and Peter put his arm around my shoulder, pulling me in close.

He was guilty.

Tears welled in my eyes, and I didn't even try to stop them. Tears of anguish, of pain, humiliation, shame, and loss rolled down my cheeks. My final grief for all that he took. I somehow knew in my heart that I'd never cry because of him again. That was it. The very last time. It was over.

He was guilty.

The judge handed down her final words in a blur. I heard her say he was to serve twelve months in a minimum-security facility, and I didn't even care that he only pled guilty to get a lighter sentence in a nicer prison.

He *was* guilty.

And he was going away for his crimes. He deserved to.

We all stood, and as the uniformed men took Lance away, the last thing Lance would have seen was me hugging Tyler and then being engulfed by Peter in a crushing embrace. It was the icing on the cake for me. That Lance would see me truly happy, thriving even. Tyler too. And Tyler and me standing side by side was poetic justice. But I knew what would have bothered Lance the most was that I was in the arms of a man who wore a more expensive suit than him.

We walked out into the LA sunshine and everyone hugged again. Mrs Landon had glassy eyes. Mr Landon beamed. "Let's have a celebratory lunch! All of us," he said including my roommates and Tyler of course. "My treat!"

I put my hand on Tyler's arm, who was standing with Spencer and Andrew, and interrupted. "Will you join us for lunch? Please?"

He nodded, so I went to my roommates next. Jordan gave me a teary smile. "I'm really proud of you. I know how nervous you were."

"It's like the perfect outcome," I said. "I'm happy with what he got."

"Guilty," George said. His black-painted lips quirked upwards.

I nodded again. "Yep. And I hope his cellmate is the creepy guy who has headless dolls lined up on his bed."

Skylar laughed. "We can live in hope."

"Thank you all for being here today. It really means a

lot. Please say you'll come for lunch," I said, looking at all of them.

They agreed and started to follow the Landons. Mrs Landon had her arm around Tyler, Mr Landon was walking between Andrew and Spencer with his arms on their shoulders, telling them both that "Grace" was the best Jeff Buckley song after "Hallelujah," and that left me and Peter.

He stood there, watching me with a look on his face that I couldn't quite name. Happy? Proud? Pained? "Hey you," I said softly.

"Hey." He frowned.

I took his hand. "What's wrong?"

He let out a deep breath. "I'm sorry for how I behaved in there."

I was confused. "What do you mean? You were perfect," I said. He huffed, clearly pissed at himself. "Peter, what's wrong?"

"I wanted to jump the balustrade in that courtroom and beat the ever-living life out of that piece of shit. I swear, if you hadn't been holding my hand, I think I might have. Only twice in my life have I ever wanted to inflict pain on another person." His whole face crumpled. "Once, when I beat the crap out of my old man when I was seventeen. And today. God, Yanni, I wanted to hurt him so bad." His chest was heaving and he rolled his shoulders like he couldn't contain his emotions. "I swore to protect you and to never hurt you," he said sadly. "And I would never, *ever*, raise my fist at you. But I wanted to inflict a world of pain onto that slimy shitbag."

"So?"

"Don't you see? That makes me no better than him."

I threw my arms around his waist and clung to him. "You're nothing like him. You're so much more a better man than he could ever be. Please don't ever compare yourself to him."

He tentatively put his hand on my back, then his other, and eventually he melted into me. "You're not upset?"

"Why would I be upset?"

"You don't think an act of violence is the same as another?"

I pulled back to look at him. "He did what he did to me for the power and the control. If you *did* hit him, which you didn't, by the way, so this is completely hypo-thetical, it would be out of vengeance." I shook my head. "You have nothing to be worried about, Peter. You are the gentlest, most loving man I know." Then I broke out in a grin. "And that slimy shitbag, as you called him, admitted his guilt and is going away. I feel, I don't know… free."

He cupped my face and kissed me. "You are a remark-able man, Yanni."

I smirked up at him and gave him a wink. "Don't you mean 'boy'?"

He finally smiled, just as Mr Landon called out to us. He was at the corner of the block. "Hey, are you two coming or not?"

Grinning, I took Peter by the hand and dragged him forward. "Come on. Can't wait all day. I've got a life to live."

EVERYONE HAD TOLD me I'd come so far. Mr and Mrs Landon, Patrice, Peter. They all kept saying I had more than turned a corner; I'd practically moved ahead in leaps and bounds. But it wasn't until three weeks later that I real-ized just how far I'd come. It was just like any other

Wednesday. I'd walked into school just before class to a scene that made my blood boil.

Christopher was upset, holding his mop in his hand, trying not to cry. "What's wrong?" I asked him quietly.

He wouldn't speak at first, so I looked around the foyer. His *Caution Wet Floor* sign was lying down and there was a group of first-years standing off near the corridor. They had their backs to me, but one looked over like he was trying not to watch. He said something, and one of the guys with his back to me laughed.

"Did they knock your sign over?" I asked Christopher, gently putting my hands on his arms.

He nodded sadly. "Him in the red shirt. Took my mop."

And that was it. Me, meek little Yanni Tomaras, who never speaks up, who runs from confrontation of any kind, saw red. Literally.

"Hey, you," I yelled at the group of guys. "Asshole in the red shirt."

The whole group turned to look at me. Red shirt asshole smirked. "You talking to me?"

"You're the only asshole in a red shirt, so yeah." A quick dash of *What the hell are you doing?* raced through me, but my anger was louder than my fear. "Does picking on someone who won't fight back make you feel bigger? Need to feel like a man by ridiculing someone smaller than you?"

He tried to laugh it off. "It was just a joke, man. Lighten up."

"A joke?" I spat back at him. I pointed to Christopher. "Is he laughing?" I looked at red-shirt's friends. "Do you find it funny? Or do you just laugh along because you're too spineless to stand up to him?"

Not one of them answered.

Other people had come in now, and we had an audience. I looked back at red-shirt asshole. "Pick the sign up."

He scoffed. "What?"

"Pick it up. Now."

He looked around at the people watching on. "No way, man."

I glared and took a step toward him. "Pick it up now, and apologize to Christopher."

He stood there for a second or two and finally rolled his eyes. Like a spoiled brat, he righted the sign and stared at Christopher. He mumbled something that sounded like an apology, and that just pissed me off some more.

I turned to Christopher. "May I borrow your mop, please?"

He handed it to me, and I walked over to stand in front of red-shirt asshole and held the mop out for him. "Now finish mopping the floor."

"What the…? No fucking way," he said like the idea offended him.

"You're a bully, and everyone knows bullies are just cowards with self-esteem issues. So be a man," I said, holding his gaze, shoving the mop at him. "And finish mopping the floor."

He looked at me like I was shit on his shoe, but I didn't care. He sneered at me. "Who's gonna make me? You?"

"I am," a loud, stern voice boomed over the foyer. Mr Landon stood there in the crowd watching. "Take the mop, Fitzgerald. Finish mopping the floor. And if you want to keep your place here, you'll be here at seven o'clock tomorrow morning to help Christopher clean the bathrooms." Mr Landon stared at him, arms crossed, unblinking. "Do you have a problem with that?"

A pale Fitzgerald took the mop and mumbled something unintelligible. Mr Landon spoke up for everyone to hear. "No one in this institute is less than anyone else. Christopher's job here is no less important than mine. If anyone here thinks they're better or more valuable than the person standing next to them, you're not welcome here. Am I clear?"

A brief round of applause went around the audience, Fitzgerald grumbled as he did a poor job at mopping the floor, and everyone dispersed.

Christopher stood with his arms folded and watched Fitzgerald like a hawk, and Mr Landon clapped his hand on my shoulder.

I stared at him. The adrenaline was wearing off and my hands began to shake. "What did I just do?" I whispered.

"Come with me," Mr Landon said. He gave a smile to Christopher and said, "Tell me what kind of job he does, won't you, son?"

Christopher nodded seriously. "Yes."

"When you're done, Fitzgerald. My office," Mr Landon called out over his shoulder as he walked down the hall. I went with him, feeling suddenly nauseous.

He closed his office door behind us. "God, I feel sick," I said, with my hand on my stomach. "I just did that." I motioned to the door. "Out there, I just did that."

Mr Landon put both hands on my shoulders. "You okay?"

My eyes burned with tears and my stomach twisted. "I just almost had a fight. Oh God." I breathed in and out a few times. "I'm sorry. It was out of line and it wasn't my place to speak up, but Christopher was upset—"

"Yanni," he interrupted. "You did the right thing. Actually, what you did just now was more than the right thing. You saw an injustice and you acted. It was brave."

I held out my hands. They were still shaking. "I've never done that before."

Mr Landon was practically beaming. "Yanni, I'm so proud of you right now."

"You are?" I thought he might be mad...

"Hell, yes. The Yanni I met all those months ago would have never stood up to a bully, but look at you now!"

I was all jittery, like the adrenaline had left some kind of residual energy in its wake. I let out a laugh. He was right. I wouldn't have before, but I was different now. Everything I'd been through had made me stronger, more resilient. And a whole lot less tolerant of other people's crap.

"I guess I did, didn't I?" I said. "That guy was a real jerk."

He smiled. "Don't worry, I'll deal with him. You better get to class." Then, just as he was leaving, he said, "Oh, Helen wanted me to ask if you're still coming for dinner tonight?"

"Yes, of course."

"Peter too?"

"Yeah, he's picking me up from Patrice's office." Peter was picking me up because Mr Landon had something else going on this afternoon and had asked me to make other arrangements.

He just smiled. "Okay, I'll let her know."

There was a quiet knock on his door, and I opened the door to leave. Fitzgerald was standing there, looking a mix of fuming and scared. I huffed at him as I walked past, and all I heard was Mr Landon say, "Close the door and take a seat," to him as I headed to class.

I didn't think any more about why Mrs Landon had asked if I was coming for dinner until we walked into their kitchen and there was a cake on the kitchen counter with a bunch of candles. Mr and Mrs Landon were there, with Spencer, Andrew, and Sarah, all standing around before they broke out into a very theatrical rendition of Happy Birthday.

Peter shot me a horrified look. "It's not your birthday?"

To be honest, I hadn't given my birthday a thought. "Not until Saturday."

They finished singing, and Mrs Landon told me to make a wish before blowing out the candles. I closed my eyes and blew them out. "What did you wish for?" Sarah asked.

"He's not supposed to tell or it won't come true," Andrew said, squinting at his sister.

"I didn't wish for anything," I said. "I have everything I need, so I just kind of sent out a thanks to the universe instead."

"Oh." Mrs Landon burst into tears. Everyone stared at her. "Ignore me," she said, mumbling about stupid hormones. Mr Landon gave her a hug and told Spencer to hurry and serve her some cake.

Peter gave me a kiss to the temple. "I thought for a minute I'd missed your birthday."

"No, we're early because Wednesdays are our day, and I thought it'd be better early than late," Mrs Landon said, dabbing a napkin to her eyes. "Yanni, I heard you had a moment before class this morning."

I shot Mr Landon a look. "Oh, yeah. That."

"What happened?" Peter asked.

So we ate cake and I told them what had happened with Christopher and then we ate a dinner of Greek take-out, in my honor, of course. It was quite possibly the best early-birthday dinner I'd ever had.

I wasn't kidding earlier when I'd said that I had every-thing I needed instead of making a wish. Not material possessions, of course. I didn't have much in that regard, but I had people who loved me, my family of choice, and that made me pretty damn rich.

When dinner was all cleared away and Andrew and Sarah were arguing over a game of charades, Mrs Landon pulled Peter and me aside. She sat us down in the living room and looked hard at me. "Yanni, I want to ask you something."

That sounded ominous. I frowned. "Okay."

"You're doing so well," she said. "We're all very proud of you."

That wasn't a question, but I nodded slowly. "Thanks. Patrice thinks so too."

"Well, about that…" She hedged. "We're very busy at the Acacia Foundation, as you know. And we've had a case come in that's similar to yours, but maybe closer to Jordan's."

My heart sank. "Oh. Are they okay?"

She smiled sadly. "He will be. He's quite young, not even eighteen. But we need a place for him to stay. We're so overwhelmed at the moment, and your house would be ideal, and I'd really like him to spend time with Jordan. I think she could help him heal, and she'd benefit from helping someone."

"Okay." I thought about what she was saying…

Mrs Landon paused, then said, "Placement housing is never meant to be permanent, as you know. Now, George has been there for sixteen months—"

"He can't leave," I said, cutting her off. "He's just getting on track with Ajit's family. They've worked really hard at proving they're committed, and if he had to move and couldn't find somewhere close, well, Ajit's mother might think he's being unreliable, and I'd hate for that to happen. And you can't split Skylar and Jordan up. I don't know if this is against the rules, and if it is, just pretend I didn't say anything, but they've become close. Like really close, if you know what I mean. Jordan trusts her and Skylar's good for Jordan. They're like, just starting out, ya know? It's new but it's a beautiful thing. You can't break them up. It'd kill Jordan."

Mrs Landon gave me a knowing look and frowned.

"Me." I nodded. "I can move out. I have money saved. And I'm ready. I really am. Patrice is super happy with where I'm at." It was daunting as hell and a whole world of the unknown, but I could handle it. I had no doubt.

"You could move in with me?" Peter said. The hope in his voice made it a question.

I stared at him. "What?"

He licked his lips. "I know your independence is important, and I don't want to take anything away from you." He looked directly at Mrs Landon. "If that's not a good idea for him in any way, please just say. I don't want to overstep, but I just thought…"

She smiled. "I thought you might say that."

Now I stared at her. "Pardon?"

She cringed. "Well, you're so in love, and I know you're a perfect fit for each other. Yanni, I would never suggest it if I didn't think it was right for you." She gave me her serious-mom eyes. "I only want what's best for you, you know that, right?"

I nodded. "Yeah, I know that."

"And I wouldn't even suggest you move out at all if I didn't think you were ready. But I've seen you grow so much. Over the last twelve months, you've really become the man you were supposed to be." She sighed. "And you've always said Peter makes you feel safe."

I gave Peter a shrug. "True."

"And I just want you to be safe," Mrs Landon said. "It's

all a mother ever wants for her kids. I just want you to be happy and safe. I do think of you as one of my kids, Yanni. You know we love you very much. Which is why I'm also offering you your old room here as well, as an alternative. It's your choice."

Well, that was a loaded speech. I didn't know where to start with a response. "Move back in here with you?"

"You'll always be welcome here."

I scrubbed my hands over my face. "I love you both as well, in case you didn't already know. You're like the parents I should have had."

Her face softened. "Thank you, sweetheart."

"How long have I got?" I asked. "When does this guy need to move in?"

"Well, ideally, as soon as possible. Three or four weeks at the latest."

My head was spinning. "He can have my room. As for my decision about what I'll do, can I let you know in a few days?"

"Of course," she said. She stood up, so I did too and gave her a hug. When she pulled away, she patted my arm and looked at each of us in turn. "I'll leave you to talk. After that bombshell, I'm sure you have much to discuss."

When we were alone, I fell back onto the sofa with a plop. "Well, I think bombshell is an understatement."

Peter chuckled and took my hand. "I meant what I said. I'd love nothing more than to offer my home to you. But I'd prefer if we asked Patrice first." He ran his free hand over his jaw. "Maybe we could organize a joint visit, where we both see her together, and she can tell us if it's too soon. I don't want to rush you. If it's not the right time, then it's not the right time. And if you don't want to, that's okay too. I won't mind, I promise. I just want you to know it's an option. You could have the spare room if you think we'd need some space…"

"Then I'd have to call your cell for you to talk to me at night when you're in the room next to mine. That wouldn't make much sense."

He chuckled. "True. But still, I wouldn't mind."

I sighed. "I have so much to think about." I hardly knew where to start. I squeezed his hand and looked him square in the eye. "It's not a no. I just need time to think about it. And thank you for the offer. I really do appreciate it."

He kissed me softly. "Anytime. Whenever you're ready. The offer will always stand."

We went back into the kitchen where, thankfully, charades were over. "Coffee?" Mr Landon asked.

"No thanks," I said. "We're gonna head off. Thank you for a wonderful early-birthday dinner. It means a lot."

I hugged Mrs Landon extra hard and told her I loved her before I climbed into Peter's car. It was a quiet drive home. My mind was still spinning, and I wondered how my roommates would take the news of me moving out and where I'd end up living. And with whom.

When Peter pulled the car up to my place, I kissed him goodnight. "Call me when you get home," I said, just like always.

"Of course." His eyes were warm and full of love, and I almost told him to take me back to his place. But I didn't.

I needed space and time to think clearly and rationally.

Which lasted all of twenty minutes. I was in bed, staring at the darkened ceiling, wondering what the hell I was going to do, when my phone rang. Peter's name flashed up on screen, and I felt a familiar warmth bloom in my chest as soon as he spoke. "Hey."

"Trip home okay?"

"Very uneventful."

"Good."

"So, interesting evening, huh?"

I let out a laugh. "You could say that."

He never pressured me. In fact, he never mentioned it again. At the Landons', he'd told me the offer would always be open, and he gave me the thinking room I'd asked for.

But his voice didn't lull me to sleep like it normally did. My mind was too wired, and when I was antsy like this, there was only one way I could sleep. And that was in his arms.

It dawned on me, slowly at first, then all at once, that he was my home.

How many times had I crawled into his lap and thought *home*? How many times had he held me and everything wrong in my world was right?

How stupid was I?

I shot out of bed, flipped on the light, and pulled on my jeans. "Yanni, what are you doing?" Peter asked down the phone.

"Something I should have done an hour ago."

"Uh…"

"I know it's late, but don't go to sleep just yet." I pulled on my sweater. "I'm on my way."

"You're what?"

I laughed and ended the call, pulled on my shoes, and grabbed my backpack. As a last-minute thought, I picked up the purple orchid flower he'd given me and raced downstairs. I booked an Uber, and before I knew it, I was on my way to Peter's place. At midnight. Holding a potted plant. More excited than I'd ever been.

I didn't even have to knock. He opened the front door when I was still getting out of the car, with a worried, puzzled look on his face. He looked at the orchid, then at me. "Yanni, what are you doing?"

"It's your housewarming gift," I said. "I mean, you gave it to me as a housewarming gift, and so now I'm bringing it here. For my housewarming gift. God, it made better sense in my head."

He laughed, though still confused. "What are you saying, Yanni?"

"I'm bringing the orchid here because I want to live here. With you."

He broke out in a grin. "Did you want to run it past Patrice first?"

"No. It's my birthday in three days. I spent my last birthday black and blue, alone and homeless. I want to spend my next one with the man who taught me what home really is."

"Oh, Yanni." His eyes were so full of love. "Are you absolutely sure?"

"Yes. I know what I want, and I know what's right for me. I was stupid really, not to agree sooner. But I was lying in bed wishing to God I was here with you like I do every single night. And I'm here three nights a week anyway, and I spend the other four nights wishing I was or wishing you were at my place, and it makes sense, yeah? It feels right? We'll have to work out the money side of things because I want to pay rent, which I know you'll object to, but I'm putting my foot down with that. And I know you offered me the spare room, but I think that'd be a waste of time—"

He grabbed my face and crushed his lips to mine in a smiling kiss.

"You're squashing my orchid," I mumbled against his lips.

He laughed, took the plant, and placed it on the dining

table, then took my hand and led me to his room. *Our* room. I dumped my backpack, kicked off my shoes, and stripped down to my briefs. I climbed into bed, and he pulled me into his arms, wrapping me up safe and warm. With my face buried in his neck, I sighed contentedly.

I was, without a doubt, home.

CHAPTER TWENTY-FIVE

Fifteen Months Later

WEARING my newest silk gown and briefs, I floated around the house, dusting, cleaning. Peter was at work and I was being the perfect houseboy. I smiled to myself. Peter had laughed when I first called myself that. I'd graduated from college and managed to somehow get signed with one of LA's best stage performance agencies and had done a few productions. I was still working at the coffeehouse, but with nothing but a few days a week at the community theater and some auditions to fill in my time, I spent most of my days at home being a well-kept houseboy.

Peter's houseboy.

And I loved every minute. My friends would shake their heads at me, but there was something deeply satisfying for me to look after him. To make my Daddy happy. He certainly looked after me, in every possible way.

He was a born protector and provider. Nothing pleased

him more than to ensure I was happy and well cared for. And I very happily returned the favor.

I also wore his ring on my left hand. Not a wedding ring. Not yet, anyway. Peter had given me this ring as a promise to one day replace it with a wedding ring when I was ready. And it was really just a matter of time. I would spend the rest of my life with Peter. I had no doubt.

I'd spent the day doing some reading and research on a role I was getting ready to audition for. I'd annoyed Neenish until she glared at me to leave her alone. I was also working on a screenplay. The one Patrice had me start almost two years ago was being fleshed out—if it ever saw the light of day it would be a miracle, but it was cathartic to write.

I'd cleaned and straightened as well, and dinner was in the oven. Now all I needed was my daddy to come home and tell me what a good boy I was.

My balls ached at the thought.

When my phone rang and Peter's name flashed on screen, I answered with a purr. "Hello, handsome."

I could hear sounds of traffic and knew he was in his car. He sighed. "Well, your voice just improved my day by ten thousand percent."

He sounded miserable. "What's wrong?"

"Just a shit day. Shit meetings, shit clients, shit boss. Even the traffic is shit." He very rarely swore, so I knew his day must have been bad. He let out a frustrated growl. "Just one of those days when everything went wrong."

I leaned against the back of the sofa. "Well, if it's any consolation, I can't wait for you to get home. Dinner's cooking and I'm wearing the new dressing gown you bought me." This new one was purple, like they all were—something about the color purple spoke to me, reflected the inner me—and it came to my thighs and tied off around my waist. It was flowy and light and felt divine against my skin. It made me feel sexy, and Peter loved it.

Now he groaned. "Sounds like a perfect night."

I leaned over the back of the sofa, pressing my hardening dick against the leather, imagining Peter was standing behind me. "How long will you be?"

"Twenty minutes. Traffic is bad."

"Mmm." I rolled my hips, enjoying the friction the sofa provided, letting my imagination run wild. "That's just enough time."

"For what?" His voice had an edge to it. "Yanni, what are you doing?"

I smiled, knowing exactly what I was going to do. "You've got twenty minutes to get yourself nice and hard, thinking about how much you want to be inside me. Because the second you walk through that door, I'll be bent over the sofa with my ass ready and waiting. All you'll need to do is unzip your fly and slide right into me——"

"Jesus Christ, boy."

I moaned dramatically into the phone. "Eighteen minutes, Daddy," I said, ending the call and throwing my phone onto the couch. I went to our room and fetched the lube and walked back to the living room. We really should consider leaving some out here on the coffee table.

After my final stage play at the academy, to another standing ovation, I might add, we'd celebrated with everyone—my classmates, the Landons, Andrew and Spencer, Jordan and Skylar, George and Ajit—and afterward, we came home but made it no farther than the living room. Lube on the coffee table would have been handy that night...

I leaned over the back of the sofa again, lifting my gown up and pulling my briefs down just far enough to get my hand in. I slicked and stretched myself. Never as good as when he did it for me, though. Nothing could compare to the time and care he took getting me ready for him.

But I was soon ready enough, and an ache to be filled had spread from my balls to my belly. I was getting desperate.

I heard his car pull up and my stomach clenched. His keys in the door made me smile. The sound of the door closing behind him made me grind my cock against the couch. The sound of his groan followed by his zipper made my knees go weak.

Oh, God, yes.

He stood behind me and pressed his hot, hard erection against my briefs, along my ass crack. With a strong arm around my waist, he stood me up straight and whispered in my ear. "You made me speed. You almost made me wreck my car."

I panted, desperately wanting more. "Sorry, Daddy. You had a bad day, and I wanted to make it better."

He turned my head and slanted his mouth across mine for a messy kiss. "You make everything better," he grunted and pushed me back down. He slid my briefs down to my thighs and pushed the gown up my back and slid his cockhead over my hole. "You ready for me, boy?"

"Yes, Daddy."

He pushed into me, slow and deep, until he was fully buried inside me. I gripped onto the cushions, groaning loudly at the beautiful intrusion. His huge cock throbbed inside me, and then he began to move. He gripped my hips and pushed me against the back of the sofa, filling me over and over with each thrust.

This was perfection. Being everything my daddy needed, making him happy, making a bad day good was a need that burned in my heart. Letting him have me as he wanted was heaven, demanding yet still gentle, still Peter, always Peter.

His pace quickened and I knew he was close. I wanted it so bad…

He scooped one arm around my chest and brought me upright so my back was against his chest. I was impaled on him, my feet barely on the floor, and he came inside me. Pulse after pulse spilled into me, and he roared as his orgasm took hold.

It was everything.

He eventually sagged, his breathing ragged, his chest heaving. He kissed my back, my shoulder, my nape. "I love you," he murmured over and over.

I basked in his tenderness, his complete adoration.

Eventually, reluctantly, he slid out of me. He quickly pulled up my briefs and turned me in his arms, kissing me thoroughly until we both needed air. He held my face and kissed my forehead, my eyelids. "You're such a good boy," he whispered.

I chuckled. "And you're such a good daddy."

He hummed and stepped back, his spent cock hung heavy out of his suit pants. "I should have bad days more often."

I smirked. "I can greet you like that every day if you'd like?"

Now he laughed. "Shower now? Or later?"

"Later," I replied. "There will be round two after dinner."

He kissed me again with smiling lips. "What did I ever do to deserve you?"

I stared into his eyes. "You loved me in all the right ways."

"Correction. I *love* you in all the right ways. There is no past tense on that word. There will never be past tense on that word. Forever, Yanni."

"Forever, Peter." I meant it every time I said it. He was it for me. *Forever.* I reached down and gave his ass a squeeze. "Now go get changed. Dinner will be ready soon."

He kissed the side of my head and walked away, peeling off his suit as he mumbled something about his bossy boy. I hummed in satisfaction, aching in all the right ways, just as my phone rang. I picked it up off the sofa and saw Spencer's name on screen.

"Hey Yanni," he said. "Hope I'm not interrupting."

I laughed. "Ten minutes too late for that. What can I do for you?"

"I have a favor to ask," he said. "And it's a big one."

By the time Peter walked back out in his old, comfy jeans and a T-shirt, I'd told Spencer I would do anything he needed me to. Now I just had to tell Peter.

"Who was on the phone?" he asked, checking the tray of bubbling *kartoshnik*, a Russian-inspired dish I'd made decidedly Greek, which Peter loved. "This smells divine. Can we eat it already?"

I turned the oven off, smiling. "It was Spencer."

Peter grabbed two plates. "Oh? How's he doing?"

We'd only seen him last week to congratulate him on Andrew and his engagement. "He's great. He uh, wanted to ask me a favor. Well, both of us, actually."

Peter started to pour two sparkling mineral waters but stopped and stared at me. "What was it?"

"You've been to Australia before, right?" I bit the inside of my lip. "Not that it matters, I guess, because he asked if I'd like to be a guest speaker at the grand opening of his Sydney foundation for LGBT youth, and I said yes. Which means you have to come because I can't go without you."

Peter stared. "Uh… When?"

"In seven weeks."

He blinked, then sighed. "You already said yes?"

I nodded quickly, then leaning up on my toes, I kissed him and fluttered my eyelids a little. He was a sucker for my eyes and long lashes. "Thank you, Daddy."

He fought a smile. "You're lucky I love you."

Tell me about it. I was the luckiest man on the planet. "I know."

WHEN SPENCER ASKED me to be a guest speaker at the Archer Cohen Foundation's opening night in Sydney, I said yes without thinking. Of course, I would help him. He'd basically saved my life—well, he was the one who put the wheels in motion—and I owed him everything.

So Peter and I found ourselves in Sydney, Australia, four days before opening night. Spencer and Andrew were staying on for an extended holiday with Lewis, Spencer's brother, but Peter and I had to go home.

Not only did Peter have work to do, but I did too! I'd scored a role in a play at Geffen Playhouse, LA's most glittery theatrical venue. It was only a small role in a local production of the *Carol King Story*, but it was a huge step for me. And I needed to be back in LA a few days after my speech for Spencer.

I had no clue what I was supposed to say. It would be a full house of not only struggling LGBT people but also people and representatives of companies who had donated huge sums of money. And it was a monumental life-changing moment for Spencer and Lewis. They were doing this to honor their brother, Archer, who they'd lost to suicide.

I had to get it absolutely perfect. I couldn't let Spencer down.

Peter and I walked into our hotel room in awe. It was *very* nice and didn't cost us a cent. Spencer had booked us into Bondi Beach's Atoll Hotel, a five-star executive suite, and told us the only thanks he wanted for our accommodation was for us to have a lot of sex on any flat surface we could find. He spread his hands like a rainbow. "We need to put the gayness everywhere," he said brightly. "I hear the owner would love it."

Peter and I stared at him, wide-eyed, and Andrew burst out laughing. "Ignore him," Andrew said, pushing Spencer toward the door. Then Andrew stopped and made a thoughtful face. "But, just so you know, the owner would really appreciate it if you could leave lube everywhere."

Spencer laughed some more and pulled Andrew out the door. "Have fun, boys. See you at dinner tonight."

After they'd gone, I turned to Peter. "Do you know what that was about?"

He shook his head sadly. "No clue." After we'd unpacked, Peter was googling stuff to do in Sydney when he turned his laptop around to face me. "Check out the name of the guy who owns this hotel."

There, in black and white, on some financial subsidiary listing of the Atoll Hotel chain was the name Cohen & Sons. I shot Peter a look. "Do you think…? Cohen, as in Spencer *Cohen*?"

Peter laughed. "I'd put money on it. I could look a little further." Tracing financial histories was part of Peter's job, and he was clearly very good at it. "But Spencer did say *the owner.* I'd bet it's his father."

I chuckled. "Well, then. We best do our part of spreading the gayness," I said, doing the rainbow thing with my hand.

Grinning, Peter picked me up and spun me around. "On every flat surface, I believe was the official request."

We were both laughing as we fell onto the bed. It was flat, after all.

———

SITTING ON THE BALCONY, overlooking the glorious Bondi Beach, I scrunched up my fiftieth piece of paper and growled in frustration. This was worse than penning my damn screenplay. "What the hell am I supposed to say? It needs to be perfect."

I'd been trying to write this damn speech since we arrived three days before. Peter had suggested sightseeing, a walk on the beach, shopping, anything to clear my head. Nothing had worked, and at this rate, I'd be walking out on that stage and doing a mime performance.

Peter had tried to explain that I could get up in front of packed audiences and put on a Tony-worthy performance, and I should treat this no different.

"I'm not worried about stage fright," I replied. "I don't know what to say. Why did Spencer even ask me to do this?"

Peter pulled his chair around and took my hand. "I'll tell you why. Because you're living proof that it works. Cities need these places because there are people, kids—human beings—that get treated like garbage, like they don't even exist. And that has to stop. Every kid on the streets is you. They have the potential to be happy, to be safe and healthy, and to dream. Just like you. Yanni, you are proof that it works. That what Spencer and Lewis are doing is a very good thing. It shouldn't take private funding. It should be a government-led initiative." He took a breath to calm down. He was as passionate about this as we all were. "Just get up there and speak to them like you spoke to Tyler. Like you spoke to the homeless people on Skid Row. Tell this audience what you told them. Imagine you found a young kid on the street who had lost all hope. What would you tell him?"

And just like that, it was crystal clear. I kissed him, then picked up my pen and began to write.

WHEN IT WAS time for my speech, I wasn't even nervous. I was ready like I'd always been ready for this.

Sure, the venue was packed, there were youth caseworkers bumping shoulders with Sydney's elite, champagne was flowing, checkbooks were open. Spencer and Andrew looked incredible wearing tuxedos, and it was a truly touching moment when Spencer and Lewis unveiled the name and logo of their brother's memorial foundation.

Other people spoke before me, and one or two were due to speak after me. But Spencer welcomed me on stage. "I've invited a personal friend of mine," he said to the audience. "He's come all the way from LA to speak tonight with an insight, firsthand, of how foundations, such as this one saves lives... Please give a warm welcome to Mr Yanni Tomaras."

I walked out and was given a hug by Spencer before he left me alone in front of the podium. This was it. Hundreds of faces, a few flashing bulbs, a few rolling cameras. Peter stood in the wings, my pillar of strength, and gave me an encouraging nod. His ring on my finger bolstered me even more.

"Good evening," I started, looking out at the audience. My voice was loud and clear, as was my path. I could do this, without a doubt.

"Thank you, Spencer, for the warm welcome. Before I start, I just want anyone in the audience tonight who questions their worth, or who is without hope, to know there are good people in this world. If there is anyone here who doubts what The Archer Cohen Foundation is capable of, I want you to know, I have stood where you stand. I have been where you are. I can tell you, there *is* hope. There is a way out. It's not easy, but the Archer Cohen Foundation will save lives. I know this because Spencer Cohen saved mine."

I took a deep breath. "My name is Yanni Tomaras, and this is my story."

The End

WHERE ARE THEY NOW?

George and Ajit

George and Ajit's persistence did eventually pay off. Ajit's mother, a devout Sri Lankan, Hindu woman, eventually relented and accepted George as Ajit's chosen partner. She never truly warmed to George until he converted to Hinduism so he and Ajit could be married. Seeing this as a true commitment to her son, she welcomed him with open arms. Though she still laughs every time he almost dies trying to eat her spicy Dahl curry. The last time Yanni spoke to George, he and Ajit were planning a trip to Cambodia.

Jordan and Skylar

Jordan graduated with honors. She works in her chosen field of psychology, trying to unravel the disturbing dark minds of convicted sex offenders. Yanni still doesn't understand her burning desire to figure out why monsters behave in such ways, but he supports her completely.

Jordan and Skylar finally made their relationship official two years after Yanni moved out. It was a long and winding road, but one most definitely worth traveling. They're very happy, have two rescue dogs, and Jordan remains one of Yanni's best friends.

Tyler

Tyler gained his degree in business college and is now in marketing. He and Yanni kept in touch for a few years but now only really speak on social media with a comment or message every so often. He's done well for himself financially, but it took him years before he found someone to fall in love with.

Lance

Lance Nader went to prison, where his cellmate was the creepy guy who decapitated cockroaches and kept records of how long they lived thereafter. He served every day of his sentence, lost his job and his expensive apartment, and all his Armani suits. His car was repossessed. He now works in the accounts department of a truck company somewhere in Utah. He has a nervous tic and has therapy every other week.

His therapist can't stand him.

ABOUT THE AUTHOR

N.R. Walker is an Australian author, who loves her genre of gay romance. She loves writing and spends far too much time doing it but wouldn't have it any other way.

She is many things: a mother, a wife, a sister, a writer. She has pretty, pretty boys who live in her head, who don't let her sleep at night unless she gives them life with words.

She likes it when they do dirty, dirty things... but likes it even more when they fall in love.

She used to think having people in her head talking to her was weird, until one day she happened across other writers who told her it was normal.

She's been writing ever since...

ALSO BY N.R. WALKER

The Spencer Cohen Series, Book Three

The Spencer Cohen Series, Yanni's Story

Blood & Milk

The Weight Of It All

A Very Henry Christmas (The Weight of It All 1.5)

Perfect Catch

Switched

Imago

Imagines

Red Dirt Heart Imago

On Davis Row

Finders Keepers

Evolved

Galaxies and Oceans

Private Charter

Titles in Audio:

Cronin's Key

Cronin's Key II

Cronin's Key III

Red Dirt Heart

Red Dirt Heart 2

Red Dirt Heart 3

Red Dirt Heart 4

The Weight Of It All

Switched

Point of No Return

Breaking Point

Starting Point

Spencer Cohen Book One

Spencer Cohen Book Two

Spencer Cohen Book Three

Yanni's Story

On Davis Row

Free Reads:

Sixty Five Hours

Learning to Feel

His Grandfather's Watch (And The Story of Billy and Hale)

The Twelfth of Never (Blind Faith 3.5)

Twelve Days of Christmas (Sixty Five Hours Christmas)

Best of Both Worlds

Translated Titles:

Fiducia Cieca (Italian translation of Blind Faith)

Attraverso Questi Occhi (Italian translation of Through These Eyes)

Preso alla Sprovvista (Italian translation of Blindside)

Il giorno del Mai (Italian translation of Blind Faith 3.5)

Cuore di Terra Rossa (Italian translation of Red Dirt Heart)

Cuore di Terra Rossa 2 (Italian translation of Red Dirt Heart 2)

Cuore di Terra Rossa 3 (Italian translation of Red Dirt Heart 3)

Cuore di Terra Rossa 4 (Italian translation of Red Dirt Heart 4)

Intervento di Retrofit (Italian translation of Elements of Retrofit)

Confiance Aveugle (French translation of Blind Faith)

A travers ces yeux: Confiance Aveugle 2 (French translation of Through These Eyes)

Aveugle: Confiance Aveugle 3 (French translation of Blindside)

À Jamais (French translation of Blind Faith 3.5)

Cronin's Key (French translation)

Cronin's Key II (French translation)

Au Coeur de Sutton Station (French translation of Red Dirt Heart)

Partir ou rester (French translation of Red Dirt Heart 2)

Faire Face (French translation of Red Dirt Heart 3)

Trouver sa Place (French translation of Red Dirt Heart 4)

Rote Erde (German translation of Red Dirt Heart)

Rote Erde 2 (German translation of Red Dirt Heart 2)